C000297766

# SONG OF THE EIGHT WINDS

## *RECONQUISTA*

Oasis-WERP

# SONG OF THE EIGHT WINDS
## *RECONQUISTA*

- An Epic Tale of Medieval Spain -

**by**

**PETER KERR**

Oasis-WERP

Published by Oasis-WERP 2012

ISBN: 978-0-9573062-1-9

Copyright © Peter Kerr 2012

**All rights reserved**

No part of this book may be reproduced, stored in a retrieval system, or transmitted in any form or by any means, without the written permission of the copyright owner. The right of Peter Kerr to be identified as the author of this work has been asserted in accordance with Sections 77 and 78 of the Copyright, Designs and Patents Act 1988.

A catalogue record of this book is available from the British Library.

**www.peter-kerr.co.uk**

Cover design and maps © Glen Kerr

Printed and bound by CPI Group (UK) Ltd, Croydon, CR0 4YY

# TABLE OF CONTENTS

# ALSO BY THIS AUTHOR

Thistle Soup
Snowball Oranges
Mañana, Mañana
Viva Mallorca!
A Basketful of Snowflakes
From Paella to Porridge
The Mallorca Connection
The Sporran Connection
The Cruise Connection
Fiddler On The Make
The Gannet Has Landed

# ABOUT THE AUTHOR

Bestselling Scottish author, Peter Kerr, is a former jazz musician, record producer and farmer. His award-winning 'Snowball Oranges' series of humorous travel books was inspired by his family's adventures while running a small orange farm on the Spanish island of Mallorca.

Peter's books are sold worldwide and have been translated into several languages. This is his first book of historical fiction.

**www.peter-kerr.co.uk**

# MAPS

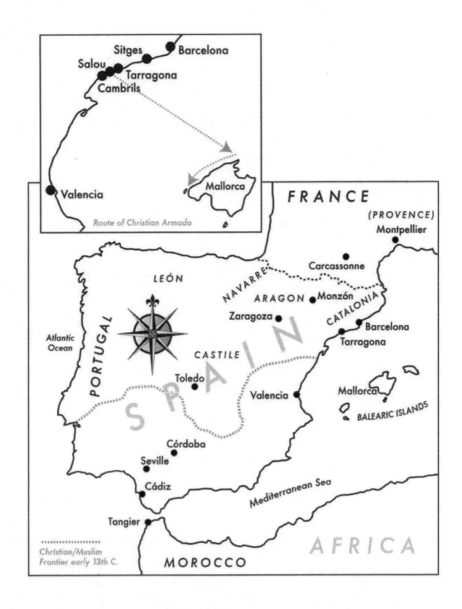

**MAP OF SPAIN**

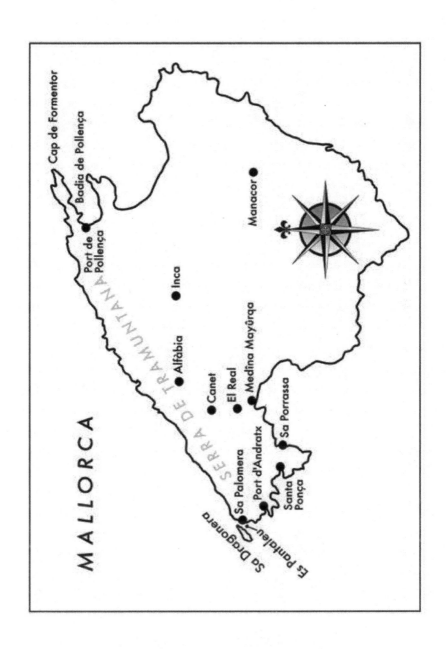

**MAP OF MALLORCA**

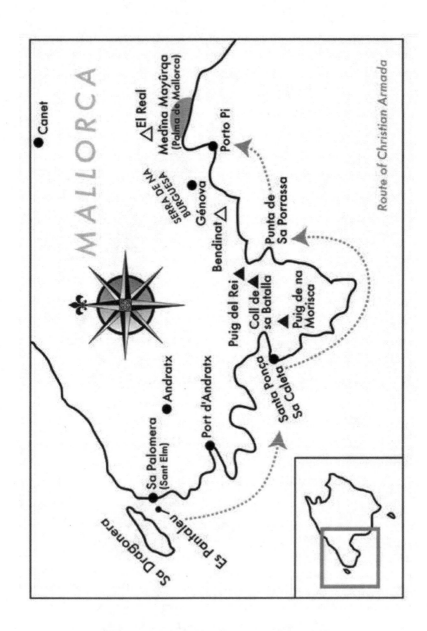

**MAP OF MALLORCA (DETAIL)**

Tramuntana

Mestral

Gregal

Ponent

Llevant

Llebeig

Xaloc

Migjorn

"The Eight Winds of Mallorca"

# IN PRAISE OF MALLORCA...

'One of the most fertile and best cultivated lands
that God ever made, and the most abundant
in provisions of all kinds.'

*(Abú al-Walid Ismail [aka Ash-shakandí]*
*- Medieval Moorish chronicler)*


'Land to which the collared dove has lent its ruff
And the peacock has clad in its cloak of plumes;
In it, the rivers are like old wine
And the courts of the houses cups for drinking it.'

*(Ibn al-Labbana – Medieval Moorish poet)*

# INTRODUCTION

In the second decade of the eighth century AD, Christian Spain was invaded from North Africa by the Moors, an Islamic people of predominantly Arab and Berber blood. They named their new Iberian dominion *al-Andalus* – a derivation of the Berber *Tamarus Wandalus*, 'The Land of The Vandals'.

Historians tell us that this Muslim incursion resulted in a change for Spain that could be likened to an emergence from darkness into light. A seat of power was established at Córdoba, where a city was created to equal the grandeur of Damascus, the jewel in the crown of a vast Arab empire that now stretched from the mountains of India in the east to the Pillars of Hercules and the shores of the Atlantic Ocean in the west.

During the Sultanate of Córdoba's first 250 years of sovereignty, Moorish Spain, with its magnificent palaces, mosques and fountained gardens, its sophisticated methods of irrigation and agriculture, its gifted architects and builders, its scholars, poets, philosphers and physicians, raised the torch of civilization and culture to the rest of Europe.

It was said that the prosperity and refinement of Spain shone like a beacon of enlightenment over a continent still struggling to emerge from the barbarism of the Dark Ages. Without doubt, the country's reputation became greater than it had ever been before – or, as fate would have it, might ever be again. For, despite the Moors' religious tolerance and liberal attitudes towards their non-Muslim subjects, the embers of resistance to this 'Saracen subjugation' glowed defiantly in the small Christian enclaves that survived in the mountains of Spain's northern frontier.

With the passage of time, the effect of the Moors' progressive attraction to opulence began to erode their allegiance to the more disciplined ways of their forefathers. Consequently, by the middle of the eleventh century, much of the great nation of *al-Andalus* had fragmented into a collection of small fiefdoms, or *taifas*, each with its own king, and all eventually severing their allegiance to Córdoba, just as, on reaching the zenith of its power almost three hundred years earlier, that first Islamic capital on Spanish soil had renounced its fealty to the once-indomitable Caliphate of Damascus.

Moorish Spain, for so long the epitome of order in a disorderly world, was now in danger of descending into turmoil.

While the rulers of the *taifas* squabbled among themselves, the resolute Christians of the north were pushing ever southward and establishing, on land long held by the Moors, their own individual kingdoms, such as Navarre, Castile, León and Aragon, as well as Catalonia, with its formidable maritime countship of Barcelona. So disorganised had the *taifas* become, in fact, that some even called upon the Christian armies to help resolve their differences with fellow-Muslim neighbours. And the Christian kings, though not immune to intrigue and rivalry themselves, siezed every resultant opportunity to press their territorial advantage.

Following the demise of Córdoba, the Moorish centre of power – at least in the south of Spain – had shifted to Seville, and it was from there that a plea for help to counter these Christian advances was sent to the *Almoravids*, a warlike Afro-Berber tribe of Islamic fundamentalists who now ruled Morocco.

In response, the Pope threw down the gauntlet by authorising a crusade against the Moors. The Christian *Reconquista* of Spain was now officially under way.

This was the era of *El Cid*, the legendary Spanish hero, who, in 1094, ventured deep into Moorish territory to take their 'impregnable' coastal city of Valencia. Despite that glittering prize being reclaimed by the Moors after his death, *El Cid*'s daring exploits had succeeded in stirring Christian hearts and galvanizing their resolve to rid Spain of its 'Saracen yoke' for ever.

For a century, the border between the two adversaries ebbed and flowed with the tide of battle. To add to the confusion, yet another Moorish incursion took place. The *Almohades*, an intolerant Islamic sect from the Atlas Mountains, rose up in Morocco and invaded Spain, eventually ousting the *Almovarids*, as well as checking the southerly advances of the Christian armies.

It was during this turbulent period that the future King James I of Aragon first saw the light of day. The child who was destined to become *El Conquistador*, 'The Conqueror', a champion of Spain to compare with the great *El Cid* himself, was born in 1208 in the southern French province of Montpellier, the only son of an ill-starred marriage between King Pedro II of Aragon and María, daughter of the Count of Montpellier.

The infant prince became a pawn in the marital games of expansionist chess that were the convention within the ruling classes of Christian Europe. At the age of three, he was given over to the care of Simon de Montfort, a ruthless nobleman from northern France, who was bent upon seizing southern French lands belonging to the Cathar allies of Aragon and Montpellier. As an act of appeasement, James's father had agreed that his son would be 'educated' at de Montfort's Carcassonne fortress, as a preliminary to being married to the tyrant's daughter.

After King Pedro's death in 1213 (ironically, in a battle against Simon de Montfort), his son, now all of six years old, became King James I of Aragon and Catalonia, as well as Lord of Montpellier and Count of Barcelona. In the troubled and treacherous times that followed, James owed his survival to the goodwill of the Pope, who arranged for him to be released from de Montfort's 'care' – and also from his nuptial commitments! He was taken under the tutelage of Guillen de Montredon, the head of the Spanish Knights Templar, in their castle at Monzón in Aragon.

The duty of the Templars in Spain was, at the behest of the Catholic Church, to assist their monarch in ridding the country of the 'heathen' Moor. So it was that young King James was taught the warring ways of a Christian knight, in preparation for the crusading campaigns that he would one day lead. Part of this preparation was his arranged marriage, aged thirteen, to Doña Léonor, the daughter of the King of Castile, whose territories conveniently bordered those of James's own kingdoms of Aragon and Catalonia. Here was a good example of how the wedding ring could be more powerful and, with luck, less bloody than the sword.

Although appearing to be, perhaps, merely the puppet of a coterie of Machiavellian guardians, James grew up to be a self-assured young man, with a strength of character to match his imposing physique. He was also to show that he was sufficiently astute and persuasive to win over the support of his nobles, some of whom had long been opposed to his accession to the throne. Here was a young king with the heart of a true warrior and blessed with all the qualities required to inspire an army in battle.

Who better, then, to lead a Christian reconquest of Mallorca, a large and strategically-placed island only 120 miles off the coast of mainland Spain, and a valuable asset that had been under the rule of successive Moorish kings for well over three centuries? Mallorca had also become a haven for Moorish pirates, who were the scourge of Christian shipping in the western Mediterranean and were now daring to make raids on the Catalonian coast, where not even the great city of Barcelona had been safe from attack.

In December, 1228, a meeting of the *Cortes* (Parliament) took place in Bercelona, where the heads of the church and civil dignitaries from all over the realm were joined by the *Ricos Homes*, knights of high rank who served as the King's counsel and were members of families that had enjoyed positions of power since long before the arrival of the Moors. It was enthusiastically agreed by this august assembly that it would fund and equip a massive naval expedition to reclaim Mallorca for Christendom. The youthful and charismatic King James – or Jaume, to give him his Catalan name – was duly endorsed as leader of the campaign.

Eight months later, a huge fleet had been assembled at the ports of Salou, Cambrils and Tarragona in north-east Spain. The *Reconquista* of Mallorca was about to begin.

This is the story of one of King Jaume's followers, a young man with a background just as disrupted as the monarch's, but singularly lacking the advantages that come with a privileged birthright, no matter how steeped in treachery and intrigue…

# 1

# FAIR STANDS THE WIND
# FOR MALLORCA

*OFF THE PORT OF SALOU, NORTH-EAST SPAIN, ON THE
MORNING OF WEDNESDAY, SEPTEMBER 5$^{TH}$, 1229 – ABOARD
THE GALLEY OF KING JAUME I OF ARAGON-CATALONIA…*

\*

'A-A-A-YOS … A-A-A-YOS … A-A-A-YOS!'

The slow, rhythmical chant of the sailors resounded across the
wide waters of the bay as anchor after anchor was hauled up and the
great armada bearing an army of 15,000 foot soldiers and 1,500
cavalry prepared to put to sea. There were some 150 vessels in all:
twenty-five large sailing ships, eighteen undecked horse transports
called *taridas*, a flotilla of flat-bottomed *brices* loaded with supplies
and engines of war, plus squadrons of oar-and-sail-driven galleys
carrying the nobles and the elite of their men-at-arms, in addition to
the mandatory members of the clergy, including Berenguer de
Palou, the Bishop of Barcelona himself.

The royal galley was lying at anchor some distance landward of
the main body of the fleet, which had been assembling off the Cape
of Salou. Clad in a long, scarlet surcoat trimmed with gold, the
young king stood tall, broad-shouldered and proud on the raised
poop deck, his blue eyes ablaze with anticipation, his flowing
flaxen hair swept back from his face by an off-shore breeze which
augured well for the forthcoming voyage. He raised his eyes to the

top of the galley's mast, where the royal pennant was fluttering now against a cloudless sky. A look of satisfaction lit his face.

'At last, the day that will change my life,' he murmured. Then, sensing someone behind him, he half turned to see a young sailor checking the coupling of one of the galley's two side-mounted tiller shafts. In a tone of regal self-assurance, though diluted by the merest hint of embarrassment, the king said, 'Did you ... that is, I take it you heard what I said just then, *marinèr*?'

There was a wry smile on the young helmsman's lips as he lowered his head in deference. '*Sí, Majestat*, and I daresay there's no man among all the thousands who sail with you today who wouldn't agree.'

King Jaume surveyed the helmsman's features for a few seconds, trying to decide if that lopsided smile of his indicated derision or was merely an attempt to convey some sort of empathy. If it was the former, then the lad had little respect for his own neck, and if it was the latter ... well, that was a reaction from a subordinate the monarch had seldom experienced before, and was one, therefore, that he would regard with due suspicion.

'Wouldn't agree with what?' he enquired warily. 'That this is the day that will change *my* life, or theirs?'

The helmsman arched his eyebrows. 'Well, both, *senyor* ... both!'

The King said nothing, but his stare remained fixed on the sailor's face.

The helmsman's smile broadened and, turning his head seaward, he said, 'For you, another land to add to your existing kingdoms of Aragon and Catalonia lies just forty leagues over that horizon. Also, when you've claimed Mallorca, your reputation as a great champion of Christian Spain will be written on the pages of history for ever. So, as a king, this could well be the day that will change your life.'

With a slightly exaggerated nonchalance, the king nodded his head. '*Sí*, if it pleases the Almighty, that may well be the case. But,' he added both swiftly and with an air of piety, 'it is for *His* glory, not for mine, that the battle for Mallorca will be fought. I act merely as God's vassal – a Christian soldier, chosen by Him to help retake all of Spain from the infidel Moor.'

The helmsman was tempted to point out that the Moors would have believed that their occupation of Spain five centuries earlier had also been undertaken in the name of God, albeit that they called him Allah. But he knew all too well that such a statement would be regarded as blasphemy. Hides more valuable than his had been flogged for daring to utter such unthinkable thoughts.

Instead, he dipped his head again. 'Therefore, *senyor*, God will surely grant victory to his chosen vassal, and your reward will be the tenure of the kingdom of Mallorca.'

The king shrugged. 'Which is no more than my right. Equally, the churchmen and barons who accompany me and have provided the ships, men and wherewithall to make this holy mission possible will also be entitled to their division of the lands and wealth of Mallorca.'

'Just as their men will be entitled to *their* share of the plunder?'

The king gave a little laugh. 'The men who follow me today have come, not just from Aragon and Catalonia, but from all over Iberia, from France and from as far away as Italy, Hungary, Germany and even Britain. How else can such an army be mustered – and paid for – if not by the promise of a fair allotment of whatever bounty a God-given victory may provide?' A look of suspicion came into his eyes. 'But do I detect a note of disapproval in your attitude, sailor? I hope not, and I suspect not – for what else but the prospect of increasing your own wealth, meagre as it doubtless is, would be your reason for embarking on such a perilous quest as this?'

The helmsman shook his head, the smile now gone from his lips. 'Strange as it may seem, my decision to follow you wasn't motivated by any desire to benefit from the spoils of war. No, *Majestat*, even if God has decreed that such is the right of His chosen vassal and *his* vassals, I didn't join the *Reconquista* for personal gain.' Motioning towards the teeming main deck of the galley, where sailors and oarsmen were now busying themselves with their respective tasks in preparation for putting to sea, he continued: 'Although I own little more in the world than the clothes I stand up in, I seek no material riches in Mallorca, unlike the motives of this crew and every other in the fleet.' He paused to assess the king's reaction, which, as could be expected, was a mix of puzzlement and simmering displeasure. 'With due respect to each and every man,' the helmsman prudently appended, 'and to their allegiance to God and your Majesty, of course.'

Still the king said nothing, although he was thinking plenty. There was something about this young sailor he couldn't fathom. Although he spoke with the accent of a common man, the way he spoke and the smack of intellect in what he said belied his status as a humble seaman. And while he was clearly being careful to show an acceptable degree of reverence in the presence of his king, there remained a suggestion of independence in his manner – a further hint that there was indeed more to this fellow than his occupation would have one believe. There was also an air of honesty about him, a frankness that was the very anthithesis of the fawning and backstabbing ways of so many of the 'nobility' that King Jaume had been associated with since childhood. He was intrigued. More than that, something told him that perhaps, just perhaps, here was someone he could trust, no matter how modest his position in life. Yes, he would have to find out more about this fellow.

'So, tell me, *marinèr* – what do they call you?'

'Call me? Why, Blànes, *senyor*. Pedro Blànes is my name. Although…' He hesitated, rolling a shoulder uneasily.

Now it was the king's turn to smile. 'Don't be shy, Master Blànes. If you have another name – a nickname, perhaps, by which you're better known – then you must tell me.' With a jerk of his head, he gestured towards the bustle of seamen going about their duties on the open deck immediately forward of where they were standing. 'On a cramped vessel like this, nothing can remain a secret for long anyway.'

The helmsman lowered his eyes.

The king was delighting in the young sailor's embarrassment. 'Come on, *marinèr*!' he taunted. 'Tell me – what do your friends call you, eh?'

The helmsman sighed. 'Well, *senyor*, if you must know, it's … well, it's Pedrito.'

4

'Pedr*ito*?' the king laughed. 'But that means *little* Pedro – a child's name!' He strode over and stood beside the young seaman. 'And look at you! You're as tall as I am, and I stand a good palm's width above most of my knights, and as much as two palms above many of them. Yet you're called *little* Pedro?'

'It's what my parents called me when I was a baby,' Pedrito indifferently explained, 'and the name just sort of, well, stuck – even after I started to grow.'

The king took a pace back, grinning while he looked the helmsman up and down. He noted his shock of black, wavy hair, his suntanned skin, his fine-boned features framing dark, deep-set eyes that twinkled with good humour, yet revealed a suggestion of melancholy as well. His baggy linen shirt and trousers were ragged and stained, though long exposure to the elements had bleached them salty white, as was typical of the garb of seafaring men. However, for all that he was fated to climb no further up the ladder of life than the lowly rung he stood on now, the fellow exuded a definite freedom of spirit, with even his bare feet looking as though they might never welcome the restriction of shoes.

It was obvious from his lean, muscular frame that this sailor was no stranger to hard physical effort. Nothing unusual about that. More interesting, perhaps, was that his appearance had more than a hint of the Moor about it. But, as the king was then obliged to concede, there was actually nothing unusual about that either. After all, it was said that no women had accompanied the first Moorish armies that overran Spain all those centuries ago, so there had always been plenty of Arab blood flowing through the veins of the peasantry. By the same token, the king could hardly deny that his own physical appearance reflected the characteristics of the Visigoths, the Germanic peoples who had occupied Spain after the Romans had been driven out many centuries earlier than the arrival of the Moors. Therefore, being a fair and just man, he bore no grudge against people who looked a bit like the current occupiers – provided, naturally, that they worshipped the true Christian God and not the Muslim Allah.

'How old are you?' he asked the helmsman.

'Twenty-one, *senyor* – as far as I know.'

The king stroked his chin. 'Interesting. The same age as myself. But why do you say "as far as you know"?'

'Because the people I call my parents never knew exactly when I was born. It may have been a week before they found me, maybe two weeks, maybe three.' Pedrito Blànes hunched his shoulders. 'Who knows?'

But the king was only half listening. 'Hmm, but by the look of your arms, you could wield a two-handed sword with ease. *Sí*, and I'll wager those legs of yours are more than capable of supporting a heavy coat of mail.' He gave Pedrito a hearty slap on the shoulder. 'So then, how would you like to fight at my side when we attack the Saracen armies on Mallorca? You could be one of my squires.' There was an impish glint in the king's eyes now. 'That's if you're an able horseman, of course. And I presume you *can* handle a horse, can't you, En Blànes?'

Pedrito resisted the inclination to frown. He was aware that he was being teased, but he had no intention of giving the king the satisfaction of thinking it bothered him. Accordingly, instead of answering the king's questions, he promptly countered them with one of his own.

'Why do you call me *En* Blànes, *Majestat*? I've told you my name's Pedrito, so why call me something else?'

A smile played at a corner of the king's mouth. 'It seems, then, that your life at sea has taught you little of the ways of chivalry.'

Pedrito gave a dismissive snort. 'The only chivalrous thing I learned during five years pulling an oar on a galley was not to fart in the face of the rowers sitting immediately behind me.'

The king threw his head back and bellowed with laughter. 'And as a measure of their respect, they called you Pedrito, but never En, right?'

'A man can be called many names when he's at the bottom of the heap, *senyor*, and few of them are complimentary.' Then, giving King Jaume a look that was as chastening as prudence allowed, young Blànes added, 'It always helps to understand what the insults mean, though.'

'Ah, but calling you En is no insult, *amic*.' King Jaume shook his head vigorously. 'On the contrary, you should feel flattered.' He went on to explain that in much of Spain the Castilian term 'Don' was put before a gentleman's name as a mark of respect. 'In Castile, all noblemen, even kings, are addressed as Don,' he continued, 'as in "the King Don Alfonso", for example. But in the language of my kingdoms of Aragon and Catalonia –

'*Sí, sí,*' Pedrito cut in, unable to quell his mounting irritation, 'you say En instead of Don. I know all that!' Noticing that the king was taken aback by this sudden show of testiness, and acutely aware that such apparent impertinence could result in severe punishment, he promptly adopted a more deferential manner. 'I realise that no one is less entitled to be addressed as En than I am, *senyor*. But my position at the bottom of the heap doesn't mean that I don't have some pride, and I feel less than flattered by being mocked' – he paused to look King Jaume in the eye – 'even by someone as exalted as your royal self.'

There were a few tense moments as the two young men stood with their eyes locked, their expressions stony. It was Pedrito who eventually spoke, his desire for his head to remain attached to his shoulders rising above the overwhelming compulsion to stand up for himself that the harsh lessons of life had instilled in him.

'However, let me assure you, *senyor*, that having respect for myself doesn't mean that I have any less respect for you, or for anyone else … *if* he deserves it.'

The king's eyes burned into Pedrito's. 'But isn't being your king reason enough to deserve your respect?'

The young helmsman swallowed hard, his brain sending urgent messages to his mouth that it should now remain firmly shut.

Slowly, the king lowered his right hand until it found the hilt of his sword. Pursing his lips, he stroked the sword's pommel with his thumb.

Unblinking, Pedrito watched as the glistening blade was withdrawn from its scabbard, inch by buttock-clenching inch. And still the king's gaze remained fixed on his face, from which he could feel the blood starting to drain.

In a flash, the king withdrew the last few inches of sword from its sheath, and in a single stroke thrust its point into the deck between Pedrito's naked feet.

Pedrito closed his eyes, tightly. He heard a faint splintering of wood as the sword was prised upwards, then waited for the regal grunt that would tell him his intestines were about to experience their first breath of sea air. But there was only silence, followed, after a few apprehensive moments, by the touch of a hand on his shoulder. Pedrito opened his eyes, gingerly.

Although the king's smile was warm, a shadow of uncertainty lurked in his eyes. 'I'm not accustomed to such candour from my subjects, Master Blànes,' he said in a matter-of-fact way.

The enquiring look that Pedrito cast him was tinged with foreboding. Was the king merely lulling him into a false sense of security before testing the sharpness of that sword on his worthless guts? Everyone knew that King Jaume was well-trained in the ways of a knight. And, despite never having mixed in their company, Pedrito knew that knights were trained to kill. What's more, he'd heard that some, like cats, took great pleasure in toying with their victims before putting them out of their misery.

The king pouted again. 'I'm still waiting for your answer, Master Blànes. I repeat – isn't being your king reason enough to deserve your respect?'

Pedrito nodded mechanically. 'As a mouse respects a cat,' his mouth blurted out without resorting to consultation with his brain.

The king scowled.

Pedrito silently resolved that, in the unlikely event of his internal organs being fortunate enough to survive this fraught encounter intact, he would sew a button on his lip.

His promise of self-retribution was, however, premature. The king's scowl gradually dissolved into a smile, which in turn graduated into a broad grin.

'But I suspect you're no mouse,' he beamed. '*Sí*, and I respect you all the more for that!'

Too surprised to venture a reply, Pedrito inclined his head briefly to one side as a tacit gesture of appreciation.

The king acknowledged in like manner, then, pointing to his sword, he added, 'And lest you may have heard otherwise, I can promise you that *I* am no cat!'

Pedrito took the point, canting his head again as confirmation, while thanking his lucky stars that his head was still suitably situated for the undertaking of such a gesture.

His relieved expression didn't go unnoticed by the king. With a knowing smile, he raised his sword and rested its blade on the palm of his left hand. 'Toledo,' he said. 'The finest steel there is.' He looked Pedrito in the eye. 'So, we can say the Saracen invader brought at least *one* useful skill to Spain, no?'

'I've heard it said, *senyor*, that they also brought skills for the *saving* of life.' Pedrito immediately wished he hadn't made such a potentially provocative reply, true though it was.

However, if the king was annoyed, he didn't let it show. 'I have several such swords, Master Blànes,' he smiled. 'So, will you accept my invitation to carry one of them at my side when we fight the Saracens on Mallorca?'

Pedrito took time to think carefully before replying this time. 'You, uhm – you said you respected my frankness, *Majestat...*'

King Jaume indicated the affirmative.

Nervously, Pedrito tweaked the lobe of his ear.

'Come on, *marinèr*,' the king urged, still smiling, 'if it's the prospect of handling a horse that worries you, I can promise –'

'It's not that,' Pedrito interrupted. 'I'm well used to horses, *senyor*.' He rolled a shoulder uneasily once more. 'Well, when I say horses, I actually mean *a* horse – singular.'

The king knotted his brows. 'But surely one horse is pretty much the same as another, when you get down to basics?'

Pedrito offered a weak smile. 'Except when a horse is not a horse, maybe?'

'A horseless horse?' The king gave an impatient shake of his head. 'I've no time for riddles, *amic*.'

Pedrito noticed that the king's attention was now beginning to drift. Those penetrating blue eyes had started to wander, first towards the prow of the vessel, where a huddle of sailors were awaiting the order to weigh anchor, then to admidships, where another group were preparing to unfurl the galley's sail. Suddenly, Pedrito could see that, king or no king, this man was human after all. His nerves, royal as they might be, were on edge. And Pedrito wasn't about to make any criticism of that. All *he* had to concern himself with, after all, was steering this ship towards Mallorca – a simple matter of using his physical strength to heave rudder paddles one way or the other according to the commands of the captain. King Jaume, on the other hand, had to bear the responsibility of being in charge of the greatest seaborne expedition ever undertaken in the name of Spain, a daring and complex military operation that would eclipse any purely land-based assault against the Moors that had taken place to date.

This, possibly, was what had been going through the king's mind when Pedrito had overheard him declaring that this was the day that would change his life. Yet, as Pedrito had sensed, no matter how much the king had been trying to convince himself, there had been an element of doubt in his general demeanour as well. And little wonder, since the risk of failure was real and its consequences dire. The Moors, with their vastly larger army, would defend their dominion of Mallorca fiercely, and in the associated battles many lives would be lost, including, perhaps, that of young King Jaume himself. So, his train of thought at this pivotal moment in his reign would have been manifold. A glorious victory would indeed immortalise him as a great champion of Christian Spain, whereas being forced into ignominious retreat would commit his name to history's register of also-rans. Alternatively, death in action would send him to meet his maker, who would either heap honours upon him for his success against the infidel, or would condemn him to purgatory for his lack of it. With such onerous matters weighing on his mind, it was very likely, Pedrito concluded, that the king's dalliance with him had been but a light diversion from the gravity of his present situation.

And indeed it had been, for the most part, but not entirely. The king's curiosity had been aroused by this enigmatic young sailor, and for all that he was preoccupied with thoughts of the forthcoming campaign, he was still of a mind to find out more about Pedrito's background. He turned to him again...

'You were about to tell me about a horseless horse, I believe?'

Pedrito couldn't help chuckling. 'I said a horse that isn't a horse, *senyor*, not a horseless horse. There *is* a differnce.'

The king raised an eyebrow. 'Really?'

'*Sí*. Surely a horseless horse would be nothing at all, no?'

The king's expression was blank.

'Whereas,' Pedrito went on, 'a horse that isn't a horse is *some*thing – even if it's something other than a horse.'

'Get to the point, Master Blànes,' the king bristled. 'I told you, I've no time for riddles.'

Pedrito got to the point. 'It's my father's horse – or rather the man I call my father.'

The king bared his teeth in a smile, though with scant evidence of humour. 'The horse that isn't a horse, belonging to a father who isn't a father?' He scowled again. 'You're beginning to test my patience, *amic*.'

Pedrito duly apologised, then explained that the man who was the only father he'd ever known had actually found him, abandoned as a tiny baby, behind a heap of fish baskets on the quay at Medîna Mayûrqa, the Moorish capital of Mallorca. The man, Gabriel Blànes, was a fisherman from the little port of Andratx, some eighteen miles distant from the capital on the south-western tip of the island. To supplement the meagre income from his fishing, he farmed a small *finca* a short way inland from the port, keeping some livestock as well as growing enough vegetables and fruit to feed a family of four – himself, his wife, their natural daughter and the foundling Pedrito – with any surplus produce being taken by boat to the capital for sale on market days.

'Ah, so you're from Mallorca?' said the king, his curiosity whetted. 'But the man you call your father – Gabriel – this is hardly an Arabic name, no?'

'Nor is Pedro, the name he gave me after the patron saint of fishermen, and there are no Muslim saints.'

'Meaning?'

'Meaning my parents are Christians, or Mozarabs, as the Moors call those who live under the rule of Islam, but choose to practise their own religion.'

'Mozarabs,' the king muttered, 'meaning would-be Arabs in the Moorish tongue, I believe. Hardly a complimentary term for a Spanish Christian, in my opinion. Typical of the patronising arrogance of the Saracen, however.'

Pedrito shook his head. 'In fairness, *senyor*, the Moors of Mallorca, in my family's experience at any rate, never showed any disrespect for our faith or objected to us worshiping Christ – provided we didn't try to build a church in his name, that is. Nor did they object to us speaking in the same *Latina* tongue as yourself, as many fishing families still do in that little corner of the island, having kept the language alive by sea-trading with Catalonia over the centuries. Of course, we speak Arabic as well – just as everyone does in Muslim Spain.'

'A humiliation which is going to cease the moment we've driven the Saracen hordes back to Africa,' the king declared through clenched teeth. 'Catalan, or *Latina* as you call it, will be spoken throughout my kingdoms, and the Arab language, like everything else that reeks of the Moors, will be stamped out for ever. This I have promised in the name of God.' Then, as if to put such daunting obligations to the back of his mind for the moment, he adopted a less austere manner. 'But what of this strange animal of yours – the horse that isn't a horse?'

A wistful smile traversed Pedrito's lips. 'My father's mule,' he murmured. 'But he always insists on calling it a horse – his *cavall*.'

The king's eyes lit up. 'Or *caballo*, as they say in Castile. And if, as you claim, you're accustomed to handling your father's *caballo*, then you're entitled to be called a *caballero* – a horseman, a gentleman, a knight!' He gave Pedrito a manly slap on the back. 'There, I told you that you deserved the title of En before your name. So then,' he grinned, 'I take it you will fight at my side as one of my squires, *En* Pedrito Blànes?'

Pedrito lowered his eyes. 'Ah, but I know your Majesty's merely jesting, and –'

'Oh, but I assure you I am not!'

'Then you do me a great honour, *senyor*, and I'm truly grateful. But...'

'But?'

Pedrito detected an ominous note in the king's delivery of that single word. He could only guess what the consequences of rebuffing a royal invitation to arms would be, and the prospect didn't appeal. He would have to tread extremely carefully here. He cleared his throat.

'You, ahem, you said you respected my frankness, *senyor*...'

'Yes, so if you have something to say, say it.' King Jaume squinted at Pedrito through half-closed eyes, then asked tauntingly, 'Or are you a mouse after all?'

Pedrito raised his eyes to meet the king's. 'That depends. I'm not a fighting man by nature, and I've no wish to inflict harm on anyone – not even the Moors. But that doesn't mean I'm a –'

'No wish to inflict harm on the Moors?' the king interrupted, his voice rising, a frown of amazement furrowing his brow. 'No wish to inflict harm on the disbelievers who stole our land from us?' He shook his head. 'You mystify me, Master Blànes. First you say you've no desire to benefit from the spoils of war, and now you tell me that you wish no harm to *my* enemies.' King Jaume was making no attempt to conceal his displeasure. 'I think it's high time you explained precisely *why* you came on this crusade, don't you?'

'Well, firstly because I was hired as a sailor, not as a soldier, and secondly –'

'Every sailor must take up arms if required,' the king barked. 'Surely you're aware of that?'

Realising he had talked himself into a corner, Pedrito decided to throw a measure of caution to the wind. He had no option now. 'You said you respected my frankness, *Majestat*...'

'And?'

'And I'm going to be honest with you. My main reason for coming on this expedition was because I hoped it might give me the chance to check on the wellbeing of my parents and little sister. I've been at sea for five years now, and I haven't had any news of them in all that time.'

'Then perhaps you should never have gone to sea,' the king retorted.

'I didn't really have any choice,' Pedrito came back. 'If it had been up to me, I'd still be working with my father's mule on our *finca*.'

'All of us, even kings, have to do things in life that we'd rather not!' the king admonished. Then, after a moment, his look softened slightly. 'Still, your concern for your family is commendable, Master Blànes. And I envy the fact that you have a family at all, for I've known no mother or father since I was three years old. However, we're about to go to war, and *you* are a member of my army, whether you like it or not!'

At that, and to Pedrito's great relief, the galley's captain appeared, stepping briskly up to the poop deck from between the ranks of oarsmen now settling onto the benches straddling the vessel's hull. Though obviously in a state of some agitation, the captain took a moment to bow before the king.

'Permission to weigh anchor, my lord?' He crooked a thumb over his shoulder. 'As you can see, the rowers are on the thwarts with oars at the ready, and the deck hands are waiting for my order to hoist the sail, and –'

The king raised a silencing finger. 'No one is more impatient than I am to start this voyage, Captain Guayron, but the orders I gave are clear – the fleet does not move off until the lead ship of Captain Bonet signals that the last of the vessels have come out from Tarragona and Cambrils on either side of the cape yonder. Then, and only then, does my galley join the fleet, bringing up the rear as planned.' He followed that outburst with a mumbled: 'As planned by our fine general, my cousin En Nunyo Sans, but not by me, I may say.'

The captain, though an older man than the king and doubtless much more experienced in the ways of the sea, clearly had no wish to invite his monarch's displeasure. 'I beg your forgiveness, *senyor*, and I don't wish to distract your Majesty's attention from other more important matters' – he cast his helmsman a chilly glance, then offered the king another stiff little bow – 'but if you will pardon my intrusion, I –'

'Oh, for God's sake, get on with it, man!' the king snapped. 'This is no time to stand on ceremony! What is it you want to say?'

The captain was now pointing frantically towards the seaward flank of the fleet, and to the lead ship in particular. 'B-but, my lord,' he stammered, '– look there! The flag man on Captain Bonet's ship is already signalling. You see, the remaining Tarragona and Cambrils vessels came out and took up position while you were –' he shot Pedrito another icy look – 'while you were otherwise engaged. Everyone's now waiting for your signal to proceed.' He pointed again. 'As you can see, the canvas on the sailing ships is already being raised.'

The king glared at Pedrito. 'If you had the makings of a half-decent squire,' he hissed, 'you would have told me about that flag!'

Pedrito was sorely tempted to tell the king that if he had the makings of a half-decent naval commander he would have noticed the flag himself, but he kept his own counsel. It was becoming increasingly obvious to him that King Jaume, though destined to become one of Spain's greatest heroes (if the fates allowed), was also a 'normal' young man like himself, saddled with insecurities and self-doubt, which his regal status compelled him to conceal as best he could.

Just then, a cry rose up from amid the masses of onlookers thronging the shoreline:

'Look there! See how all the sea seems white with sails!'

'And why, Captain, aren't we hoisting ours?' the king demanded. 'The royal galley having to bring up the rear in front of all those people is bad enough, but being left behind completely would be a disgrace too terrible to contemplate!'

'To Mallorca! To Mallorca!' came the concerted call from the crowds on the beach. 'To Mallorca, and go with God, King Jaume!'

'Well, Captain Guayron,' the king urged, 'you heard what they said! What in heaven's name are you waiting for? Tell your conch horn blower to sound the advance, or whatever it's called at sea!'

Without having to be asked a third time, the captain barked the required command. Then, with a pained look, he turned round to address the king again.

'The *Ponent* – I fear it may not favour the larger ships today, *senyor*.'

'The *what*?' the king frowned.

'The *Ponent* – the west wind.'

The king's frown deepened. 'But surely the west wind is what we want. The *Ponent*, as you call it, will blow us eastward to Mallorca, no?'

'*Sí, Majestat*, but look at our sail. It's hanging like a wet shirt on a washing line. The wind's just too slack. I mean, this and all the other galleys can make good headway by using our oars, but the large sailing ships – well, they have no oars.' His expression changed from concern to one of resignation. 'And any fleet is only as fast as its slowest vessel.'

The king's face fell. 'Surprise is worth a thousand men in battle, and this morning after mass the Bishop of Barcelona prayed for a fair wind to take us swiftly to Mallorca. But now your wretched *Ponent*...' His voice trailed away.

'Perhaps he didn't pray hard enough,' Pedrito Blànes suggested, aware that his wayward tongue might be putting his head on the chopping block again, but deciding nevertheless that an attempt at raising the young monarch's flagging spirits was called for. King Jaume was already renowned as a leader of land armies, but it was becoming increasingly apparent that he was sadly lacking in knowledge of how things happen at sea.

'You dare to criticise the Bishop of Barcelona's power of prayer?' he growled at Pedrito.

'I'd never criticise anyone's prayers,' Pedrito assured him, 'for I've no skill at praying myself.' He shrugged his shoulders. 'Never seems to work for me.'

'You're treading on dangerous ground, *marinèr*. Doubting the power of prayer, even your own, is tantamount to doubting the mercy of God, and that's a sin punishable by –'

The king's words of warning were interrupted by the galley master's shouted command to his oarsmen that they should take the strain.

16

Then, as the regular beat of a drum dictated the rate of the rowers' strokes, Pedrito said to the king, 'All I was about to say, *senyor*, is that, when it comes to dealing with the fickle ways of the sea, even the most skilled sayer of prayers can have his powers boosted by the age-old traditions of the seafarer.'

He then began to sing in time with the slow, steady rhythm of the galley master's drum…

> 'Sailor, you say you will do anything,
> So make me a song of the winds
> And sing it to me when night falls…
> I see the winds –
> Morning wind and evening wind,
> North wind and desert wind.
> *Llevant, Xaloc, Migjorn,*
> *Llebeig, Ponent* and *Mestral,*
> *Tramuntana* and *Gregal.*
> Make me a song of the eight winds –
> The winds of the world.
> And bring me a wind,
> A wind that will take us safe to land.'

The king's mood had mellowed somewhat by the time Pedrito had come to the end of his song. 'A pleasant enough ditty, Master Blànes, but are you really suggesting it'll bring us the wind we need more readily than would the power of prayer?'

Pedrito raised his shoulders again. 'All I can say is that, when man's at the mercy of the sea, the eight winds are God's messengers, just as Christ was His messenger on earth. So, it does no harm to pay the winds homage, even if only through an old sailor's song like that one.'

Smiling, the king nodded his head as he considered what Pedrito had told him. 'You speak more like a philosopher than a helmsman,' he said at length, then patted Pedrito's shoulder again, though more gently than before. 'However, it's good to know that your years spent pulling an oar on a Catalonian galley taught you, somehow, to nurture such worthy Christian thoughts – even though I don't entirely follow them.'

With a twinkle in his eye, Pedrito returned the young king's smile. 'Perhaps that's because the old song of the eight winds isn't a Christian one, *Majestat*.'

The king looked surprised.

'No, no,' Pedrito said, 'it's actually a Muslim sailors' chant I translated from the Arabic.'

The king stared at him, aghast. '*Mus*lim? *Ara*bic?'

'Oh, absolutely, *senyor*. You see, before I was hired as helmsman for this voyage, the years I spent pulling an oar were served, not on a Catalonian galley, but aboard a Moorish pirate ship.'

Stunned, the king glowered at him, then gave the captain an even darker look.

'You hired a Mozarab *pirate* to man the helm of my galley?'

The captain was quick to point out that he hadn't hired Pedrito, raising both hands to emphasise his innocence in the event of the king's wrath being provoked, which it was clearly about to be.

King Jaume lowered his voice to a menacing snarl. 'Then who, in the name of Saint Mary, *did* hire him?'

The captain dropped the corners of his mouth. 'My information is that the order came directly from one of your nobles, En Guillen de Muntcada, who sails in the lead ship of Captain Nicolas Bonet, and it was Captain Bonet who relayed the order to me.'

Mulling that over, the king rubbed his jaw. 'But En Guillen de Muntcada is one of my most battle-seasoned nobles, and one of my most trusted as well.' He looked askance at Pedrito. 'I'd have expected him to be a bit more careful when selecting members of my crew.'

Pedrito was now adjusting the angle of the tillers, setting course for the rear of the fleet, his head raised, his gaze directed beyond the king towards the prow of the galley. He was fully conscious of the king's confusion, however, and he couldn't help smiling.

'Don't look so smug, helmsman,' the king muttered. 'You may think it's too late to replace you now, but I swear that if you put a finger wrong during this voyage, I'll personally throw you overboard and steer the ship myself!'

Pedrito suppressed the urge to laugh as he stole a brief glance at the captain, whose face was a picture of bewilderment. Then, with his eyes focused on the galley's direction of passage, he gave the king a sideways nod of his head. 'It's fair enough to call me a Mozarab if you choose to, *senyor*, but I'm no pirate and never have been.'

'You're talking in riddles again,' the king replied frostily, 'and I told you I've no time for them. It seems you have a poor memory, no?'

'No poorer than your own, if you'll permit me to say, because you obviously forget what I told you only a few minutes ago.'

The captain, fearing a right royal eruption at what he regarded as Pedrito's show of insolence, excused himself and made a swift exit from the poop deck. Nautical matters, he claimed, required his urgent attention.

But the king was too busy glaring daggers at Pedrito to bother about what the captain had said. 'You're pushing your luck again, helmsman,' he growled through his teeth.

Pedrito smiled. 'Only being candid, your Majesty, and you did tell me you appreciated my frankness.'

'Except there's a thin line between respectful frankness and disrespectful impertinence, and you're coming dangerously close to crossing it!'

Staring dead ahead, Pedrito continued to concentrate on manipulating his tillers. 'I merely wanted to remind you, *senyor*, that I said I'd no choice about going to sea those five or so years ago.'

'I remember you said that,' the king retorted, 'but I don't recall you saying anything at the same time about joining a pirate crew!'

'And I don't remember anything about joining the pirate crew either. And that's the whole point. One minute I'm ploughing my father's field with the old mule, a minute later I see a bunch of Arabs leaping out at me from behind a wall, and the next thing I know I'm lying on the deck of a Moorish pirate ship with a lump on my head and stars in my eyes.'

'Ah, I see,' said the king with a contrite dip of his head, 'you, uh – you were kidnapped, then – taken into bondage. Is that what you're saying?'

'That's where I did have a choice, *senyor* – either become an oarsman on that pirate galley or be sold to the highest bidder in a Moroccan slave market.' Pedrito shuddered at the thought. 'A fine strong boy, they said I was. Would fetch a handsome price as a plaything for some rich, wizzened crone in Tangier or Casablanca, they reckoned. *Vaja*! I couldn't get them to shackle me to that rowing bench fast enough!'

King Jaume was more intrigued than ever now. 'So tell me, how did all that time spent on a Moorish pirate ship lead to you being taken on as helmsman on a Christian king's galley, especially by a high-ranking nobleman such as my trusty friend En Guillen de Muntcada?'

While maintaining his set heading in the wake of the hindmost vessels of the fleet, Pedrito proceeded to relate how he had managed to escape from his pirate captors during a slave-taking attack on the Catalonian fishing hamlet of Sitges. It was the first time in his five years as a galley slave that he'd been able to convince his masters that they could trust him to be included in such a raiding party. And he'd grasped the opportunity as though his life depended on it – which, in reality, it probably did. Men doomed to the drudgery of propelling Moorish pirate ships by the power of their muscles weren't noted for their longevity.

From Sitges, he'd made his way southward along the coast to the city of Tarragona, where the topic on everyone's lips was the impending reconquest of Mallorca by King Jaume himself. That had been some three months ago, when many vessels committed to the expedition were already beginning to assemble at Tarragona and the neighbouring ports of Salou and Cambrils. In a harbourside tavern one evening, Pedrito had chanced to fall into the company of a happy-go-lucky, red-haired young fellow from northern Britain by the name of Robert St Clair de Roslin, a novice Knight of the Temple who happened to be one of En Guillen de Muntcada's train. The new royal galley, the cost of its construction having been provided by the king's native city of Montpellier, had just been launched and a crew was being put together prior to the start of the vessel's sea trials. The hiring of the sailors had been entrusted to the master of En Guillen de Muntcada's galley, Captain Bonet, who, as chance would have it, was also in the same tavern as Pedrito and Robert St Clair that evening.

'So, *Majestat*,' Pedrito concluded, 'Robert St Clair introduced me to Captain Bonet as an experienced sailor, who'd not only known the waters around Mallorca since childhood, but could also speak Arabic and was well acquainted with the practices of the Moors at sea. Don't forget,' he cautioned, 'that they may well launch an attack on your fleet between here and the island.'

King Jaume stroked his chin in the now-familiar way, though his expression was more penitent than pensive this time. 'It seems, then, that I owe you an apology, Master Blànes.'

Pedrito gave him a reassuring smile. 'You owe me nothing, *senyor*. As I said before, all I seek from this mission is an opportunity to see my family again, and being a member of your crew is giving me that chance. So, by my way of thinking, the only person who's indebted to anyone is me.'

A moment or two passed as the king gathered his thoughts, all the while studying Pedrito's face, as he in turn concentrated on holding steady the galley's course against the swells and currents of the open sea into which they were now sailing. Yes indeed, King Jaume told himself, there was a lot more to this young sailor than his lowly status might suggest.

'And by *my* way of thinking,' he said at last, 'the old song of the eight winds wasn't the only thing you learned during your five years as an oarsman on a pirate ship.'

Pedrito gave a chuckle. 'That's right. I also learned the etiquette of farting in company.'

'No doubt, no doubt,' the king laughed, then resumed a more thoughtful mien. 'Yet something tells me you learned a lot more besides, no?'

Pedrito remained silent, his gaze still fixed on the way ahead.

'However,' the king said with a sigh, 'as long as your old song brings us a fair wind to carry us in all haste to Mallorca...'

'Keep the faith, *senyor*, keep the faith. Sometimes God answers a prayer, sometimes the winds answer a song.' Pedrito turned his head to look the king in the eye. 'And this time, I've a feeling my old song will bring you the very wind you need.'

## 2
# IT'S AN ILL WIND…

*LATE AFTERNOON OF THE SAME DAY – ABOARD THE ROYAL GALLEY, TWENTY MILES INTO THE VOYAGE…*

The galley's sail was flapping, as was Captain Guayron.

'*Majestat*!' he shouted over the howling of the wind. 'Give the order to turn back, I beseach you. This *Llebeig* will be the ruin of us!'

The king was standing at the vessel's stern, his back to the weather, his hair and robes soaked by the spray being whipped off the whitecapped waves. He was peering into the gathering gloom, one hand raised to shield his eyes, the other holding on grimly to the gunnel rail while the deck rolled and pitched beneath his feet.

'*What* will be the ruin of us?' he yelled at the captain.

'The *Llebeig* – this south-west wind, *senyor*. It's driving us off course.' The captain pointed forward. 'And just look – the galleys were ordered to encircle the large sailing ships to protect them from any Moorish attack, but now the formation of the fleet is being blown into total disarray!'

The king glared at Pedrito, who was struggling gamely to control his kicking and tugging tillers. 'You and your unholy Moorish sea shanties!' he bellowed. 'No doubt Mohammed himself answered your call by sending this wind to scupper our crusade before it's even begun!'

Pedrito's logical answer to this accusation would have been that the negative results of the Bishop of Barcelona's prayers could have been equally to blame for this unfortunate turn of meteorological events, but he held to his earlier resolution of self-preseravtion by keeping his lip tightly buttoned.

The vessel's galley master and sailing master now clambered onto the heaving poop deck. After paying the king the obligatory courtesies, Berenguer Sagran, the sailing master, told him that they had come to support the captain's view, stressing that they also spoke on behalf of the entire ship's company.

'We'll never reach Mallorca with this wind, *senyor*. We'll miss the island by miles and end up somewhere in the Gulf of Genoa off the north-west coast of Italy!'

Their expressions deadly serious, his two companions muttered in agreement.

'While intending no disrespect to your competence as mariners,' the king began, 'I suggest you may be exaggerating the situation slightly, Master Sagran.' He was obliged to pause while he grabbed the gunnel rail with both hands as the galley was hit by a huge wave. 'As I was saying,' he continued with all the composure he could muster, 'although we seem to have encountered a slightly turbulent patch of weather, we must continue undaunted for Mallorca.'

Then up spoke the captain again. 'My lord, as your subjects, we're bound to guard you life-and-limb and to give you the best advice we can. For that reason, I must stress that it's absolutely impossible to make Mallorca with this south-west wind. So, if you take my advice' – he gestured towards his two senior crewmen – '*our* advice, you will put about and go back to land.' He gave the king an imploring look. 'God will give you a wind for crossing soon enough, I promise you.'

Out of the corner of his eye, Pedrito watched King Jaume silently weigh the captain's words for a few moments. Inexperienced in naval matters as he doubtless was, and impulsive as he appeared to be in certain ways, it had become obvious to Pedrito that this young monarch did give due consideration to the opinions of others before coming to any decision. In this case, the king quickly came to the decision that his own judgement was best.

'Your concern for my safety is much appreciated, gentlemen, but it's entirely unfounded. You see, it was for the love of God that I launched this crusade against the disbelievers, and it was my solemn vow that I would either convert them to the faith of our Lord, or destroy them.'

The captain and his two subordinates exchanged worried glances.

'We understand what you say, *Majestat,*' the captain piped up, 'and as righteous as your motives are, the fact remains that the *Llebeig* is driving us off course and –'

'And the fact remains,' the king cut in, 'that since God knows we go in His name, He will surely see us safely to Mallorca.' King Jaume then scrutinised the faces of the three men, quickly arriving at the conclusion that, being common seamen and not blessed with the unshakeable faith of a God-chosen king, they would require some more convincing. Common seamen though they were, the continuation of the mission now depended totally on their nautical skills, so he knew that all of his powers of persuasion would never be more crucially put to the test.

Pedrito, eavesdropping while still valiantly wrestling with the tillers, realised this as well, and although the wailing of the wind and the crashing of the waves against the galley's hull made it difficult to hear all of the king's words, he strained his ears to pick up as much of his address as possible.

'You're all well-seasoned men of the sea,' the king told the captain and his two cohorts, 'master mariners with salt water in your veins. But, you know, not everyone in this armada can boast those qualities.' He pointed in the direction from which they'd sailed. 'You must have noticed the dozens of *barcas* that followed us out from Salou – little boats carrying perhaps a thousand men – not hardened soldiers, but peaceable fishermen and coastal villagers, who joined this expedition at the last moment of their own free will, simply to support me, their king.'

The captain and his shipmates nodded their heads, a tad sheepishly.

'Well,' the king continued, 'how do you think these brave men would react if they saw the royal galley turn tail and head back to the mainland at the first puff of an unfavourable breeze?'

The captain was about to venture a reply, but the king cut him off.

'And what of all the hardened soldiers crammed into those sailing ships and transports ahead of us – the booty-seeking mercenaries from all over Europe who are strangers to the sea, who mistrust, hate and fear the sea, and would scurry back to a safer land battle anywhere, irrespective of reward, if they saw the leader of this venture succumb to a threatening wave or two?'

The captain made to say something, but the king got in first again.

'I'll tell you what would happen if we put about and returned to the mainland as you advise, gentlemen – this crusade, which took me the best part of a year to prepare, after gaining the support and financial backing of all the leading clergymen, city elders, merchants and nobles in my realm, would be sunk, never to resurface. Ever! So, Captain Guayron, I suggest that you and your shipmates here take courage from the brave villagers who followed us out of Salou in their little *barcas*, and use your superior seamanship to do as they're doing by pressing on determinedly for Mallorca.'

This time, the king did allow the captain to speak.

'As you wish, my lord,' he said, bowing reverently, but with a note of reluctance in his voice. 'We'll do our best for you, and as you lead us in the name of God, surely He will help us make safe passage to Mallorca – somehow.'

King Jaume wagged an admonishing finger. 'God helps those who help themselves, Master Guayron, and it's up to you to use your skill to help this ship stay on the correct heading, whichever way the wind blows.'

'As you say, *Majestat*, as you say,' the captain replied, though still without much conviction. He pointed forward again. 'As you can see, all order has been lost, with vessels mixed together like twigs in a whirlpool, and all struggling to make headway in the right direction. And anyway, if you'll permit me to ask, *senyor*, how are we to convey our intentions of trying to maintain our proper course to the rest of the fleet in a storm like this?'

At that very moment, the bow of the galley was submerged when a mighty wave crashed over it and lashed the rest of the ship with sheets of water. Caught unawares, Pedrito lost his footing on the soaking deck timbers, allowing one of the tillers to be snatched from his grasp by the surge of the wave.

In an instant, the king was at his side, gripping the flailing shaft with both hands and fighting to control it as he would a rearing horse.

'You ask how we're to signal our intentions to the other ships,' he shouted to the captain. 'Well, we'll do it by overtaking all of the fleet and leading the way to Mallorca, that's how. This galley and the lead ship are the only two vessels showing a lamp, so the rest will know who we are well enough as we pass them.'

'But, my lord,' the captain protested, 'that would take a superhuman effort by my crew at the best of times, but in these conditions...'

'I never ask anyone to do anything I wouldn't do myself,' the king yelled back, while fighting with all his strength to align his tiller with Pedrito's. 'And just as I'll help your helmsman steer the ship through this storm, I'll gladly take over from any crewman who isn't up to his job either.' His blue eyes shot arrows at the captain. 'Now, be about your business, Master Guayron, and show me what you and your sailors are made of!'

Although the captain didn't waste a second in detailing a capable seaman to take over from his overlord, the young monarch insisted on standing firm by Pedrito's side until the end of the evening's two-hour dog watch. Since he was facing the ranks of rowers, King Jaume's determination to successfully control his tiller against the violent pitching and yawing of the ship served as an inspiration to all of the crew to redouble their own efforts. And, sure enough, by nightfall the royal galley had overtaken all of the fleet and was drawing level with the leading ship.

The king's strength and tenacity at the helm had certainly impressed Pedrito too. Yet it took more than just persistence and brute force to maintain the correct bearing in such heavy seas. When two helmsmen were on the tillers, each had to mirror the other's movements precisely, and that required a degree of mutual understanding that usually only came with experience. King Jaume, though totally unschooled in the discipline, had taken to it like a veteran. And Pedrito told him so when they were relieved at the end of the watch.

The king gave him a world-weary look. 'Believe me, *camarada*, when you've worn a full hauberk of chain mail in battle at only nine years of age, as I did, and if you've swung a heavy sword for your life when surrounded by a sea of enemies as many times as I have, then spending an hour or so grappling with a wooden pole on a bucking ship isn't all that demanding – not to demean the honed skills of you and your fellow helmsmen, of course.'

Pedrito acknowledged that backhanded compliment with a wry smile.

'However, Master Blànes,' the king said, while raising a cautioning eyebrow, 'it could be said that I've done you a favour today, no?'

'*Sí, senyor,*' Pedrito readily agreed, 'and I promise you it's a favour I'll make a point of returning.'

'Indeed you will, Master Blànes,' the king replied, in a way that left Pedrito in no doubt that he meant what he said. '*Sí, sí,* indeed you will.'

With a flamboyant sweep of his surcoat (sodden though it was), he stepped down from the poop deck and, as if cocking a snook at the rolling of the deck, made his way like a victorious gladiator between the cheering ranks of oarsmen all the way to the galley's prow. He then hailed the sailor guarding the lantern of the leading ship, which was was now off the galley's port side…

'*Oy del vaixell!*' he yelled. 'What ship is that?'

'The ship of En Guillen de Muntcada,' the sailor called back. 'And what galley is it that asks?'

'My galley, *marinér*! The galley of King Jaume of Aragon and Catalonia! There,' he shouted, pointing to the lantern mounted at the galley's stern, 'you can see my lamp – the only lamp showing in the fleet tonight, bar your own.'

As the sailor squinted in disbelief through the darkness, the king laughed into the windblown spray. 'So you can tell my noble friend *El Gran Senyor* Muntcada that I'll see him at Mallorca – *if* he manages to get there in time for the invasion!'

Thus the royal galley headed off in defiance of the persistent south-westerly, running all night without shifting or shortening sail. And the rest of the ships followed suit, close hauled to the wind as possible. By dusk the following day, the king's galley was so far ahead as to be out of sight of the rest of the fleet. Then, just as the mission-threatening Llebeig finally abated, the island of Mallorca appeared in the distance, the saw-toothed peaks of its mountains floating like a mirage above the eastern horizon and shimmering pink in the glow of the setting sun.

On the king's orders, his galley hove to. After a while, two solitary ships approached from astern, one of them being that of En Guillen de Muntcada, who shouted to the king that the others were following as best they could. However, when last seen by him, several vessels had been faring badly in the storm. He feared that some of them might even have foundered.

This, in an additon to a possible attack by Moorish ships, was an eventuality the king had dreaded. At least the latter hadn't happened, yet. However, it did nothing to diminish the increased danger of having to face the enemy's land forces, which would already greatly outnumber his own, with perhaps many hundreds of his troops and horses now lost to the sea. But the thought of aborting the crusade when so much had already been committed to the cause wasn't one that King Jaume was prepared to entertain.

'We'll wait here to see who's made it this far,' he called over to Guillen de Muntcada, whose ship had now drawn alongside. 'And to let the fleet know we're here, each of our three vessels will show a lamp, with blankets shielding their light from Mallorca.'

This prompted a response from Muntcada that was anything but optimistic. 'I fear, my lord, that, although we've lowered sail, the Moorish lookouts on the island will already have seen us, distant though we are.'

The king made his irritation blatantly obvious. 'Well, my friend,' he bristled, 'you're more experienced in naval tactics than I am, so just what do you propose we do, eh?'

Guillen de Muntcada was a member of one of Catalonia's most eminent aristocratic families. A stern-looking man of stocky build, he had formerly been leader of a group of renegade nobles who had vehemently resisted King Jaume's accession to the throne. He had also deeply offended the king by later attempting to lay waste lands in southern France that had been bequeathed by Jaume's father, King Pedro, to his cousin and staunch ally, the Count of Provence. Although King Jaume had been but fourteen years of age at the time, his fierce defence of the rights of the Count and his son Nunyo Sans had served as an abrupt lesson to Guillen de Muntcada that his own interests would be best served by admitting the error of his ways and swearing allegiance to the boy king. He had since become one of King Jaume's most faithful liegemen, and it was for the king's good that he now offered his advice...

'Under the circumstances, there's only one thing we can do, *senyor*, and that's to head back out of sight of the island until we know how much of the fleet has survived. With luck, the Moors will think that, after being battered by the storm, we've given up hope of –'

'No!' the king barked. 'Not even as a ploy to dupe the enemy! If our ships see us heading back towards them, they'll think the worst and about turn themselves. No, no, *amic*, I didn't risk life and limb leading the way here just to yield to the same faint hearts who would have scurried back home at the first puff of wind yesterday.'

'I understand that, *Majestat*, but what I suggest perhaps poses less of a risk than holding our position, which may invite a pack of Saracen ships to sally forth from the island and attack us before our own have been able to join us.'

The king rejected that speculation with a shake of his head. 'At least, if we hold our station here, we'll be able to see any enemy ships that *do* set out from Mallorca, whereas, if we slink back out of sight...'

Guillen de Muntcada said no more. He'd learned enough of the young king's doggedness over the years to know that, when in this mood, there was nothing to be gained by arguing with him. Besides, as he was obliged to concede (albeit only to himself), the king was in all probability right on this occasion.

As it transpired, no Moorish ships did set out from Mallorca, and by midnight the king was counting the lamps of more than forty vessels of his fleet being lit as they came over the western horizon. Standing beside the captain at the galley's stern, his face was wreathed in a self-congratulatory smile.

'There, just as I said, Master Guayron – they've seen our lanterns and have read the situation perfectly.'

'Indeed they have, *senyor*,' the captain replied, then added toadishly, 'A just endorsement of your wise decision earlier, if I may say so.'

'You may indeed say so,' the king grinned back. 'You may indeed.'

The moon was shining bright in a cloudless sky, so the outline of Mallorca was still clearly visible away to the east.

'What headland is that on the left of the island?' the king asked the captain.

'It's called the Cape of Formentor, *Majestat* – the northernmost point of Mallorca.'

'So, behind that is the Bay of Pollença, our planned landing place, correct?'

'*Sí, senyor*. I've only sailed past there once, but I recall that the bay is wide and well-sheltered. A perfect place for the fleet to anchor and for your men and horses to rest before starting the advance southward to the capital. Again, if I may say so, you made a wise choice, *senyor*.'

'Again, you may indeed say so, Captain Guayron,' the king replied with a gracious smile, conveniently passing over the fact that it had been his cousin and most experienced general, En Nunyo Sans, who had made all such crucial campaign decisions. After all, King Jaume told himself, even royalty can benefit from accepting a bit of reflected kudos when the opportunity arises. Helps keep the the regal profile suitably high in the eyes of the populace.

A light breeze that had started to blow from the west a few minutes earlier was now freshening, setting the galley rolling gently on the swell. The king couldn't have been more pleased.

'Your *Ponent* wind has returned at the perfect time,' he told the captain, then turned to Pedrito Blànes, who was resting with his arms draped over one of the tillers. 'And with more air in its lungs than when we left Salou yesterday, Master Blànes, no?'

'And at the perfect time, as you say, *Majestat*.'

'Yes, with that wind behind us we can reach Pollença, and no better time than now!' King Jaume nudged the captain with his elbow. 'Well, Captain Guayron. What are you waiting for? Give the order to get under way.'

The captain frowned. 'But what about the rest of the fleet?'

The king glowered at him. 'What about them?'

'Well, it – it's just that I,' the captain flustered, 'it's just that I thought you'd want to wait for the rest of the fleet to arrive. I mean, if the Moors send out ships to attack us when we draw close to the island, we'll need strength in numbers and –'

The king raised a hand. 'There's an expert in the seafaring ways of the Moors standing right here, so let's ask *him* what they're likely to do, shall we? Well?' he said to Pedrito, cocking his head inquisitively.

Pedrito motioned towards the setting sun. 'No need to worry, *senyor*. The Moors won't attack us at night. It isn't their way. Besides, word of your huge fleet being assembled back at the mainland will have reached them long ago, you can be sure. And what's more, they don't know any better than we do how many of our vessels survived last night's storm, so it's unlikely they'll commit their ships to anything until they know what they're going to be up against.' Pedrito stole a glance at Captain Guayron, whose looks in his direction were anything but cordial. 'And that isn't a Moorish tactic in particular,' he added pointedly, '– just common sense.'

The look that the captain then shot Pedrito informed him in no uncertain manner that he might ultimately rue the day he'd slighted him in such a way, and especially in front of the king. Not that

Pedrito was unduly bothered. He had nothing against the royal galley's captain, but his overriding concern was to return to his family on Mallorca, and if this man had his way, the landing would be delayed until his father's mule had grown a beard.

As for the king, his only reaction to Pedrito's advice was to vent his mounting impatience on the captain. 'Well, you heard what the helmsman said! So I repeat – give the order to get under way, and give it *immediately*!'

## 3

# THE MEETING PLACE OF THE WINDS

*OFF THE NORTH-WEST COAST OF MALLORCA –*
*FRIDAY 7ᵗʰ SEPTEMBER...*

And so the voyage continued in fine weather and on a calm sea until the next morning, when the royal galley and those vessels which had caught up with it were finally approaching Mallorca's Cape of Formentor and preparing to sail round into the Bay of Pollença. Not a single Moorish ship had been sighted since dawn, however, and this was something that puzzled the king as much as it pleased him.

'What do you make of it?' he asked Pedrito, who was once again manning the twin tillers by himself. 'Surely the Saracens have seen us and will have planned *some* sort of resistance.'

'If I had a free hand, I'd be scratching my head,' Pedrito confessed. He thought for a moment. 'In all honesty, I'd never claim to know the finer workings of the Moorish mind – no one can, unless he's a Moor – but I can't fathom why anyone, even the Moors, wouldn't engage us at sea now, if only to weaken us for whatever battles might follow if we do manage to establish a foothold ashore.'

King Jaume scrutinised Pedrito's face again. 'You intrigue me, Master Blànes, you really do. The way you speak, the things you say. First I said you talked more like a philosopher than a helmsman – now you talk more like a military man than a philosopher.'

Pedrito allowed himself a little chuckle. 'Let's just say you can develop more than your arm muscles during five years on a Moorish pirate galley – if you're lucky, and keep your ears open.'

'Hmm, intriguing, intriguing,' the king murmured. He stroked his chin in his habitual way. 'You must tell me your story sometime, for I've an idea it may be as colourful as my own, though doubtless in very different ways.'

Just then, they were joined by the captain and his sailing master, both of whom appeared to be in a state of high anxiety.

'Look yonder, *Majestat*!' the captain urged. He pointed to the northern sky. 'That cloud above the summit of the cape.'

'What about it?' the king shrugged.

'It comes from the quarter of the Provence wind,' the sailing master said. 'It doesn't bode well for us, *senyor*.'

'Master Sagran's right,' the captain affirmed. 'If a Provence wind hits us as we try to round the cape, we'll be blown onto the rocks. We'll never make it into the Bay of Pollença.'

The king turned to Pedrito. 'You know the ways of the Mallorcan weather better than any of us. So, what do you say? Are these gentlemen right about this wretched wind from Provence?'

Pedrito looked up at the clouds already forming above the mountain range that ran fully forty miles the length of the coast away to the galley's starboard side. 'The *Tramuntana* is what that wind's called in Mallorca. The same name as these mountains, and just as cruel and unforgiving to the unwary.' He nodded his head gravely. '*The Meeting Place of The Winds* is what the Mallorcan fishermen call the Cape of Formentor. It can be a wild and unpredictable place. And it's true – any ship sailing broadside to a *Tramuntana* in these waters would be in real danger of being smashed against the cliffs. *Sí*, and it can happen with very little warning too.'

As if on cue, an eerie silence fell as the sky leadened. Then, of a sudden, a sharp northerly rose up, whipping the sea into a seething foam and slapping the sails of the ships back against their masts.

'A white squall!' the captain shouted, raising his forearm to protect his eyes from the stinging spray. 'Quick, Master Sagran, make ready to strike your sail before it's torn to shreds!'

The command '*Cala! Cala!*' – 'Hold fast!' was soon being called from vessel to vessel, followed by the order, '*Carga! Carga!*' –

'Lower sail!'

Confusion reigned as the buffeting wind made the hauling of ropes and the furling of canvas well nigh impossible for sailors already in danger of being swept overboard by wave upon wave breaking over their decks. For all that, every ship in the vicinity was eventually under bare poles, though now being tossed perilously close to each other by the angry sea.

The king's expression was grim. He may not have had much experience of naval matters, but he realised well enough that he was now in very real danger of losing his life, and with it his chance of having his name engraved in the annals of Christian glory. There was nothing he could do now but pray, so pray he did.

Falling to his knees on the rain-lashed poop deck, he beseeched Christ and his Holy Mother to deliver him and those with him from their present danger. Then, with hands clasped and eyes closed, he raised his face to the storm and implored God Almighty to remember that he, His chosen vassal, was undertaking this mission to exalt the faith that God Himself had given him, and to abase and destroy those who did not share it.

From his position at the helm, Pedrito was close enough to hear the young king's entreaties. He couldn't help but compare them to his own humble prayers while a captive of Moorish pirates; earnest pleas to be released from the purgatory of slavery and returned to the bosom of his family. As yet, his prayers remained only half answered at best, and he wondered if the king's unshakeable conviction that his royal rank had been granted by God Himself would stand his exhortations in any better stead than his own.

'Save us, dear Lord, from this terrible tempest,' King Jaume begged, 'so that the good work I have begun in Thy name may not be in vain. For remember that Thy loss will be greater than mine, if my mission to spread the teachings of Thy dear Son to the disbelievers should be allowed to fail.'

But pray as he might, the storm continued to rage, and the plight of the royal galley and all the fifty or so vessels presently with it grew ever more critical.

'This is yet another of your eight winds sent to plague us,' the king barked at Pedrito, his mounting feelings of desperation inciting him to lash out at the person nearest to him. He slashed the air with his hand. 'Damn your Saracen song and its heathen winds!'

Though struggling to keep the tillers from being torn from his grasp as the galley was driven ever closer to the base of the cliffs, and sympathetic as he was to the king's state of mind, Pedrito felt sufficently maligned by what he regarded as this childish outburst to take a deep breath and shout back, 'To curse the wind, *senyor*, is to invite the wrath of God.' He gave himself a moment to confirm that the king had been adequately taken aback before making the deliberately provocative qualification: 'According to an old saying of Moorish sailors, that is.'

He was fully aware that, under less fraught circumstances, he would have been inviting perhaps worse than the wrath of God by goading the monarch in this way. However, as both he and King Jaume were now equals in the life-threatening situation in which they found themselves, his instinct compelled him to respond bluntly to what he had been taught by the school of life to regard as the futility of pitting one religion's god against the other – given that he remained to be totally convinced of the existence of either.

The king's view was less ambivalent, however. 'Spare me your Moorish proverbs!' he snarled. 'I fear the wrath of God, as do all good Christians, but I care nothing for Muslim gibberish!' Raising a hand, he jabbed a finger into the eye of the gale. 'If Allah has sent this damned *Tramuntana* wind to overwhelm us, then I *do* curse it, and I call upon the one true God to restore, in His infinite mercy, the wind that will take us to Pollença!'

But still the *Tramuntana* howled down from the north, while panic began to spread through the crews fighting to contain the chaos into which their ships were being hurled.

Captain Guayron clambered back onto the poop deck, consternation staring from his eyes. 'We'll have to bear away southward from this wind, my lord,' he cried. 'It's our only chance.'

'No!' the king shouted back. 'You were the one to tell me yesterday that God would send a wind to take me to Mallorca, *if* we turned back then. Well, we didn't turn back, yet He still sent me such a wind, and I'll keep faith in Him again.'

The captain was becoming frantic. 'This Provence gale is likely to blow for hours, perhaps days – I've seen it many times – but we've only minutes to save ourselves from being being smashed against those rocks. We have to harness the wind to take us out of here!'

But his entreaties fell on deaf ears. The king was adamant: the grace of God was without limit for those who believed in Him, and those who truly believed owed it to God to stand firm when their faith was being tested – as it was now.

No less was Pedrito's will to live being tested, however. Although he realised that the king's upbringing by the Knights Templar had instilled in him an unquestioning belief in the benevolence of God, Pedrito didn't understand how even this could blind him to the fact that to ignore the captain's warning was tantamount to committing suicide and, in all probability, mass murder as well. He decided to tackle the king's ideology head-on – though with as much subtlety as he could. The prospect of feeling the thrust of King Jaume's sword was no more attractive, after all, than the likelihood of going down with his ship.

Hesitantly, he reminded the king of the seafarers' belief that the eight winds he had sung about were actually God's messengers. Then, before the king had a chance to erupt into another anti-Moorish rant, he offered the suggestion that, for any benefit to be realised, such messages might have to be read correctly.

King Jaume scowled. 'I told you I've no time for riddles! If you have something worthwhile to say, then say it straight!'

'What I'm saying, *senyor*, is that perhaps God has sent this *Tramuntana* wind to tell you that there may be a better landing place than Pollença.'

The king's frown deepened, but he said nothing, his silence suggesting to Pedrito that he should expand on what he had just said – but quickly, and it had better make sense!

Thinking fast, Pedrito advised him that to sail from here on a broad reach ahead of the wind would ultimately take them under the lee of the southern extremity of the Tramuntana mountain chain, where there was an uninhabited island sheltering a bay which would make a safe haven for his entire fleet – or as much of it as might yet survive this storm.

The king still said nothing, but his expression had become slightly more receptive.

'What's more,' Pedrito swiftly continued, 'the place I speak of is just round the headland from my own home of Andratx. I know it well. It's not much more than sixteen miles overland from the city – just half the distance you'd have to march from Pollença.'

'And how far by sea?' the king enquired, his interest kindled.

'About three leagues – nine or ten miles, maybe.'

'And the name of this place?'

'The island is called Sa Dragonera. It's mountainous, narrow and over two miles long, lying off the bay of Sa Palomera, or Sant Elm, as the Christian fishermen call it. And there's ample anchorage in Es Freu, the channel between Sa Dragonera and the shore.' Pedrito was warming to his theme. Perhaps there was something in the old sailors' belief that the winds were God's messengers after all. Anyway, if espousing the belief would help persuade the king to desist from committing himself and his followers to a watery grave, then espouse it Pedrito would. 'Sí, senyor,' he enthused, 'and the place is well protected from this north wind and easily defended too.'

'And fresh water for our men and horses?' the king queried.

Yes, there was a good spring on Sa Dragonera, Pedrito confirmed. 'Clear, sweet water, senyor, and plenty of it, with none to share it with but lizards and a few wild goats.' As it was now obvious that the king was becoming more sold on this idea by the second, Pedrito added the clincher: 'And better still, there's a little islet called Es Pantaleu, tucked into the bay at Sa Palomera, which would make a perfect place for your Majesty to take rest and discuss fresh tactics with your nobles.'

King Jaume promptly turned again to the captain. 'Well,' he

barked triumphantly, 'I told you my faith in God would be rewarded. So what in heaven's name are you waiting for, man? *Ràpidament*! Give the order to go with the wind for Sa Palomera, and see that word is relayed for all the other ships to follow on!'

# THE WORTH OF UNSHAKEABLE FAITH

*SATURDAY, SEPTEMBER 8ᵗʰ – THE BAY OF SA PALOMERA
(SANT ELM), SOUTH-WEST MALLORCA…*

After arriving in the bay on the Friday evening, King Jaume and the key members of his entourage had set up camp on the islet of Es Pantaleu. All the other vessels that had followed him southwards from the Cape of Formentor had also made it safely through the storm, which by then had blown itself out. It was a thankful young king, therefore, who finally fell asleep that night, exhausted by the harrowing experiences of a voyage that had almost cost him his life, and still fearful that some, or even all, of the ships that had been delayed by the first day's storm might not yet complete the crossing to Mallorca.

His anxiety was to increase considerably at dawn the following morning, when he emerged from his tent to see a huge army of Moors amassed on the shore not much more than what he reckoned to be a good crossbow shot away. They were armed to the teeth, flashes of light from the rising sun glinting off the silvered bosses of their shields. Turbanned and loose-robed, they stood perfectly still. Their silence, broken only by the occasional whinnying of a horse, was eerie and more menacing than a fanfare of war.

King Jaume was with his cousin, En Nunyo Sans, who, along with two more of the expedition's most able and experienced military campaigners, En Guillen de Muntcada and his older cousin, En Remon, had been summoned to discuss how best to revise the original invasion plans, which had been nullified (due to divine intervention or otherwise) by the previous day's *Tramuntana* gale.

'Now we know why they didn't attack us at sea,' the king murmured.

'*D'acord*,' Nunyo Sans replied, his voice thick with foreboding. 'Why risk their ships when they knew they'd outnumber us as heavily as this on land?'

Solemnly, the two other nobles expressed their agreement.

'There could be upwards of five thousand men there,' Remon de Muntcada muttered as he scanned the shoreline, 'and fully two hundred horse, perhaps.'

En Guillen cast his eyes towards the channel between the coast and Sa Dragonera Island. 'And with only a third of our fleet here, we'd be hard pushed to assemble a landing force big enough to challenge even half that amount.'

The immediate outlook was bleak indeed, and even the usually-optimistic king was obliged to admit as much. All the same, he wasn't about to capitulate without making a wholehearted attempt at taking Mallorca, no matter how unfavourable the eventual odds.

'God has brought us this far,' he stressed, 'and as we do this in His name, I believe no less than before that He will see us through to victory.'

But En Remon de Muntcada ventured a more pragmatic view. 'As much as I admire your faith, *Majestat*, it would take a miracle equal to that of the loaves and fishes for us to mount a successful attack on such a superior force as is facing us now.'

Nunyo Sans was quick to back him up. 'En Remon speaks as a good general, and although he's as God-fearing as any man, what he says makes sense. To pit our limited forces against those Saracen hordes would be too great a favour for even a king to ask of the Almighty.'

King Jaume shrugged off that pronouncement with a firm reminder that, in good time, God would deliver enough of the fleet to swell their current numbers to an adequate level – *if* they had faith.

His three nobles said a concerted amen to that, though swapping anxious glances.

For all that the mounting risks of the mission lay heavily on his shoulders, and despite the cautioning words of his trusted noblemen jarring his impatience for action, a serene smile spread over King Jaume's face as he gazed for the first time above and beyond the Moorish troops assembled rank behind rank along the curve of the shore. His eyes had been drawn to the mountains that protected the bay like enfolding arms. Their lower slopes were carpeted in swathes of evergreen oak, their rugged flanks cloaked by pinewoods, their sunbathed ridges glowing gold against a cloudless sky like the points of a giant's crown. Languorously, he inhaled the resinous scent of the island drifting over the water on the still morning air.

'Now I know why God has blessed me with the task of reclaiming this land from the infidel,' he murmured, his eyes alight with almost childlike wonder. 'Did you ever see such a beautiful place?' He savoured the view for a moment or two, then turned to his companions and said, 'You know, when I was a child being brought up by the Templars in Aragon, one old knight told me of a Muslim legend which has it that, when Allah created Earth, each land was given five wishes. Al-Andalus, as the Saracen thieves named Spain, asked for a clear sky, for a sea full of fish, for beautiful women and plentiful fruit. The final wish, which was for good government, was rejected by Allah on the grounds that it would have completed the creation of an earthly land to rival Heaven itself.' A look of grim determination was on the king's face as he concluded, 'But with God's help, we will surely show our contempt for Allah's lack of benevolence by establishing a true Christian Heaven right here in Mallorca!'

En Nunyo Sans respectfully though pointedly replied that, while the king's motives were unquestionably pious and worthy of the steadfast support of all his followers, there was still much to do before he'd be in a position to create a government of *any* kind in Mallorca. 'Firstly,' he went on, 'there's the matter of finding a suitable landing place for our forces. The logic behind our chosing the northern Bay of Pollença was that our advance on the city of Medîna Mayûrqa would be made by traversing southward over the island's central plain – an easy route for our men and horses, while providing precious little opportunity for ambush by the Saracens.' He gestured towards the mountains the king had just been admiring. 'Now we're faced with an altogether more daunting route to our target, I fear.'

To which En Guillen de Muntcada quickly replied, 'Unless, of course, there's a landing place with a more even terrain between here and the city.'

'But that's where we're at a loss,' En Remon put in, 'because we've no detailed knowledge of this southern coastline.'

With a wry smile, En Guillen shook his head. 'You should never jump to a negative conclusion so readily. Remember, an essential of any military campaign is to be prepared for at least the most likely contingencies.'

En Remon raised his shoulders. 'You have the better of me.'

'And me,' King Jaume admitted.

Nunyo Sans smiled knowingly, but maintained a diplomatic silence.

With mischief in his eyes, En Guillen gave the king an enquiring look. 'Are you forgetting the captain of my ship's controversial appointment of a certain ex-pirate to the crew of your Majesty's galley?'

'Certainly not!' the king retorted. He gave an imperious toss of his head. 'In fact, I was just about to summon him myself.' Snapping his fingers, he beckoned a seaman who was standing in attendance nearby. 'Take the skiff to my galley and bring the helmsman Pedrito Blànes to me immediately!'

\*

A wiggly line drawn with a stick into the sand of Es Pantaleu's tiny beach comprised Pedrito's improvised map of the south-western coastline of Mallorca. The king and his council of war, which comprised a selection of senior nobles and the shipmasters of most authority in the fleet, looked on attentively.

'So, *senyors*,' Pedrito said, pointing with his stick, 'this mark here denotes where we are now.' He moved the stick eastwards along the crude chart. 'And here we have the inlet to the port of Andratx. An excellent natural harbour, but still with a mountain pass to negotiate before gaining a level approach to the city.' He moved his pointer farther in the same direction. 'And this curve is the *Ensenada* of Santa Ponça, a cove quite wide enough to accommodate a large fleet, and with the creek of Sa Caleta at the far end a handy place for unloading vessels directly ashore.'

Mutterings of approval were exchanged.

'Then, *senyors*,' Pedrito continued, while moving his twig even farther eastward, 'you have an unobstructed crossing over the Sa Porrassa peninsula for the final approach along level ground skirting the coast to –' he jabbed his pointer into the ground '– the city of Medîna Mayûrqa!'

Further positive-sounding murmurs ensued.

'How far from this Santa Ponça to the city?' asked En Nunyo Sans.

'Eleven miles, maybe twelve.'

And was the route overlooked by high ground, Remon de Muntcada wanted to know?

Indeed it was, for at least the final five miles, Pedrito informed him.

Pensively, En Guillen de Muntcada scratched his beard. 'Hmm, the enemy on the high ground and our men on the low. Never the best of positions for engaging in battle.'

'We'd be at the mercy of their archers,' En Remon warned. 'And with our backs to the sea at that.'

Mutterings of disapproval were exchanged.

'Enough!' barked the king. 'The only way to gain the initiative in such a situation is to *take* the high ground from the enemy.'

'Ah yes, but we could suffer heavy losses,' Nunyo Sans advised.

'And what in heaven's name do you think waging war is all about?' the king bristled, his patience stretched to the limit. 'I expected more of my nobles than the girlish whimpering of nuns!'

'That may well be, my lord,' said En Guillen dryly, 'but we're already dangerously inferior to the enemy in numbers, so –'

'So, we just have to fight all the more fiercely! Have you *really* so little trust in the succour of God for those who bear arms in His name?'

Heads were hung in silence for a few moments before Nunyo Sans plucked up the courage to tell the king that, although they all realised how committed he was to the holy cause, they, in their experience as generals, were only trying to ensure that no unnecessary risks would be taken. For to do so, he cautioned, would surely be to hand victory to the Saracens and to commit many good Christian knights and soldiers to a pointless death.

Despairingly, the king shook his head. 'As our Lord Jesus Christ said, "Oh thou of little faith..."'

At that, a cry rang out from one of the galleys standing lookout to the seaward of Sa Dragonera island:

'*Vaixell a la vista*! Look – a ship! A ship!'

And sure enough, approaching from the west was a sail, and another, then another, and yet another still. Soon there were twenty or more, making good headway towards Mallorca from the direction of mainland Spain.

'It's our fleet!' one of the king's squires shouted. 'See, on the mast of the lead ship – the banner of the Knights Templar!'

'Oh thou of little faith,' a patently self-satisfied king repeated to his crestfallen barons. 'Wherefore didst thou doubt?' He then dusted off his hands and declared, 'Now, gentlemen, I suggest that you, En Remon, take Master Blànes here aboard your galley and let him guide you along the coast so that you can assess his suggested landing place at Santa Ponça.' He turned to his cousin Nunyo Sans. 'And it's best that you follow in your galley as an escort. *Sí*, and make sure both vessels carry the biggest complement possible of first-class crossbowmen in case of a Saracen attack.' He paused to look directly at each of his senior nobles in turn. 'Even our protector, the Lord God Almighty, is entitled to expect a little human assistance occasionally!'

\*

As it transpired, the reconnoitering mission attracted no response whatever from the enemy. Indeed, not one Moorish vessel ventured forth from any of the small coves that nibble the coastline in that part of the island, nor was there evidence of the two Christian galleys being observed from the shore. It was taken for granted by the king's two commanders, nevertheless, that their every move was being watched by countless pairs of dark eyes on the wooded hillsides bordering the sea.

While it was unnerving for King Jaume to know that the Moors were in the fortunate position of being able to play a waiting game, he was able to take considerable encouragement from Nunyo Sans and Remon de Muntcada reporting, on their safe return to the islet of Es Pantaleu later in the day, that Pedrito Blànes' description of the Bay of Santa Ponça had been absolutely accurate. It was indeed an ideal landing place, with the added advantage of being overlooked by a hill large enough to accommodate an advance party of at least five hundred knights and foot soldiers – sufficient, they calculated, to hold off any Moorish attack while the rest of the army was being disembarked.

The king's rising spirits were elevated even more when, towards sunset, the last of the main body of the fleet finally dropped anchor in the channel between Sa Dragonera island and the bay of Sa Palomera. His faith in the benevolence of God had been totally vindicated. Every one of the vessels that had left the mainland with him four days earlier had now arrived at Mallorca, and not a single man, horse or item of battle equipment had been lost during the two great storms.

For Pedrito's part, a feeling of melancholy tempered his gladness for the king and the successful start to his attempted reconquest of Mallorca. For, deep down, he had no real wish to be involved in this crusade, or rather in the bloodshed and destruction that would accompany it. He had been as happy as any boy could be when living and working with his adoptive parents on their little farm near the Andratx coast, and, as he had told the king himself, the fact that they'd lived under Muslim rule hadn't been of any significant hardship at all. No more and perhaps even less, Pedrito privately mused, than might have been the case under the strict auspices of the Christian Church.

Yet it wasn't so much these unfathomable religious contentions and the inevitable violence they spawned that was troubling him as he sat outside the king's tent that evening. No, it was the fact that he was now so near his family that he could actually walk to them in under an hour from the beach opposite, on which that huge Moorish army was assembled. Even greater had been his urge to make immediately for home when sailing past the mouth of the Andratx inlet earlier in the day. In the distance, he had seen the two tall palm trees that stood guard over his parents' little farmhouse on a rise just half a mile inland from the head of the cove. The temptation to jump ship and swim ashore had been almost overwhelming, particularly on the return trip, when the merits of the Santa Ponça landing place had already been confirmed by the king's two barons. But what would have been the point? If he hadn't been shot by the galley's archers for desertion, he would probably have had his throat cut as a spy by one of the many Moorish soldiers who were doubtless lying in wait on shore.

How many times had he and his father welcomed the sight of those tall palms when rounding Sa Mola headland on their way home from a fishing trip? And how many more times had he longed to see them again during those five hellish years chained to the sweat-stinking ribs of an Arab pirate galley? Home. Now he was so close that he could almost smell the olive-wood smoke from his mother's bread oven drifting over Es Tres Picons ridge across there to the right of the bay. Home. His mother, his father and his little sister Esperança. 'Hope' was her name, and hope was what the memory of her laughing eyes brought to him every time he was in danger of being drawn into the depths of despair while slumped gasping for breath in the reeking belly of that damned galley. Esperança. She'd be almost seventeen now. A beauty to break the hearts of many a young village lad, if she cared to put those eyes of hers to best use – as undoubtedly she would. She was a girl after all. Pedrito smiled wistfully at the thought.

'Your thoughts are far away, *amic*. Surely you aren't longing for your pirates and their barren shores of Morocco, when this Garden of Eden awaits you.'

Pedrito looked up to see the king gazing over the water of the bay towards that selfsame ridge of Es Tres Picons. Admiration was in his eyes, but there was also a trace of avarice. Pedrito was coming home, and he wanted nothing more, but King Jaume was coming to take, to conquer, to change and, in his own words, to destroy those unwilling to convert to his own faith. In the process, albeit in the name of God (or *a* god), something of the truly heaven-sent allurement of the island and the contented lives of its people would be forfeited for the material gain of relatively few. And all of them strangers – even the king.

'All I'm longing for is home,' Pedrito replied. 'I can't wait to see my family again.' He then told the king how he had been tempted to swim ashore when passing the Andratx inlet earlier in the day.

'Pah,' the king scoffed, 'Nunyo Sans would have given the order for you to be shot before you'd swum half your own length.'

'Why do you think I didn't dive in?' Pedrito swiftly retorted.

The king stared at him for a sign that he might be joking.

Pedrito's face remained expressionless.

King Jaume looked genuinely hurt. 'Your allegiance to me is as fragile as *that*?'

Pedrito allowed a few strained moments to pass, then said, 'Show me one man in all the thousands with you who'd rather have an arrow in the back than delay seeing his family for a few days.'

The king smiled awkwardly, not knowing quite how to take that.

'But anyway,' Pedrito continued, straight-faced, 'it really wasn't fear of En Nunyo's bowmen that bolstered my allegiance to you.'

The king's look of relief was tinged with uncertainty. 'It … wasn't?' he checked.

'Absolutely not, because with luck I could have swum underwater for long enough to get out of arrow's range. No, no, what persuaded me to stay aboard the galley was the fear of having my gizzard slit by a Moor's scimitar when I did make it ashore.'

The uneasy smile on the king's face graduated into one of hesitant good humour. 'I, ehm, I believe you may be teasing me,

Master Blànes.'

Pedrito's expression remained inscrutable. 'No more, *senyor*, than you teased me about being called Little Pedro.'

A few more tense seconds passed, then, as a playful grin spread over Pedrito's face, the king started to chuckle. Pedrito joined him, and soon their unbridled laughter was ringing out over the bay – an incongruous sound, which probably intimidated the encamped Moorish army as much as their own ghostly silence had disconcerted the king earlier in the day.

'You're a brave man, Little Pedro!' he beamed, slapping Pedrito's back.

'Not brave enough, though, to risk a Christian arrow up my arse or a Moorish blade across my windpipe.'

'No, but brave enough to take risks with your king's sense of humour. What if I'd thought you were making fun of me, instead of having fun *with* me?'

Pensively, Pedrito stroked the lobe of his ear. 'Well, I suppose I'd probably have had the honour of being the *Reconquista*'s first victim of your Majesty's sword.'

'Indeed you would, *amic*,' the king chortled. 'Indeed you would. And you're all the braver in my eyes for admitting it, even though your opportunities for doing anything other than staying within the ranks of my troops appear to have been somewhat limited.'

Pedrito got to his feet, looked squarely at the king and said, 'I'm not a brave man, *senyor*, but I am a man of my word, and I promised you I'd repay the favour you did me when you took a hand at the helm during that first storm.'

The king canted his head to one side. 'And that repayment is?'

'My willingness to do your bidding during this crusade … provided you don't expect me to kill anyone, whatever his colour or creed.'

A little snort of disdain escaped the king's nostrils. 'Fine sentiments for a lady in waiting, perhaps, but of little value to a soldier. *Sí*, and if such grand principles withstand the heat of battle, as God is my witness I'll eat my chain mail!'

'Well now, that'll take a fair pinch of salt, and no mistake,'

Pedrito quipped. 'But don't worry, *Majestat*, I know where the best *salines* on the island are, and I'll happily take you there to season your hauberk when the time comes.'

'And I'll hold you to that, *if* the time comes,' the king replied with an owlish wink. Then, ushering Pedrito a few paces down from his tent to the tiny beach where the impromptu council of war had gathered earlier, he said, 'But I've summoned you here this evening for another purpose entirely, and that's to take my mind off what lies ahead by having that promised talk with you about what lies in the past – both your past and my own.'

# 5

# FOOD FOR THOUGHT

*THE SAME EVENING – THE ISLET OF ES PANTALEU,*
*IN THE SOUTH-WEST OF MALLORCA ...*

As bizarre as it was for the king of such a large realm as Aragon-Catalonia to be conducting an informal pre-hostilities conversation with a mere seaman, the location did at least match the occasion. The entire islet of Es Pantaleu would have fitted inside the walls of one of King Jaume's more modest castles, though without the most basic of amenities. It was nothing but a turtle shell of rock with a few scrubby thorn bushes scattered about, and without even the simplest of moorings for a boat. For why would anyone want to tie up there anyway? After all, not even the lizards of Sa Dragonera Island had bothered to swim over and colonize Es Pantaleu. And the two boulders that had been selected by the king as makeshift seats for himself and Pedrito would never have been considered suitable stools for court milkmaids, far less the base of a royal throne. But the rocks were rounded by the age-old attentions of the sea, so were comfortable enough for the present purpose, while boasting the added benefit of providing an unobstructed view of the attendant Moorish army and any moves it might make.

'I see they're pitching their tents now,' the king observed.

'Making ready for a long stand-off?' Pedrito suggested.

'Then they'll be disappointed. Tomorrow is the sabbath, so we rest, but then... Well, En Nunyo and the Muntcadas are finalising details for the invasion with the other leading barons on the ship of the Bishop of Barcelona even as we speak.'

It was ironic, Pedrito silently considered, that the expedition's most senior prelate should host a conference aimed at devising the maximum loss of life for the 'disbelievers', while one of the linchpins of his own belief was 'Thou shalt not kill'. But that had been the paradox of so-called holy wars since time immemorial, so why should it change now?

A servant brought a simple supper of bread drizzled with olive oil and topped with slabs of pork that had been preserved in vinegar and garlic. He also brought a goatskin of wine, a jug of fresh water and two horn beakers.

'I'm afraid the bread's a mite stale now,' the king told Pedrito, while pouring himself a goodly measure of wine, 'but it's still a whole lot better than the hardtack we'll be eating for a while after this.'

'Mmm, bread,' Pedrito pondered, helping himself to a cup of water. 'It's funny how little things like the smell of fresh-baked bread can remind you of home.'

'Oh?' queried the king, clearly unfamiliar with this particular line in nostalgia.

Pedrito pointed towards the mountains to the east of the bay. 'In fact, I thought I could almost smell the smoke from my mother's bread oven drifting over that ridge a bit earlier.'

A humourless little laugh escaped the king's lips. 'I've had more homes in my life than I care to remember, and the only smells I associate with them are the stench of sweat, rust and dried blood drifting out of suits of mail – oh, and the mustiness of priests' bibles.'

'Armour and bibles,' Pedrito murmured. 'War and religion – constant companions.'

'And it will be ever so until the whole world learns to follow the path of Christ.'

'But I've heard it said that Jesus was also a prophet of Islam, according to the followers of Allah.'

'Ah yes, but they'd say anything to suit their own ends,' the king pooh-poohed.

'Maybe, but there's much in common between the Christian and

Muslim religions – the Jewish religion too, because it came before either of them, and many Christian and Muslim beliefs are based on what the old Hebrew scribes laid down.'

The king gnawed at a chunk of pork and washed it down with a slug of wine. 'None of those old fairy tales matter. No, no, all that matters is converting the followers of Allah to the true teachings of our Lord Jesus Christ, the Son of God.'

'So, you believe there are two gods, just as the ancient Romans and Greeks believed there were several?'

'The gods of the Romans and Greeks? Pah, more fairy tales! No, no, *amic*, as you must be well aware, having been brought up as a Christian yourself, there is only one god, our Lord God Almighty, father of our Lord Jesus Christ.'

'But what about those who say there is no such thing as *any* religion?'

The king looked at him in utter amazement. 'You're speaking in riddles again, aren't you? At least I hope you are!'

Pedrito knew well enough that his tongue might be leading him into dangerous territory once more, but he couldn't resist the urge to find out how much thought, if any, the king had put into the beliefs that were the driving force behind what he saw as his God-given mission in life. And what better time to find out than when the king was succumbing to the sedative influence of the grape.

'Not that I necessarily see eye-to-eye with those who support it,' Pedrito began, by way of ameliorating what he was about to say, 'but there is a line of thought that all organised religions came about because of our fear of dying.'

The king's look of amazement morphed into one of confusion. 'But surely the whole point is that, if we believe in the word of Christ and follow his path, then we needn't fear death, because we'll live with him in the house of God forever.'

'Yes, but those who worship Allah say basically the same – as do the Jews, and Jesus was a Jew himself.'

The king lowered his eyes and stared blankly into his wine. 'What exactly are you trying to say?' he muttered, his tone exuding an odd mix of curiosity and menace.

'Oh, just that believing we'll be rewarded with eternal life in heaven if we live a good life on earth is a worthy enough belief, if it encourages us to be better people in the here-and-now.'

'And?'

'Well, some people – and I repeat it's not that I necessarily see eye-to-eye with them myself – some people suggest that this basic hope for eternal life was seized upon in ancient times by opportunists who saw a measure of power and even profit in it for themselves, if they could convince everyone else that they were the earthly spokesmen of the gods.'

'And?' the king repeated, still gazing inscrutably into his beaker.

Pedrito shifted his feet uneasily, wishing now that he'd curbed his inherent inquisitiveness. But he'd talked himself into a corner, and there was nothing else for it but to try and talk his way out again. 'Well, I *think* what these people are saying,' he ventured, 'is that those few self-appointed holy men, for want of a better description, would have had the advantage over everyone else of a certain amount of education, and may have used this to complicate everyone's hope for life after death by creating a set of rules and regulations that would be of most benefit to themselves.' He cleared his throat. 'That's, ehm, to the benefit of the holy men, I mean.'

Slowly, the king ran a finger tip round the rim of his beaker. '*Complicate* everyone's hope for life after death? What do you mean by that?'

'Well, I – I can't speak for the people who say these things,' Pedrito stammered, 'but, you know, I suppose they mean holy men confusing and mystifying the uneducated by, well, let's say preaching in Latin to people who can't understand Latin. And, some would say, by also setting themselves apart, and even above, everyone else by dressing up in fancy clothes.'

King Jaume raised his head and looked at him coldly, but, as Pedrito was becoming accustomed to at such awkward moments, the young monarch said nothing.

Nervously, Pedrito tugged at the lobe of his ear again. It was becoming increasingly apparent that King Jaume wasn't prepared to even discuss the complexities of this thorny though, to Pedrito, fascinating subject. And while he had no desire to offend the king, of whom he was an extremely privileged guest after all, he felt he had to put him right on one important point.

'Although I was brought up as a Christian, I was never preached to by a priest, simply because our Moorish overlords in Mallorca prohibited them.'

'That'll change soon enough, never fear,' the king grunted, then quaffed a mouthful of wine.

'Yes, but what I meant was that I learned the teachings of Christ from my parents, who had learned them from their parents, and so on. All word of mouth, of course, because none of them could read or write. And neither could I.'

'So?'

'So, no one had an axe to grind – no religious organisation to support, no priests to pay, no churches to build and maintain, no evangelical motives, nothing but a simple belief that it was right to pass on this good code of living from one generation to another.'

'There you are then – proof enough that the Christian faith can survive in even the most barren of situations.' The king poured himself another cup of wine.

Pedrito rubbed the tip of his nose to conceal a smile. It was refreshing to see the young king relaxing again, and amusing to note that he was also becoming a little tipsy. Pedrito took a sip of water.

'But what I'm getting round to,' he went on, 'is that we were taught to tolerate and respect those in Mallorca who worshipped Allah, just as they tolerated and respected us Christians – by and large anyway.'

King Jaume swiped the air with a chunk of bread. 'Allah? Puh! He was only one of many pagan idols who existed long before Mohammed came along with his weasel words for the gullible. *Sí, sí, sí,* I learned the truth about all that Islamic mumbo-jumbo from the Knights of the Temple even before I was old enough to lift a sword.' He prodded Pedrito in the chest. 'Take it from me, Allah was never the God of the Bible. He was the pagan Moon-god the Arabs built Mecca in homage to. Nothing but a myth created by the infidel to further his own selfish ends.' He raised a resolute eyebrow. 'Why do you think the Moors took Mallorca in Allah's name?'

Pedrito was sorely tempted to fire the king's question straight back at him, but substituting Christians for Moors and God for Allah. However, he doubted if even the consumption of the whole goatskin of wine, never mind a few swigs, would make King Jaume receptive to such a profane proposition.

'Nevertheless, life under the Moors in Mallorca wasn't a bad one for us,' Pedrito said instead, 'and it proves that the two religions can co-exist reasonably well.'

The king's expression grew deadly serious. 'Yes, and that's something else that will change soon enough. Those who worship Allah will convert or die. It's as simple as that!'

Pedrito dipped his head in mute acknowledgement, having promptly decided it was time to button his lip again.

The king seemed to read his thoughts. 'And I'll give you a word of advice, my friend. I'm an open-minded fellow who's prepared to listen to the views of others, no matter how misguided, but if you ever come out with the abominations you've said to me here in front of the likes of the Bishop of Barcelona, he'll have your tongue cut out, then have you burned alive as a heretic. *Sí*, and if the Bishop asks me to, I'll gladly light the fire!'

Pedrito dipped his head once more, though with considerably more reverence this time.

A slightly woozy smile replaced the glower that had been darkening the king's handsome features. He punched Pedrito lightly on the arm. 'But why are you drinking water when we have wine, man?' He let out a snigger. 'When I was a boy, an old drunkard of a monk who was my tutor told me, never drink water, my child – fish shit in it!'

After the king's burn-as-a-heretic remark, Pedrito was glad to join him in a hearty guffaw, even though he'd heard the same old joke a thousand times from pirate-galley oarsmen when long at sea and obliged to slake a searing thirst with rancid wine they'd willingly have swapped for water any day, fish shit and all.

The king raised his beaker. 'But as sacrilegious as some of your utterings are, Little Pedro, at least they're more scholarly than one expects from a common sailor, and that's why I summoned you to talk with me this evening.' He clicked his beaker against Pedrito's. 'So, come on – tell me your story, *marinèr*. Explain how an illiterate peasant, turned slave of Moorish pirates, could blossom into a philosopher before a Christian king.'

Pedrito began by informing him that, from the day he was captured, he had shared an oar with an Arab known simply as *al-Usstaz*, 'The Professor', a tall, wiry fellow in his late twenties or early thirties, who would reveal no other name. According to shipboard rumour, he'd once been a highly respected academic in the court of the Sultan of Seville, but had fallen out of favour and had been banished to a deliberately short life as an oarsman on a pirate galley. No one knew what crime, if any, had justified such a fate, and the man himself would brook no question on the subject. Indeed, it was said that he hardly spoke a word to anyone until Pedrito was shackled beside him and established a bond by revealing a genuine hunger for knowledge.

'I'd always been an inquisitive sort of child,' Pedrito continued, '– asking my father why the sky was blue and the clouds were white, and where the rain came from and where the sun went at night. That sort of thing.' He chuckled quietly. 'I can't remember what answers my father came up with, but I'm sure he did his best to explain many things he knew precious little about himself.'

'In that respect,' said the king, nodding absently, 'your father had much in common with the drunken monk who taught me for a while.'

Pedrito cast the king a sardonic glance. 'Well, I know nothing of drunken monks, but that's how it is with illiterate peasants, you know.'

'Quite,' said the king. He gestured imperiously with his beaker. 'Do, uh, do carry on.'

'Quite,' said Pedrito, then revealed that, while they were resting between the usual twenty-minute bursts of oar-heaving on the galley, the Professor would tell him stories about history and faraway places, and would gladly answer any questions he cared to put to him. Then, at night, when crammed like grilling sardines beneath the galley's rowing thwarts, he'd lie and listen to more of the Professor's teachings, while all around the crew snored, whimpered and passed wind in their despairing sleep. 'It may seem strange,' Pedrito admitted, 'but, just as the smell of new-baked bread reminds me of home, the stench of urine, excrement and sweat will always make me think of education.'

The king smiled a rueful smile. 'Just as the smell of blood, sweat and bibles does for me. But tell me – you said you translated the old song of the eight winds from the language of the Moors. Surely you don't mean that this Professor fellow also taught you read?'

'Well, as I told you before, I could already speak both languages, just as most of the fisher folk around Andratx can. But yes, it was the Professor who taught me to read, and to write as well.'

'But how? I mean, with all that rowing … when did you have time?'

'Ah, but we didn't spend *all* our time at sea,' Pedrito laughed. 'No, no, truth to tell, pirates probably spend most of their time ashore, either lurking up some concealed creek waiting for a passing ship to pounce on, or roaming the surrounding countryside looking for plunder and capturing sellable natives.'

'And what do their galley slaves do in the meantime?'

'Well, a few of them, if they've earned enough trust, will be taken along on these pillaging raids – more or less as pack animals, really – you know, to lug the booty back to the ship.'

'And the others?'

'They'd be put to work fetching water or firewood, carrying back slaughtered livestock or sacks of grain stolen from nearby settlements, or doing maintainance jobs on the ship – caulking timbers, scrubbing decks, mending sails, scraping barnacles off the hull. Things like that. And in their rest time, most would sleep, a few would huddle together whispering plans for mutinies that would never happen, sometimes one or two would even die.' Pedrito fell silent for a bit, his eyes downcast. 'Then we'd draw on what little reserves of energy we had to dig graves – give them a decent burial – or as decent as you can when all decency has gone out of life.'

King Jaume gave a knowing grunt. '*Sí*, that's why we Christians always take priests into battle with us.'

Although it struck Pedrito that the king had missed the point entirely, and thoughtlessly so at that, he prudently elected to continue with his story as if he hadn't heard him. He went on to relate how listening to the teachings of *al-Usstaz*, the Professor, had not only satisfied his thirst for learning, but had also helped keep him from going insane during the seemingly endless years spent on that hellish ship. This and the conviction that he would one day return to his family on Mallorca.

'The minds of so many galley slaves die first, *senyor*. And if they've also lost the will to live, it's just a matter of time before the body gives up the ghost as well.' Pedrito smiled reflectively. 'So you see, I was lucky on both counts. I had stimulation for my mind and I also had the pull of my parents and little sister to prevent the spark of life from being stifled.'

'Hope springs eternal, even from the depths of adversity,' the king sagely acknowledged, '– *if* you believe in the teachings of our Lord Jesus Christ.'

'Or even if you accept the generosity of a Moorish galley slave, who had nothing but his knowledge to offer, but gave it willingly – even to a Christian.'

The king chose to let that observation pass without comment, although Pedrito knew from the look on his face that the point hadn't been lost on him.

Both young men sat silently with their own thoughts for a while, Pedrito sipping his water and gazing longingly towards the crests of Es Tres Picons, King Jaume savouring his wine and staring bitterly at the Moorish army encamped across the still waters of the bay.

'I suppose, Little Pedro,' he said at length, 'it was also this Professor fellow who encouraged you to question the motives and merits of *organised* religion, no?'

Pedrito readily confirmed that indeed it had been.

King Jaume then took on a more assertive manner. 'Well then, just remember, my friend, that although you may have learned a bit more than most men in your humble position, a little knowledge can be dangerous.' He brandished an admonishing finger. 'And don't ever forget that it's organised religion, and the power and wealth it wields, that supports kings like me.' He paused to look Pedrito directly in the eye again. 'And organised religion – the Church – can crush anyone, even kings, if they dare doubt that the Lord appointed the clergy, from the lowest village priest to the Pope himself, as His mortal custodians and conveyors of the Truth.'

Pedrito could have said that the king, albeit unwittingly, had just endorsed the Professor's point perfectly, but prudence, and concern for the welfare of his neck, prevented him.

The king yawned, stretched, then eased himself from his stone cushion and lay down sideways on the sand, his upper body supported on one elbow, his free hand gripping his beaker, which he held out to Pedrito for replenishment. Behind them, the warm September sun was descending towards the Puig de Na Pòpia summit of Sa Dragonera Island, bathing the bay in the golden glow of evening and sending shadows of the fleet's masts creeping over the hushed Moorish encampment like the legs of spiders.

'So beautiful, yet so fearsome,' the king murmured, as if to himself. 'Soon, this tranquil Garden of Eden will be watered by rivers of blood.' Then, realising that Pedrito was staring critically at his empty cup, he smirked and said, 'So, Little Pedro, you think I'm drinking too much, eh?' He laughed as Pedrito passively raised his shoulders. 'Aha, but you forget I was born in France. I was weaned on wine, *amic*, so a few cupfuls with my supper now will do me no more harm than my mother's milk did then.' The smile gradually faded from the king's lips. 'Although it's highly unlikely that I ever tasted much of that.' Glumly, he dipped his head. 'I'd have been clamped like a limpet to the tit of a wet nurse at the earliest opportunity, just as I was bundled off to the citadel in Carcassonne at the age of three, to be *educated* – and by my father's enemy, of all people.'

Without saying anything, Pedrito looked on as the king's regal poise seemed to melt away, lending him the appearance of a little boy lost, with more hurt and loneliness in his heart than the lion-like courage of *El Conquistador*, The Conqueror, the dashing young monarch who now aspired to become Christian Spain's greatest hero of all.

He raised his eyes to Pedrito with the look of a sad puppy. 'Mind you, none of that necessarily means that my parents didn't love me. Perhaps they did. I'm sure my mother did … in the little time I was with her. But she certainly didn't love my father, nor he her.' He thought for a few seconds before adding that theirs had been a marriage arranged for the usual purpose of expanding a monarch's domain. 'All my father wanted out of the relationship was a son and heir. Gambling was only one of his vices, you see, and once I arrived, I suppose he regarded me as just another stake to wager when circumstances suited. Yet despite all that, I admired him, his bravery in battle, his generosity towards others.' The king then shook his head forlornly. 'Maybe I've even grown to forgive his weaknesses. Oh yes, he had plenty of those all right – and he passed at least one of them on to me.'

King Jaume fell silent again, and although Pedrito was eager to hear more about his troubled childhood, he was aware that he was being made privy to thoughts which may never have been divulged to anyone before. He therefore showed respect for the king's silence with an equal measure of of his own.

After a while, the king picked up where he had left off, though there was now an edge of resentment to the way he spoke.

'The ruthless Simon de Montfort was the guaradian my father entrusted me to at the age of three.' King Jaume uttered a sharp, mocking laugh. 'Entrusted me to? No, *threw* me to would be more accurate. *Sí*, thrown by my father like dice loaded in de Montfort's favour in hopes of curbing his brutal, land-grabbing ways. He was already the Earl of Leicester in England, and with extensive lands in the north of France as well. Yet he was hungry for more, and the lands he'd been seizing in the south of the country belonged to my father's Cathar allies, close to the territory of Montpellier, which my father had received as my mother's dowry.'

Pedrito listened enthralled as the young king related how the deal of appeasement his father, King Pedro II of Aragon, had struck with Simon de Montfort included an understanding that he, the king's son, would marry de Montfort's daughter, thereby extending de Montfort's sphere of influence into the royal circles of both southern France and northern Spain. There had been nothing particularly extraordinary about any of this, King Jaume conceded, although the fact that his mother was a blood relation of de Montfort might have created ethical issues with the Church, should the marriage between himself and his 'cousin' ever have neared realisation. Then again, a politically blind eye might have been turned to the event. That, after all, was the accepted way of things within the religious establishment.

Pedrito could detect a note of cynicism creeping into the king's speech. Interesting. He topped up the proffered wine beaker, from which the king took a generous slurp. Suitably refreshed, he continued with the story of his early life...

As it turned out, his marriage to de Montfort's daughter never materialised. Despite his covenant with the tyrant, King Pedro had eventually been lured into armed conflict with him, and died on the field, as much the victim of his own debauchery on the eve of battle as the sword of the man who killed him. Prince Jaume, though by this time only six years old, became King Jaume and, his exiled mother having died earlier that same year in Italy, an orphan as well.

On being told this, Pedrito immediately offered the king his deepest sympathies.

'Oh, don't feel sorry for me,' he replied with an air of insouciance, which Pedrito suspected was more well-practised than spontaneous. 'My situation wasn't all that different from your own, after all. You never knew your real parents, and I knew mine only briefly. Oh, yes, by the age of six, I had *long* forgotten how to cry for them, believe me.'

Somehow, Pedrito didn't quite buy such a glib assertion, even from this warrior king, whose reputation for self-reliance was legion.

Regardless, King Jaume carried on with his lifestory...

Thanks to the intervention of the Pope himself, he was released from Simon de Montfort's southern French citadel and taken to the castle of Monzón in his newly-inherited northern Spanish kingdom of Aragon. There, he was given over to the care of En Guillen de Montredon, the powerful Master of the Knights Templar in northern Spain and southern France, thereby baulking the tyrannical de Montfort's ambitions in both areas.

The king shot Pedrito a cautionary glance. 'As I said, the Church can be the maker and breaker of kings.'

He then revealed that, after his father King Pedro died, it emerged that, as a result of his degenerate lifestyle, all the 'tribute' revenues he had in Aragon and Catalonia had been pledged to money-lending Jews and even to some Saracens of the same pursuit. More than this, however, he had sold, given away or pawned the rental income from many of his most valuable fiefdoms.

'In short,' said King Jaume with a frown of resentment, 'when I inherited my father's throne, I also inherited his empty purse.' He bit off a chunk of bread and chewed it pensively, then swallowed it with a slug of wine. He motioned Pedro to lean in close. 'In fact, Little Pedro,' he confided, 'when I first arrived in Aragon, the land was so wasted and mortgaged that there wasn't a scrap of food to eat in the castle of Monzón for whole days at a time.'

Pedrito was flabbergasted, and it showed. 'I'm beginning to think, *senyor*, that I was lucky to be born a humble peasant instead of a king!'

The king struck a sagacious pose, his wine cup raised like the torch of wisdom. 'But luck doesn't come into it, my friend. You see, God decreed that I should be a king, just as, in His infinite wisdom, He determined that you should be a peasant.'

There was no simple answer to that pronouncement, so Pedrito didn't attempt one.

But the king wasn't finished. 'However,' he continued airily, 'despite God's will being done at one's birth, it doesn't mean that I, for example, shouldn't strive to be a *great* king, while you, by the same token, should try to make the most of whatever gifts the good

Lord bestowed upon you – no matter how modest.'

There was even less of a simple answer to that one, so Pedrito gave the king an evasive little smile and waited for him to get on with his story.

## 6

# A SKINFUL OF CONFESSIONS

*LATER THAT EVENING – THE ISLET OF ES PANTALEU ...*

With the setting of the sun, an almost palpable peace had descended on the bay of Sa Palomera. There was a noticeable chill in the air now too, and a servant of the royal household had dutifully set a fire of dry twigs and driftwood close to where the king was reclining. Over on the shore, fires could also be seen flickering here and there within the Moorish camp; gossamer smoke spiralling lazily upward in the still evening air, the reflection of flames flitting and glittering on the water like a swarm of floating glow-worms.

Pedrito breathed in the scent of burning olive wood wafting over the bay, and he thought again of home. Automatically, his eyes were drawn to the ridge of Es Tres Picons, whose outline now rested dark and serene against an indigo sky, in which little stars had started to blink as twilight faded into night. On the wooded hillsides below, an owl hooted, heralding the first liquid trills of a nightingale, while in the air above Es Pantaleu, tiny bats dashed to and fro like fleeting splashes of shadow. Then, somewhere on a distant mountain farm, a dog barked a warning to imagined marauders skulking by his master's gate. Mallorca was preparing to sleep.

Pedrito looked over his shoulder towards the silhouette of Sa Dragonera Island – a giant dragon, true to its name, basking on an inky-blue blanket flecked with the dying embers of dusk. It was a scene he had marvelled at many times on the way homeward from a day's fishing with his father. Back then, their tiny boat would most likely have been the only craft afloat in this remote and peaceful corner of the island, but tonight the shimmering lanterns of the great Christian fleet painted an altogether busier picture – a pretty picture, yet a stark reminder of the approach of war and all the ugliness that would follow in its wake.

The king, however, gave the impression of being too immersed in thoughts of the past to take much notice of this vast array of ships lying silently at anchor, their bellies full of fighting men awaiting the command to do his royal bidding. And Pedrito could understand why the king was wearing this cloak of detachment. Here was a young man with the weight of the world on his back, and as aware as he doubtless was of the gravity of the tasks facing him, such concerns would be best put to the back of his mind for as many precious moments of distraction as he could presently steal.

'Yes, from the age of six,' King Jaume said, 'I was kept in the castle at Monzón for fully two and a half years, being taught the ways of a knight by the Templars and being educated in the ways of Christ by their priests. And I accepted it all without question, because I'd known no different way of life before that anyway.'

Pedrito was slightly puzzled. 'But although you were only a child, you were also now the king, so how could you – ?'

'Rule my kingdom?'

'Exactly.'

'Well, the simple answer is that I didn't. I couldn't, even if I'd had the experience, which I clearly hadn't. No, all such affairs were handled for me by a council of high-ranking barons – regents who were approved by the Church, naturally.'

Pedrito listened spellbound as King Jaume related how, in the meantime and unknown to him, his right to the throne was being fiercely contested, and by rival factions of his own close family to boot. Then, when he was only nine years old, a group of loyal liegemen took him away from Monzón with the declared intention of installing him as the rightful monarch in Aragon's capital, Zaragoza. But treachery was afoot, and en route to the city he found himself donning his first coat of chain mail in battle against the forces of a coterie of renegade barons.

Somehow, the boy king and his supporters prevailed against all odds – not just in that encounter, but in many others during the ensuing years. His kingdom was in turmoil, and to such a convoluted extent that it became difficult at times to recognise which nobles were true to him and which were against. Consequently, by the age of fourteen, King Jaume was already a battle-seasoned campaigner, and invloved in fierce armed conflict with En Guillen de Muntcada, who had previously been one of his most infuential counsellors, but who had now turned his coat and was attempting to overrun lands in southern France bequeathed by King Jaume's father to his cousin, the Count of Provence, the father of the king's foremost general, En Nunyo Sans

A look of assured self-satisfaction came to the king's face. 'Yes, I may have been only fourteen, but I took one hundred and thirty fortresses, castles and towers from En Guillen in that campaign. Oh yes, I taught him the price of treachery, and no mistake!'

This latest revelation came as a surprise to Pedrito. 'Forgive me, *Majestat*, but I'm a bit confused. Is what you're telling me – I mean, are you really saying that the En Guillen de Muntcada you defeated in those battles is the same baron who – ?'

'Is now one of my top commanders on this crusade? Yes, he is indeed.'

'But I don't understand how – '

'How a traitorous turncoat can become a trusted ally?'

Pedrito nodded his head.

The king hunched his shoulders. 'I've seen many such changes of loyalty since the day I left the castle of Monzón as a naïve child of nine. Why, even my cousin Nunyo Sans, in whose interests I risked my life fighting Muntcada, later turned against me and sided with Muntcada himself.'

Baffled, Pedrito frowned. 'But En Nunyo Sans is now your senior general. How can you trust people like that?'

The king took a sip of wine and smiled bleakly. 'Every man has a price, and even after En Guillen and En Nunyo had pledged their allegiance to me, I had to pay them twenty thousand *morabatins* – a huge amount of money – and grant them fiefdoms in Aragon in order to cement that loyalty. Then, to heap hurt upon hurt, they promptly gave those fiefdoms to their friends, simply to raise their own standing in the eyes of the beneficiaries.' He lowered his voice with his eyes. 'Why, even my own uncle, En Fernando, who had tried to wrest the throne from me and whom I'd forgiven, was in league with the other two in that affair. I was little more than a boy, and they took advantage of that.' The king then squared his shoulders and stated firmly, 'But let's just say that I put my trust in God, and as all the nobles with me have come to fight in God's name, I have nothing to fear from any of them.'

'And their promised share of the lands and riches of Mallorca has nothing to do with their newfound loyalty?'

King Jaume gave Pedrito a forbearing look. 'As I told you before, *amic*, no matter how just the cause, an army has to be paid, and that stands good for the generals and knights just as much as for the common foot soldiers.'

'And for the clergy too?' said Pedrito, though immediately regretting having put such a provocative question to the king.

His response, however, was surprisingly complaisant, for which Pedrito silently thanked the placating effects of wine.

The king readily admitted that, during the meeting of the Barcelona Cortes at which this *Reconquista* was initiated, he had been obliged to make a pact with the hierarchy of the Church whereby they and the fighting men whose services they contributed would receive a just share of the lands and 'moveables' of Mallorca. King Jaume then appeared to be struck by an appropriately pious afterthought. 'But their *real* reward, Little Pedro, will come in the joy of spreading the Truth to the heathen Saracen multitudes. *Sí*, and the Church has spared no commitment to make sure that this *will* happen. I mean, even the Archbishop of Tarragona himself swore that, but for his advanced years, he would have come to fight at my side. As you know, however, the Bishop of Barcelona came instead, and with more than a hundred knights in his train! *Sí, sí*, and the Bishop of Gerona came too, with thirty knights!'

King Jaume's sudden show of excitement reminded Pedrito of a child on the eve of a birthday. For, no matter how hard he was trying to suppress thoughts of the impending war, the responsibility of carrying the expectations of so many prominent people was obviously having its effect.

'Also,' the king added with undisguised pride, 'you can be sure that His Holiness the Pope, God's personal emissary here on earth, has given his blessing to my great campaign and to each and every one of his clergymen who are with me. And they in turn, according to the direct instruction of His Holiness, granted full absolution and the guarantee of eternal life in God's house to those men who confessed their sins before joining this crusade.'

Pedrito looked over to the shoreline, pitch black now except for the glow of the camp fires, and he wondered how many mullahs attached to that massive Moorish force would be saying similar words of encouragement to their soldiers waiting tensely for battle. He also wondered what God and Allah, if either of them even existed, would think of the blood that would soon be spilt in their respective names. But these were thoughts that would have to remain unspoken, at least in the present company.

'Well,' he said with as much awe as he could affect, 'little did I imagine, when tilling the land with my father's mule, that sleepy old Mallorca would one day become such a coveted prize in the eyes of someone so important as God's personal emissary himself.'

Ah, but Pedrito was forgetting one very important thing, the king came back. God looked after his own, be they men of the cloth spreading His word, or men of commerce creating the wealth that can help spread His word. Pedrito should understand that many rich merchants had also contributed men, ships and money towards this reconquest of Mallorca, not for the glory of God *directly*, it had to be admitted, but because Mallorca had become a hornets' nest of pirates whose galleys plundered the trading ships of Christendom throughout the western Mediterranean. Then, of course, there was the broader aspect of the crusading movement to consider; namely the strategic importance of Mallorca as a stepping stone for pilgrims and crusaders alike on their way to the Holy Land – the former to pay homage to Christ in the country where He was born, lived and died, the latter to recover and safeguard all of the Kingdom of Jerusalem from the infidel Saracens.

'Which is why so many Knights Templar have accompanied you on this mission?' Pedrito asked rhetorically.

'Precisely. It's essential for the Christian Church to have a secure haven here for the soldiers of the Cross and *its* followers, if their virtuous journeys eastward are to be made in reasonable comfort and safe from Saracen terror on the high seas.' King Jaume offered Pedrito a reassuring smile. 'Have no fear, here on Mallorca the Knights of the Temple will lay firm foundations for the sanctity and expansion of the one true faith, which is another reason why I and they will emerge victorious from the battles that lie ahead.'

With this, the king breathed in deeply, exhaled a slow, relaxing breath and raised the cup of wine once more to his lips.

To Pedrito, it seemed that King Jaume had been delivering a kind of sermon, but a sermon intended not so much to enlighted Pedrito, but to reassert in the king's own mind the religious principles which had been instilled in him since infancy, but which nevertheless required occasional reinforcement, particularly when his unwavering trust in those beliefs was about to be put to the test – as it soon would be, and more severely than ever before.

Just then, a loud splashing noise disturbed the gentle sough of the sea lapping onto Es Pantaleu's little beach, its waterline barely visible in the flickering firelight, though only a few steps away. Startled, the king sat upright, peering into the darkness. The splashing stopped momentarily, only to be replaced by a frantic shaking and shuddering, mingled with the jingling of a chain and the rasp of heavy breathing. A black shape emerged out of the gloom and bounded towards the fire, leaping at the king with such ferocity that he was knocked flat on his back.

Pedrito froze. Behind him, by the royal tent on Pantaleu's tiny summit, the swish of swords being drawn by two of the king's guard carved a vigilant warning through the night air.

'*Qui va*? came the urgent call from the sentries as they started down the slope. 'Who goes there?' Thoughts of an attempt on the king's life by a Moorish assassin made their blood run cold – just as surely as it would run free should he come to any harm during their watch.

To their surprise and even greater relief, however, the response they got was an outburst of laughing from their king. It was all right, he shouted to them. It was only his dog. Nothing to worry about. 'Relax, men. Back to your posts. *Tranquíl*, eh!'

Pedrito was fascinated by the king's almost childlike giggling as he tried to shield his face from the dog's slobbering tongue. This was more an image of a boy and his pet than of a conquering hero with one of his dogs of war. Pedrito looked at the animal while he playfully fought his master's good-natured attempts to push him away .

'I mean no disrespect, *senyor*,' he said, 'but he looks more like a lop-eared black sheep than a dog.'

'You may well be right,' the king grinned, 'but he's a dog all the same – a French water dog, given me by my subjects in Montpellier. They said his breed is good for carrying messages from ship to ship at sea. Would be a real asset on such an expedition as this, they said.' He laughed again. 'Well, I've had him six months, since he was a little pup, and this is the first time I've known him go anywhere near water. Hates it!' He nodded towards a ship anchored nearby. 'Yet he must have swum over from the transport that brought him from the mainland with my horses. Must have slipped his tether, I suppose.' King Jaume indicated the leftovers of their supper lying on a plate by his side. 'Most likely attracted by the smell of this pork.' He popped a scrap of gristle into the dog's dribbling mouth. '*Vaja*! You're welcome to it, boy!'

The dog promptly released the king and gave his undivided attention to gobbling up every remnant of pork and bread that remained on the plate. Then, as if noticing Pedrito for the first time, he lunged at him and proceeded to honour him with the same boisterous greeting he'd given his master.

'He obviously likes you,' said the king.

'It takes a long time to get a galley slave's smell out of your pores,' Pedrito gasped amid an onslaught of licks to his mouth and nose. 'He probably thinks I'm another dog.'

He laughed along with the king for a few moments, then stopped abruptly and declared, 'But I think I've discovered the *true* reason why he's called a water dog.'

'Yes?'

'Yes. You, uhm, you probably can't see it in this light, *senyor*, but by the feel of my shirt front, I'd say he's just pissed all over me!'

'Aha, a true sign of affection in a water dog!' the king pronounced.

'What's his name?' Pedrito asked after the ensuing howls of hilarity had subsided.

'Nedi – I call him Nedi.'

'Nedi?' Pedrito tilted his head. 'A nice name, but an unusual one. I don't think I've ever heard it before.'

'Yes, well, that's because I made it up myself, you see.' That look of assured self-satisfaction spread across the king's face again. 'Short for *El Nedadór*, the Swimmer. You know – him being a breed of water dog and everything.'

Pedrito glanced down at his sodden shirt. 'Fair enough, but maybe *Pee-pee* would've been nearer the mark, no?'

More waves of laughter rippled over Sa Palomera bay.

After a while, the king wiped a tear from the corner his eye, then lay back and gazed at the stars, his hands clasped behind his head. 'Ah, Little Pedro,' he sighed, 'I can't remember when I had so much fun.' He pondered that statement for a bit. 'Maybe not at all. *Sí*, and certainly never when so close to battle.'

Pedrito allowed the king to submerge himself in the privacy of his own thoughts again.

Clearly, the young monarch was relishing the simple pleasures of eating, drinking and communicating one-to-one with someone of his own age; with someone who wasn't part of the same cloistered and double-dealing establishment as himself, and who didn't have any self-interested motive for being friendly towards him. He was enjoying the theraputic comfort of the situation, wallowing in a feeling of mellow relaxation, which was likely to be the very antithesis of the turmoil he would be exposed to in the coming days, weeks and months. Perhaps even an entire lifetime, *if* he survived the perils of the looming conflict.

Pedrito understood this, and he remained silent until the king, in his own good time, decided to pick up the threads of conversation once more.

'Have you ever been married?' was the unlikely question he eventually chose to open with.

Pedrito's response was a mocking laugh. 'Married? Me? Well, firstly, weddings weren't all that high on the pirates' list of treats for their galley slaves. And secondly, I was only sixteen when I was captured. So, no, I've never been married.'

'Sixteen's nothing,' the king countered. 'I was married at thirteen. Not that I had any choice in the matter, mind you. No, the decision was made for me by some of my most powerful vassals, En Guillen de Muntcada of the fluctuating loyalties foremost among them. Yes, they said that, since I was my father's only son, I would have to produce a son of my own, if my family's royal bloodline was to continue. At the time, my kingdom was still riddled with treachery and opposition to my monarchy, and I was continually told that my life was in grave danger. The risk of my murder, whether by poison or other foul means, was said to be both real and always imminent.'

'Yet your decision-making vassals couldn't have believed your murder was *that* imminent,' Pedrito put in.

'How do you mean?'

'Just that it would have taken nine months at least for you to produce the son and heir they wanted, wouldn't it?'

A sheepish smile vied with a squirm of embarrassment as the king scratched his beard. 'Even allowing for that timespan, they'd have been disappointed, I'm afraid. I was still a child, you understand, not yet a man.' He feigned a cough. 'Well, even if I was a – a *man*, I didn't know how to...' He coughed again. 'What I mean is that you don't learn much about the ways of the flesh when you're educated by priests and monks ... not with regard to the opposite sex at any rate.'

It was all Pedrito could do to stop himself from bursting out laughing again, but he recognised that the king was feeling understandably uneasy about divulging these highly personal details, so he maintained an appropriate air of composure.

After a third cough, King Jaume continued, though even more awkwardly. 'It was, ehm – it was actually fully a year before I did the … you know, consummated the, uh, with my bride.' He glanced over at Pedrito while putting on a semblance of man-to-man frankness. 'She was the daughter of the King of Castile – La Infanta Doña Léonor – lovely girl – very gifted in the, uhm-ah, in the consummation procedures, if you know what I…' His words trailed away as he took a steadying slurp of wine.

Pedrito stepped swiftly into the conversational hiatus by stating that his own youth now seemed like a sweet, uncomplicated dream compared to the nightmare of the king's. 'A child king who never had a childhood,' he pondered aloud, then prudently added, 'No offence intended, *senyor*.'

'None taken,' the king replied, but in a way that suggested his thoughts were elsewhere anyway. 'Ah *sí*, my queen,' he mused, his eyes closing, 'the lovely Doña Léonor. She was made to suffer many discomforts after marrying me – even being kept captive with me for three weeks by so-called loyal nobles in my own palace in Zaragoza. Why, it was only my own skill in negotiating with those traitors that saved us from even worse deeds of treachery – perhaps even death. *Sí*, and I was still only a child myself.' He promptly opened his eyes and turned his head to look squarely at Pedrito. 'But I *have* fathered that required son and heir. Born this very year, the year destiny decreed that I, with the blessing of God, would help change the history of Spain.' He fell silent again, lying back and staring blankly up at the stars. 'Ah *sí*, my little son Alfonso … like me, born to be a king.'

He remained lost in his reverie for a moment or two, then raised himself up on one elbow again and said in confidential tones, 'You'll recall, Little Pedro, that I told you how I'd inherited at least one of my father's many faults.' He smiled leniently as he noticed Pedrito looking askance at his beaker. 'No, no, not the wine,' he laughed. 'Admittedly, I do enjoy it, but unlike my father, I drink in moderation only.' He lowered his voice again. 'No, the fault, the weakness I'm talking about is – how can I put it? – yes, let's say Cupid's little arrows. Do you know what I mean?'

Pedrito did, but he diplomatically indicated that he didn't.

'All right, I can tell you,' the king disclosed, 'that one of those arrows in the eye can blind the wisest and strongest of men – even kings. Well,' he added with a frown of self-reproach, 'this one at any rate.'

He held out his beaker, which Pedrito dutifully refilled from the goatskin.

'And I have to admit, *amic*, that I'm an easy target. *Sí*, and the irony is that it was that first, you know, *consummation* procedure with my young queen that gave me the taste for being shot in the eye – figuratively speaking, of course.'

Without saying a word, Pedrito continued to lend a willing ear.

The king took a pensive sip of wine. '*Sí, sí*, Cupid's little arrows. If only they'd been aimed better at myself and Doña Léonor.' He heaved a doleful sigh. 'But we were only innocent children – two lambs whose young lives were sacrificed to the scheming ways of our shepherds. *Sí*, and Cupid's arrows had nothing to do with it.'

It was obvious that the king was drifting into a maudlin mood, partly brought on by the effects of the wine, no doubt, but also, Pedrito guessed, because he harboured an element of guilt about a certain aspect, or aspects, of his relationship with his wife, the queen.

'My father was unkind to my mother, they say – ignored her, neglected her, deserted her, was unfaithful to her, never went near her bed until urged by his senior barons to produce a son – me.' King Jaume was mumbling now, thinking aloud. 'At least I haven't been unkind to Doña Léonor ... although I *have* been unfaithful. Then again, maybe I wouldn't have been, if I'd been allowed to chose my own bride. But maybe I *would* have been. I *am* my father's son, after all. Hmm, Cupid's arrows, indeed...' He sank into several moments of morose contemplation, then looked at Pedrito and said earnestly, 'You do believe I'm not really an ungodly man, don't you?'

Pedrito thought it wiser not to respond to the king's question, and it became apparent that he wasn't expected to either. It seemed that he was now being used as some sort of mute father confessor – a secret, though secular, font in which the king could wash away his sins before the very real possibility of an early meeting with his maker.

King Jaume lay back and retreated into his self-appraising shell again. 'You see,' he murmured, 'I have to admit that, like my father, I'm just not capable of being faithful to my wife – or, perhaps, to even more than one wife, even if they're not mine.'

So, Pedrito told himself, two of the Ten Commandments which were the basic tenets of the Christian religion had already been abandoned by the man who had aspirations of being its champion against the alleged disbelievers.

'Thou shalt not commit adultery. Thou shalt not covet thy neighbour's wife,' his mouth said of its own volition.

He expected the king to instantly threaten to have the offending tongue ripped out by the roots, but instead, he merely shook his head and said offhandedly, 'Ah, but you can't always take these things too literally, *amic*. Circumstances dictate the interpretation of the scriptures. For instance, God's Commandments also tell us that "Thou shalt not kill", yet when we're compelled to do it for the furtherance of His glory, killing clearly isn't a sin, but a virtue.'

'One of the many complexities of theology that *al-Usstaz* warned me about,' Pedrito said with deliberate lack of contention, despite being totally unconvinced by what he'd just heard. 'Too much for a simple peasant like me to grasp, I'm sure.'

The king gave a condescending little laugh. 'Ah *sí*, the teachings of your pirate-galley Professor. Trust a Muslim to be confused by the obvious.' He heaved himself up on one elbow once more and stared into the darkness of the bay. 'And yet those Moors over there do have one aspect of their religion which even I am tempted to envy … at times.'

'The, uhm – the right to have several wives?' Pedrito hesitantly put forward.

The king didn't answer – not directly anyway. 'Those harems of their kings,' he began, still gazing into the void, 'full of concubines, beautiful young women, hand-picked and pure, and each one available to satisfy her master's needs whenever he snaps his fingers.' He savoured that thought for a while, then, his eyes alight, he turned to Pedrito and said, 'You must have seen many such beauties taken as slaves, Little Pedro. And don't tell me that you and all those other shackled men didn't hunger for each and every one of them. It must have been torture for you, no?'

Being chained up was a great cooler of ardour, Pedrito told him. And those men whose lust burned hotter than their shackles, though never enough to melt them, would take their release whenever and in whatever way they could. The results were only further indignities to pour onto to the depths of inhumanity that victims of slavery are plunged into.

The king stroked his nose. 'A-a-a-ah, not only the victims of slavery, *amic*. Believe it or not, but I myself have been obliged to witness such sinful bahaviour by soldiers encamped in no-man's-land during a siege. *Sí*, and many times at that. Masturbation. I've often thought its prohibition should have replaced adultery in the Ten Commandments. That is, ever since those initial consummation procedures with my queen, I mean.'

Yet again, it was clear to Pedrito that the king had misssed the point entirely. Perhaps the privilege of being brought up in ivory towers, no matter how restrictive, had blinkered him to the harsh realities of life at the bottom of the castle midden. It occurred to him now that it might not go amiss to make him aware of a slave's perspective on the matter.

'It's one thing to have some rutting, pox-ridden gargoyle trying to interest you in satisfying his needs in the piss-slopping bilge of a galley – you either have to bend with the wind, so to speak, or give him such a kick in the plums that he'll think twice about bothering you again – but it's another thing entirely to look on helplessly as lines of frightened young girls are herded like pigs into the tiny *zuga* holds below decks.'

Pedrito glanced at the king to check his reaction. There was none. Indeed, if he had been shocked by what he'd just been told, it certainly didn't show on his face. Undaunted, Pedrito continued...

'No, far from being aroused by the sight of newly-captured girls, I thought of my own sister and I how I would have felt if she'd been one of them.' Pedrito paused, an icy shiver running up his spine as vivid images of such moments returned as clear as daylight to his mind. 'The pitiful wailing, the frantic screams and cries for their mothers that came from those poor creatures, some little more than children, was like a bucketful of freezing water onto the lap of all but the most sadistic of men. And, sickened as most of us were by the sound, we had to sit there chained to the thwarts and listen to it, hour after hour, day upon day, night after night, until we reached port and the girls were herded away to be pushed around, ogled, prodded, groped and bid for in the teeming souks of Morocco. Yes, and what might have happened to them after that hardly bears thinking about.' He shook his head vigorously. 'No, no, *Majestat*, I can assure you that hungering for them was the opposite of what I felt.'

In turn, the king nodded his head, but slowly. 'Now that you explain it, I can see that having a sister could have its difficulties.'

Pedro could hardly believe his ears. Was this man's regard for others so shallow and self-centred that all he cared about was whether or not a sexually-attractive victim of a slave trader was a sibling of his or not?

Yet again, however, it seemed that the king had been reading his thoughts. 'Being brought up as a fighting knight, who takes – as is his right – the victor's spoils, doesn't mean I'm a cruel and heartless person,' he murmured, as if thinking aloud again. 'The little birds will vouch for that on Judgement Day, I know.'

Pedrito was puzzled. Little birds ... on Judgement Day? Was this a biblical fable his parents hadn't mentioned, or was the king's mind flying away on the wings of wine?

'Excuse me, *senyor*, but did you say little birds ... on *Judge*ment Day?'

The king twitched, like someone waking from a daydream. 'Little birds?' he repeated, the vague look in his eyes gradually changing to one of unease. '*Si, si,*' he scowled, brushing the question aside with a flick of his hand, 'it's, uh, it's nothing that would interest you.'

Pedrito allowed a few respectful moments to pass before gently reminding the king of his oft-voiced assertion that he had no time for riddles. 'And now,' he said, his fingers firmly crossed, 'you come out with a right royal one of your own.'

A wary look was the king's immediate response. 'Do you *really* want to know?'

Pedrito assured him that he did indeed. 'My thirst for knowledge didn't end when I bid my final *adéu* to *al-Usstaz*, you know.'

Well, the king conceded with a shrug, his story of the little birds wasn't one that any professor would consider educational, but it was true and meant a lot to him. That said, it might just suggest a trait of weakness in his character to some, so it was essential that Pedrito should keep it to himself himself – on pain of death.

On that understanding, King Jaume proceeded to relate how, during a long siege of the castle of a renegade noble a few years earlier, it had become necessary to move his camp forward to a more advantageous position. However, in the preceeding days he had watched enthralled as a pair of swallows built their nest in the eaves of his tent. Their unwavering dedication to the task and the limitless energy they put into it had been an inspiration to the king. So, even in the face of well-founded urging from his military advisors, he forbade anyone to move a single guy from that tent until the parent swallows had completed their work, had raised their young and had led them safely to the freedom of the skies. And, as God Himself had witnessed this event, it came to pass that He blessed the king's army with a successful sacking of the castle, and without any ultimate need for the tent to have been moved in any case.

Until the king started this story, it had slipped Pedrito's mind that he'd already heard it being told in the quayside taverns of Salou prior to the fleet's departure for Mallorca. And, contrary to what the king clearly feared, even the most hardened seafarers and cynical mercenaries had been moved by his compassion and consideration for the welfare of these little creatures. Pedrito gave no hint of this to the king, however. It was better, he decided, to leave him lulled in the security of believing that he was seen by his followers as a monarch of iron will and uncompromising resolve.

As, one by one, the lanterns of the great armada went out and the waters off Sa Palomera became shrouded in the blanket of night, King Jaume yawned, turned on his side and rested his head in the crook of his arm. Nedi, his dog, was already sound asleep at Pedrito's feet, little clicking sounds coming from his tongue while he dreamed toothsome dreams of stale bread and pork gristle.

Pedrito lifted the goatskin and gave it a shake. There was still some wine swilling about in there, but not a lot. The king had enjoyed a nightcap well and truly fit for someone of his regal standing.

'You know, Little Pedro,' he muttered sleepily, 'as God has endowed me with the gift of honesty, I have to confess that, in fairness to my wife – and I tell you this in strictest confidence – I initiated proceedings earlier this year to have my marriage to her annulled.'

Pedrito's mouth fell open, but, fortunately for him perhaps, no words emerged.

'I was fairly sure the Church would condone it on the grounds of consanguinity,' said the king, then looked directly at Pedrito through drowsy eyes. 'Consanguinity – do you know what that means, Little Pedro?'

'In-breeding' had been the term chosen by The Professor when telling Pedrito about the typical family trees of Christian royalty, but rather than risk the consequences of admitting that, he shook his head.

'It means that the queen and I are actually close relations – and were, even before we married, I mean.' The king released a pensive little grunt. '*Sí*, I was fairly sure the Church could be persuaded to consider the marriage invalid – particularly when we were both more or less forced into it.'

This was fascinating stuff – so much so that Pedrito couldn't contain his curiosity. 'But wouldn't such an annulment mean that your baby son will be declared a – well, with all due respect, a –'

'Bastard?'

Pedrito nodded his head.

The king shook his. 'When everything I've done for Christendom is weighed at the end of this *Reconquista*, I'm sure the leaders of the Church will be in a sufficiently obliging frame of mind to allow the purity of my son's origin to be preserved. As it has in the case of kings, Little Pedro, the Church has the power to make bastards or, in a manner of speaking, make them disappear.'

Pedrito was learning something every time the king opened his mouth now, and intrigued as he was, he didn't feel particularly comfortable about it. Why, he wondered, was he being made privy to such sensitive royal thoughts? He put that very question to the king.

'I felt in need of telling someone,' came the reply, 'and who better to tell than you?'

Pedrito felt flattered, but the feeling was to be extremely shortlived.

'After all, even if you did betray my confidence, *amic*, who would believe such outrageous claims when coming from a humble sailor?' His eyelids closing, King Jaume swallowed a yawn. 'And anyway, apart from anything else, I could always have you beheaded for treason.'

A chortle rumbled in the king's chest after he'd said this, but Pedrito had no way of telling whether its message was intended to be benign or malignant. He plumped for the latter and gave the king his word that his lips would be tightly and permanently sealed.

He might as well have saved his breath, however, for while he awaited the king's response, the sound of snoring told him that his promise had fallen on deaf ears.

## 7

# A FORECAST OF THE WIND OF CHANGE

*THE ISLET OF ES PANTALEU – SUNDAY 9<sup>th</sup> SEPTEMBER ...*

Pedrito was summoned to Es Pantaleu again about noon the following day, but the king's purpose this time was neither social nor theraputic. This was strictly business. When the skiff that had taken him the short distance from the royal galley rounded the side of the islet, Pedrito noticed a flurry of excitement on the little beach where he had spent the previous evening. The king was in the midst of a group of his men, all of them shouting words of encouragement to someone swimming over the bay towards them from the Mallorcan shore, on which a line of Moorish archers appeared to be doing their level best to *dis*courage the swimmer – permanently. A hail of arrows was splashing down all around him, yet he somehow made it to Es Pantaleu, where he was helped ashore by the same pair of royal guards who had been moved to rush to the king's aid when he was being 'savaged' by his frolicsome dog Nedi the night before.

King Jaume saw Pedrito coming. 'Quick, Master Blànes!' he shouted. 'We may have a Saracen deserter here, and I'll need you to translate for me.'

As Pedrito approached, he could see that the alleged deserter was a slightly-built, doe-eyed youth a few years younger than himself. He was wearing only a loincloth, so it could be presumed from the swarthy colour of his skin that he was indeed a Moor. There was also something vaguely familiar about him.

'What's your name and why have you come here?' Pedrito asked him in Arabic.

The lad told him his name was Ali and that he had been sent by his mother to deliver a message to 'the great Sultan of the Christians'.

Accordingly, Pedrito introduced him to King Jaume, whereupon Ali fell to his knees and kissed the monarch's feet.

'Take him to my tent and give him clothes,' the king told one of his men. '*Sí*, and let him have a cup of water. No doubt he could do with one.'

Pedrito relayed the king's instructions to Ali, who immediately protested that his mission was too important to delay for even a single minute. On being told this, the king motioned Ali sit down on the rock on which he himself had sat the night before, then, with a sweep of his hand, indicated that he should proceed with what he had to say.

In need of a rest as he may well have been, Ali made it clear that he was unworthy to sit in the presence of a king. Pointing towards the shore, he indicated where, on the brow of a hill behind the Moorish encampment, there was a fortified tower in which his mother lived. He said that, from its ramparts, she would survey the heavens and decipher the writings created by the movements of mysterious, distant stars. He told how her great knowledge of astrology had enabled her to prophesy that King Jaume was destined to rule Mallorca, and she had been so convinced of this that she had risked the life of her son by bidding him carry the message to His Majesty personally.

'So you may be absolutely certain, Sire,' he informed the king through Pedrito, 'that this land will soon be yours to command.'

As pleased as the king would normally have been to be given such an encouraging prediction, he was yet to be convinced that this young Saracen could be trusted. He was one of the enemy, after all, so his motives might well be subversive. The king said so, and his doubts were endorsed by the members of his train.

He turned to Pedrito. 'What say you, Master Blànes? You're familiar with Moorish guile. Is this bedraggled *jove* a traitor to his own or a snake in the grass?'

Pedrito had no hesitation in offering the opinion that, if this young fellow was a spy, he appeared to be a suicidal one. 'From what I saw, those arrows were hitting the water a bit too close to suggest that the Moors were happy about him reaching here.' To emphasise the point, he indicated a trickle of blood oozing from a graze on Ali's shoulder. 'A hand's breadth to the left and that one would have been lodged in the middle of his back.'

'A fair enough appraisal,' the king conceded, 'which suggests that he must therefore be a traitor to his own. So, Master Blànes, ask him what he is. Is he a defecting soldier? And if so, why?'

Pedrito did as instructed, and when Ali replied that he was no soldier but the son of the major-domo in the palace of Abû Yahya Háquem, the Moorish King of Mallorca, it finally dawned on Pedrito why he had sensed something familiar about this lad. It all came back to him now: the exalted head steward of the royal household, robes flowing and with several porters in his wake, ambling imperiously along the palm-shaded quayside of the city, where Pedrito and his father would offer their freshly-caught fish for sale in competiton with so many others of equally humble ilk. The king's major-domo would usually favour them with a more than generous purchase, not because their fish was necessarily better than anyone else's, but rather because it had become a custom for Pedrito's father to give the man's young son, who often accompanied him on these excursions, a few *boqueróns* as a titbit. It was unusual for a child to like the acidity of the vinegar in which these little anchovies were pickled, but after an involuntary screwing up of his face, young Ali would grin ecstatically and gobble down as many as were offered. It was a gesture that the boy's father, although a stern-looking and somewhat overbearing man, would acknowledge with an almost imperceptible nod before instructing one of his lackeys to pick up and pay for whatever specimens of the day's catch had caught his eye.

When Pedrito reminded Ali of this, the young Moor didn't go quite so far as to kiss his feet, but his uninhibited show of delight at meeting up again in such unlikely and potentially hazardous circumstances caused Pedrito considerable embarrassment. He was well aware that the king and his attendants would have been more than a little perplexed at the sight of an ex-galley slave being treated like royalty – or almost so.

How he'd grown, Ali told Pedrito as he felt his biceps and looked him up and down approvingly. He'd only been a skinny kid when they'd last met, but look at him now! Tall as a house and with the muscles of a bear-wrestler. And that thick, dark stubble on his face! No wonder he hadn't recognised him at first. Allah be praised, Pedrito was a *real* man now!

After Ali had finished hugging him again, Pedrito thought it sensible to advise the king and his company that, contrary to what they might have heard about the *deviant* habits of some Arab males, Ali's display of affection was quite normal for a member of a race who harboured no inhibitions when showing emotion of any kind.

That was all very well, the king said with evident impatience, but of no immediate consequence. What he wanted to know was why this young Saracen had decided to throw in his lot with the Christian invaders when he was the son of someone with a responsible and respected position in the Moorish king's household. Wasn't this change of allegiance an insult to his own father?

Without the slightest compunction, Ali related how his mother had originally been his father's favourite wife, but on being replaced by another had chosen to retire to the seclusion of the tower yonder, the occupancy of which King Abû Yahya, in his infinite bounteousness and as a token of his regard for Ali's father, had assigned to her for the rest of her days. This arrangement made no difference to Ali's relationship with either of his parents. It was the way of things in his society, and he remained equally close to both his mother and his father.

Again, this was all very well, the king declared, but hadn't it been foolhardy of Ali to court death by a hundred arrows for the sole purpose of relaying the omen of a hermit soothsayer to the enemy?

Pedrito was careful not to use the potentially demeaning terms 'omen', 'hermit' and 'soothsayer' when translating the king's question. Ali seemed sincere enough to him, so why risk insulting his mother? In any case, Ali's reply was that he had total faith in the unfailing reliability of his mother's reading of the stars, and swimming out to convey her word to the man who would be the future ruler of Mallorca was also intended as an act of homage on his own part. This done, Ali deduced, Allah in his mercy would surely make certain that he and his parents would be treated well by their new Christian overlord.

On being told this, King Jaume smirked knowingly and muttered under his breath that this seemed very reminiscent of what his gambling father might have called betting your shirt on the favourite in a two-horse race. Then, adopting a more authoritarian manner, he said to Pedrito, 'Tell him that nothing he's said so far convinces me that he may not be an infiltrator. Ask him to give me one good reason why I shouldn't have him put to the sword right now.'

Ali responded to Pedrito's translation with the a wry smile, saying that he believed the great Christian king was not just a compassionate man but a prudent one as well. For why would he have offered him clothes a few minutes ago, if his ultimate intention was to have them soiled by Moorish blood?

Arching his brows in acknowledgement of this subtle piece of reasoning, the king nudged Pedrito and said out of the corner of his mouth, 'So, Little Pedro, the sea has delivered me yet another unlikely philosopher, eh?' He then raised his voice for all to hear. 'But he still hasn't told us what he is. Is he a soldier? Can he prove his newfound allegiance to me by supplying some inside information about the Saracen forces on Mallorca, for example – or, perchance, where their king is at present?'

Ali was both keen and quick to oblige. He disclosed that he was no soldier, but a servant in the king's palace, an assistant to his father, the major-domo. As such, he was in a position to catch wind of anything significant that was happening in the city, and even if elements of such news turned out to be based on rumour, there was usually a fair amount of truth involved as well. 'As the great Christian king himself will know,' he said as an aside to Pedrito, 'the walls of royal palaces have a thousand ears, and all of them endowed with very sharp hearing.'

Pedrito thought it wise to skip the translation of that unintentionally disconcerting observation.

Ali duly continued with his revelations. King Abû Yahya, he divulged, was in the capital city of Medîna Mayûrqa with some forty-two thousand troops, five thousand of those mounted, and all of them well-armed and ready for battle. They were determined to relinquish not one single footprint of the island and would do everything they could to prevent a Christian landing – anywhere.

Ali looked at the king and said, 'I can tell you, Sire, that reinforcements have been summoned from Africa, and it is only because of an act of betrayal by one of the king's own family that those forces are not already here. As you may have guessed, your invasion has been anticipated for some time, and the plan was to have your fleet intercepted by Morrocan ships long before you reached here.' Ali shrugged his shoulders. 'However, the treachery which has foiled King Abú may yet work in your favour – but only if you act quickly and attack the city before support arrives from Africa.'

The king had now been joined by the principal general of his forces, his cousin En Nunyo Sans. He put Ali's suggestion to him, whereupon En Nunyo reminded the king that, during the previous day's tactical discussions with the two Muntcadas and the other senior barons, it had been agreed unanimously that a landing would be attempted at the earliest opportunity following the present day of rest. Now, in the light of this latest information, if indeed it was true, it would be En Nunyo's recommendation that all commanding nobles and ship masters be instructed to make ready to depart for Santa Ponça at dawn the very next day.

'And where would the element of surprise be in that?' the king casually enquired.

En Nunyo was visibly taken aback. 'Surprise?' He gestured towards the Moorish camp. 'Surprise? Surely there can be no element of surprise with all those eyes watching our every move, so I'm at a loss as to you what you mean.'

'What I mean is that to wait until dawn before making our move would be to play into the enemy's hands.'

En Nunyo's face was a picture of disbelief. He drew the king aside and said in a hoarse whisper, 'You can't be suggesting that we go into battle today, on the sabbath?'

'You know very well that I've more respect for our Lord's day than to do that.'

En Nunyo shook his head in exasperation. 'In all the years I've known you, you've always been straight with me, so why are you being so difficult now?'

The king canted his head to one side. 'Difficult?'

'Yes! You question my decision to undertake a landing tomorrow, yet you admit it would be wrong to launch one today. If that isn't being difficult, I don't know what is!'

King Jaume gave a mischievous little laugh. 'When I appointed you senior commander of my forces, I expected you to at least be able to work out what lies between one day and the next.'

Nunyo Sans looked at him in total disbelief. 'Don't tell me you want to attempt a seaborne assault on the island at *night*!'

'Well, you tell me – how else can we spring one on the Moors when, as you say, all those eyes over there are on us?'

Now it was En Nunyo's turn to laugh, except there was nothing mischievous about it. 'I've known you to yield to your own impetuosity often enough,' he scoffed. 'That's just the impatience and inexperience of youth, but what you're suggesting now is the height of folly, and as your kinsman and senior military counsellor I strongly advise you to – '

'As your king and supreme commander,' the king cut in, 'I strongly advise you to remember your place!'

En Nunyo's jaw dropped.

But the king wasn't finished with him yet. 'You may be eighteen years older than me, cousin, but don't forget that, although you have more experience as a commander than me now, you and your father still had to depend on the intervention of my army under *my* leadership to save your possessions in Provence from being taken by En Guillen de Muntcada. *Sí*, and I was only fourteen at the time!'

'I understand that,' En Nunyo said with an apologetic spreading of his palms, 'but all I'm trying to do now is – '

'And I haven't forgotten that you then sided with En Guillen when he turned against me, *and* to make matters worse, you both ultimately demanded to be paid for your loyalty.'

En Nunyo's face flushed.

The king was on his high horse now. 'And if it hadn't been for what you call my impatience and impetuosity, the huge fleet that's anchored here now would have turned back to the mainland on the very first day of this expedition!'

'I do truly understand that, *Majestat*,' Nunyo Sans truckled, 'but I worry that you're thinking of going against my advice – which is genuinely given in your very best interests – simply because of the word of a Saracen with a scratch on his shoulder, which could have been deliberately put there before he even got into the water.'

'You obviously didn't see what he had to swim through to reach here,' the king countered. 'Those Moorish archers must be superhuman if, from such a distance, they can aim their arrows as close as they did to a moving target while all the while intentionally missing it.'

'All the same, who's to say that he really knows about the size of the Saracen army on Mallorca and if there really are reinforcements on the way from Africa?'

'*I* say so,' the king growled, 'and if you can produce anyone with more reliable inside information, now's your chance!'

En Nunyo was clearly tempted to argue his case further, but chose to keep his own counsel, albeit reluctantly.

Up to now, it had been all Pedrito could do to catch what King Jaume and En Nunyo Nans had been saying to each other, but he'd heard enough to ascertain that the young king was asserting his authority *and* reminding his general that, blood relation or not, he was still a subordinate. No matter how subdued the king's voice had been in the exchange thus far, however, what he said next might have been heard half way across Es Pantaleu, and he obviously intended that it should be...

'My friend,' he called to Ali, 'you're welcome to be a member of my retinue. And you can rest assured that, if what you say turns out to be true, I shall grant you, your mother and your children – when or *if* you have any – sufficient rewards to allow you all to prosper. And this is my solemn promise as God's chosen King of Mallorca.'

He then turned back to En Nunyo Sans and barked, 'Tell all commanding nobles and ship masters to make ready for the voyage to Santa Ponça. We weigh anchor tonight – at midnight, the very moment this sabbath day is ended!'

## THE BAY OF SA PALOMERA (SANT ELM), SOUTH-WEST MALLORCA - MIDNIGHT, SUNDAY 9<sup>th</sup> / MONDAY 10<sup>th</sup> SEPTEMBER...

It had been decided that all lamps in the fleet should remain unlit, that strict silence be maintained and that all manoeuvres involved in setting out from the bay of Sa Palomera should be undertaken with sufficient care to ensure that the Moorish forces on the shore remained unaware of what was happening. The agreed strategy was for twelve galleys to leave first. Each of those would tow a transport carrying a body of knights, their mounts and their detatchments of foot soldiers, whose mission was to establish a defensive position on the hill called Puig de Na Morisca overlooking Santa Ponça Bay and hold it against any enemy opposition until the remainder of the vessels, including the slower sailing ships, had arrived.

The chant of '*Ayos*', customarily used by sailors to keep in time when weighing anchor, had been forbidden in favour of the discreet tapping of a stick on the prow of each galley. As luck would have it, a layer of cloud had veiled the moon, while a gentle onshore breeze sent ripples whispering onto the beach in front of the camp of the sleeping Moors, thereby masking the sound of oars delicately stroking the water out at sea.

It seemed, then, that optimum conditions prevailed for the stealthy departure of the great armada. Yet, before the twelve galleys had cleared the Punta Galinda headland at the eastern extremity of the bay, the breeze freshened enough to part the clouds, though only for a second or two. Nevertheless, a cry rang out from the shore, from where it was feared a Moorish lookout may have caught a glimpse of mastheads moving acrosss the fleetingly-moonlit horizon. Could it be that King Jaume's bold decision to make a nocturnal invasion of Mallorca was about to be baulked at the very outset?

All oars were raised, and not a word was spoken in the entire flotilla.

Then the moon disappeared once more behind the clouds. A tense hush enveloped the bay.

Pedrito had been assigned to the lead galley of En Nunyo Sans. He was to act as pilot to guide the fleet along the ragged coastline; a hazrdous enough exercise in daylight for anyone unfamiliar with these rock-strewn waters, and at best a reckless undertaking at night. But Pedrito was well up to the task. He was manning the twin tillers himself, with En Nunyo standing immediately behind him on the elevated poop deck.

He touched Pedrito on the shoulder. 'Perhaps,' he whispered, 'the shout from the Saracens was some kind of a false alarm. We'll give it a few more seconds, then set the oarsmen rowing again – but gently.'

Pedrito nodded his agreement. He knew what En Nunyo meant. Whoever had called out from the Moors' encampment hadn't actually used a recognisable word of warning – more a crude expletive of the type that might be uttered by someone who'd just had his foot trodden on by a horse. If nothing else, it was a comforting thought, but not one destined to stand the test of time. A moment later, whirls of sparks could be seen rising from the remains of the dying camp fires dotted along the shore. Then a blazing arrow shot into the sky, to be followed by an eruption of others; scores of them, their trajectories carrying them high above the bay, their flames flooding the entire area in golden glow.

'Damn them to hell!' En Nunyo growled. 'We're discovered!'

In the few seconds that the light from the arrows persisted, a flurry of activity could be seen within the Moorish camp: men running from tents while buckling on scimitars, others throwing saddles over horses, still more pointing excitedly at the departing Christian fleet as they dashed about in preparation for giving chase over land.

'*Ràpidament!*' En Nunya Sans barked at his galley captain. 'Set your men rowing for Santa Ponça! *Sí*, and don't spare their backs! If we fail to make a landing before the Saracens get there, we're done for!'

Then, as darkness closed in again, a murmur of voices, faint at first, drifted out from the shore. The sound grew louder, like the roll of approaching thunder, until the bellow of thousands of male voices filled the enclosure of the bay with a war cry intended to put the fear of death into its foes. No sooner had this roar reached a crescendo than it was augmented by the beating of drums. Again, the sound was muted to begin with, but steadily increased to an ear-splitting pitch.

This combination of frantic shouting and loud, repetitive drumming may well have had the desired psychological effect on many of the Christian soldiers at whom it was directed, but not so upon their supreme commander. Though with reluctance, King Jaume had agreed with his senior generals that, for the sake of military prudence, he, the crusading force's figurehead and inspiration, should allow the expeditionary group of twelve galleys and transports to lead the way, then follow on himself in the vanguard of the main body of the fleet.

'*Oy del vaixell!*' he cheerily hollered from the prow of his own galley as it drew alongside the stern of En Nunyo's. 'Ahoy there, *marinèrs!*'

The moon peeped out from behind a cloud at that very moment, illuminating a broad grin on the king's face. His right hand was raised in hearty greeting, his robes and hair billowing in the freshening breeze.

En Nunyo was almost speechless. Almost, but not quite. 'What in heaven's name is he up to now?' he muttered through gritted teeth. 'Holy Mary, Mother of God, his impatience will be the death of us all yet!'

King Jaume shouted over to his cousin that his royal galley had already proved itself to be the fastest in the fleet, so it made sense for it to act as pacemaker for the others at this vital time. Now that their cunning ploy had been so unfortuitously exposed to the enemy, it was crucial that they secured their landing place at Santa Ponça before the Saracens got there. 'Otherwise,' he stressed, 'we're done for!'

'My thoughts entirely,' En Nunyo called back with as much self control as he could dredge up, 'but the agreed plan was to – '

'And,' the king butted in, 'I've given instructions to be passed down the convoy that each vessel should show a lantern at its stern – a beacon for the one behind to follow. After all, now that the enemy knows what we're about, there's no point in making our fleet's passage along this treacherous shore any more hazardous than is absolutely necessary.'

This time, En Nunyo *was* speechless. Completely.

Pedrito, for his part, couldn't help smiling at the young king's determination to do things his way. Impetuous and impatient he most certainly was, and possibly to a fault, but his fervent commitment to the cause and his will to see it through had to be admired.

'Oh, and one other thing, En Nunyo,' King Jaume added, '– I'll make sure that my Captain Guayron and his crew here don't get ahead of you.' He motioned with a jerk of his head towards Pedrito. 'I haven't forgotten that Master Blànes is the only one who knows has way along this coast.' He let rip with a hearty laugh. 'But we'll be pushing you all the way, so you'd better make sure your oarsmen get their backs into it with a vengeance!'

As if on cue, the breeze then stiffened and swung round behind them.

'See,' the king cried, 'see how we've been sent yet another wind to speed us on our way.' He looked over his shoulder. 'And a wind from the north-west to boot. Perfect! So then,' he called across to Pedrito, 'what name in your song of the eight winds matches this one, Master Blànes?'

'The *Mestral, senyor*. They call this one the *Mestral*.'

'Then thank God for the *Mestral*. Why, even the sailing ships will be able to match the speed of our galleys now.'

With that, what sounded like roars of contempt rang out from the

Moorish troops striving to keep pace with them along the shore.

King Jaume laughed again. '*Ànims!*' he yelled. 'Let's go, men, and may God go with us!'

## 8

# INTO DEATH'S DARK VALE

*EARLY MORNING, MONDAY 10<sup>th</sup> SEPTEMBER –*
*THE BAY OF SANTA PONÇA, SOUTH-WEST MALLORCA ...*

The rosy flush of dawn was spreading along the skyline when the first of the galleys slipped into the pine-fringed creek of Sa Caleta at the far end of Santa Ponça Bay. Men and horses poured from the transports as they berthed on either side of the narrow inlet, soon all but clogged with vessels struggling to ease their way past one another without oars and tow ropes becoming hopelessly entangled. Meanwhile, the bay itself was alive with small boats from the next wave of ships, all pulling for shore loaded with soldiers making haste to join their peers in whatever challenges lay ahead.

To Pedrito's untrained eye, this appeared more like an every-man-for-himself stampede than the start of a carefully coordinated invasion involving upwards of sixteen thousand men.

Nevertheless, the nocturnal voyage along the coast from Sa Palomera had been completed in surprisingly quick time, the effects of a following breeze and no further need to keep the enemy unaware of their activities combining to speed the Christian expedition on its way. Also in their favour had been the fact that the deeply serrated coastline and the mountainous nature of the seaboard in this part of the island would have made it difficult, especially in the dark, for the pursuing Moorish land forces to match the progress of their seaborne adversaries.

Certainly, Pedrito could discern neither sight nor sound of the Moors from his position on the deck of En Nunyo Sans' galley, which was tied up immediately forward of the king's at the head of the creek. King Jaume himself had been one of the first ashore and could now be seen standing tall in the stirrups of his horse, a winged coronet on his head, the royal insignia of red and gold embellishing the breast of his surcoat, his sword wielded aloft, while he cantered back and forth shouting words of exhortation to the droves of men swarming onto the beach. He was the king, God's chosen leader of the *Reconquista* of Mallorca, so it behoved him to ensure that his followers' appetite for the fray should be sharpened by his presence at this critical time.

Out of all this confusion, some semblance of order began to emerge as individual commanders rallied their troops to their respective banners. Suddenly, a mighty cheer rose up when, in the half light, a junior knight by the name of Bernardo de Riudemeya was spotted hoisting the Catalan flag on the hill called Puig de Na Morisca, a short distance inland from Sa Caleta creek. Then, as had been planned, a body of cavalry and supporting infantry set off to join him, their task to prevent any Moorish advance towards the shore before the remaining bulk of the Christian forces had disembarked.

While men, horses, pack animals and supply wagons continued to spill from successive flotillas of landing craft, Pedrito secretly hoped the king would be too preoccupied with the complex logistics of the situation to remember the pledge he had made on the islet of Es Pantaleu a couple of days earlier. It had been one thing to promise to do the king's martial bidding in the relative tranquility obtaining then, but another matter entirely now that the air was charged with the pulse-quickening proximity of war. Indeed, Pedrito would have been content to leave active participation in the forthcoming conflict to those more favourably disposed to heroics than himself. But it wasn't to be.

'Ho there, Master Blànes! Your king bade me deliver his orders to you!'

Pedrito recognised the voice of Robert St Clair de Roslin, the devil-may-care young knight from northern Britain, who, back in that quayside tavern in Salou, had been responsible, even if indirectly, for his being taken on as helmsman of the royal galley in the first place. Mounted on a charger and resplendent in a long white mantle adorned with the red cross of the Knights Templar, Robert was clutching the reins of his prancing steed in one hand, while holding a rope attached to the bridle of an old she mule in the other. He was grinning from ear to ear, his expression more reminiscent, in Pedrito's view, of a little boy about to steal apples than of a soldier steeling himself to ride into the gaping jaws of eternity.

'His Majesty tells me you're skilled in handling one of these,' he called out, laughing delightedly as he nodded towards the mule. 'There's a litter strapped to her side. You've to follow behind the company of En Remon de Muntcada when they engage the enemy. Aye, it'll be your job, along with the other porters, to pick up any of our wounded and bring them back here.' Noticing the sudden apprehension in Pedrito's eyes, Robert indicated the metal helmet resting on the pommel of his saddle, then added chirpily, 'And don't worry, laddie, there's one of these – only a leather one, mind you – and a padded *gambeson* undercoat strapped to your friend here as well. They're spare ones of the king, and they've seen plenty of service.' He winked mischievously. 'All right, they're passed their best, and while the leather helmet won't absorb an axe blow and the gambeson won't stop an arrow, they'll slow them down a bit, so be sure to put them on before you set out!' He lobbed Pedrito the rope, wished him God's blessing, reared his horse in deliberately spectacular fashion and, with a loud 'whoop', galloped off through the pines to rejoin his troop.

En Remon, the older of the two Muntcadas, had been one of the earliest nobles to go ashore, and his detatchment of cavalry and foot soldiers was the first to proceed inland to reinforce the advance party already established on Na Morisca hill. This had been in accordance with the orders of the the king's foremost general, En Nunyo Sans, who had also recommended that the king should remain at the beachhead for the present, both to boost the spirits of those men still landing and for his own safety, until such time as the size and capability of the Moorish opposition had been established. King Jaume, hungry for battle, had been reluctant to comply, but had yielded eventually to the advice of his senior barons, who had reminded him that he was the figurehead and inspiration of the entire Christian army. Losing his own life – or even sustaining a serious injury – at this early stage of the campaign could have such a demoralising effect that it would be tantamount to handing victory to the enemy.

It had been calculated that, once En Remon de Muntcada's company had augmented those troops already installed on the high ground, the full complement of Christian forces set to hold this vital position would amount to approximately seven hundred infantry and one hundred and fifty horse. Consequently, it came as something of a shock when the first rays of the rising sun revealed a vast army of Moors assembling on the landward side of that selfsame Puig de Na Morisca bridgehead.

En Remon gave the order for his forces to halt. Being in the vanguard, he was only a few hundred paces from the lower slopes of the hill, therefore close enough to the Moors' position to ascertain the extent of their forces. Pedrito, conversely, was standing with a group of other supporting personnel to the rear of the main body of fighting troops, so unable to see the deployment of Moors for himself. However, word soon came back through the ranks that, because of the Moors' line of approach from the west, it could be assumed that these were the same forces that had been confronting the Christians across the bay of Sa Palomera during the previous two days. Confirmation was established as column after column of them emerged through an early-morning mist to occupy a stretch of fairly level land between the Puig de Na Morisca and a sequence of higher hills to the north.

Predictably, their number was estimated to be the same as that calculated by King Jaume's generals back at Sa Palomera – that's to say some five thousand foot soldiers and two hundred horse. So, while it might be a fairly even match for the cavalry on both sides (with the Moors enjoying a slight advantage), every Christian infantryman would be pitted against at least seven of the enemy.

The risk of this had been known in advance, of course, but the gamble taken had been that, due to the difficult terrain they'd have to traverse, the Moors would arrive piecemeal in relatively small numbers, thereby giving the Christian expeditionary force a reasonable chance of holding ground until the remainder of their own army had come ashore.

Now, while the Moors assembled in combat formation facing the hill, an unnatural silence fell on a tract of rustic serenity that was about to become a cacophonous, blood-soaked battlefield. As if directed by an invisible hand, the dawn chorus of birdsong ceased. Not a horse neighed, not a solitary leaf stirred. Death was in the air, and the things of nature smelt it.

Pedrito smelt it too, and he felt the same chill of fear that had coursed through his veins when taken captive by pirates those five years earlier.

It appeared, though, that no such feeling was troubling the Christian soldiers amassed ahead of him here. The smell now invading their nostrils was also of death, but the death of their enemies, not their own. They were hardened campaigners all, and the adrenalin-rush of impending battle, combined with the prospect of plunder to be snatched from fallen adversaries, made them impatient for the fight, no matter how unfavourable the odds against them.

Agitated murmurs began to spread from man to man; a contagious surge of hostility that could only be satisfied by making real the nebulous stench of death. And their eagerness for the kill intensified rapidly when the beat of the Moors' drums began to resound across the field – quietly at first, just as had happened at Sa Palomera, then gradually increasing in volume as thousands of Saracen voices joined in a tumult of noise meant to strike terror into the hearts of the enemy.

It had the opposite effect on this particular enemy, however. They started yelling their own threats and, despite their comparative lack of numbers, succeeded in matching the din being produced by the Moors. Hundreds of Christian foot soldiers were beating swords against shields and bellowing for the attack to commence, which in turn provoked many a knights' horse to rear up and strain impatiently at the bit. Even Pedrito's dozy old mule began to fidget, tugging against her rope, ears back, teeth bared, braying hoarsely as she finally became aware of the mounting excitement.

Just when it seemed that the entire Christian contingent might be about to descend into chaos, En Remon de Muntcada himself rode back through their lines urging restraint and, most of all, silence. As their commander, he was about to give an order, and it was plain that he wanted everyone to hear it.

He was some years the senior of his kinsman Guillen, but of a similar stocky build and with the same dour, determined look about him. 'Harnessed' in full battle attire of chainmail suit and heraldic tabard, he was sitting astride a charger with the butt of his lance resting in a stirrup, its tip pointing ominously heavenward. Looking every inch the warrior nobleman, he spurred his horse to the top of a rocky knoll, where he could be seen and heard by all the troops, including those already posted on the hill behind him.

He removed his helmet, waited for the ongoing clamour to subside, then shouted, 'Save your anger for now, men, and save your energy as well! You'll need all of it soon enough, I promise you!' He then pronounced that not everything about that great throng of Saracens might be as appeared on first impression. Numbers, after all, weren't everything. 'For this reason,' he continued, 'I'm about to have a closer look at them, and let none of you dare follow me. I go *alone*! '

'But, *senyor*,' one of his accompanying men-at-arms protested, '– their archers. They're bound to see you, so what if –'

En Remon raised a gauntleted hand. 'I'll be able to establish what I want to without venturing within arrow-shot. And anyway, if what I saw when they were trying to shoot the turncoat Ali in the Bay of Palomera is anything to go by, I'll have little to fear even if I do.'

Having made his intentions absolutely clear, he motioned the crush of troops to make way, then trotted off through a copse of wild olive towards enemy lines.

By now, the rays of the rising sun were drawing long, receding shadows over the countryside, where little farmhouses the colour of weathered straw sat amid almond groves and orchards of orange, apricot and fig. Sheep and goats still grazed the weedy stubble between the trees, though Pedrito guessed that the peasant families who shared the land with them had already fled. He noted how most of the farmsteads had a tall palm tree or two standing sentinel by their gates, reminding him once more of his own home overlooking the sea at Andratx, so near from here in times of peace, yet so far now that warring armies barred the way.

He was jolted from his musings by someone giving him a nudge in the back, then turned to see a grizzled old fellow dressed in a sleeveless quilted coat that may once have been part of a knight's battle attire, but was now fit only for a tramp. He was holding the bridle of a saddle-backed nag, its scrawny frame suggesting that it had at least one hoof in the grave. On taking a closer look at the horse's master, however, it appeared to Pedrito that he was perhaps somewhat younger than he'd seemed at first glance. Small and wiry in build, he had the calloused hands of someone who'd known a life of manual labour, and his leathery, sun-wrinkled skin hinted that he'd spent that life toiling on the land. Yet a sparkle of youthfulness still danced in his eyes.

With a sideways twitch of his head, he indicated the direction in which En Remon de Muntcada had just ridden.

'How the other half lives!' he grunted, then spat into the dust at his feet, which Pedrito now noticed were shod – no, 'wrapped' would be more accurate – in strips of sacking bound with twine. 'I tell you, boy,' the man went on, 'even that baron's horse is wearing better clothes than anyone in my village back in Aragon ever set eyes on.' His face creased into an impish grin. '*Sí*, and by the look of it, the son of a whore's horse is a hell of a lot better-fed than any of my neighbours as well! *Sí, sí, camarada*,' he chortled, 'it's an ill-divided world we're born into, but maybe next time I'll be lucky enough to come back as a nobleman – or even a horse!' He looked askance at his own pathetic animal, then muttered out of the corner of his mouth, 'Though, pray to Christ Almighty, not like this poor bastard, eh!'

He went on to say that his name was Rafael, forty years old, give or take a couple of years, and a born-and-bred peasant, who tried to scrape a living for his wife and twelve children on a patch of mean, stony land in the foothills of the Pyrenees some way to the north of the Aragonese capital, Zaragoza. He had been following King Jaume on his battle expeditions since his arrival in the city to assert his right to the throne of Aragon at the age of nine – more than eleven years ago.

Rafael patted his old horse on the forehead. '*Sí*, and that was when El Cid here could still pull a plough all day without stopping for a rest every five minutes.'

Pedrito was amazed. 'You rode *that* all the way from Zaragoza to Salou?'

Rafael smiled and nodded his head.

Pedrito frowned and scratched his. 'Zaragoza to Salou? But – but that must be well over a hundred miles!'

'Could be, as the crow flies,' Rafael shrugged, then patted his nag again. 'But it seemed more like three hundred at the speed this bag o' bones hobbles along at them days.'

'But why?'

'Because he's bloody ancient, that's why!'

'No, no, what I mean is why would you want to leave your family so far away, just to come here and lug the wounded off a battlefield – yes, and maybe even risk stopping an arrow yourself?'

'Well, like I say, I've been doing it on and off for years – following King Jaume's armies into battle – and it hasn't been because I'm all that bothered whether or not a soldier dies where he falls or at the hands of some sawbones back at camp. Hey, I may look as stupid as that mule of yours, boy, but I'm not, believe me!' As if to punctuate the point, Rafael launched another missile of spit into the dust. 'No, *camarada*, all I'm after is a chance to rip some decent swag off the bodies of them that's already croaked their last – you know, collect enough valuables to let me make a better life for my missus and the kids.'

'Ah, I see. So, you've been building a nest egg over the years, eh?'

Rafael gave a wheezy laugh. 'Sure, and Muslims eat pigs! Nah, by the time the cavalry and infantry have raked over the bodies, all that's left for us tail-enders is dross.' He looked disparagingly at Pedrio's borrowed helmet and gambeson. 'As you know well enough already, judging by that rubbish you're wearing.' Rafael shook his head. 'Nest egg, you say? Nah, truth to tell, boy, after I've made my way back to Zaragoza and flogged my miserable bits and pieces to old Moses the Jew, I've usually only made enough out of the entire exercise to get blind drunk for a couple of days before staggering back home to the *finca*.'

Pedrito frowned. 'Seems to me there must be easier ways of getting a hangover, so why keep doing it?'

'Well,' Rafael shrugged, 'it's more exciting than growing beans. Besides, like I said, I've got a wife and twelve kids – one for every campaign, as it happens! – so there's more peace and quiet on some battlefields than at home.' He winked conspiratorially. 'Also, there's a half-witted whore in Zaragoza who gives discount rates to returning war heroes. Enough said, huh!'

Pedrito rolled his eyes. No wonder this character looked older than his years.

All at once, a roar went up as the waiting troops caught sight of En Remon de Muntcada heading back towards them at speed.

'Just as I thought,' he shouted as he reined in his horse, '– those Moors are worthless – nothing but a bunch of camel milkers and carpet sellers masquerading as soldiers. I tell you, men, no matter how many there are over there, they'll be no match for us!'

This news was greeted with another roar, even louder this time and loaded with aggression.

Pedrito suspected that En Remon was deliberately stretching the truth in order to work his troops into a frenzy of belligerence. And it was having the desired effect.

Waving his shield above his head, he silenced the uproar, then proceeded to orchestrate the offensive. Firstly, he deployed detatchments of archers to the forward flanks, telling them that their first task would be to let a deluge of arrows rain down on the heads of the enemy, to 'soften them up a bit' before the cavalry charge.

'We are honoured and fortunate to have many Knights of the Temple within our number on this crusade, and our assault against this infidel mob will be led by them in their distinctive, unflinching way. The rest of you men-at-arms will heed their example and bear down on your opponents at full gallop and with a steadfast will to run them through and kill them.' He paused to address the infantry, telling them to follow the cavalry into the melee with urgency, and to show no mercy to any member of the enemy still able and willing to fight. 'You will take no prisoners. From what I've just seen, there will be few Saracens worth much in ransom anyway. Also, provisions are going to be scarce enough for a while without having to feed hostages. So, I repeat, you will take no prisoners, and neither will you dally to plunder the fallen!'

As disgruntled mutterings rumbled through the ranks, Rafael nudged Pedrito again.

'He'll be lucky! Even among his regular soldiers, there's plenty toerags like me who're only here for what they can swipe from corpses.'

'I repeat,' En Remon shouted, 'no prisoners and no plunder!' He pointed his lance eastward. 'If what the turncoat Ali told your king is true, there's a vast garrison within the walls of the capital city of Medîna Mayûrqa, just twelve miles away in that direction, so we do what we have to do here as swiftly as possible, then regroup back at the beachhead – with luck, before any Saracen reinforcements have sallied forth from the city.' That said, he held his lance aloft, stood high in his saddle and declared, 'We are in good heart, brothers, for God is with us! So, let battle commence, and may the spirit of our Lord Jesus Christ lend courage to our hearts and strength to our arms as we dispatch those spineless disbelievers to the depths of oblivion!'

No sooner had the first barrage of arrows plunged down on the Moors than the screams of their stricken horses sliced through the battle cries of the Christian troops, all of them still holding back from the charge, though reluctantly. Then, as Moorish shields were raised in anticipation of another aerial bombardment, En Remon de Muntcada gave the signal for his archers to fire directly into their front line. The sickening thud of crossbow bolts hitting unprotected bodies was the result, and not a single Moorish bowstring was drawn in retaliation. Without a moment's delay, En Remon signalled his archers to repeat the initial action of releasing their arrows on a trajectory which would enable them to pelt the enemy from above. Yells of agony and shouts of confusion resounded across no-man's-land. Then, and only then, did Remon de Muntcada commit his forces to the assault.

With banners flying and lances couched for action, a squadron of Knights Templar led the onslaught, thundering forward knee-to-knee, their horses kicking clouds of dust into the faces of the following surge of troops. But a little dirt in the eye deterred no one. Battle fever, a cantageous affliction spread by the elation and terror of impending combat, had infected the Christian soldiers, and even the possibility of their own demise at the hands of a vastly greater force could not contain it. Valour, or aspirations for it, and the power of raw bloodlust had seen off whatever vestiges of discretion still lurked in anyone's breast. The charge had become a one-way journey to victory or heaven. It would be glory – or death.

To gain a better view of the ensuing activity, Pedrito hauled his mule onto the mound from which En Remon had delivered his address. And it didn't take him long to come to the conclusion that the the baron's declared assessment of the Moors' military capability hadn't been such an exaggeration after all.

The mounted knights and supporting foot soldiers who had rallied earlier to the Catalonian flag on Na Morisca hill were now careering down its northern slopes to join En Remon's forces in the attack. Through the billowing dust, Pedrito could see that the havoc wreaked on the Moorish front ranks by the Christian arrow strikes was having a multiple effect. Those Moors who had been injured but could still run were doing just that – or trying to. Their movement wasn't intended to counter the Christian advance, however, but to get away from it. And as they struggled to force their way back through their own lines, those troops at the rear of the vast formation were pressing ever forward, unaware of the pandemonium developing ahead. Even a non-miltary man like Pedrito could see that the consequences were unlikely to be in the Moors' favour.

En Remon's stratagem for the use of his archers had been an inspired one, and his assessment of the enemy's capacity for fighting was already proving to be admirably accurate as well. The majority of the Moors were clearly not professional soldiers, but in all probability just ordinary citizens from the more modest walks of life, drafted in to make a show of numbers, which their ruler had hoped would be sufficiently intimidating to hold off the Christain invasion until his anticipated reinforcements arrived from Morocco. The outcome, though, was already promising to be the humiliating rout of his five thousand men by a force of considerably less than nine hundred.

Panic spread like wildfire throughout the Moorish lines. Carnage without reprisal would be the inevitable result. What Pedrito was seeing from the safety of his vantage point was less a theatre of war than a pageant of mass slaughter. Deadly flashes of steel glinted through a hazy blur as the Christian pack carved into the mayhem that had formerly passed as an orderly battle formation. Savage roars erupted from the attackers, while their victims' cries of distress, combined with the shrieks of pain from horses caught up in this commotion of violence, added further dimensions of ugliness to an already repugnant scene.

A cloud of dust hung above the tumult in the still morning air – still, that is, except for the whirlwind of butchery sweeping over the ground below. As the Christian forces charged, hacked and lunged their way forward, more and more men behind the Moorish van were falling over themselves in a desperate bid to escape, not only from the advancing enemy, but also from their retreating comrades. In the ensuing crush, those who stumbled were trampled and fallen upon by their own wounded. They lay pinned to the ground, cringing helplessly as they awaited their fate at the hands of an unstoppable adversary, a focused and brutal foe who had already made it painfully clear that no quarter would be given.

It now appeared that King Jaume's promise of a Mallorcan

heaven on earth would have to wait until after an embodiment of hell itself had been created on the island – and at his behest too.

Pedrito took the old mule by the bridle and led her down from the hillock, then slowly over no-man's-land towards the site of the initial clash of arms. The shallow valley they were passing through was still embalmed in a strange hush, in which the only sound was the steady, muted plod of the mule's hooves. Yet behind him, Pedrito could make out the distant clamour of troops and equipment being offloaded from the Christian ships at Santa Ponça Bay. And up ahead, there were the war cries of En Remon de Muntcada's men; the baying of hunters bearing down on a hapless quarry; the bloodthirsty noise of the chase, growing ever more faint as those Moors still capable of running scattered for their lives.

However, when Pedrito drew closer to the scene of the opening encounter, another sound came to his ears. It was the sound of men dying; grown men whimpering for their mothers, moaning pitiably, praying to Allah for deliverance, or, even more heart-rendingly, pleading for someone to put a swift and merciful end to their suffering.

Body was strewn upon Moorish body. Hundreds upon hundreds of them. Some were lying distorted and lifeless, others writhing in agony, all of them smothered in gore that oozed from wounds so appalling that it turned Pedrito's stomach to steal but the merest glance. And there was the smell, the smell of mutilated flesh mixed with the once-sweet aromas of a field now sullied by human brutality. The aberrant odour of earth soaked in blood, the putrid stench of clothing drenched in sweat and urine, the foul stink of defecation. The stuff of fear that took Pedrito back to his years as a pirate-galley slave, though the sensations now polluting his consciousness bore a more debasing stamp than he had ever thought possible.

He was standing in what appeared to have been, until a few violent minutes ago, a *horta*, a vegetable plot of the type common to many small farms in Mallorca. Indeed, there was one on his own family's *finca* – a little, dry-walled enclosure just like this, in which his father would cultivate a range of crops to augment the staple sustenance provided by the family's modest assortment of poultry, sheep and goats. Onions, cabbages, garlic, spinach, carrots, peas and beans. Plenty of beans. Always a surfeit of beans, it seemed. Which reminded him of his 'tail-ender' colleague, Rafael, the itinerant plunder-seeking peasant from Aragon.

'*Hola*! How goes your life, *camarada*?'

Speak of the Devil. Pedrito's eyes followed the voice to where Rafael, crouched like a hunchback, was emerging from behind the stone parapet of a well.

'Keep a low profile, boy – that's the secret. *Sí, sí,*' he hissed, 'you never know who might be watching from afar while you go about your business.'

Pedrito's senses were still numbed by the scenes of horror surrounding him. 'Your business?' he asked vaguely.

'Loot, plunder, booty. That's why I'm here, remember?'

Pedrito shook his head, hardly able to believe the insensivity of the man. 'And you're scared Muntcada or one of his knights might see you, is that it?'

Rafael wheezed his chesty laugh. 'Nah, I don't bother about them toffs.' He glanced furtively about. 'Nah, nah, it's other scavengers like myself I'm on the lookout for. Telling you, boy, them toerags would pick the pockets of blind lepers, given half a chance.' He flashed Pedrito one of his conspiratorial winks. 'Better get rummaging fast, if you want to grab yourself a few trinkets while the going's good.'

But Pedrito wasn't really listening. His ears were becoming deaf to everything but the heartbreaking sounds of misery all around him. Yet what could he do to help these victims of the recent orgy of bloodshed? Even if he had been armed, would he have had the courage to end even the most doomed of lives with a compassionate thrust of a sword? For the first time in his life he felt totally inadequate in the presence of the deplorable suffering of fellow human beings. Even back on the pirate galley, chained as he was, he had been able to call out occasional words of solace and support to those captives being herded into the cramped *zuga* holds beneath the decks. But here, the only comfort he could offer the afflicted would be death, and the very thought of having to administer it gave him a feeling of impotence that filled him with shame.

It seemed that Rafael had been privy to his thoughts. 'If you're thinking about putting any of them Arab sons of a whore out of their misery, there's plenty weapons lying about. Just help yourself to a scimitar or a dagger and get on with it.' He gave a mocking chuckle and glanced up at the sky. 'You're a big strong boy, but you better be quick all the same. There's scores of the half-dead bastards for you to bump off, and them buzzards circling up there have more patience than you've got energy or time.' He savoured Pedrito's perplexed look for a moment, then added with a smirk, 'Them Arabs like a nice sheep's eyeball in their rice and boiled mutton round the camp fire of an evening, see.' He smacked his lips. 'Mmm, and them buzzards up there like a nice human eye – live if possible – any time.'

His rasping laughter mingled offensively with the moans of anguish that rose and fell like waves of despair within the *horta*, where neat rows of one family's life-sustaining crops lay flattened and destroyed by the fleeting presence of two armies committed to furthering the glory of their respective gods – and, in the case of the invaders, to increasing the contents of their own purses, to a lesser or greater extent, depending on rank and, consequently, aspiration.

Rafael's aspirations may well have been among the lowest, but his dedication to the task couldn't have been bettered, nor could his scruples have been more lacking. He dipped into the pocket of his sleeveless coat and, having attracted Pedrito's attention with a shout of '*Mira*!', pulled out a severed finger. He pointed to the blood-stained ring still encircling it.

'Colours of King Jaume's banner,' he chuckled. 'Red and gold, see? Very appropriate, I reckon.' Whistling through the few teeth that still populated his gums, Rafael wiped some blood off the ring with his thumb. 'Hmm, nice piece of stuff, this. Should fetch a fair price from old Moses back in Zaragoza.' Then, with a frown, he tutted, 'Just too bad I couldn't get it off the Saracen bastard's finger!' He looked up and beamed at Pedrito. 'Might have been easier if he'd been right dead, though, eh?'

Pedrito winced.

Rafael shrugged. '*Sí*, hardhearted it may seem to you, boy, but mark my words – us scavengers haven't time to waste on them details here in the battlefield.' He shook his head and unceremoniously stuffed the finger back in his pocket. 'Nah, I'll chop the bits off either side back at the beach later on.'

While Pedrito watched in dismay, Rafael clambered over a pile of the dead and dying, his eyes fixed on a body lying on its own a few paces away. He swooped on it in a way that would have done justice to the birds of prey wheeling hungrily above.

'Must have been a right swanky bastard, this one,' he called out, stradling the man's knees and hauling at the buckle of his belt. 'Never a soldier, this one. Nah, more like a no-balls eunuch or some other pansified pervert from one of them high-class Moorish whore houses. What do they call them again? Harems or hareems or something, ain't it?' Rafael whipped the belt from the body and held its buckle up for Pedrito to see. '*Mira!* Studded with nice shiny jewels.' His eyes popping, he was grinning like a breathless cat. 'Could be rubies and emeralds and sapphires or something, eh?'

If Pedrito hadn't been gagging with disgust, he'd have told him that beads of worthless glass would have been more likely. He'd noticed plenty of baubles like those being worn by the poorer sailors who hung about the quaysides of North African seaports. It was well known that the souks there were full of such fake stuff. But, in the event, it made no difference whether he offered Rafael this information or not, because the self-styled scavenger suddenly had more important things to concern himself with.

As he made to get back on his feet, a Moorish archer, who had been lying as though dead nearby, raised himself onto an elbow and, with what may well have been his last gasp, released an arrow into Rafael's chest.

Rafael's bellow of pain appeared to serve as some kind of signal to his old horse, El Cid, who had been grazing peacefully in a patch of trampled carrots over by the well. In defiance of the arthritic appearance of his aged limbs, he took off at the canter, cleared the boundary wall with a foot to spare and galloped away to who knows where without a backward glance. It was as if he realised that his master's plight had presented him with a long-awaited chance to escape the purgatory he'd been obliged to accept as his way of life since the day he'd tasted his first handful of oats.

Rafael was now sprawled awkwardly over the corpse he had just robbed. He glanced at the departing El Cid, then, with a pained smile, grunted, 'Let the bastard go. He was clapped out anyway.' Though clearly in agony, he attempted another smile, then added, '*Si*, don't worry, *camarada*, there will be plenty better horses than him going a-begging before this war's over.'

Pedrito stepped forward to take a closer look at where the arrow had struck.

Rafael coughed, and a trickle of blood ran out of the corner of his mouth. 'Just get me back to the shore, boy,' he wheezed. 'Bound to be a sawbones or two ashore already. *Si*, one of them bastards will get that thing out and fix me up right as a trivet. *No problema!*'

Pedrito wasn't so sure. The arrow had entered the left side of Rafael's chest, and you didn't have to know much about anatomy to realise that its tip was probably lodged dangerously close to his heart. If that were the case, moving him might well be the worst possible thing to do. In any event, Pedrito told himself, Rafael was probably in no worse a state of health than some of the men whose bodies he had been in the process of desecrating, so why should he help this objectionable wretch in preference to any of the other wounded? Certainly not because Rafael was a Christian and the rest were Muslims. To Pedrito, a life was a life, irrespective of which particular divinity the owner believed he owed his existence to, though there could hardly have been a less commendable example of *any* religion's fellowship than Rafael. Neither did the total disrespect Rafael had shown for his fellow man do anything to earn him the sympathy of one of them now. He deserved to die the same lonely, lingering death that he had so callously proclaimed to be a fitting end for those he now lay among.

All of these things raced through Pedrito's mind as he unrolled and spread on the ground the litter that had been tied to his old mule's harness. A life was indeed a life, and if he could help save just one on this god-forsaken day – even a life so apparently worthless as Rafael's – then it might go at least a little way to help lessen the feeling of inadequacy that had overcome him when he first stepped into this arena of misery.

He attached the front ends of the litter's two long shafts to the mule's hip strap. Then, as gently as he could, he lifted Rafael up in his arms and laid him on the crude canvas stretcher. Rafael groaned and flinched as Pedrito heaved the other ends of the shafts onto his shoulders and, with a click of his tongue and a few quiet words, coaxed the mule into a steady plod back towards the bay of Santa Ponça.

'And another thing, boy,' Rafael spluttered, 'don't let any bastard swipe my Saracen's finger while the sawbones is working on me.' He hacked up a gob of bloody mucus, then gasped, '*Sí*, the money Moses pays for that gold ring will buy me a whole week with the halfwit whore in Zaragoza!'

Pedrito didn't waste his breath asking what the same money would have bought for Rafael's wife and twelve kids. This was a crusade, and he was doing his best to save the life of a crusader. Not a typical one, admittedly, but a crusader all the same, and maybe no less deserving of survival than some of the more illustrious stereotypes.

\*

The entire landward area of Santa Ponça cove was swarming with men and horses when Pedrito arrived back. It seemed to him that the situation was slightly less chaotic than before, despite the fact that even more droves of men were splashing ashore from the scores of ships now anchored in the bay. The standards of the various nobles that had been raised in designated areas along the sparsely wooded foreshore were obviously serving their purpose in marking the mustering points for the respective companies of troops.

Rows and rows of horses were being hitched to ropes tied

between pine trees on the fringes of each detatchment's patch of ground. Makeshift kitchens were being set up in shady spots adjacent to the wells of little farms whose carefully cultivated land was now being trodden flat by this massive influx of human and animal feet. The smell of wood smoke and vegetable broth mingled oddly with the whiff of horse droppings, though Pedrito had to concede that there was something comforting about this – at least to a homesick peasant like himself.

Amid the rallying calls of knights and their squires, the clank and thump of blacksmiths' and carpenters' tools could already be heard reverberating through the trees, as repairs were being made to equipment damaged during the storms that the fleet had encountered on its way here. To Pedrito's amazement, a veritable tented city-on-the-move had materialised in the short time he'd been absent, and it was obvious that its inhabitants planned to be moving in one direction only, and that certainly wasn't back to sea.

A baggage park had been established near the beach to accommodate supplies still being off-loaded, and it was to here that Pedrito had been directed by a priest stationed on the edge of the encampment to offer prayers for the returning casualties, of which, Pedrito had been informed, his own particular stretcher case was the only one thus far.

Rafael, his face fixed in a grotesque grin, was staring at the sky when an out-of-breath Pedrito laid down the shafts of his litter outside the tent he'd been told was serving as a field hospital.

'I hope it's God he's smiling at and not the Devil,' said the portly monk who greeted them.

'You mean he's –?'

'As a doornail. The unblinking, unseeing eyes are always a dead giveaway, my son.'

'Phew!' Pedrito panted, wiping the sweat from his brow with the back of his hand. 'You mean to say I could have saved myself all that trouble?'

The monk leaned forward and closed Rafael's eyes. 'We certainly won't need to operate on this one,' he said blandly, before muttering a few words in Latin and making several signs of the cross. He gave Pedrito a cheerless smile. 'There, that's him seen to, my son. So, you can either dig a hole for him somewhere, or we can have him buried at sea.'

Pedrito raised a cynical eyebrow. 'You mean have him rowed out into the bay and dumped overboard.'

The monk hunched a nonchalant shoulder. 'I've given him a blessing and forgiven him his sins, so he's now in the arms of Jesus – or at least his soul is. Whatever happens to his earthly body now is neither here nor there.'

Just then, the old she mule half bent her back legs, lifted her tail and squirted a jet of piss directly onto Rafael's face.

'Not to worry,' Pedrito sighed, 'it's probably the nearest thing to holy water that old rake has been splashed with in his entire life.' He uncoupled the shafts of the litter from the mule's harness, then lowered them to the ground. 'The burial at sea it is then, friar. I've spent enough energy on this one already. Oh, before I go,' he said as he took the mule by her bridle, 'there's something in the pocket of his coat that should provide a few alms for the needy.'

The monk's eyes lit up.

'Or it'll buy you a week with a halfwit whore in Zaragoza!'

Turning to leave, Pedrito could have sworn that a smirk of enthusiasm had tugged momentarily at the corners of the monk's lips. Conversely, it could have been a grimace of disgust at such an unholy suggestion being made to such a holy man as himself. By now, Pedrito couldn't have cared less either way.

## 9
# WAR IS THE SPORT OF KINGS

*SANTA PONÇA – A FEW MINUTES LATER…*

In the absence of any specific instructions, Pedrito made his weary way back to where the galleys of En Nunyo Sans and the king were moored in Sa Caleta inlet at the eastern end of the bay. As he approached through the pines, he could see King Jaume in conversation with a young knight who was wearing a surcoat emblazoned with the red and gold of Aragon. The garment was soaked from the waist down, suggesting that the knight had only just waded in from one of the recently arrived transports.

'*Hola*, Master Blànes!' King Jaume shouted when he caught sight of Pedrito. 'Back so soon from the fray? I trust you bring us good news.'

Despite Pedrito's down-in-the-mouth delivery, the king couldn't contain his delight at his depiction of the total rout and associated massacre of the Moorish force by such a small detatchment of Christians.

The young Aragonese knight was patently less pleased, however. 'Just my luck!' he griped. 'The first battle for Mallorca has already been won, and I wasn't even in it!' He took a petulant kick at a conveniently located asphodel. 'Damn the Devil in hell, I've missed the chance of a lifetime!'

King Jaume wagged a finger. 'No, no, not a bit of it! I'm as keen as you are to give the Saracens a taste of their own Toledo steel, and I'd have been in the forefront of that first battle myself if I hadn't listened to the advice of those who thought I'd give more inspiration to my people by parading about here.' He gave the young man a slap on the shoulder. 'How would you like to follow me into battle right now, *amic*? Better late than never, no?'

Without waiting for the taken-for-granted reply, the king vaulted onto the deck of his galley and shouted to the body of his company, who were tending their horses and checking equipment in an adjacent clearing, 'Are any of you ready to go with me far into the island? The Saracen foxes are on the run, so now's our chance to cut off their tails before they go to ground!'

An encouraging cheer of assent rang out as mounts were swiftly saddled, swords girt and lances taken up. Then a cloud of dust appeared, rising above the trees in the direction of the Puig de Na Morisca, from where the recent assault against the Moors had been initiated.

'Look there!' the king shouted. 'That'll be En Guillen and his men returning victorious from the first thrust against the infidel. Now, friends, without delay, let's continue the Lord's good work where our brothers left off!' He turned to Pedrito. 'And you, Master Blànes – you will come with us to show the way.'

Pedrito tried to excuse himself by saying he'd seen enough of death and butchery for one day. But the king would hear none of it. He was giving an order, not extending an invitation, so Pedrito had better look sharp and do what he was told. In the coming days, there would be many missions much more gruelling than the one Pedrito had just completed, and no lethargy or lack of commitment to the cause would be tolerated. King Jaume was being typically uncompromising in his resolve.

'You there, Lorenç!' he shouted to his armourer, a fawning little man, with a permanent, though humourless, smile on his face. 'Have a horse saddled for Master Blànes. A nice, docile hack will do, as I doubt our fine helmsman here will be doing any charging.'

'But I'm not even armed,' Pedrito objected. 'And even if I was, I wouldn't know how to use a sword or –'

'And another thing, Lorenç,' the king cut in, 'fetch Master Blànes a shield and a "morning star" as well.' He chuckled quietly to himself. '*Sí*, that should do him nicely!'

The 'morning star', when it appeared, turned out to be a wooden ball studded with metal spikes and attached to a short handle by a chain.

The king laughed when it was handed to Pedrito, who was already making himself as comfortable as possible astride his allotted horse, while looking markedly uncomfortable to be in this position at all. He was well accustomed to ambling along a farm track on a mule's back, but it was something else entirely to go galloping into battle on a *real* horse, albeit an allegedly 'nice, docile' one. Pedrito wasn't relishing the prospect.

Alongside him sat the king, duly mounted on his charger. 'There you are, Little Pedro,' he muttered through a mischievous grin, '– you don't need any soldierly skill to handle that subtle instrument. Just take care not to hit yourself on the head when you're trying to bludgeon a Moor with it. Those spikes would do no good to that leather helmet I lent you. Old and scruffy it may be, but it holds great sentimental value for me nonetheless.'

Pedrito clearly wasn't sharing the king's sense of levity about this. 'Really?' he replied dryly.

'*Sí*, it was the one I was wearing when I took a life for the very first time.' Pensively, the king stroked his cheek. 'Hmm, only fourteen I was – maybe even just thirteen.'

Pedrito cast him what almost passed as a reassuring look. 'Don't worry, *senyor*, I'll do my best to make sure it isn't the one I'm wearing when someone else takes *my* life.'

King Jaume, becoming more excited by the second at the thought of impending action, laughed heartily – and a tad manically, Pedrito thought. He was witnessing first-hand the young king's infamous impetuosity, and he could only hope that the results wouldn't be too disastrous. His hopes weren't bolstered when it quickly transpired that only twenty-five equally-impulsive young knights were ready (and willing!) to join the king in his impromtu foray into enemy territory. Even allowing for the huge casualty count resulting from the morning's encounter with En Guillen de Muntcada's men, there was still a vast number of Moorish troops on the island – forty-two thousand in the capital city alone, according to Ali – so it struck

Pedrito that King Jaume might just be biting off a little more than he could chew here.

Pedrito considered the 'morning star' which had been thrust at him by the hurrying, scurrying Lorenç. It was now occupying his right hand, while his other was gripping a shield. To Pedrito's non-equestrian way of thinking, this left him two hands short of being able to control the horse on whose back he was about to gallop off.

'With due respect, *senyor*,' he said to the king, 'I think I'll manage better without this weapon.'

King Jaume frowned. 'Are you mad, Master Blànes? Going into battle unarmed?'

Pedrito handed the 'morning star' back to Lorenç, then pulled a length of braided twine from his pocket. 'This will serve my purpose better. At least I know how to use it.'

'A piece of string?' the king scoffed. 'What's that for? Are you going to dismount and *strangle* every Moor we come across?'

This induced an outburst of laughter from those within earshot.

With a polite little smile, Pedrito rolled up the cord and returned it to his pocket. 'I'm sure it won't come to that, *Majestat*. Well, I certainly *hope* it won't come to that.'

'And so do we all, Master Blànes. And so do we all.' Laughing lustily again, the king set the butt of his lance into his right stirrup, then stood up and shouted, 'Follow me, brave lads! Let us hunt down those sickly Saracens and give them another dose of Christian medicine! *Ava-a-a-ant*! Onward, men! Onward for Spain and for God!'


Luckily for Pedrito, the king set out at an easy trot, which seemed to be to the liking of the heavier warhorses, as well as to Pedrito's hack, which did indeed appear to be a docile beast, without even a hint of the wilful tendencies typical of the mules he was more accustomed to handling. Apart from having the encumbrance of a shield on his left arm, he actually felt quite at ease atop his mount, and would probably have been looking forward to the ride had it not been for the nagging thought that he might well be riding to his death.

With the king beside him at the head of the little troop, he took the same route by which he had returned earlier while bearing the weight of Rafael's litter on his shoulders. Instead of going straight ahead through the scene of so much carnage, however, he skirted the battlefield by what he considered to be a respectful margin. But respectful though the distance may have been, it still wasn't enough to allow even the most insensitive of nostrils to escape the stomach-turning smell of death that was spreading ever wider with the rising of the warm September sun. And this wasn't the nebulous smell that had been sensed before the so-called battle. This was the unmistakable stench of putrefying flesh. The stench that oozes from a rat lying dead in a trap – but magnified here to a nauseating intensity.

Retching, the king covered his nose. '*Jesús!*' he gasped as he paused to survey the site of the massacre from the crest of a hummock they were traversing. 'I've seen the aftermath of more battles than I care to remember, but I've never seen anything to compare with that.' He blessed himself, then muttered, 'Holy Mother of God! There could be as many as fifteen hundred dead strewn over that small stretch of land!'

'Maybe not all dead yet,' Pedrito said. 'And the thought of that is even more sickening than the smell.'

But if the king heard him, he gave no such indication. '*Es coll de sa batalla.* The vale of the battle,' he murmured, staring stony-faced at the gruesome legacy bequeathed by just one small unit of his army. '*Es coll de sa batalla...*'

'The vale of one-sided butchery would be more like it,' Pedrito blurted out without thinking.

But again, the king appeared not to have been listening. '*Es coll de sa batalla,*' he repeated absently. 'And the fate of those who perished here will be the fate of every Saracen who rejects the one true faith.' He blessed himself once more. 'May God help us in our quest to rid this land of the infidel hordes.'

'Look there, *Majestat!*' one of his companion knights called out. He was pointing to a hill some way off to the north. 'Moors! Three hundred of them, maybe four – and nearly all on foot!'

'God has answered my plea even more quickly than I could have hoped,' King Jaume murmured. He stood high in his saddle again and shouted to the waiting column of cavalry, 'Brace yourselves for the kill, brave boys, for there skulks the pack of foxes!'

And off he set at a brisk canter, a long streamer fluttering from the head of his lance, his small squadron of mounted men-at-arms and their retinues in close pursuit. To Pedrito's great relief, his horse seemed to know its place, which happened to be several lengths behind the rear of the column. As a hack, his mount's purpose in life was to carry its master *to* a battle, but not *into* it. That was when the heavier chargers took over, and they could now get on with it while the hack provided emergency backup in case any unhorsed knight should require his services for a quick getaway. Anyway, this was the theory as Pedrito interpreted it. Horse sense, so to speak, and he was happy to go along with it.

As soon as the Moors saw the Christian party heading in their direction, they took flight and made for a tree-mottled hill a short distance farther north from their present position.

'We'd better waste no time if we're to overtake them, my lord,' one of the king's suite urged. 'If they reach the cover of the woods on that second hill...'

But before he could complete his sentence, King Jaume was away at a hot gallop, with three other knights chasing close behind, and the remainder of the company left to catch up as best they could.

Pedrito knew nothing of the accepted procedures of going into battle, but the same horse sense that told him it was prudent for him to be bringing up the rear of the column also told him that the king was currently letting his fighting spirit rule his head. And possibly to the point of total recklessness at that.

By the time Pedrito reached the base of the second hill, which had already been dubbed *Es Puig del Rei*, the King's Mountain, by a waggish element within this swashbuckling band of young *cavallers*, it was apparent that the majority of the Moors had, in fact, made it to the cover of the woods. Pedrito estimated that no more than a hundred remained on the open lower slopes to face the

Christian onslaught. And although this depleted Moorish rearguard still outnumbered their attackers, it was obvious even now that they would be capable of offering little resistance.

Pedrito could see that the king and his three consorts had already slain four or five foot soldiers (if, indeed, they were any kind of soldiers at all), while those Christian cavalrymen following on were dispatching the other scattering remnants of the Moorish infantry by sword, axe or lance as the opportunity arose.

The oft-vaunted policy of attempting to convert their Muslim adversaries to Christianity was clearly no more on the agenda now than it had been during the wholesale bloodletting of earlier in the day. Which prompted Pedrito to recall some words of advice put to him by *al-Usstaz*, 'The Professor', during one of his nocturnal discourses aboard the pirate galley:

'Never mistake a religious war for a holy one, my friend.'

The king and his three companions were deep in conversation as Pedrito ascended the slope towards them. From the way they were pointing in different directions, it looked as though they were assessing the number of Saracens already killed, while also taking a few minutes to give their horses a rest. There wasn't another living soul in sight, as the rest of the royal contingent had now taken off in pursuit of all the Moors still capable of running. All the Moors, that is, except one, and the direction he was running in was directly at the king.

Pedrito would have been about a hundred paces away when he noticed him, mounted on a handsome Arab stallion, breaking from a clump of trees at the gallop with his lance aimed at the king's back. From his attire, it was obvious that this was no pseudo soldier, but a member of the Moorish military elite, and a skilled horseman to boot.

Pedrito shouted a warning to the king, but the clamour of men killing and being killed in the adjacent woods drowned out his voice. Apparently, the noise had also masked the sound of the the Arab stallion's hooves thundering down the hillside behind the king's little group, who, blissfully unaware of the impending danger, continued to survey the scene below them.

With not a second to spare, Pedrito jumped down from his horse and took from his pocket the length of cord which King Jaume had made fun of before setting out on this raid. Picking up a pebble about the size of a small egg, Pedrito couched it in the little leather cradle that was attached mid-way between the two extremities of the twine, gave the device three rapid overhand whirls, then let go one end to released the stone in the direction of the charging Moor. It hit him square on the front of his steel helmet with such force that he was propelled backwards out of his saddle.

The first the king knew of this little drama was when he saw the riderless Arab stallion racing past him down the hill. Instinctively, King Jaume wheeled round to witness the stunned Moorish cavalryman getting to his feet with his lance held menacingly in his right hand. No sooner had Pedrito arrived on the scene than King Jaume told him to ask the Moor to surrender. His reasoning was that, as this Moor was clearly a knight himself, he deserved to be treated as such. The Moor's response to this chivalrous invitation, however, was to tilt at his opposite Christian numbers.

The king and his men were still on horseback, and he quickly let it be known to his subordinates that the welfare of their mounts was his primary concern.

'Horses are in short supply on this this campaign, brothers,' he said. 'The vast majority of our knights have only one apiece, so take care that this Saracen's lance does no harm to yours. *Sí*, never forget – the life of one horse is worth that of twenty Moors.'

Thereupon, he proceeded to instruct the members of his party on how best to treat this particular twentieth fraction of a horse's life.

'Let's surround him, and when he thrusts at one of us, the one immediately behind him can strike him down in such a way that he'll pose no further threat to anyone.'

While this delicate manoevre was being set up, another knight, whom Pedrito recognised as one of the king's entourage called En Pedro Lobera, came galloping out of the woods and ran straight at the hapless Moor, who reacted by plunging his lance deep into the horse's chest. Although the animal was done for, the impetus of its charge knocked the Moor back to the ground, where the king and his men fell upon him with the points of their swords at his throat.

'We'll give him one more chance,' King Jaume declared. 'Tell him once again to surrender, Master Blànes!'

'*Lé!*' the Moor growled, his negative body language obviating the need for King Jaume to ask Pedrito for a translation. '*Lé!*' he snarled again, then went to draw his sword, which determined that his one-word declaration of defiance had been the last word he would ever speak.

'By my reckoning, that makes something like eighty Saracens killed on this outing,' the king remarked as he wiped the blood from his sword with a leaf from a handy fig tree. 'And that isn't counting those still being done away with by our lads in the woods there.' He gave En Pedro Lobera a comforting pat on the shoulder. 'So, *amic*, this tally should more than compensate for the loss of your horse, no?'

'I'm responsible for one of those deaths,' Pedrito admitted, but with a distinct lack of pride. He was too preoccupied with his own thoughts to take any notice of what En Pedro's reaction to the king's questionable words of comfort had been. 'Responsible – at least in part,' he added as an afterthought.

'How so, Master Blànes?' the king queried. 'You're talking in riddles again, I fear.'

Pedrito took what the king had called 'a piece of string' from his pocket and dangled it from his fingers. 'Remember this, *senyor*? You thought I might use it for strangling Saracens?' He then pointed to the dent on the front of the dead Moor's helmet.

The king nodded his head slowly as he put two and two together. 'I've heard stories of the great prowess of the slingers from these Balearic Islands of Mallorca, Menorca and Ibiza in ancient times. The legendary Balearic Slingers – the pride of the Roman legions, weren't they? Indeed, it's said that Mallorcan mothers wouldn't give their little sons a morsel of bread to eat until they'd knocked it from a branch with a slingshot.' A grin spread across his lips. 'Did your mother also treat you in this cruel way, Little Pedro?' he teased. 'Is that how you gained such skill with your piece of string?'

'She didn't have to encourage me,' Pedrito replied matter-of-factly. 'No, us kids around Andratx had listened to tales about the Balearic Slingers since we were in the cradle. *Los Honderos* were our heroes. And, by the way, they were the pride of Hannibal's Carthaginian army long before they fought for the Romans.' Only now did a faint look of pride come to his face. '*Sí, senyor*, we could make a sling and hit moving targets a hundred paces away when we were still only knee-high to a gecko.'

'Well, it was playtime well spent,' the king pronounced, 'for today you and your piece of string may well have saved my life!' His congratulatory thump on the back was hearty enough to make Pedrito cough. 'Come, lads,' King Jaume laughed, 'let's round up the rest of our band and make our way back to camp. A good day's work has been done, and we must give our thanks to God for that.'

*

It was late afternoon by the time they'd covered the three miles back to Santa Ponça. After dismissing his company, King Jaume told Pedrito to stay close by him. He was now to be a fully-fledged member of the king's train, and as such would be required to be on call at all times for whatever duties might be required of him.

They dismounted at the edge of the clearing which had been established as the royal compound and walked towards the king's tent, from where two figures emerged to greet them.

King Jaume nudged Pedrito with his elbow. 'En Guillen and En Remon de Muntcada. Something tells me that my two eminent military counsellors won't be too pleased with me for having set off on that little unplanned mission.' He wasn't wrong.

En Remon's face was a picture of utter exasperation. 'What in heaven's name have you been doing?' he barked at the king, prompting Pedrito to surmise that this young monarch's impetuosity had become such a thorn in the flesh of his more cautious generals that this one at least was prepared to risk a royal backlash by berating him as he would a wayward child. Even more significantly, En Remon was prepared to bring the king to book in front of

Pedrito, a bottom-of-the-heap underling in his aristocratic eyes. 'Did you want to kill yourself and all the rest of us as well? If luck had gone the other way and you'd lost your life – and I've no doubt you ran the risk of it – then your army and all that's been put into this crusade would have been lost. You are the figurehead and inspiration – irreplaceable! How often must you be told?'

Pedrito held his breath for the royal retaliation, but none materialised. On the contrary, King Jaume merely smirked like a misbehaved schoolboy and raised his shoulders in an all's-well-that-ends-well shrug.

Sheer frustration glowed crimson in En Remon de Muntcada's cheeks. He swatted the air with his hand. 'Pah! Sometimes I wonder why I bother!'

But his kinsman En Guillen took an altogether more pragmatic approach to the situation – an attitude, Pedrito suspected, born of the prospect of the riches and lands of Mallorca that the king would be granting them and their fellow barons on the successful conclusion of this campaign.

'It's true, En Remon, that the king has done a very foolish thing, yet it was also the act of a true knight. Any one of us would have been angry and impatient at not being included in the first battle for the island. And, lest we forget, the king surely has more reason than any for wanting to be involved in every aspect of winning the war.' He then addressed the king. 'But you must restrain yourself, *Majestat*, for in you lies life or death for us all.'

'I know, I know,' King Jaume sighed, '– the figurehead and inspiration. I've been told it often enough, believe me.'

En Guillen gave him an understanding smile. 'But you can comfort yourself with one thing, my lord – that from the moment you set foot on Mallorcan soil, you became its rightful king. And we will do all in our power to help you hold it for your own, just as God Himself decreed you should. But,' he concluded with a sage look, 'you will do more for the glory of His name alive than dead.'

## 10

# HELL IS WHERE HEAVEN IS NOT

*SANTA PONÇA – SHORTLY BEFORE DAWN –*
*TUESDAY 11ᵗʰ SEPTEMBER,*
*IN THE TENT OF KING JAUME I OF ARAGON-CATALONIA…*

So congested had the waters of the cove become the previous evening that the masters of the hindmost ships, which had fully three hundred knights and their horses still onboard, found it impossible to find places to moor. Again, Pedrito's navigational knowledge of the local coastline was called upon by the king's senior generals, who decided he should set out aboard a small *barca* and lead the larger vessels eastwards round Sa Porrassa peninsula to the cape of the same name, where, as he had advised them, they would find good anchorage. The Punta de Sa Porrassa was little more than three easy miles overland from the current base camp, its location affording an unobstructed view across the wide bite of the island's southern bay towards the capital city of Medîna Mayûrqa, from where it was assumed the main military threat of the Moors would ultimately emerge.

Although it had been almost nightfall when they arrived off Sa Porrassa point, a lookout on Pedrito's boat spotted a large army, which was taken to be that of Abú Yahya Háquem, the Moorish King of Mallorca, already encamped on the side of a mountain called Na Burguesa. The Moors' position overlooked the little haven of Porto Pi, just over a league away from the Punta de Sa Porrassa on the western flanks of the city. Without delay, Pedrito sought out En Pere Ladron, the nobleman commanding this arm of the fleet, who decided that, while it would now be risky for the large ships to do anything other than anchor here for the night, Pedrito should return immediately to Santa Ponça in the *barca* to inform the king of the situation.

*

It had been midnight when Pedrito finally accomplished his mission. However, all the king could do at that hour was send messengers to the individual quarters of his chief barons, telling them to post scouts far enough from the camp to allow a warning to be relayed back in time for preparations to be made in the event of an enemy advance.

Now, with the dawning of the new day, it emerged that no such precautions had been taken, due to the relative state of disarray that the travel-weary commanders and their troops were still in. This, at least, was the excuse given to King Jaume by En Guillen de Muntcada.

The king was not best pleased. 'Only yesterday you told me that I would serve God better alive than dead!'

'Yes, my lord, but the men have endured much and were suffering from total exhaustion – especially those involved in the skirmishes yesterday, so –'

'So, if the Moorish king had chosen to fall upon us with his army while we slept, how many of us would still be here to continue the crusade?'

'I understand what you're saying, *Majestat*, but –'

'But it's a pity more people in this army of brave Christians don't share my *fault* of impetuosity! If they did, an appropriately large guard would have ridden out in the early hours, even if their commanders were too tired to enforce my order!'

En Guillen was suitably contrite. 'You've made your point, *senyor*.' He gave a respectful nod of his head. 'But I'm sure you would agree that an army of soldiers who take it upon themselves to do things on a whim would be an ineffectual army indeed.'

'Ah, but there was no whim involved, *amic*. I sent a firm order to my barons, and not one of them chose to obey it. So, I'll put to you the question your cousin En Remon put to me yesterday – did they want to kill themselves and all the rest of us as well?'

Pedrito had been listening to this tense exchange from the most discreet distance that the limited space within the tent allowed.

En Guillen now gestured towards him. 'While I continue to take your point,' he said to the king, 'I'd prefer it if you didn't embarrass me by making it in the presence of a lackey.'

A wry smile came to the king's lips, but it was accompanied by a steely look in his eyes. 'Are you referring to Master Blànes?'

En Guillen replied somewhat caustically that he didn't see anyone else in the tent.

The king inhaled sharply, his nostrils flaring. 'And you regard Master Blànes as a mere lackey, do you?'

En Guillen hunched his shoulders. 'What else?'.

The king scowled. 'Yet you never paused to think that you might be embarrassing me, your king, by berating me in front of him, a mere lackey, when I returned from that *skirmish* yesterday?'

It was obvious that En Guillen couldn't defend himself with an acceptable answer to that one, so he went on the offensive instead. 'I'm bound to tell you,' he said with an air of confidentiality, 'that your trusting of this ex-pirate is the talk of your nobles. They believe you are both lowering yourself and risking the security of your forces by accepting a person of such dubious origins into your suite.'

The king's frown deepened. '*Lower*ing myself?'

'That's what's being said behind your back, *senyor*, and I believe I serve you better by saying it to your face.'

The king narrowed his eyes. 'A person of such *dubious* origins?' he repeated, his voice oozing resentment.

En Guillen's mounting unease was betrayed by the colour rising in his cheeks, yet he maintained a façade of self-confidence. 'He told you himself that he's a foundling, and now it's common knowledge throughout the –'

'And what objection have you to foundlings?' the king butted in, his demeanour quickly shifting from displeasure to an ostensibly benign curiosity.

'Foundlings?' En Guillen released a mocking little laugh. 'Ha! We all know what that means within the peasant classes.'

'Do we indeed?' said the king, his head tilted to one side.

Pedrito cleared his throat. '*Perdona, Majestat*, but I – well, I apologise for interrupting, but I think it may be better if I take my leave until –'

'I summoned you here to advise my barons on the situation as you saw it at Na Burguesa and Porto Pi, Master Blànes, and I'll be grateful if you'll do me the service of remaining right here until the rest of them arrive.' King Jaume then calmly addressed En Guillen again. 'Now, you were about to tell me the meaning of "foundling" within the peasant classes, I believe.'

'It's just a euphemism,' En Guillen pooh-poohed, 'a crude cover-up of the truth.'

'And the truth is?'

En Guillen glanced over at Pedrito before replying. 'I've no wish to decry your – your *retainer* here, my lord, but foundlings are usually the bastard offspring of whores. It's well known that much of the population of seaports is made up of generations of so-called foundlings.'

Pedrito felt his hackles rising, but he kept his composure. What else could he do anyway? His pedigree, or lack of it, was being discussed by a king and a high-ranking aristocrat, both of whom, if the notion took them, could have him flogged for no particular reason. He decided that confronting them now would give them reason enough, so he held his tongue.

The king, however, was in a position to take a more robust stance. And, to Pedrito's great relief and no little surprise, he did just that.

'The bastard offspring of ... *whores*?' he checked.

'Absolutely! I mean, how else would harlots manage to continue in business if they didn't leave their unwanted brats somewhere where they'd either be found and cared for by other members of the lower orders, or eaten by stray dogs?'

En Guillen now found himself on the receiving end of a distinctly disapproving look from the king, who cautioned him that he would do well to be mindful that high rank does not justify arrogance.

'Rank? Arrogance?' En Guillen shook his head. 'I don't follow.'

'Let me put it this way – what difference is there between a common whore and a high-born woman whose marriage to a nobleman is arranged for the material benefit of one or even both parties?'

It was now the king who was subjected to a dark look. 'That, *Majestat*, is tantamount to saying that those of us born into the aristocracy have whores for mothers!'

'It could be taken as such – in some cases,' the king shrugged, 'and if their offspring, bastard or otherwise, are given away in infancy to be *educated*, as is often the case, it could also be said such children aren't all that far removed from your definition of foundlings.'

Pedrito recalled that the king had divulged to him the less-than-enviable details of his own parentage. He had also admitted that, at the tender age of three, he had been handed over by his father to the tyrannical Simon de Montfort, allegedly for his education, but actually to be used as a pawn in a complex and unsavoury game of land grabbing. So, he was clearly not excluding himself from the provocative proposition he had just put to En Guillen de Muntcada. For this, Pedrito thought all the more of him.

But not so En Guillen. He glared at the king. 'You demean all those of high rank by making such inappropriate comparisons, *senyor*!'

The king gave him an exaggeratedly genial smile. 'Oh, I don't think so, my friend – merely expanding on what I told you a few moments ago.'

'Which was?'

'That having high rank doesn't justify arrogance. Nor does it justify a lack of respect for the lower orders, as you choose to call them. After all, as I suggested, the only real difference between them and the upper classes is the privilege that comes with inherited wealth – or the semblance of it.'

This took the wind out of En Guillen's sails. Suddenly, his

manner became less self-assured, almost submissive. 'Again, I take your point, my lord. And let me assure you that I didn't intend to offend your, uhm, your –' he glanced briefly at Pedrito again '– to offend Master Blànes. It's merely that I was a little surprised that you'd called on someone other than an experienced military man to brief us on the situation at Na Burguesa.'

'And I'd have thought you would have realised that I did so for the same reason that En Pere Ladron sent Master Blànes back here last night instead of coming himself.' King Jaume then proceeded to remind En Guillen that Pedrito had more knowledge of the coast and seaboard in this part of Mallorca than anyone else in his entire army. 'Which, as you may recall, was the main reason that Nicolas Bonet, the captain of your own ship, hired him as my helmsman back in Salou.'

En Guillen acknowledged that with a somewhat grudging, 'Yes, of course, and a wise decision it was, I'm sure.'

'And so,' the king concluded, a triumphant twinkle in his eye, 'when Master Blànes has briefed you on the situation of the Moorish army as he saw it from Sa Porrassa point and has described the lie of the land in the vicinity of Na Burguesa mountain, you and the other generals can make the requisite military decisions, no?'

'Absolutely, *senyor*.' En Guillen dipped his head. 'And I meant you no personal discourtesy when I questioned the wisdom of putting your trust in Master Blànes. I was merely trying to –'

The king cut him off with a snap of his fingers. 'Save your breath for fighting Moors, which is what we're here for. And one final thing – when you're next discussing my choice of aides with the other nobles, you may wish to remind them that none of us would have reached here at all if it hadn't been for helmsman Blànes. One, he steered my galley – with a little help from myself, admittedly – through that first storm, when others had begged me to turn the fleet back to the mainland. Two, his advice saved fifty of our vessels, including your own, from being wrecked during that second storm when we were trying to round Cape Formentor for the original landing place at Pollença. Three, he guided those same ships south to the shelter of the bay at Sa Palomera, where the remainder of our fleet was able to join us in safety. And four, he directed us to our present location, from where, on this very day and with God's help, we will launch a victorious battle against the pride of the infidel forces.'

En Guillen managed a sheepish smile. 'Indeed, *Majestat*, you have chosen your local advisor well.' He cast Pedrito a cold glance. 'And I'm sure you will reward him well for his ... assistance.'

King Jaume didn't like the tone of that remark. 'For your information,' he snapped, 'Master Blànes seeks no personal gain from his involvement in this campaign, even though his *assistance* in getting us here ensures that everyone else, not least yourself, will have the opportunity to benefit from the spoils of war.'

'As is my right!' En Guillen bristled. 'Why else do you think I pledged four hundred armed knights to this crusade?'

The king canted his head again, then asked softly, 'For Spain, your king and the glory of God, perhaps?'

Clearly riled, En Guillen growled that this surely went without saying.

'Indeed it does, my friend,' the king replied impassively. 'Indeed it does. And I respect you for that. However, I respect no less Master Blànes' reason for being here, which, although perhaps less *noble* than yours or mine, is a source of envy for me, nonetheless.'

At first, Pedrito's face mirrored En Guillen's look of puzzlement. Then it dawned on him what the king was coming to, and a shiver of emotion ran down his spine.

King Jaume stared inscrutably at En Guillen for a few seconds, then asked, 'What better cause for embarking on a perilous journey could any man have than the simple wish to be reuinted with his family?' He hesitated before adding in a hushed voice, 'Would that I could look forward to the same opportunity.'

While En Guillen struggled, unsuccessfully, to come up with an apt response, the king strode over to Pedrito, laid a hand on his shoulder and said, 'In the little time I've known this fellow, he has proved himself to be a good companion, without any thought of what might be in it for himself.' He looked directly at the baron again. 'It's the first time I've encountered such a person in my entire life – a life which, you may be interested to know, he was on hand to save yesterday. Yes indeed, En Guillen, a foundling he may be, a soldier he's not, but a friend he is, and I believe him to be a true and selfless one at that.'

Pedrito felt a lump rise in his throat. Yet, as much as he was touched by the king's words, he felt it best to remain circumspectly silent. When all was said and done, he was still nothing more than a fly on the wall, witnessing a young king tactfully but firmly reminding one of his most powerful vassals that, no matter how staunch his present motives might be, his disloyalties of the past, though long forgiven, were certainly not forgotten.

\*

With the first light of day, the king and his nobles heard mass in the royal tent from En Berenguer de Palou, a rather grey and gaunt man, with a grave look that befitted his status as the Bishop of Barcelona. He was dressed, however, not in his customary ecclesiastical robes, but in the garb of a fighting knight. He addressed the assembly as follows…

'Barons, this is not the time for a long sermon. The occasion does not allow it. But bear in mind that the enterprise in which the king, our lord, and you are engaged is the work of God, not ours. Therefore, you should reckon upon this, that whoever should die in this meritorious work will die for our Saviour, and will pass through the gates of Paradise and have everlasting glory therein for all time. And they who shall live will have honour and praise in life and a good end at death.

'So, strengthen yourselves in God, because our lord the king and all of us here desire to destroy those who deny the name of Jesus Christ. Accordingly, each man should, and can, trust that the Son of God and His Mother will not depart from us, but rather will help us triumph over our foes.

'For this reason, you should have good heart and trust that we will overcome all.'

He paused to look into the face of every man in turn, then lowered his voice and said, *'The decisive battle, gentlemen, will be this day.'*

He then raised his eyes and smiled a pious smile, before declaring dramatically, *'But comfort you well, barons, and rejoice, for we go with our good liege lord, the king. And God, who is over him and over us all, will guide us onward to victory!'*

Pedrito, as was right and proper for someone of his humble status, had left the tent immediately after giving the king and his nobles the benefit of his local knowledge in relation to what he had seen of the Moorish army's mountainside position the previous night. Since then, he had been listening to the bishop's sermon from outside, and not for the first time on this campaign was he prompted to wonder if the same exhortations would be preached to the Moors, but in the name of Mohammed and Allah instead of Christ and God. The promise of everlasting life in Paradise would certainly be a common element of both sermons, although the Christian version had stopped short of guaranteeing a generous supply of full-breasted virgins to its own potential martyrs and victims of war. That detail aside, it did still strike Pedrito that there was something basically flawed about any doctrine that offered eternal sublimity as a reward for dying while engaged in the destruction of those who didn't happen to share your belief in 'the one true faith' – no matter which variety you opted for.

As a child, he had heard his parents quote things which they said were the very foundation stones of the Christian religion: simple maxims along the lines of, 'Blessed are the meek, for they shall inherit the earth,' and, 'Blessed are the peace-makers, for they shall be called the children of God.'

Well, from what Pedrito had seen of the two rival armies here on Mallorca, it wouldn't be the meek who would inherit this little corner of the earth, and the only people likely to be called the children of God would be those who proved to be best at making peace with the point of a sword. Strange anomalies indeed, but wholly acceptable, it seemed, to those high-ranking Christian soldiers gathered here to pay pre-battle homage to their chosen divinity.

It prompted Pedrito to recall what the king had said to him back on the islet of Es Pantaleu three nights earlier: 'God's Commandments tell us that "Thou shalt not kill", yet when we're compelled to do it for the furtherance of God's glory, killing clearly isn't a sin, but a virtue.'

Then the words of *al-Usstaz*, the pirate galley 'Professor', came back to him: 'Never mistake a religious war for a holy one, my friend.' Here was a once-confusing tip that was beginning to make more sense to Pedrito by the moment.

Just then, he overheard the Bishop of Barcelona state that the king and all his barons, with the exception of one, had celebrated holy communion before leaving the mainland. Now, through a chink in the tent's canvas, Pedrito caught a glimpse of the usually self-assured En Guillen de Muntcada, kneeling before the bishop to belatedly receive the body and blood of Christ. En Guillen was sobbing, the tears running down his face like those of a lost child. At length, he stood up and approached the king, fell to his knees again and vowed to God in His mercy that he would prove his unswerving loyalty to the young monarch in whatever trials lay ahead.

It was a moving scene, but one which brought home to Pedrito how fragile these warrior nobles could actually be when faced with the stark reality of their potential death. They were men of violence who lived by the sword and were prepared to die by the sword. Yet, beneath all that, they were normal human beings with normal human frailties and fears. For them, therefore, religion and its rites served as crutch, comfort, stimulus and shield at such critical times as this.

The king laid a hand on En Guillen's head and motioned him to stand up, then embraced him warmly, but without saying anything. There was no need for words, as it was obvious to everyone present that he was deeply touched by his nobleman's public demonstration of devotion.

It occurred to Pedrito that what he was witnessing now was in stark contrast to the friction that had existed between these two men only a few minutes earlier – an example, perhaps, of the diametrically opposite ways in which the tensions, elations and terrors of impending battle can be minifested, even in the bravest of hearts.

Meanwhile, the news which Pedrito had conveyed to the king at midnight had clearly spread like wildfire through the camp by dawn. While the barons had been engaged in their reverential proceedings inside the royal tent, the rest of the vast Christian army had been coming to life, refreshed by a good night's sleep and fired up by the prospect of confronting at last the elite of the Moorish forces on Mallorca. Without any apparent order or organisation, horses were being harnessed and men were arming themselves while exchanging shouted words of encouragement from one division's compound to another. The euphoria of war was in the air and, as Pedrito was becoming ever more accustomed to noting, its effect was both virulent and overwhelming.

Inside the king's tent, conversely, the atmosphere was altogether more controlled. Matters had moved on from the solemn and sacred to the militarily practical. Pedrito could hear the voices of En Nunyo Sans and the two Muntcadas discussing the final tactics of engagement. The question of who should lead the attack came first.

'You take it, En Nunyo,' said Guillen de Muntcada.

'No, I think it's better that you take it today,' Sans replied.

This drew a cynical little chortle from Remon de Muntacada. 'En Nunyo, we know well enough why you say that. I'm sure you're speaking out of love for the hard blows we're bound to get in this battle, aren't you?'

A nobleman's honour was being questioned here, but this was hardly the proper time to debate it. Accordingly, En Guillen was quick to snuff out any flame of animosity that might be about to flare up. 'Anyhow,' he shrugged, 'none of this matters to me one way or the other.' He then addressed En Remon. 'To settle it, you and I will ride together in the vanguard and we won't spare our horses until we reach the Saracan lines. Agreed?'

At that very moment, the king, looking understandably harrassed, exited the tent and beckoned Pedrito. But before he could say anything, one of the royal porters came running towards them through the pines.

'*Majestat*,' he shouted, 'a large body of our infantry – maybe as many as five thousand men – is heading out of camp! They're hell bent on advancing on the Moors immediately!'

'On whose orders?' the king demanded. 'My three top generals are still inside the tent here, so the command didn't come from them.'

The porter indicated that he had no idea what had spurred the foot soldiers into this impromptu act. All he knew was that they were on the march without even waiting for the customary cover of cavalry to lead the way.

King Jaume punched the palm of his hand. 'Damned idiots! God knows I'm all for a measure of spontaneity in my fighting men, but this is complete stupidity.' He threw his head back in anguish. 'Holy Mother, how could they! Yet again I'm tormented by people who risk scuppering the *Reconquista* before it's even started!'

Pedrito assumed that the king's immediate reaction to the porter's news would be to rush back into the tent and alert his generals, but instead he grabbed Pedrito by the elbow and hustled him towards the nearest stabling enclosure.

'Let's take the first two saddled horses we see!' he growled. 'We'll have to head off these blockheaded infantrymen before the Moors catch sight of them!'

Pedrito hardly had time to contemplate what might be the difference, to the king's way of thinking, between spontaneity in his men and his own impetuosity before he was being given a leg-up into the saddle of the same 'nice, docile' hack he'd been teamed up with for the king's spur-of-the-moment incursion into enemy territory the previous day. For this stroke of good fortune, he offered up a silent prayer to the god (or gods) of horse sense. Then, with the king mounted on a markedly more spirited beast, Pedrito dashed off through the woods behind him in pursuit of the miscreant mob of foot soldiers.

If this was to be one of the most glorious military operations in the history of Christian Spain, it appeared to Pedrito yet again that it would be due more to good luck than good guidance.

*

When they caught up with the renegade band of infantry, its rearguard was spread out shoulder-to-shoulder over a wide area of open country, where the only cover comprised clumps of dwarf palms and copses of shrubby mastic and juniper which the local folk called *monte bajo*.

'Make way for your king!' the king hollered as he hurtled towards the unsuspecting backmarkers. 'Out of the way, for Christ's sake!'

As the great body of men opened up like Moses' fabled parting of the Red Sea, Pedrito could see the undulating summits of Na Burguesa ridge up ahead, though still far enough off to keep the Christian troops out of sight of the Moorish army encamped on the seaward slopes away to the right. It was now a question of whether or not the king could put a stop to this uncontrolled advance before it was spotted by enemy scouts, thereby setting in motion the inevitable disintegration of the entire Christian campaign.

When King Jaume had eventually barged his way to the front of column, he wheeled round, reared his horse and shouted a command for the forces to halt.

'What in the name of the Virgin Mary do you think you're doing?' he bellowed. He was in a blind rage and made no attempt to disguise the fact. Pointing to the wooded hillsides stepping upwards to the soldiers' left, he yelled, 'You have no cavalry protection, neither have you archers deployed on that flank. So, if a large troop of Saracen horse charged down on you from there, you would be killed to a man.'

A hush of embarrassment descended on the huge throng, before a young man-at-arms stepped forward, bowed before the king, then called out to his colleagues, 'What His Majesty says is right. We were acting like an army of blockheads – letting our excitement blinker our common sense.' He turned to the king. 'I beg your forgiveness, my lord, for we have let you down badly.'

There was no doubt that these men had been guilty of an act of utter folly, but the king preferred to tell himself that they had been swept along by some kind of mass hysteria for action, rather than by any sense of mutinous self-interest, as, for example, in a frenzied lust for plunder. Also, it was essential to bear in mind that each and every one of them would be expected to fight to the death for his king, country and God in the mighty battle that awaited them. Accordingly, amelioration and encouragement were what was required now – not chastisement. Prudently, then, King Jaume adopted a suitably conciliatory mien.

'I understand your impatience,' he called out with a sympathetic nodding of his head, 'and I share it. You are all brave fighting men, and many of you have come from faraway lands to join me in this great crusade against the infidel, for which you have my heart-felt gratitude and my reaffirmed royal promise of generous rewards.' He half turned in his saddle and pointed towards the ridge of Na Burguesa. 'But in the hills yonder there lurks a huge Saracen army, which, if my information is correct, consists, not of puny fakes like those who were so easily defeated yesterday, but of seasoned and fearless professional soldiers like yourselves, who are committed to killing us or to driving us back from this island which was stolen from our Christian forefathers three hundred years ago.'

The vast assembly was now hanging on King Jaume's every word.

'We face an able adversary today, men, but we have God on our side, and if we put our trust in Him, we surely have nothing to fear.'

Mutterings of assent rippled through the lines of troops.

'That said,' the king went on, 'we cannot be complacent. We cannot expect God to be our guardian if we ask too much of Him. God helps those who help themselves, but it is up to us, his vassals, to help Him by going into battle in a way that will be a credit to ourselves, His chosen defenders of the Christian faith.'

King Jaume allowed a few dramatic moments of silence to elapse before adding, 'I have the most experienced generals in Spain with me, as well as the foremost Knights of the Temple and their mounted retinues. Therefore, with such military excellence to guide us – and to bring out the best in you, the bravest fighting men in Christendom – those Saracen thieves on the mountainside yonder will be eliminated, and this heaven on earth, with all its riches, will be returned to God ... and to *us*, His obedient and faithful servants!'

## 11

# BETTER LATE THAN NEVER

*A FEW MINUTES LATER –*
*ON THE WAY TO NA BURGUESA MOUNTAIN...*

The storm of cheering which the king's oration whipped up could
well have been heard by the waiting Moors, who, if not alarmed by
its ferocity, would surely have been put on their guard. So, it was
not a moment too soon that three large platoons of Christian cavalry
now approached at the gallop to join King Jaume at the head of the
successfully restrained yet freshly stimulated horde of foot soldiers.

The mounted troops were following the banners of En Guillen
and En Remon de Muntcada and that of the Count of Empúries, the
first two detatchments comprising four hundred and one hundred
knights and their squires respectively, the latter made up of sixty
knights and their followers. Together they made an impressive
sight, the steel of their helmets, lances and chain mail glinting in the
morning sun, their colourful surcoats and coordinated trappings of
their horses completing a picture that would have done justice to the
most spectacular of victory parades. But the prospect of victory was
still a long way off, and no matter how uplifting their young
monarch's words had been, many who had heard them would never
live to see that day.

The frown on En Guillen de Muntcada's face indicated that he
was both surprised and displeased to find the king here. 'What
brings you to this place, my lord? I expected you to wait in your
tent to hear our final battle plans, but you simply disappeared.'

'And if I hadn't, the five thousand or so foot soldiers you see assembled before us here would have marched on to their deaths, and to the likely end of this crusade.'

En Guillen's expression became slightly less chastening. Leaning in towards the king, he lowered his voice to almost a whisper. 'It was a foolhardy thing you did, *Majestat*, and I'm bound to say yet again that your impetuosity is a constant source of worry to all of us who know how essential your wellbeing is to the success of this mission.'

'Though perhaps no more essential right now than the wellbeing of some five thousand foot soldiers, no?'

The irrefutability of the king's observation was acknowledged with a deferential dip of En Guillen's head. 'You have done right well, my lord. But I must now ask, no *beg*, that you remain here to await the arrival of En Nunyo Sans' reinforcements. Meanwhile, we will press onward to confront the Moors with the cavalry and infantry forces already here.' He gestured towards the scrub-dappled slopes of the foothills immediately ahead. 'The enemy will have had lookouts posted there, so the sooner we attack their camp, the less time they will have had to prepare a welcome.'

Pedrito could see that this request for his personal abstinence went right against the grain with the king, whose appetite for being in the forefront of the approaching showdown was keener than anyone's, and doubtless more insatiable as well. Yet, for once, he agreed to his general's proposal without objection. The logic of restraint, it seemed, had finally tempered his inherent response to a challenge.

While the troops were being mustered into orderly formations for the advance, and tactical orders relayed for the engagement of the enemy, Pedrito approached the king, who was watching proceedings from an elevated position nearby.

'Excuse the intrusion, *senyor*, but this is the first chance I've had to ask you why you beckoned me when you came out of your tent this morning.'

King Jaume gave him a vague look, thought for a moment, then replied, 'Oh that? I'd all but forgotten. I just wanted to ask you to skip along to the nearest field kitchen and grab me a bite to eat.' He rubbed his stomach. 'I'm starving, and God only knows when any of us will next see a decent meal – in this life, at any rate.'

Pedrito looked at his mount grazing a tuft of shrivelled weeds. 'Yes, as Rafael the scavenger told me, maybe we'd all be better off coming back as horses.'

The king glowered at him. 'There you go talking in riddles again, and, as ususal, this is neither the time nor place!'

It was obvious that the king was not only preoccupied with the enormity of the task facing his army today, but was also itching to be involved from the outset himself. Pedrito withdrew a few respectful paces as the king watched the great body of his men head off, banners fluttering, shields raised, lances and swords at the ready, towards the foothills of Na Burguesa ridge and the battle that would surely decide the fate of this momentous campaign.

Pedrito took advantage of this temporary lull to dismount from his horse and give his saddle-sore backside a much needed rest. He sat down on a tree stump and cast his eyes over the surrounding landscape. Behind him, the land rose steadily through woods of evergreen oak to the westernmost heights of the Serra de Na Burguesa chain, where wisps of white cloud drifted upward and evaporated in the warmth of the early autumn sun. This was the time of year Mallorcan country folk called the season of 'Winter Spring', so benign was the climate in the wake of the equinoctial storms that farmers chose now to sow and plant crops that would not have survived the fiece heat of summer. Beans came immediately to mind again. Beans. As long as he lived, he would never forget what, as a small boy, he regarded as the drudgery of shuffling through the *horta*, plopping seed beans into drills that his father was opening up ahead of him with his hoe. Drudgery indeed. How little he knew then, and how much he now longed to to be doing that same chore again – except that his father would now expect Pedrito to do the *real* work with that old hoe. The thought made him smile.

In front of him here, almond trees dotted with harvest-ready nuts descended in neat, evenly-spaced rows towards the sea, which seemed so close on this fine morning that Pedrito felt sure a well-delivered pebble from his sling would reach the shore with ease. He was tempted to try, just for the fun of it, but one look at the king's expression persuaded him to desist. Fun was clearly the last thing on King Jaume's mind at this moment in time, and understandably so. His destiny would be decided this day, and its deliverance lay in the hands of others – at least for the present.

Pedrito looked out to those clear-as-crystal azure and emerald waters that he had sailed so often with his father. Over to the right, there was the Punta de Sa Porrassa, a rugged, pine-fringed finger of rock pointing eastward to where the rear squadron of the Christian fleet had been resting at anchor overnight. From this distance, with their masts swaying lazily on a gentle swell and only a few sailors going unhurriedly about their duties on deck, there was no indication of the manpower and machinery of war that waited within their hulls, ready to be brought to bear on the enemy at the most opportune moment. And, if all went according to the Christian commanders' plans, as revealed to the troops by En Guillen de Muntcada a few minutes earlier, the vital cargoes of those vessels would be brought ashore at the little harbour of Porto Pi, only just visible across the vast bay to Pedrito's left. A short way beyond that again lay Medîna Mayûrqa, the City of Mallorca, nestling in the lee of the green-cloaked Serra de Na Burguesa mountains, the only sign of its existence a gossamer haze of wood smoke floating motionless above in the limpid September air.

Pedrito couldn't help marvelling at the beauty of this spot, which he thought even more stunning viewed from here than from the sea. Mallorca really was an island blessed with the most precious of nature's gifts. Little wonder, then, that it had been regarded as an earthly paradise by all the different peoples who had invaded and inhabited it since prehistoric times – Pheonicians, Carthaginians, Romans, Vandals, Byzantines, Arabs. Now Mallorca had been invaded again, and Pedrito wondered if the damage that was bound to be inflicted upon it during the ensuing struggles would destroy much of the qualities that had made it one of the brightest jewels in the Mediterranean crown to all those fortunate enough to have known it down the ages.

A hoopoe bird, flitting like a giant butterfly on black-and-white striped wings, landed on the branch of a nearby olive tree. Normally, this dandy of a creature, with its pink breast, its long, curved beak and striking, fan-like head crest, would announce its presence with a rather haughty 'Poop! Poop! Poop!'. But not today. As had happened before the hostilities of the previous day, the island's feathered occupants had fallen silent, as if sensing the human violence that was about to erupt within their peaceful habitat. It created a weird ambience, totally at odds with the visual charms of the surroundings.

'Why so gloomy, Little Pedro?'

The king's words, spoken in a strangely detatched sort of way, stirred Pedrito from his musings.

'Not gloomy, *senyor*,' he lied, '– just, you know, just admiring the scenery. Yes, I was actually thinking that this must be one of the prettiest views on the island. Maybe not the most spectacular, but a truly beautiful one, nonetheless.'

The king was pacing up and down, first looking in the direction of the departed troops, then towards where those of En Nunyo Sans would be expected to appear. 'Well then,' he said absently, 'once the war for Mallorca is won, we'll call this stretch of coast after you. The Costa d'En Blànes. How would that please you?'

Pedrito was about to reiterate his original judgement that, flattered though he was, he didn't warrant the lofty prefix of 'En' before his name, when the silence was shattered by the clamour of battle bursting forth from the direction of the seaward extremity of Na Burguesa ridge.

'Holy Mother of God, Saint Mary!' the king exclaimed. 'Our men have fallen in with the Saracens already, and still En Nunyo and his reinforcements aren't here! How in heaven's name could he serve me so badly, and today of all days?' He turned to Pedrito. 'Mount up, *amic*! Get back to camp as fast as that old hack will carry you and tell En Nunyo to delay not a moment longer.' Agitatedly, he looked towards the intensifying noise of the fray. 'How can any general allow his rearguard to be so late as this? It

146

can't be right for them not to be at least within sight of the advance forces – which could be getting hacked to pieces even as I speak!' He gave Pedrito a boost up onto his horse. 'Quick, Little Pedro, go like the wind!'

Pedrito wasn't happy about this. 'But I can't leave you here alone,' he objected. 'I mean, you're not armed. What happens if you're attacked by an enemy patrol?'

'And what difference would having you with me make? A slingshot expert you may be, but I doubt if you'd be able to scare off a pack of murderous Moors with just one piece of string.' He slapped Pedrito's horse on the rump, though notably to no avail. 'Get back to camp with that message for En Nunyo and don't worry about me. I can look after myself.' He smacked the horse's hind quarters yet again, but still it didn't budge. 'Dig your heels into its ribs!' he growled at Pedrito, then whacked the horse one more time. 'Yah-h-h-h! *Arri-i-i-i!*'

And to think that Pedrito had originally believed this old hack to have none of the self-willed tendencies of a mule! The more he spurred it and the more the king yelled abuse, the further back the horse pinned its ears and the more rigidly it planted its hooves in the dirt. It wasn't going anywhere for anyone. Not surprisingly, the king had almost burst a blood vessel through sheer exasperation by the time the reason for the beast's obstinacy became apparent.

Through the almond groves from the direction of Santa Ponça came cantering the cream of the Christian cavalry, wave after wave of them, following the banners of En Nunyo Sans and several other barons. Horse sense had prevailed yet again, it seemed, and had saved Pedrito an unnecessary journey – while also sparing his backside even more saddle sores.

'What are you doing here, my lord?' En Nunyo called out to the king, scowling as he pulled up his horse in a flurry of dust. 'I thought you would be with the Muntcadas.'

Hurriedly, King Jaume explained how he had been obliged to take it upon himself to rush out of camp in pursuit of an unauthorised expedition by the infantry. He then alerted En Nunyo to the sounds of battle emanating from the slopes of Na Burguesa.

'The fight has already started, and I fear our advance troops may be fatally outnumbered.' He shot Sans a reproachful look. 'I thought you were never going to come, so for God's sake let's not waste another second!' He then shouted instructions for word of the commencement of battle to be urgently conveyed to the nobles whose cavalry units were now arriving on the flanks of the main body. 'Tell them to be on their guard and, whatever happens, to fight for the glory of God!'

'Rather tell them to watch my banner!' En Nunyo chipped in. 'They know their orders, so let no man take matters into his own hands!'

An almost palpable friction was building up between the king and his cousin, a feeling of antagonism exacerbated by the impatience permeating the ranks of barons and their trains now so frustratingly halted on their final approach to the battlefield.

'I take it that *my* banner and its followers are among your number?' King Jaume asked En Nunyo.

'In your absence, I instructed them to bring up the rear of the main column.'

'Then we shall bring them forward to advance alongside your own men. *Sí*, and I will lead the charge!'

En Nunyo drew him aside. 'I think you have forgotten, *Majestat*,' he said out of the corner of his mouth, 'that you are neither armed nor harnessed for battle.' He nodded at the hack the king was riding. 'And frisky as that animal apparently is, it's about as useful a war horse as my wife's cat!'

Much to King Jaume's chagrin, there was no denying that he was well and truly undone. What En Nunyo Sans had pointed out was painfully true. So desperate had the young king been to head off the 'over-zealous' infantry at dawn that he had neglected to gird himself with even a dagger or to clad himself in anything more protective than his surcoat.

'You have acted bravely,' En Nunyo conceded, 'but, as ever, with a rashness that will be the downfall of us all, if it isn't curbed. Why didn't you take a moment to tell someone you were about to rush out of camp so suddenly this morning?'

'I'm the king, so I needn't tell anyone anything,' King Jaume retorted with what was a fair affectation of authority, though also with a hint of almost childlike guilt.

It was a chink of vulnerability in the king's armour that didn't go unnoticed by his cousin. 'You are indeed the king, my lord, but you have appointed me to be your senior general on this crusade, so when it comes to a battle situation –'

'You are indeed my senior general,' the king interrupted, 'but I'm your commander-in-chief, and if I say I'll lead the charge...' His words trailed away as he realised the futility of this attempted show of superiority. He was totally ill-equipped for combat, and the more he argued with En Nunyo, the longer it would be before the cavalry support now present would reach those Christian forces already engaged in fighting for their lives up ahead. The best the king could do to save face was to stand high in his saddle and shout at the top of his voice that every nobleman, knight and his squires should now follow En Nunyo Sans into battle. 'And may God bless you all!' he bellowed. 'I, your king, will be behind you and with you all the way!'

Whether to steal the king's thunder, or merely to put a premeditated plan into action, En Nunyo then instructed one of his company to signal the ships lying off the Punta de Sa Porrassa to weigh anchor and set sail for Porto Pi. 'That'll distract the enemy long enough for us to hit them with a surpise attack!' he called out to the king, a trace of smugness in his smile as he finally led his troops away.

*

Fortunately for King Jaume, Lorenç, his personal armourer, had followed En Nunyo's forces mounted on the royal charger, while also leading a pack mule carrying the king's coat of mail, his helmet, shield, sword and lance.

'Knowing that your Majesty, in all your indomitable courage, would wish to be equipped for battle whenever and wherever you saw fit,' he truckled, 'I thought it best to come prepared for that eventuality.'

The king couldn't hide his delight – or his relief. 'Lorenç, you're an absolute genius!' he grinned, swiftly undoing the ropes that tied his accoutrements to the mule's back. 'Now,' he panted, 'help me get dressed for the conflict. I must make all haste to catch up with the others. Hurry, man – my gambeson first!'

The self-satisfied smirk that had been on the armourer's lips gradually faded as it became evident that the vital garment hadn't been packed.

'And if I'm hit on the chest by a Saracen's axe, a fat lot of protection my mail hauberk will afford my ribs without the padded undercoat to soften the blow!' The king was livid. 'Lorenç,' he snarled, 'you're a complete cretin!'

While the hapless Lorenç struggled to come to terms with his rapid demotion from brilliance to idiocy, Pedrito took off the quilted coat he'd been handed by young Robert St Clair de Roslin at Sa Caleta creek the previous morning.

'It's an old one of yours anyway,' he told the king, 'so you may as well make use of it again now. For once,' he added with an impish smile, 'I seem to have chosen the right time and place, no?'

King Jaume accepted the gambeson with alacrity. 'It may have seen better days,' he grunted, while slipping his arms into the sleeves, 'but it'll have to do.' He fired a hostile glance at Lorenç. 'Certainly better than nothing! But what about you?' he asked Pedrito as he struggled into his cumbersome hauberk. 'You can hardly follow me into battle wearing only a linen shirt.'

'My thoughts entirely,' Pedrito replied, wide-eyed and unashamedly perturbed. 'And the fact that I'm also unarmed troubles me ever so slightly as well.'

Flustered as the king was, he acknowledged Pedrito's drollery with a smile, albeit a cursory one. He then asked him to help Lorenç heave him up into the saddle of his charger.

'But ill-prepared as I am,' Pedrito said with a stoical shrug, 'I did promise to do your bidding in this conflict, and I won't go back on my word now.'

'Never fear, Master Blànes,' King Jaume puffed, adjusting his steel helmet and arranging his weaponry while his warhorse snorted and stomped irritably under his weight, 'I wouldn't expect you to get within range of the enemy archers. However, I'll still need you to hitch the reins of my hack to yours and follow on behind me. If I'm unhorsed in the field, I'll be relying on you to bring a spare mount to get me out of there.'

Pedrito couldn't resist another quip. 'Let's hope you're unhorsed well away from *all* of the enemy then, *senyor*. My sailor's shirt is just as vulnerable to swords and lances as it is to arrows.'

But the king didn't hear him. With a yell of 'God be with me!' and a kick of his spurs, he was off towards the slopes of the Serra de Na Burguesa, and whatever God – or Allah – had in store for him there.

*12*

# PATIENCE PROVOKED TURNS TO FURY

*LATER THE SAME MORNING OF 12<sup>th</sup> SEPTEMBER –*
*THE FOOTHILLS OF THE SERRA DE NA BURGUESA…*

Presently, the king and Pedrito came to a glade, where a makeshift medical post had been set up. A few monks were tending the wounds of a line of soldiers who, despite some fairly serious injuries, had managed to make it back from the combat.

'How far to the battlefield?' King Jaume asked a young knight, still gamely straddling his horse, though with an arrow embedded in his thigh.

'Just over that next rise, *Majestat*. About a mile – not much more.'

'And how goes it for our people?'

'I was in the mounted company of the Count of Empúries. We attacked the enemy's centre with the Knights Templar, while En Guillen and En Remon de Muntcada led the charge to their left.'

'And you know no more?'

'Only that it was a hellish fierce fight, especially having to battle our way uphill. We drove the Moors back three times, and they did the same in return.'

Suddenly, worry was writ large on the king's face. 'Are you telling me the Saracens have the better of us?'

'I was one of the lucky ones. I saw many slain on both sides before I took this arrow in the leg. But I'd say our men were more than holding their own, although we're up against a much larger army, *senyor*, so things could still go badly.'

152

Just then, another knight came trotting into the clearing.

The king recognised him. 'En Guillen de Mediona! Well met, but why aren't you still fighting?'

'Because I'm injured, my lord. I came to have my wound treated by the good friars.'

The king squinted at him. 'Are you badly hurt? You seem able to ride well enough.'

The knight pointed to a smudge of blood beneath his nose. 'I was struck by a stone, *Majestat*.'

This revelation was greeted with a gasp of disbelief from the king. 'Struck on the *lip*? And you think that's reason enough to quit the battle?' He then made a point of attracting everyone's attention. 'Can you believe this, men? We have here a brother knight renowned throughout Catalonia for his jousting prowess. None bolder in the lists or more skilled with the lance, it's said. Indeed, many's the time I've seen him in action myself, and he can tilt at the best of them. Yet he retires from a *real* fight with nothing more serious to hamper him than a grazed lip!' King Jaume wasn't about to spare the knight's blushes now. 'Well, let me remind you, Guillen de Mediona – this isn't a tournament, and there are no pampered damsels looking on and swooning at the very thought of your handsome features being bruised by a pebble. This is war, the real thing, and a true knight would have been enraged by such a trifling blow – not used it as an excuse to cut and run. So, *amic*, you will turn about right now and ride back into the thick of it!'

Suitably conscience-stricken and visibly contrite, En Guillen de Mediona did just that.

The king and Pedrito followed in his tracks until they caught up with En Nunyo Sans, who was mustering his troops at the foot of the rise where the first clash of arms had taken place. Even here, on the periphery of the action, the ground was strewn with bodies, all of them showing evidence of the brutality of hand-to-hand combat.

Surveying the carnage surrounding him now, Pedrito was struck by how different this scene was compared to those he had witnessed the day before. Then, he had passed through killing fields that bore all the hallmarks of an unequal massacre, whereas here, it was evident that a fierce battle had taken place, with both sides giving no quarter and suffering a corresponding share of the losses.

However, the first surge of hostilities appeared to be already over, the Moors having been put to flight – at least temporarily. Christian cavalrymen and foot soldiers were coming down from the hill, some in orderly fashion behind their respective banners, others straggling alone or in little groups, either nursing personal wounds or helping injured comrades and horses back to the safety of their own lines. There would be no question of these men and animals taking part in any further fighting this day, or, in many cases, for some considerable time to come.

Yet the king had the smell of victory in his nostrils, and he was keen to press any advantage already gained by his advance troops. He drew En Nunyo Sans' attention to a large group of Moorish soldiers on top of the hill from which the Christian vanguard was now descending.

'Look there – in the midst of that body of infantry – all clad in white astride the white horse. See the red-and-white striped standard flying beside him. It's the flag of the Amir, the Saracen King of Mallorca!'

En Nunyo nodded his agreement, but without saying a word.

The king's eyes were ablaze. 'And can you see what's adorning the top of his lance? A head! The head of one of my people! A severed Christian head impaled on a heathen's spear!' King Jaume's show of bitterness was rapidly degenerating into a fit of blind hatred. 'The disbelieving swine will pay for this!' he snarled. Then, turning to En Nunyo Sans, he declared, 'And no time like the present!' He pointed to the hilltop again. '*Mira*! You can see they're still in a state of disarray, so they'll be easily beaten if we launch a fresh attack immediately.' Goading his steed into readiness for the charge, he shouted, 'Call your troops to order, En Nunyo, and have them follow me!'

At this, En Nunyo and two other barons who had been listening to this royal outburst grabbed the bridle of the king's horse.

'Your madness today is going to be the death of us all!' En Nunyo hissed. 'For God's sake, *Majestat*, have patience!'

He and his two companions were tugging at the reins of the shying horse, while the young king struggled fiercely to retain control of it. This wasn't presenting a particularly inspiring image to the droves of fighting men who were milling about awaiting orders from their commanders. En Nunyo told the king so in no uncertain manner.

'All right, all right!' King Jaume barked. 'I'm not a lion or a leopard or some kind of wild animal, so there's no need to manhandle me like one! If you think it's all that imprtant, I'll hold back.' He glared at his three nobles. 'But you'd better pray that no ill comes of it, or you'll live to rue this moment. *Sí*, and you have my solemn oath on that!'

Then, out of the surrounding mass of troops rode a nobleman, and although Pedrito was positioned at what was becoming his customary 'respectful' distance from the king, he was close enough to see that this man boasted a presence which commanded the immediate attention, not only of En Nunyo Sans and his two fellow barons, but of the king himself.

'Who's he?' Pedrito asked an archer who was standing in the shade of an adjacent carob tree tensioning his bowstring.

'Him? Oh, that's En Jaspert de Barberá. *Sí, sí*, I've served in many a campaign under him. A real gentleman, a brave knight and a fine reader of a battle. No better tactician, in my experience, and the best engineer, too, when it comes to a siege.'

'He certainly seems to be held in some regard by the top men over there – even by the king himself.'

The archer's reply was accompanied by a rather cynical smile. 'Yes, well, En Jaspert probably knows more about warfare and how to conduct it than the king and all his *cousins* put together. But he isn't a member of that noble clique – all cock-connected, even the bishops, you know – so he hasn't been given the position he deserves on this crusade.'

In some respects, this made sense enough to Pedrito, but he was intrigued by one of the archer's expressions. 'Cock-connected?' he queried.

The archer was more interested in his bowstring, to which he gave an appraising 'ping'.

'Cock-connected?' Pedrito repeated.

'Absolutely,' muttered the archer, looking at Pedrito in a wearily-tolerant way. 'The ancestry of that lot is more intertwined than a grapevine. I mean, that's why they're all so-called cousins, no matter how many times removed. *Sí, sí*, plenty of branches on their family trees, but grown from very few nuts – if you see what I mean.'

Pedrito did, and he left it at that.

As soon as he'd paid his formal respects to the king, En Jaspert addressed Nunyo Sans directly, and with a demeanour that exuded as much censure as respect.

'Although I defer to your military rank, *senyor*, I'm bound by my allegiance to the king to tell you that you delay at your peril.' He gestured towards the Moors on the hilltop. 'Now's the time, when they're battle-bruised and disorganised, to attack with your fresh wave of troops.' En Jaspert then motioned towards the sea. 'Behind us, we have the harbour of Porto Pi, where the last of our ships are about to offload the remaining detatchments of our horse and infantry – all of them well-rested and ready for battle. The enemy will be watching and, no matter how superior their numbers, the arrival of our backup troops will be sowing the seeds of indecision in their minds. And lest you've forgotten,' he added, 'there's also the very real possibility of Moorish reinforcements arriving by sea from Africa at any time. Therefore, I implore you, *senyor* – launch a new offensive without delay.'

En Nunyo had been caught on the horns of a dilemma. What En Jaspert said made perfect sense, but it also echoed the king's instinctive reaction to the present situation – a reaction that En Nunyo had only just rebuffed. In the meantime, he had a huge body of men standing by, primed for the fight.

'My thought was for our horses,' he said, and there was no hint that he was telling anything but the truth. 'They've had a long trek from Santa Ponça this morning, and they need to be rested before –'

'Our horses are bred for long treks,' King Jaume interrupted, 'and if En Jaspert says we should attack now, then that's what we'll do, and I'll lead!'

'And why you? En Nunyo retorted, clearly nettled at having his authority superseded. 'Have you suddenly become a lion or leopard after all?'

King Jaume was too taken aback to come up with a swift riposte.

But En Nunyo was unrelenting. 'Don't delude yourself into thinking there won't be a Moorish knight up yonder who's as good as yourself, and probably better!'

The bickering that followed between the two men was drowned out by the sound of En Jaspert de Barberá leading his company of some seventy knights and their followers into a headlong rush up the hill. He had clearly decided to ignore earlier orders by taking matters into his own hands. Insubordination of this sort, he probably thought, would only be punished if he failed in his mission. And if he failed in his mission, the likelihood was that he wouldn't be alive to face the consequences anyway.

It seemed to Pedrito that here was a man after King Jaume's own heart.

Even so, En Nunyo Sans' drowned-out words must have had a tempering effect on the young monarch's impetuosity once again, because, while En Nunyo now marshalled his men and followed those of En Jaspert into the attack, King Jaume remained behind and busied himself gathering his own train of knights to his banner.

To Pedrito's non-military eyes, the scenario that had developed here suggested a total lack of any overall organisation. Men were still arriving back from the first encounter, while others were either embarking on or preparing to embark on the next. It seemed that orders were being shouted by all and sundry to all and sundry, also that the Christian troops' frantic coming and going risked doing as much injury to themselves as did any potential counter offensive by the enemy. It reminded Pedrito of the chaos that had prevailed during the first mass disembarkation onto the beach at Santa Ponça. Yet, just as had happened then, order somehow began to emerge from apparent confusion now.

While he left appointed squires to group the main body of his men into battle formation, the king and a few chosen knights rode a short way up the hill, to a point where they could see what progress, if any, was being made by the forces of the new vanguard. Pedrito rode with them, though at a distance that showed both respect for his lowly status and the vulnerability of his sailor's shirt.

The Moors, and there could have been as many as two thousand of them, began to shout as their attackers ascended towards them. In the apparent absence of any archers, the Moorish front line then started to hurl stones and to venture a little way forward. En Jaspert de Barberá's men held their ground, while those following the standard of Nunyo Sans immediately turned and headed back down the hill.

'*Vergonya*! *Vergonya*!' King Jaume roared at them. 'Shame! Shame on you!'

At that very moment, one of his companions noticed the troops of the royal banner, led by a hundred knights, advancing up the slope towards them. King Jaume immediately rode down to join his company, then, eagerly grasping the opportunity that had been denied him for so long, spearheaded an all-out charge against the army of his loathed adversary, Abú Yahya Háquem, the Saracen King of Mallorca.

## 13

# WAR IS DEATH'S FEAST

*ONE HOUR LATER –*
*THE FOOTHILLS OF NA BURGUESA MOUNTAIN...*

Although the Christians were heavily outnumbered, their second offensive was to prove successful, but not without paying the price in a substantial loss of life. True to his promise, Pedrito had followed behind the fighting forces mounted on his old hack, while leading the other horse that King Jaume had ridden on his impulsive dash from base camp at dawn. Whatever the reason for the Moors' dearth of archers at this stage of the battle, it had clearly handed the advantage to the Christians, as had the equally-curious absence of Moorish cavalry in any significant numbers.

So great was the mass of troops between Pedrito's position and the front line of the conflict that at no stage could he make out the figure of King Jaume. Nevertheless, he could see that, within the melee, the royal banner was always well to the fore, so he presumed that the young monarch was making his presence felt where it counted. Not so, however, the hapless En Guillen de Mediona, who had been so curtly commanded by the king to take his bruised lip forthwith from the medical post and back into combat. On his way uphill through the fallen and walking wounded, Pedrito noticed the handsome young jouster lying on his back in a pool of blood. His throat was cut. Evidently, he had fought what his king would have considered to be the fight of a true knight after all, though this would be small consolation to the pampered damsels of Catalonia, who would have to find themselves another hero to swoon over at tourneys in future.

*

The battle was well and truly over by the time Pedrito had finally made his way through the debris of butchery to the crest of the hill. There, En Nunyo Sans was congratulating the king, whose apparel and weapons were adorned with the gory proof of his hands-on involvement in what had finally resulted in yet another rout of Moorish forces.

'A good day for you, my lord, and for us all,' Sans gushed. 'All is ours, for your courageous action today has won us a momentous battle!'

To Pedrito, it seemed incongruous that such a dramatic change in attitude should have taken place in so short a time. Suddenly, the young king's impetuosity had graduated from being scorned as a potentially-disastrous liability to being hailed as a triumphal asset. It was a manifestation, Pedrito supposed, of the gulf that exists in a man's psyche between the fears and uncertainties of an approaching fight and the elation of ultimate victory – and, doubtless, of personal survival as well.

However, King Jaume appeared to be less carried away by the result of this latest encounter than was his senior general. He pointed to the north, to the brow of a hill where the remnants of the Moorish forces had retreated.

'The Saracen king is still in their midst. See, there in the white robes.' He looked around at the state of his own surviving troops, then shook his head despairingly. 'Now would have been the time to put an end to the Amir and his pack of heathen dogs, but our men and horses are worn out. Too much has been asked of our people already today, and they have done me proud. Nevertheless, there's still much for us to achieve before the war is won.'

At that point he noticed Pedrito standing a short way off, holding the reins of the hack he had dutifully delivered for the king's evacuation in the event of things going against him. 'You have done well to come unscathed this far wearing no more protection than a sailor's shirt, Master Blànes,' he smiled. 'If only you'd brought a hundred more mounts, perhaps we could have found a hundred men still up for the fight. But anyway, we can only thank God for what He has already given us this day.'

He then spoke again to Nunyo Sans. 'While the Amir is skulking in the hills yonder, we must sieze the opportunity to isolate him. Let's muster the fittest of our men and make our way to the low ground between him and the city. Even if there's only a handful of us, a message can be sent to our people landing at Porto Pi to come and add strength to our number.'

En Nunyo Sans looked far from persuaded that this was a wise course of action, but his newly-declared admiration for the king's impulsiveness stood in the way of his making any objection. However, one of his suite who had been listening to the king's proposal wasn't obliged to be similarly restrained.

'*Majestat*, what you suggest is folly. I beg your forgiveness for being so outspoken, but no general who has won a battle ever risks more without first passing the night on the field to assess what has been won *and* lost.'

'I appreciate your frankness, En Remon Alaman, and I know you speak with our best interests at heart. Even so, you must accept that what I intend doing is right, and that's the end of it.'

And so a precariously small company of cavalry and infantry set out behind their king in the direction of the Mallorcan capital, with Pedrito bringing up the rear, as had become his wont. They had only gone about a mile, however, when the Bishop of Barcelona, looking drawn and covered in grime from the battlefield, galloped up from the rear.

'*Majestat*!' he called out. 'For God's sake, don't make such haste!'

With patent reluctance, King Jaume halted the column. 'Why not?' he asked as the bishop pulled up his horse beside him. 'It seems to me the right thing to do.'

Clearly in a state of some distress, the bishop took him aside. 'Oh, my lord, my lord,' he gasped, 'you've lost much more this day

161

than you imagine.'

The king knotted his brows. 'And perhaps I've gained much more than *you* imagine.'

Looking the king squarely in the eye, the bishop shook his head. 'I heard of the great victory you won when attacking the enemy's centre, but I've just come from where our advance troops engaged them on the left some time earlier.'

The king's frown deepened. 'And?' he asked, hesitantly.

His chest heaving, the bishop swallowed hard.

'Please,' the king urged, '– I need to know the truth.'

The bishop gathered himself. 'Well, as you know,' he began, his voice quavering, 'our people were always going to be hopelessly outnumbered, yet our knights inflicted massive hurt to the enemy cavalry.' He lowered his head. 'They fought valiantly for you, *senyor*, but without reinforcements to back them up, they were bound to suffer huge losses.' He looked into the king's eyes again. 'If only our rearguard hadn't waited for so long…'

There were endless moments of silence before the king quietly asked: 'And the Muntcadas? How fare En Guillen and En Remon?'

Once more the bishop cast his eyes downward. 'Dead, my lord. Both killed while fighting alongside their men in the fiercest mounted combat some of our most seasoned soldiers have ever seen.'

Tears welled in King Jaume's eyes, and it was clear that the emotion which the bishop's news evoked was genuine, despite the history of animosity that had existed between the king and his two illustrious nobles. Equally, his attitude towards En Nunyo Sans, whose delaying tactics the bishop had so pointedly lamented, reflected not a hint of incrimination.

'Let no man weep for our lost brothers, En Nunyo. Their death is like a stab in the heart to us all, but we mustn't be seen to grieve, for that would only kill the spirit of our people and weaken their resolve to overcome the struggles that lie ahead. Therefore, let us seem emboldened by the Muntcadas' example, rather than openly mourn their loss.'

Any feelings of remorse that En Nunyo Sans might have been

experiencing were kept hidden behind a convincing façade of military poise. 'So, *Majestat*, we march on towards the city, *sí*?'

With a despondent look, the king shook his head. 'No, I think not. In the light of the bishop's news, I believe it's best to follow the advice of En Remon de Alaman after all. We must take time to assess our losses before committing what's left of our troops to any more fighting. For we musn't forget, if what the Moor Ali told us is true, there's still a sizeable part of the enemy garrison waiting within the city walls.' He then told En Nunyo to make camp for the night by a nearby stream. 'Post lookouts all around – and be sure it's done this time! And send dispatches to the rest of our units telling them we'll regroup here in the morning.' Pensively, he stroked his chin in his customary way. 'Meanwhile, I think I'll use what's left of the daylight to see how the land lies between here and the city. Whoever controls the island must first control the capital. *Sí*, and it's there for the taking.'

After assembling a small bodyguard of knights, King Jaume summoned Pedrito to accompany them to the top of an adjacent rise. 'If I guess correctly, Master Blànes, we should be able to see all the way to the City of Mallorca from there, and as you're familiar with the landscape hereabouts, your counsel will be much appreciated.'

What a difference becoming the victor of a crucial battle makes, Pedrito mused. No longer was the king the posturing figurehead who showed all the outward signs of self-assurance to his troops, while harbouring an almost juvenile subservience to a certain coterie of nobles, who were, in the final analysis, perhaps only superior to him in years. King Jaume was now taking control of matters, and instead of consulting his hitherto mentor, En Nunyo Sans, he had just put him firmly in his place. 'Post lookouts all around – and be sure it's done this time!' How many long-suppressed retaliations were being released in the scathing codicil to that one command?

\*

It was dusk when they reached the top of the hill. Above them towered the rolling crests of Na Burguesa ridge, the gulleys in its wooded slopes already filling with the milky mists of night. In the other direction, the sea was a mirror reflecting the glow of the setting sun, its rays draped over the waters of the bay like a vast, sequined veil.

'Breathtaking,' the king murmured. 'Truly breathtaking…'

His eyes were then drawn eastward by something glinting down by the shore. 'The city of Medîna Mayûrqa,' he whispered. 'My God, just look at those buildings catching the light of the sun. Gold! It's like discovering a city of pure gold!' A look of awe spread over his face. 'Never have I seen such a wonderous place. The finest city I have ever cast my eyes upon.'

His sentiments were echoed by his accompanying knights, who stood transfixed by the sheer opulence of what was spread out below them.

'And,' the king marvelled, 'just look at the tall date palms lining the curve of the waterfront there. Palms – a city of palms. And the fine houses – each one a palace. And their gardens – one lush oasis after another – orange trees everywhere, and apricots, and pomegranates too. And look at the fountains in those palm-shaded courtyards – see how their waters dance like a thousand spangles in the sunset.' He stared dumbstruck for a few moments, then whispered, 'My God, what a prize! What a veritable Garden of Eden!' His look of awe was now replaced by one of steely determination. 'And it's all mine – mine for the taking!'

It was as if the king was talking to himself, unaware of the presence of anyone beside him. Once more, Pedrito was prompted to compare his own regard for Mallorca with the king's. All Pedrito craved was to be back at home with his family, living the simple life they had always known, and working hard in the magical, yet modest, environment they had lovingly cared for in the same way as generations of country folk before them. In contrast, King Jaume was bent on taking for himself and his supporters the island's attributes that had been created by others. And, Pedrito pondered, how many of these man-made wonders of Arabian civilisation would remain unsullied by the Christian *Reconquista*, should it prove successful?

Yet again, King Jaume seemed to have been reading his thoughts, though not entirely accurately.

'I've been following your gaze, Master Blànes, and I can see that, like mine, your eyes have been drawn to that magnificent building overlooking the city's harbour down there. An architectural marvel to equal the most splendid in the entire Caliphate of old Damascus, perhaps?'

Pedrito nodded. 'The principal mosque of Medîna Mayûrqa – and a finer example of the Moorish craftsman's skills would be hard to find anywhere, they say. But I've only ever been able to admire it from the quayside before now. And yes, you're right – when viewed from up here, I think it's beauty is even more, well – breathtaking.'

The king seemed lost in a trance of approbation. 'The gilt domes, the white marble minarets and turrets piercing the sky, the sweeping archways shaped like the upturned keels of ships, the delicately carved stone of the windows. And the mosque's position dominating the city on one side and the entire expanse of that magnificent bay on the other. Surely there could be no more impressive a location for a sacred building.' He fell silent for a while, gazing intently at the mosque, before declaring to his companions, 'I swear here and now to our Lord God Almighty that, if He helps me retake this land from the infidel thieves, I will build to His glory – and on that very site – a mighty cathedral to His glory that will be the envy of every city in Christendom. And you, gentlemen, are witness to this, my solemn vow.'

The animated mutterings of approval from the king's bodyguard suggested to Pedrito that his concerns for the survival of even the most treasured of Moorish legacies might well be justified. Time, and the respective wills of God and Allah, would tell.

The sun was now dipping beyond the western horizon, sending shadows creeping from the summits of the Serra de Na Burguesa down over its foothills towards the city, where little pools of amber light began to appear one-by-one within the maze of streets.

The king looked enquiringly at Pedrito.

'I've never seen it before now,' Pedrito confessed, 'but I'd heard about it. At nightfall, men go about the town lighting oil lamps fixed to the outer walls of the houses.'

'To light up the streets for the ordinary citizens?' The king cocked his head, a frown of disbelief wrinkling his brow. 'A charitable gesture, I'm sure, but a somewhat extravagant way of spending public revenues.'

'Depends where your priorities lie,' Pedrito thought to himself, glancing seaward to where the hindmost vessels of the great Christian armada were lining up to berth at Porto Pi. How many streets in how many cities, he wondered, could be lit by the revenues collected to fund just one of those?

'I see you're looking at our ships,' remarked the king, reminding Pedrito of just how observant this young monarch could be, despite his occasional bouts of apparent daydreaming. 'Even that one squadron makes an impressive sight, no?'

Pedrito had no hesitation in agreeing.

The King then nodded farther round the bay towards the city's main harbour, its wharfs and piers huddled snugly beneath the sea walls of the great mosque. 'But what do you make of those ships lying there. There may be no more than a dozen, but they could be a threat nonetheless, don't you think?'

Pedrito told him that they were more than likely just peaceful merchantmen going about their normal trade, and caught unawares here by events. Anyway, there was no need to worry about them. They wouldn't be looking for trouble.

The king was still to be convinced. 'No pirate galleys among them? It's well known that the port of Medîna Mayûrqa is a hornets' nest of Saracen sea bandits.'

Pedrito gave a little laugh and suggested that most of the hornets would now have scurried off to the safety of one of the neighbouring islands of Menorca and Ibiza. 'Even if there are one or two pirates still in port there, they won't come out to mix it with a fleet of warships. No, they always operate with the odds stacked in their favour – a pack of them versus one poorly-defended cargo ship. That's more their style.'

King Jaume seemed reassured by this, while also declaring that the harbour would be blockaded, just in case. Then, looking out to the open sea, he said, 'There's also still the danger of an enemy fleet arriving from Africa, so we must position sentry vessels out towards the southern horizon in the morning.' With these naval decisions made, he directed his attention to purely land-based military matters. He gestured towards the city. What, he asked Pedrito, did he know about its fortifications?

With the light fading fast, the best Pedrito could do was to point out the battlements of the watchtowers that marked the position of the city's main gates – five of them located at intervals round the inland arc of the city wall, three others along its sea face. 'But to be honest,' Pedrito confessed, 'as a simple fisherman, I had no reason to learn any more about the city's defences than was common knowledge among the townsfolk who frequented the quayside markets.'

The king was unconcerned. 'No matter, Master Blànes. From what I've already seen, the fortifications of Medîna Mayûrqa are fairly typical of any city I've attacked. But what about a ditch? Do you know if the walls are protected by a ditch or moat?'

Pedrito hunched his shoulders. 'All I know is that the western wall, the section closest to us here, follows the course of a *rambla*, a river bed that's dry except following a storm, when flash floods in the mountains can turn it into a raging torrent.'

The king pursed his lips. 'Hmm, which would make it difficult to undermine the walls at this side of the city.' He stood surveying the scene intently for a while, then, with daylight almost gone, he sighed and said, '*Va bé*. All right. That establishes a good enough picture in my mind's eye.'

At this point, they were joined by En Nunyo Sans, who reported that the making of camp for the night was under way, as instructed.

'Fine, fine,' said the king distractedly. He rubbed his stomach. 'By God's faith, I'm hungry! I've eaten nothing all day, and the rump of Master Blànes' old hack there is looking more appetising by the minute!'

'No need to go to such desperate lengths,' En Nunyo laughed. He pointed westward down the hill. 'A gallant friend from my own fiefdom of Roussillon, En Oliver de Termens, has pitched his tent on the far side of the camp site there. He has food and a good cook in his train.'

'Trust a Frenchman!' the king quipped.

'Indeed,' Sans acknowledged with a little dip of his head, 'and that one invites you to dine with him this evening.'

*

While King Jaume and a small group of his barons were served inside the tent, Pedrito sat round the camp fire with some lesser mortals, including, on this occasion, Robert St Clair de Roslin, the novice Knight Templar from Britain, who had played a pivotal part in Pedrito being hired as helmsman for the royal galley back in Salou. Pedrito knew that Robert had been assigned at the beginning of this crusade to serve under En Guillen de Muntcada, so it was with some hesitancy that he broached the subject of the noble's death.

'He was a brave man,' Robert replied with surprising nonchalance, 'and a good man too, I think. But many other brave and good men died today, and even if they weren't of such blue blood as En Guillen and En Remon de Muntcada, their death is no less tragic. However,' he shrugged, 'we're all soldiers, and we dice with death every time we go into battle.'

Pedrito had no way of telling if Robert's cavalier attitude towards death was authentic, or was only a show of bravado born of the necessity for a knight to appear fearless in the face of danger. Either way, Pedrito decided not to pursue this line of conversation further. He did notice, though, that there was a definite sadness in the eyes of Robert and the handful of other survivors from the Muntcada troops sitting round the fire here. He had already heard the king personally tell them not to show any sign of sorrow at the loss of their commanders, but to put a brave face on things for the sake of overall morale within the army. They were clearly doing their best to obey this order, albeit that there had been tears in the king's own eyes when he gave it.

Nevertheless, in true knightly fashion, King Jaume had quickly covered that momentary lapse of aplomb by announcing with an ostensibly spontaneous laugh that their host, being a true Frenchman, had ensured that supplies loaded onto one of his pack mules when leaving the Santa Ponça base camp that morning had included a few skins of wine. Each man here would be welcome to a cup or two – deserved it, in fact. The king stressed, however, that nobody should be tempted to over-indulge, since there would be an abundance of work to do in the morning in preparation for laying siege to the city. Provided, of course, they weren't attacked by the Moors in the meantime.

The night was still, the sky cloudless. The place that had been chosen by En Oliver for this simple little refuge of rest and refreshment was only a short distance from where Pedrito and the king had awaited the arrival of En Nunyo Sans' rearguard troops that morning. The view down the gentle slope towards the sea was therefore similar, although the almond groves that occupied the land now appeared only as a faint filigree of spidery branches silhouetted against the moonlit waters of the bay.

Inland, the dark bulk of the Serra de Na Burguesa rose majestically, providing a serene and silent backdrop to a scene which, even in those tense moments of war, exuded an almost tangible tranquility. From somewhere in one of the high valleys, the tinny sound of sheep bells drifted down through the pine woods, to be followed by the high-pitched bleating of a lamb calling for its mother. Yet again, Pedrito was reminded of his own mother, and how she aways took charge of their small flock of sheep at lambing time. It took a woman to help with a birth, she always said. It was second nature, after all. Now, his fervent hope was that his family's life on their little *finca* would be allowed to continue unchanged under the Christian aristocracy who aspired to be the island's new overlords.

At that moment, another sound wafted down from on high: a plaintive, humming sound which was comfortingly at one with the ambience of the mountains, yet strangely disturbing as well, particularly to the unaccustomed ear.

Young Robert St Clair de Roslin sat rigidly upright, his ears pricked, his eyes on sticks. 'What in the name of Saint Mary is *that* unholy din! My Good God Almighty, it sounds as if the Devil himself is castrating all the tomcats in hell!'

Pedrito had to stop himself from laughing at this unlikely mix of the sacred and profane. 'That's just the shepherd's *xeremía*,' he said.

'His cherry *what*?'

'*Xeremía*. Bagpipe.'

Robert winced. 'Bagpipe! Is that some sort of instrument of torture – like the rack? How does it work? Do they put your head in a bag and hit it with a pipe? That's certainly what it sounds –'

A soldier sitting on the other side of the fire cut him off abruptly. 'No, no, no! *Xeremíes* aren't instruments of torture, they're *musical* instruments.'

'*Musical*?' Robert spluttered, pointing towards the source of the sound. 'You call that *music*, laddie?'

'*Sí, sí*,' the soldier calmly assured him. 'In the Asturias region of northern Spain, where I come from, we also have bagpipes. We call them *gaitas*.'

'It's an ancient instrument,' Pedrito told Robert. 'Some say it came to Spain with the Romans.'

'Well, I'm not surprised they abandoned it here when they left,' Robert retorted.

'Maybe so,' Pedrito chuckled, 'but at least the shepherds are glad they did.'

In response to Robert's puzzled look, the Asturian soldier explained that the monotonous buzzing of the bagpipe drones had a calming effect on sheep, while the more strident sound of the chanter, or melody pipe, let the sheep know where their shepherd was while they grazed the mountain slopes at night – just as the clanking of the sheep's bells helped the shepherd keep track of any members of his flock that might wander away from the rest.

'Very interesting, I'm sure,' said Robert, 'but in northern Britain, in a country called Scotland, where *I* come from, we prefer hunting stags to herding sheep, and the infernal squealing of your bagpipes would scare the deer back up the mountains!' He wagged an emphatic finger. 'Never will such a frightening abomination ever be tolerated in Scotland!'

'Very interesting, I'm sure,' the Asturian soldier muttered, disinterestedly. He was clearly more stimulated by the arrival of the cook, or at least by the promise of the food he was bringing.

'*Chireta*!' the cook announced, while placing a large dish on the ground. 'A great delicacy in Aragon, where I come from.'

'Yuk! I hope it tastes better than it looks,' said the Asturian as he peered at the pulpy substance gushing from a slash along the length of what appeared to be a large, portly sausage. 'It looks like you've just disembowelled a piglet.'

'Nothing to do with pigs,' the cook replied indignantly. 'A *chireta* is made from the chopped liver, heart and lungs of a sheep, all spiced up and bulked out with some onion and coarse-ground meal – or maybe rice, if you have it.'

The Asturian wrinkled his nose. 'Then you stuff it all into the skin of a dead piglet, right?'

'I told you,' the cook snapped, 'pigs have nothing to do with it! The prepared ingredients of a *chireta* are stuffed into the intestines of a *sheep*!'

The Asturian squirmed. 'Jesus wept! I think I'm going to throw up!'

Robert St Clair de Roslin, who had been taking a very close interest in this conversation, then leant forward and scooped up some *chireta* on the blade of his dagger. 'Mmm,' he crooned after taking a speculative taste, 'not bad, but it could do with a bit more seasoning. Some crushed mustard seeds, maybe. Give it a bit more of a kick.' He took another nibble. 'Aye, definitely needs more kick, laddie.'

The cook glared at him. 'And what would you know about *chiretas*, young sir? You don't sound Aragonese to me!'

'And you don't sound Scottish to me!' Robert pointed his dagger at the plate. 'What you have there is a poor imitation of a haggis – a great delicacy in Scotland, where *I* come from! And for your information, the recipe was brought to us many centuries ago by the Vikings. Yes indeed, and I'm not surprised our friend here was retching. You should have stuffed the haggis mixture into a sheep's *stomach*, not it's intestines!'

The cook was outraged. 'I've never heard of Scotland and I've never heard of your haggis. And for *your* information, the Vikings never came to Aragon, but the Romans did, and it was the Romans who brought us the recipe of the *chireta*!'

'Which explains everything,' Robert deduced. 'The Romans must have stolen the recipe for haggis when we kicked them out of Scotland. They probably stopped off in Aragon on their way back to Italy to pull the tails from between their legs.'

Such duels of repartee, mostly good-natured, about bagpipes, sheep, deer, haggis, *chireta*, Vikings, Romans and all manner of things associated and not associated with them, eventually involved everyone and continued round the fire while they ate. And whatever the true ancestry of the *chireta* – and the advantages or disadvantages of sheep's intestines being used as a casing – the proof of its tastiness lay in the emptiness of the serving platter at the end of this rough-and-ready feast.

Any residual scraps of intestine and gristle had been devoured by a shaggy black shape that had appeared suddenly out of the darkness. Once it had ascertained that not a smudge of *chireta* remained, the black shape lay down and fell asleep at Pedrito's feet.

'It's Nedi, the king's dog,' Pedriro said to Robert St Clair. 'God only knows where he appeared from.'

'Anyway, he seems to have bonded with you quickly enough.'

Pedrito shrugged. 'Yes, well, we have a kind of religious association, I suppose.'

'Religious association? You … and a *dog*?'

'Yes, I know it's seems strange,' Pedrito conceded, 'and I won't bore you with the details, but let's just say I was baptised by him – recently.'

Robert gave him a wary look, and left things at that.

Although Pedrito hadn't contributed much to the general chitchat, he had observed the rest of the company with interest. They were mostly all young men about his own age, a few perhaps even younger. In some respects, the way they were acting reminded him of how he and his fellow galley slaves had spent precious 'off-duty' moments, exhausted like these men, and preferring to be anywhere else than where they were at present. The banter of the oarsmen had also centred on topics that related to their respective backgrounds – each recalling the place he came from and boasting about its unique qualities, whether deserved or not. The telltale symptoms of homesickness, no doubt.

Time spent bragging and swapping mild insults constituted a respite, no matter how temporary, from the harsh realities of their present condition. On a pirate galley, thoughts were always of escape and a longed-for return to family and the comforts of home. Here, Pedrito presumed, the underlying thoughts of these soldiers would be whether or not they would survive the next battle. Gruesome thoughts indeed, though offset by the material attraction of plunder. Which, of course, was the primary reason for some of them being here at all – avowed religious considerations aside. In any event, this was all just a way for tired, combat-traumatised men to release the pressures of war in a harmless way, which a few slugs of wine helped promote. What better reason, Pedrito pondered, for the wine being given to them in the first place?

After a while, the king emerged from the tent accompanied by En Nunyo Sans. They were carrying pitch torches, which they lit from the fire. They were going, the king said, to recover the bodies of En Guillen and En Remon de Muntcada from the battlefield, and a small party of able-bodied men from within the Muntcada ranks would be required to lend their assistance. The affection in which the two nobles had been held was evidenced by every one of the half dozen of their troops present standing up and volunteering their services.

Being a member of the king's own company, Pedrito thought it proper to do likewise. The two horses he had been minding all day were tethered nearby, and he suggested to the king that they might finally be put to good use now.

The king laid a hand on his shoulder and said under his breath, 'Much as I appreciate the gesture, Little Pedro, a porter has already been detailed to fetch a couple of mules from the stabling enclosure at the main camp. They're more sure-footed than horses in the dark and will serve our purpose better.'

'Well, at least I can lend a hand myself,' Pedrito replied. 'I'm well rested and well fed, so...'

'Well fed, indeed,' the king smiled. 'Our Aragonese *chireta* may be simple fare, but there's nothing better to fill the belly of a hungry man at the end of a battle.' He patted his own stomach and said in Aragonese for everyone to hear, '*Bé hem dinat*! We have eaten well, lads, *sí*?'

'*Bendinat, Majestat!*' the men agreed with a nod and a wink at the cook. '*Bendinat!*'

'Which,' the king announced, 'would be a fitting name for this spot once we have rescued the rest of the island from the Saracen interlopers. *Bendinat*, the place where your king celebrated a great victory for God and Christian Spain with a humble but wholesome dish from his own kingdom of Aragon.'

'With a dish borrowed from Scotland,' Robert St Clair de Roslin mumbled grumpily in the background.

Seemingly oblivious to this remark, the king lowered his voice as he turned to speak once more to Pedrito. 'You've done well by me today, my friend, and I greatly appreciate that you're willing to help bring back the bodies of my two noble compatriots. But – and I mean no offence – this is a task for the men of the Muntcada companies alone. They will see it not just as their duty, but as an act of honour.'

Pedrito canted his head. 'Whatever you say, *senyor*, and no offence taken. I promised to do your bidding during this campaign, and I'll be here to do just that when you return from the field later.'

'I think not,' said the king, frowning.

Pedrito was about to protest his sincerity when the king's frown was replaced by a smile.

'I think you've earned some time off to make that longed-for visit to see your family, no?'

Pedrito could hardly believe his ears. '*Really*? But when? You mean ... *now*?'

'Whenever you want,' the king beamed. 'You can even borrow the old hack to ride on, if it'll make the journey easier.' He then assumed a serious look. 'But I trust you to return just as soon as you've spent a little time at home – two or three days at the most. Tomorrow, we start unloading the war engines from our ships at Porto Pi, and once the siege of the city has been laid, I'll be depending on you to undertake a very special mission for me.' Seeing Pedrito raise a confused eyebrow, he patted his shoulder again. 'And don't worry, Little Pedro – I won't even ask you to bear arms, far less kill anyone.

## 14

# GOING HOME

Perhaps it was the proximity of the scene of slaughter which the king had dubbed 'The Vale of the Battle' that made Pedrito feel uneasy as he passed by in the night. Then again, no matter how hard he tried to tell himself it was just his imagination, he'd also had a strange feeling of being followed ever since leaving the sanctuary of En Oliver de Termens' campfire at Bendinat in the early hours of the morning. Even the old hack he was riding seemed less 'nice and docile' than usual, occasionally taking it upon herself to come to an abrupt halt for no apparent reason other than to turn her head and peer wide-eyed into the darkness. And no amount of coaxing, tongue-clicking and rein-flicking on Pedrito's part would make her move a hoof until she was satistfied it was safe, for the present at least, to proceed.

All in all, then, the journey had added up to a fairly uncomfortable few hours for Pedrito – until, that is, he reached *Es Coll d'Andritxol*, a narrow pass between the mountains of Biniorella and Garrafa at the top of a long and tortuous track from the fishing hamlet of Camp de Mar. The horse, by now somewhat ironically named *Tranquilla* by Pedrito, was clearly relieved to have reached the end of the climb, and the first glow of dawn spilling over the high ridges of Garrafa seemed to dispel the edginess she'd been plagued by during the night.

The overwhelming sensation now felt by Pedrito, however, was the sheer joy of homecoming that the view from the pass engendered. Down there in the valley was Andratx, a cluster of honey-coloured and whitewashed houses clinging to the lower slopes of Abidala mountain on the southern reaches of the mighty Tramuntana chain, and appearing from this distance more like a scatter of little trinket boxes than a real village.

Early though it was, he could see that people were already up and about and making ready for the day ahead. Village-dwelling farmers were setting off to work on their little *fincas*, some of which, like his father's, occupied the gently rolling terrain that stretched the two miles or so down to the cove of Port d'Andratx, while others were in the form of narrow strips of land stepping all the way up the mountainsides to where the only signs of vegetation were gravity-defying pines sprouting from clefts in the craggy rock face. These terraces, or *bancales*, on which the soil was retained by beautifully crafted drystone walls, were the work of the Moors, who, over the centuries, had skilfully and tirelessly carved them from the previously barren slopes of the island's mountains.

A creaking sound and the splashing of water then drew Pedrito's attention to another Moorish innovation which had helped turn Mallorca into the fertile Garden of Eden now so avidly coveted by King Jaume and his Christian followers. Just a few paces from the side of the track, an elderly man in scruffy peasant garb was drawing water from a well, using a mule harnessed by a long pole to the shaft of a water wheel, called a *noria*. By a simple though ingenious system of cogs, the vertical wheel turned as the mule trudged round and round, while a succession of earthenware jugs attached to a rope looped over the wheel scooped up water from the depths and decanted it into an adjacent adobe holding tank, or *cisterna*. Stone-lined channels then led the water down into the valley, where it would be used to irrigate the patchwork of little fruit- and vegetable-growing *hortas* that surrounded the village.

Tranquilla the horse neither had to be led to the water nor made to drink. The seventeen miles from En Oliver's encampment had been taken at a relaxed enough pace, but this was the first refreshment she'd had all night, and the noise of her slurping the cool, sweet water was proof enough of her thirst *and* her gratification. Pedrito was no less relieved to wash the dust of the journey from his face and splash the drowsiness from his eyes. Nevertheless, what he saw when he opened them again took him completely by surprise, though with yet another wave of relief.

'Nedi!' he called to the ragamuffin black shape lapping up water at his side. 'So, it was *you* following us all night!' Grinning delightedly, he ruffled the tousled head. 'You nearly scared the wits out of me. *Sí*, and I think old Tranquilla here almost had heart failure a few times as well, eh!'

'Your dog, *amic*?' the well minder asked with a scowl.

Pedrito was about to divulge that it was actually King Jaume's, but thought better of it. Even if the man had believed him, which was highly unlikely, there was no knowing whether his allegiance lay with the Christian or Moorish sides now vying for occupation of the island. '*Sí*,' he said instead. 'My dog, *amic*.'

The man squinted at him. 'You look a bit like a Moor, but no Moor would let a dog drink from the same place as himself.'

Pedrito knew there was no denying that. 'Which must mean I'm not a Moor, no?'

The man cast him a cautioning look. 'Well then, you'd better watch out for your dog if you meet any Moors on your travels. You know what Muslims think of dogs – fit only for killing, unless you use them for hunting food or guarding your property.'

Pedrito shrugged. '*No problema*. I'd just say Nedi's both a hunter *and* a guard dog.'

The man released a little snort of derision, generated, Pedrito guessed, by the apparently gormless smile on Nedi's face and the water-dripping tongue dangling from the side of his mouth. 'Doesn't look much like either to me!' the man grunted. 'Anyway, whatever he isn't, he *is* black, and a black dog is the living Devil himself in a Muslim's eye.' He drew a forefinger across his throat. 'Meet a Moor and you'll have a dead dog on your hands.'

Having been brought up in a predominantly Christian community, Pedrito had heard such rumours about Muslims and black dogs before, but he'd never had personal experience of the allegations and, frankly, found them hard to believe. By the same token, he'd also heard it said that Muslims didn't drink alchohol, yet he knew that some of the best wine produced anywhere was made from grapes grown on a wonderful amphitheatre of steep *bancales* that rose from the sea on the mountainous north-west coast of Mallorca at Banyalfubar, which tellingly meant 'little vineyard by the sea' in Arabic.

'Thanks for the advice about the dog,' he smiled at the well keeper. 'But don't worry – I'll take good care of him.'

'Better keep good control of him as well,' the man came back. 'We've got sheep and goats grazing on these mountains, and no one wants his livestock savaged by a crazy dog.'

'That won't happen,' Pedrito assured him. 'He's a well-trained animal.'

Right on cue, Nedi let out a loud bark, pricked up his ears, focused on something in the undergrowth on the other side of the track, then took off like a black streak up the wooded hillside.

The water man responded to Pedrito's unheeded yelling of Nedi's name with a sardonic smile. 'Answers well, doesn't he?'

Pedrito returned the sardonic smile with a sheepish one. 'Probably saw a rabbit or something. Anyway, I've got to go. He found his way here, so he'll just have to find his way back home again.'

'And who pays for any livestock he savages?' the man called after Pedrito as he trotted off.

'King Jaume of Aragon-Catalonia,' Pedrito shouted over his shoulder, caring little now whether the man was sympathetic to the *Reconquista* or not. 'Just send the bill to the king!'

He couldn't make out what the man barked in reply, but he assumed it wasn't, 'Have a pleasant day.'

But a pleasant day it was anyway – or promised to be. The elation Pedrito felt at being just a few minutes from home after five years of enslaved exile was immense. His chest was almost bursting with the anticipation of seeing his family again. And all around, there were the sounds of nature that had been so ominously absent immediately before the recent battles: the chatter of sparrows in the pines, the muted tinkling of sheep bells, the sough of a morning breeze rippling the stillness of the forest. The sounds of life. It was difficult to imagine, while passing through this unsullied idyll, that so much death and desruction lay only a few hours' ride away on the approaches to the city.

A dog barked somewhere up the mountainside, and Pedrito's thoughts were brought abruptly back to Nedi. He whistled and shouted his name a few more times, but still to no effect. And the urgency to reach home that was gnawing at Pedrito far outweighed any obligation he might normally have felt to retrieve a runaway dog. Not that he didn't care about Nedi's wellbeing. He did, deeply, for he had grown fond of the big mutt during the couple of occasions they'd met so far. But, much as he was concerned about Nedi's current situation, he felt sure he could take care of himself. He might not be the sharpest arrow in the quiver, but, like all dogs, he was a survivor, and a resourceful one at that. Yes, Pedrito told himself, Nedi would be all right. He would find his way back to the Christian camp whenever his rabbit-chasing adventure was over.

Skirting the fringes of Andratx village, Pedrito followed the winding course seaward of the little *Torrent de Saluet* – paradoxically not really a torrent at all, except following a storm, yet sustaining lush breaks of cane in hollows where the merest trickle of water would linger, even in the parching heat of summer. Over on his left rose what Andratx folks called Turtle Mountain – in reality no more a mountain than the *Torrent* was a torrent, but it was shaped a bit like a turtle and, to the local kids at least, it was bigger than just a hill.

This was the countryside of Pedrito's childhood, and he could hardly contain his absolute delight at being back in these cherished surroundings. Impatient as he was to see his family, he reined in old Tranquilla to allow himself a few moments to savour it all. His gaze wandered down the valley to the little bridge that led eventually to his father's *finca*, which was situated on gently rising ground shielded from the chill, northerly Tramuntana winds of winter by the southernmost folds of the eponymous mountain range. From each one of the farm's four little stone-walled fields there were views of the sea at nearby Port d'Andratx, a wide, horseshoe cove enclosed by the arms of steep, pine-cloaked hills. There, his father, like the handful of other small farmers in the vicinty, had a tiny waterside shack, where he kept his boat and fishing tackle, and where Pedrito and his young friends had spent many an endlessly sunny summer's day swimming or playing pirates on rafts made from bits of driftwood. For, as Pedrito now knew from first-hand experience, the natural attributes of Port d'Andratx had long made it as much an occasional haunt of real pirates as it was a permanent haven for honest local fishermen.

But awful as those five years as a galley slave had been, he had resolved to banish all thoughts of them from his mind should he ever be granted the chance to see his home again. That craved-for opportunity had come at last, and he was going to make the most of every precious moment of it.

Crossing over the dry bed of the stream, he caught his first glimpse of the tall palms that guarded the gateway to the family farm; the same palm trees he had looked at so longingly when passing the cape of Sa Mola at the mouth of Andratx inlet on the reconnoitering mission to Santa Ponça just a few days earlier. The palm trees and all they represented had been tantalisingly out of reach then, but now they were a mere slingshot away. With tears welling in his eyes and his heart beating wildly, he urged old Tranquilla on.

And then, as he rounded a bend in the path, he saw him – his father, his back stooped in typical fashion as he worked away with his short-handled hoe in the *horta* by the house. With tears running down his cheeks, Pedrito giggled like a child as he was struck by the thought that his father was probably preparing to plant beans, a chore that had been such a bane of his own boyhood during this 'Season of Winter Spring'. Now, he couldn't wait to plop the hard, wrinkled seeds into the drills between the fruit trees. Or, better still, to take the hoe from his father and do the *real* work for a change.

He was about to shout a greeting, but then thought that, perhaps, this would spoil the surprise. On the other hand, if he walked up behind his father and laid a hand on his back, the shock of seeing his long-lost son when he turned round might do his heart more harm than good. It was a dilemma solved a moment or two later by Tranquilla, who decided to whinny loudly when she caught sight of a mule pulling a plough between ranks of almond trees a little farther down the valley. Instinctively, Pedrito's father looked over his shoulder and waved a hand at the approaching horseman.

It was only then that Pedrito, to his dismay, realised that the man wasn't his father after all, but old Baltazar Ensenyat, another small farmer, whose *finca* was located just a short distance away on the other side of the *Torrent*. His initial concern for the wellbeing of his father was quickly allayed, however, when he realised that Baltazar would only have come over to lend a hand, as neighbours hereabouts often did. Pedrito breathed easily again, secure in the knowledge that his father would more than likely be out in his boat doing a bit of early-morning fishing. It was a common enough practice of his, particularly on beautifully calm mornings like this.

'*Hola*, Baltazar!' Pedrito called out. '*Bon dia!*'

The old fellow returned the salutation, but Pedrito could see from his puzzled expression that he didn't know who he was actually greeting. He'd always been a bit short-sighted, as Pedrito recalled, so he waited until he was only a couple of horse lengths away before announcing with a grin, 'It's me, Baltazar – Pedrito! Don't you recognise me?'

Baltazar's jaw dropped. Then he mouthed Pedrito's name, but without a sound passing his lips.

'Getting ready to sow beans, eh? Hoping to steal my favourite job, were you?' Pedrito joked as he dismounted and strode, arms spread, towards the old man.

Baltazar's chin began to quiver and his eyes glazed over. 'Little Pedro,' he whispered, his whole body trembling while Pedrito gave him a manly hug. 'Little Pedro,' he repeated, pulling back from the embrace and staring at Pedrito in patent disbelief. '*Jesucrist*! Just look at you! I – I sometimes thought I'd never see the day when...' Choking on the words, he began to sob. He covered his eyes with one work-gnarled hand and steadied himself against Pedrito's arm with the other. '*Un desastre!*' he whimpered. '*Un desastre terrible!*'

Pedrito took him by the shoulders and gave him a gentle shake. 'Well, that's a fine way to welcome me back from my travels, I must say. Come on, Baltazar, it can't be that bad to see me again, surely.'

The old fellow was doing his best to pull himself together. 'No, no, Little Pedro,' he blurted out, 'I mean – that is, I only meant that – well, what I'm trying to say is that no man deserves such a thing to happen to him.'

Pedrito pulled him into another hug, patting his back the way one would an upset child's. 'Well, all right,' he said soothingly, 'I have to admit that spending a few years as a galley slave wasn't all that pleasant.' He leaned back, looked into the old man's upturned face and smiled. 'But don't you fret. It could have been worse. The main thing is that I survived, and I've come back – back here, back home, where I belong.'

The look that Baltazar now gave Pedrito sent a shiver down his spine. It was obvious that the old neighbour was struggling to find the right words to say.

'Something's wrong, isn't it?' Pedrito prompted, his heart in his mouth. 'If anything's wrong, just tell me. It's better I know if something's –'

Baltazar silenced him with a raised hand. 'So, you – you didn't talk to anyone in the village as you came through?'

Pedrito told him that he was so desperate to see his family that he'd taken a short cut and had come straight here.

Baltazar inhaled slowly, making a supreme effort to control his emotions. He gestured towards the higher gound on the opposite side of the *Torrent*. 'I was grazing my goats on one of the *bancales* there on the day you were taken. I saw it all, but – well, I was too far away to...' His lowered his voice with his eyes. 'What could I have done anyway – you know, one old man against a raiding party of Moorish pirates?'

Pedrito assured him that there was nothing any one person could have done to alter what had happened to him, so Baltazar shouldn't feel guilty. He repeated that the main thing was that he'd survived the ensuing years of bondage and had come safely home at last.

But the look on Baltazar's face throughout this increasingly forlorn attempt at stoicism told Pedrito that what had been on the tip of the old man's tongue all along concerned something much more painful than his own abduction, regrettable though that had been.

'I saw it all,' Baltazar repeated, his eyes downcast, his voice quavering. 'But there was nothing I could do.'

Several tense moments passed, before Pedrito braced himself and said, 'It's my father, isn't it? Something's happened to my father, hasn't it?'

Tears were filling Baltazar's eyes again. 'If only you'd come though the village, they would have said ... and I wouldn't have to tell you that the...' Again, his words faded away and he began to sniffle.

Although Pedrito knew that he would have to face the truth, no matter how unpleasant, he just could not bring himself to press the old neighbour further at this moment. His feelings were too confused: anticipation having become elation, elation having turned to joy, joy having been tempered by apprehension, and now the blood-chilling dread that he was about to be confronted with news of a type he had refused to even contemplate during the long years of separation from his family.

Eventually, it was Baltazar who recovered enough composure to speak again. 'They – the Moors, when they took you – they came at you from behind that wall by the *Torrent* down there, while you were working the ground with your mule, no?'

Pedrito indicated the affirmative. How could he forget that?

'Well,' Baltazar continued, 'you were slung over the back of your own mule and taken down to the bay by a couple of Moors, while some more of them – maybe five or six – crept up here to the *horta*, where –'

'Where my mother and father were working. *Sí, sí*, I remember that.' A sudden surge of anger was now beginning to vie with the dread churning Pedrito's stomach. 'But why would they want to take my father? A fit man, certainly – fitter than most men his age – but too old to be sold as a slave, so why would they want to...?'

Baltazar feigned a cough, steadying his voice. He motioned towards a corner of the *horta* nearest the house. 'They, uh – we, that is – well, you know that your father and mother's favourite view of the bay –'

'Is from there. *Sí, sí*, I know, I know!' Pedrito snapped. He didn't mean to sound blunt or unsympathetic towards the old man's feelings, which he could tell were just as much in disarray as his own, but he was being controlled now by a terrible inner conflict between a need to know the truth and a fear of being presented with it.

Baltazar could sense this too. Searching for the right words, he nodded again towards the same corner of the *horta*. 'We put little wooden crosses – two of them, side by side – in the same place they used to sit and watch the sun setting over the...' He heaved a great, shuddering sigh, tears dripping from the end of his nose. 'I'm sorry, Little Pedro,' he sniffed. 'I'm truly, truly sorry.'

It was as if an icy arrow had pierced Pedrito's very soul. He had witnessed so much cruelty and sorrow during his years as a galley slave and had seen death and suffering on a hitherto unimaginable scale over the past few days, yet none of those horrors had prepared him for this, the loss of his own parents – or the only parents he had ever known. He stood silent for a while, stunned, unable to even think, hardly aware of anything but the depths of emptiness into which he was sinking. But there was one thing he still needed to know – the only thing that could now light a candle of hope in his enveloping darkness.

'And my little sister,' he said after a bit. 'Little Esperança. Pray to God that she's still safe. She is, isn't she, Baltazar?'

Baltazar looked at Pedrito in a way that sent another chill through his bones. Again, it was obvious that Baltazar was trying to find words which might lessen the pain of what he had to say. Yet the very fact that he was hesitating merely added to Pedrito's agony.

'Please, Baltazar,' he said softly, '– I need to know.'

'I saw it all,' the old man repeated, wringing his hands. 'I saw it all, but there was nothing I could do.'

Pedrito patted his shoulder. 'I know, I know,' he murmured. 'And please don't blame yourself for whatever happened. Believe me, I know only too well the torture of being powerless to prevent –'

'It was Esperança they wanted,' Baltazar interrupted, spitting out the words as if ridding his mouth of a bad taste that had been endured too long. 'You see, after they took you, they looked up here and saw her coming from the house. Carrying a jug of water to your mother and father, maybe? I don't know, but they noticed her anyway. I saw them – five or six of them, creeping up here from the *Torrent.*' The old fellow looked appealingly into Pedrito's eyes. 'I shouted a warning – honestly I did – but I was so far away – too far away for them to hear.'

Pedrito stood as if turned to stone while Baltazar went on to tell of how his parents had fought frantically to protect their daughter, of how Esperança herself had put up a desperate struggle to free herself from the clutches of the pirates. He spared Pedrito the details of how his mother and father had met their deaths, while assuring him that he and the other neighbours had laid them to rest with all the love and respect they deserved, side-by-side in the place that everyone knew was not only their favourite view of Port d'Andtratx bay, but also of the sea on which their son and daughter had been taken away and, God willing, would one day return.

Pedrito remained motionless, gazing through misty eyes at that very view, hardly hearing Baltazar's assurances that the land on their *finca* had been tilled diligently by himself and other neighbours during the intervening years, and only half taking in what he said about the little house having been maintained in the same trim that it had been left on that awful day. There was always the hope, he said again, that Pedrito or Esperança, or both of them, would indeed come back home … one day … somehow.

Pedrito thanked him, though absently, for his thoughts were already racing back to the morning of his capture. 'You say they took Esperança as well,' he said quizzically, 'but I saw every one of the captives being herded off the galley for the slave market on Ibiza the following day. I saw every one of their faces – terrified, desperate, lost. I looked at every one of those poor souls as they passed between the rowing thwarts, and Esperança wasn't among them. She wasn't on that galley, Baltazar. I'd have known if she was, believe me.' Suddenly, hope was springing from the depths of Pedrito's depair. 'Maybe she escaped! Maybe there's a chance she's still...' But his words trailed off as he noticed the doleful look in Baltazar's eyes.

Gravely, the old man shook his head. 'Two galleys came into the bay that morning, Little Pedro.' He gestured out towards the mouth of the bay. 'They must have been anchored all night behind the Punta Moragues headland there – hiding, waiting for the dawn.'

Pedrito felt his heart sink once more.

'When the galleys left,' Baltazar went on, 'one of them headed north, the other south.'

Pedrito shuddered, rubbing his forehead. 'My God, and to think that I saw so many frightened and humiliated young girls crammed into the holds of that damned galley over the years. Little more than children, screaming, crying for their mothers night after night, until they were bundled out again, to be sold at whatever market the captain thought would bring the best prices.' He stared unblinkingly at the ground, tormented by his own thoughts. 'How many times did I pray for them?' he murmured. 'And how many times did I thank God in his mercy that my own little sister was safe at home here with Mamà and Papà?' A cold tremor raked his body again. 'God in his mercy?' he muttered, his lips quivering. 'What God? What mercy?'

After a few more moments of strained silence, Baltazar touched Pedrito's arm lightly. 'I'll leave you to ... I mean, you'll want to be on your own here for a while now, so I...' The old man was too upset to continue. With a nod in the direction of his own house on the other side of the valley, he indicated without need for words that Pedrito would be welcome there at any time. '*Adéu*, Little Pedro,' he whispered through his tears. '*Adéu.*'

As if in a trance, Pedrito wandered over to the house. It was just as he'd remembered it, though seeming smaller in a strange way. Parting makes the heart grow fonder, it was said, so perhaps time and distance had made his home grow larger. Anyway, it was virtually as he'd pictured it in his mind every day without exception during the past five years. The same stout walls built from the island's straw-coloured stone, the same wooden shutters covering the windows, the same arched entrance shaded by a canopy of vines, the same old well in the back yard, the same oven set into the wall by the kitchen door.

That oven. The same stone oven in which his mother would bake her bread. The oven, the smell of its wood smoke. The bread, the aroma of his mother's freshly-baked loaves. How the merest suggestion of these simple things had transported him back here from however far his Moorish masters had driven him.

He reached out and touched the charred stonework round the oven's mouth. It was cold. Dead. Just as dead as the woman who used to sing her cheerful songs while she tended it.

He looked around the little yard. Still the ancient fig tree shading the well, and beneath it the stone bench on which his mother would sit and tell his little sister stories while the bread baked. He could almost hear little Esperança's gasps of delight and cascades of laughter even now. Almost. But no, not even almost, for in truth there was nothing here now but silence – the still, eerie hush of a once-happy home from which the pulse of life had been wrenched.

His heart aching, Pedrito approached the corner of the *horta*, where Baltazar had told him his parents had been laid to rest. And there they were, just as the old man had said – two little crosses, side-by-side. The crosses couldn't have been more simple; nothing more than two bits of almond branch bound together. And the graves couldn't have been less ornate, their perimeters market by rough chunks of limestone of the sort that ploughs had nudged from Mallorcan soil since time immemorial.

Yet it was obvious that someone, perhaps old Baltazar or his wife, had cared for this humble little burial ground as fastidiously as if it had been the marble-decked tomb of some grand lord and lady. Not a weed had been allowed to grow within its confines, the ochre soil meticulously raked into furrows that ran from head to foot like the neatly arranged folds of a shroud. There were even two little posies of wild flowers placed in earthenware cups of water at the base of each cross. And the freshness of the blooms revealed that they had been picked that very morning.

Pedrito felt a lump rise in his throat as he thought of how such kind-hearted neighbours – simple country folk of modest means and devoid of any self-interest beyond the wellbeing of their families – had honoured the memory of his mother and father so unfailingly and for so long. He fell to his knees, all the pent-up feelings of those long years of exile coming to the surface at last. Burying his face in his hands, he began to sob uncontrollably, his body raked by spasms of grief, his mind gripped by an all-consuming sense of desolation.

There had been so many times on that galley from hell when all that had kept him from despairing to the point of insanity had been thoughts of returning here – to his family, to his home. Times, when pulling an oar in mountainous seas, wet, aching, exhaused and lashed both by the chill of the waves and the burning sting of the galley master's whip, when his only source of strength was the belief that he would one day be welcomed back into the bosom of his family – right here, in the very spot where they had sat together on so many summer evenings, watching the sun set over the sea beyond the Punta Moragues headland; that same rocky bluff behind which the destroyers of his family had anchored that night, lying in wait for the right moment to strike.

Pedrito didn't know how long he had knelt in front of those two little crosses, shedding silent tears, his face buried in his hands. All he knew was that he felt totally lost, alone in a world that now seemed to hold no place for him, a world in which greed, violence and man's inhumanity towards his fellow man had become the bywords of life for so many. And so much was in the 'holy' cause of religion, fought and killed for in the name of God – or Allah. Yet Pedrito knew that allegiance to no deity other than the god of evil had been the motivation for the actions of those plunderers who had stolen everything that was dear to him, had taken away his very reason for living.

But wasn't that precisely what King Jaume was set on doing on a vast scale for the glory of God? And wouldn't his adversary, the Moorish King of Mallorca, match this spreading of human suffering to protect and preserve the interests of Allah?

What hope, Pedrito asked himself, was there for anyone?

He was staring now into an abyss of misery, a black hole from which there was no escape. No escape, except by one route. For the first time ever, his thoughts began to drift towards ways of ending a life that no longer held any meaning for him. Without his family, it wouldn't be a life at all, merely an existence in a dark and hopeless world that promised him nothing but loneliness and despair. It was a form of torture more cruel than any he had suffered at the hands of the slave masters, and his will to resist was draining away.

Just then, he felt something cold and moist touching his hand. Startled, he glanced between his fingers, and there, peering at him through a fringe of shaggy black hair, were two brown eyes, exuding a curious mix of puzzlement and understanding.

'Nedi!' Pedrito gasped. 'But – but I thought you would have gone back to...' He paused, realising that the dog had *chosen* to come here, rather than return to the camp at Bendinat and his master, the king. He ruffled the tousled head. 'But how on earth did you find me, boy? Do I smell *that* bad, eh?'

Usually, Nedi would have responded to this sort of attention by jumping up and, tail wagging frantically, slobbering doggy kisses all over the face of his 'playmate'. But not this time. Instead, he laid his head on Pedrito's lap and looked up at him, the puzzlement gone from his eyes and replaced now by a look that said more in the way of sympathy and commiseration than any number of words could ever have done. Somehow, Nedi knew that Pedrito was grieving, and he was trying to tell him, in the only way he could, that he was here to help him find a way though.

Fresh tears welled in Pedrito's eyes, but instead of tears of sorrow, these were tears of release. These were tears that come when a sense of hope suddenly replaces one of despair. The quiet, bitter-sweet laughter that escaped Pedrito's lips now was both involuntary and healing. At once, he felt the leaden weight lifting from his heart.

Sensing this, Nedi raised his head and canted it to one side, as dogs do when they invite humans to share their innate optimism. His ears were pricked, his eyes shining like little black beads, his face smiling, his tongue dangling from one side of his mouth in the same way that had appeared gormless back at the Coll d'Andritxol water well only a little while ago. But now his open smile and dangling tongue conveyed an entirely different message.

Just then, a soft breeze wafted up through the valley, carrying on its breath the tang of the sea and, although faint at this time of year, a hint of the heat of Africa, the land of the Moors.

This was the *Migjorn*, the southerly note of the 'Song of the Eight Winds', the wind that Pedrito's father had always said blew the shoals of sardines into the fishermen's nets. This was the wind of hope. Hope, the meaning of his little sister Esperança's name.

Nedi tilted his head to the other side. 'Well,' his expectant grin seemed to say, 'shall we sink, or shall we swim?'

He was, as Pedrito recalled, a breed of water dog, so who better to teach you how to keep your spirits afloat than him?

## 15
# THE STRANGE
# CONTRARINESS OF TEARS

*THE FOLLOWING MORNING, 14ᵗʰ SEPTEMBER...*

While making his way back to the King's encampment, Pedrito was stopped by a small patrol led by Robert St Clair de Roslin, the tyro Templar Knight, who, perhaps in jest, had lately revealed a dislike of bagpipes, but a taste for Aragonese *chireta*, which he judged to be a rather poor immitation of his native country's great delicacy, haggis. There was nothing even faintly jocular about his demeanour now, however. He and his men were stationed by the roadway skirting *Es Coll de Sa Batalla*, scene of the massacre of so many Moors in their first confrontation with the Christian forces just three days earlier. It was the same stretch of road on which Pedrito had experienced a creepy sensation while passing along in darkness two nights ago.

Even now, with the first light of day, there was something unsettling about the place. The surrounding fields and orchards bore the scars of two armies having stormed through, one in retreat, the other in attack, but both paying scant respect for the crops that had been so carefully husbanded by the local Moorish farmers until a few hours before the so-called battle. There were even signs that some of the houses and farmsteads had suffered wanton damage, perhaps as part of a crudely conducted scorched earth policy by the fleeing Moors, perhaps as an act of subjugation by the victorious Christians. In any case, the homes and livelihoods of many innocent people had been ruined, and the victims, wherever they were now, would have to pick up the pieces by whatever means possible, if or when they were given the opportunity.

'You may as well dismount and give your backside a rest, laddie, because you'll have to wait here for a while,' Robert St Clair told Pedrito. Grim-faced, he indicated a spot about fifty paces ahead, where a huddle of men were standing, heads bowed, under a solitary pine tree. 'It's the king and a few of his high-ranking nobles. Sentry pickets have been posted all around here.'

Pedrito frowned. 'Why? What's going on?'

'They've just buried the bodies of En Guillen and En Remon de Muntcada. Aye, and I don't mind telling you, man, there's been much weeping and lamenting, even by the king, no matter what he said about everyone putting a brave face on things for the sake of army morale.' He motioned again towards the funeral party. 'A really sad affair, but it'll soon be over now, I think. Looks like the Bishop of Barcelona has started the benediction.'

The stench of death still hung in the air here, close as it was to where thousands of Moorish corpses lay where they had fallen in the first clash of arms. Somewhere, someone would be lamenting the loss of each and every one of them, but there would never be any grave to weep over, never any man of the cloth to conduct their passage to a better place. Such was the outcome of battle, Pedrito supposed, and such was the difference between the deaths of a few high-ranking victors and the mass slaughter of the vanquished.

With the dawn, a light rain had started to fall, the accompanying grey skies adding another element of gloom to an already morose scene. Dismal weather was the last thing Pedrito needed in his current state of mind. He glanced down at Nedi, who was already looking up at him, his panting face still radiating canine bonhomie and optimism.

Pedrito gave him a pat on the head. 'You're a good boy,' he said, then added, a tad apprehensively. 'Don't go making a beeline for your master just yet, though. I don't think he'd appreciate one of your rough-and-tumble reunions at this particular moment in time.'

Nedi tilted his head in a way that seemed to say that he was perfectly aware of this blatantly obvious fact, thanks all the same. This quirky little gesture brought a much-needed smile to Pedrito's face.

Away to the north, the hill that had been dubbed *Es Puig del Rei*, or The King's Mount, in recognition of King Jaume's impromptu military action on its slopes during the first day of the invasion, was hidden under a hood of cloud, swirling slowly in the grey light like the cape of a passing ghost. Pedrito shivered. He was still clad in the only clothes he owned, a baggy linen shirt and *pantalons* of the same coarse material. Once, a long time ago, they'd been white, but now the grubby, travel-soiled cloth was clinging to his body in damp, uncomfortable wrinkles. These same clothes had been soaked through by waves breaking over the pirate galley's rowing deck more often than he could remember, but that had never seemed as unpleasant as the effects of this persistent, misery-inducing fall of light rain. He confessed as much to Robert St Clair.

'Ach, it's nothing!' Robert retorted. He swatted the air. 'No, no, no, it's just a wee sprinkle of drizzle, and that never hurt anybody!' He held out the palm of his hand and looked up at the sky. 'Man, where I come from, we don't even call this rain! Scotch mist, that's all it is, and that never hurt anybody, so cheer up, for heaven's sake!'

Pedrito immediately felt like telling him that he had a lot more to be miserable about than a downturn in the weather, but thought better of it. After all, hundreds of Robert's colleagues, including many good friends, had also met their deaths over the past few days, so why would he want to hear about Pedrito's own bereavements? He forced a smile instead and asked jokingly if the twist of red hair protruding from Robert's helmet was a result of all that Scotch mist having rusted his head.

Robert, however, had a keener sense of perception than Pedrito had given him credit for. Ignoring Pedrito's attempt at levity, he shot him an enquiring look.

'What are you doing here anyway? I thought you'd be spending a bit more than one day with your family, after all those years away.'

Pedrito hung his head, but he didn't say anything.

Robert nodded knowingly. 'You can tell me, Pedrito, no matter what it is.' He waited for a response, but when none was forthcoming he gently reminded Pedrito that, although the Templars were warrior knights, they were also monks. 'I don't claim to be a very godly one myself – not yet anyway – but I've been taught a little about compassion and forgiveness, so if there's anything you want to get off your chest...'

Pedrito struggled to hold his emotions in check as he related, albeit reluctantly, everything that had happened during the previous twenty-four hours: how old Baltazar had broken the news about his parents' murder and his little sister's abduction by the same band of Moorish pirates that had taken him as a slave; how he had mourned at his parents' grave for much of the day; how Nedi had followed him and had given him succour; how he had eaten, or, to be more accurate, had picked at the food Baltazar's wife had made for him; and how, unable to bring himself to enter his own home with all the poignant memories it held, he had snatched a few hours of fitful sleep in an abandoned stable on his way back here.

Robert looked at him, his eyes revealing that any lessons he'd been given in compassion had been well enough learned. 'Don't be ashamed of your grief, Pedrito,' he said, quietly enough to avoid being heard by any of the other guards, 'and don't be afraid to cry. It's all part of the healing process – not a sign of weakness.' He jerked his head in the direction of the Muntcadas' burial party. 'Even the bold king and his gallant nobles there have shed buckets of tears over the deaths of their brothers in arms today, so why shouldn't you weep over the loss of your family?'

Pedrito thanked him for his kindness and understanding, before adding that he had wept so much since first looking down on the graves of his parents that he didn't think he had another teardrop left to shed.

'Ah, but there will be, my friend, there will be.' Robert draped an arm round Pedito's shoulder. 'And I can tell you this from personal experience, having lost my own mother and father when I was a child.' He looked into Pedrito's eyes again. 'There will be times, even years from now, when some little thing – a sound, a smell, a flower, a sunset, a word, a song – will bring the fond memories flooding back, and with them the tears.' He smiled and pinched Pedrito's cheek. 'So don't be afraid to cry, man – ever. It's nature's way of soothing the pain… which does ease in time, believe me. Oh yes,' he declared, his smile broadening, 'no matter how much it rains, the sun always shines again – even in Scotland, where I come from!'

Robert's chuckle at this self-mocking quip was followed, almost uncannily Pedrito thought, by a gentle breeze. Soon, the chilly fog that had been lying in banks on the valley floor began to drift away, and as the rain clouds rolled from the hilltops, so did a hazy glow appear in the eastern sky.

It was Pedrito, looking heavenward, who chuckled now. 'You say you're not yet all that godly, Robert, but if this is anything to go by, you must be in touch with *some*one with a bit of influence up there!'

'Well, I have to admit,' Robert said with contrived coyness, 'my miracle-working *has* been coming on leaps and bounds of late.'

And the gloom lifted with the rising of the sun. And as its warmth dispersed the last of the lingering mists, the magical aromas that permeate the Mallorcan countryside after rain intensified apace. Luxuriantly, Pedrito inhaled the musty smell of damp earth, the resinous tang of the pinewoods, the intoxicating perfumes of myrtle, thyme, rosemary, heather and countless other herbs and wild flowers that inhabit the island's landscape.

And memories of home did come flooding back, just as Robert had predicted. But the tears they brought to Pedrito's eyes weren't tears of sadness and despair, but tears of gratitude and hope. Gratitude for having been blessed with the love and care of a wonderful family after such an ill-omened start in life, and hope that one day he would find his little sister Esperança.

Esperança – hope – the shining light at the end of what would otherwise have been an interminable tunnel of darkness. Pedrito owed it to his parents to find her, and he vowed on their memory that he would … one day … somehow.

## 16
# PREPARING THE ENGINES OF WAR

*LATER THAT MORNING – ON THE SOUTHERN FOOTHILLS OF THE SERRA DE NA BURGUESA…*

The temporary encampment that En Nunyo Sans had set up two nights previously had been dismantled by the time Pedrito reached the place the king had named Bendinat, but he could see in the distance that another base was already being established to the north of the city. This vast new camp was within the projectile-throwing range, he presumed, of the war engines presently being brought ashore from transports at Porto Pi.

The nearer Pedrito got to the site, the more obvious it became that this was intended to be the permanent centre of operations for the Christian siege of the city. A ditch was being dug around the camp's perimeter, and within that a stout wooden palisade was under construction. From what he knew of the countryside around here, it seeemed that the location had also been chosen because it straddled a stream which ran from a spring rising some way farther north at a place called Canet, nestling in the lower folds of the Tramuntana Mountains. He did wonder, however, why this main camp was being built almost four miles inland from the supply base at Port Pi. Then it occurred to him that this was, in all probability, the nearest suitable site on the opposite side of the deep *torrent* channel which served as a moat on the western perimeter of the city and which, as the king himself had already perceived, would have been an extremely difficult obstacle for assault forces to overcome, even when dry. It appeared, then, that Nunyo Sans' reconnoitering scouts had done their work well.

In contrast to the chaotic conditions that had prevailed when the first landing was taking place at Santa Ponça, this operation was being conducted with a conspicuous degree of order. It was an ants' nest of activity, involving, in one way or another, every surviving soldier and sailor in this mighty invasion force. Not a moment was being wasted and not a man spared in the effort to establish what was to be the main tented barracks for the fighting troops, a launching pad for missiles from the huge timber-framed catapults now being made ready, and headquarters from where the king and his generals could orchestrate the siege and the ultimate taking of the great city of Medîna Mayûrqa.

Pedrito had waited a suitably respectful time before following King Jaume and his accompanying barons from the burial place of the Muntcadas, but had reported to the royal compound immediately on his eventual arrival at the camp. The king, although understandably preoccupied with logistical matters in hand, had made a point of conveying his condolences to Pedrito on his tragic personal loss, details of which had been told to him by Robert St Clair de Roslin. And the fact that the king chose not to dwell on the subject actually came as a relief to Pedrito. His emotions were still in a fragile state, and any overly effusive show of sympathy would only have risked an embarrassing onset of self-pity.

'Life must go on, Little Pedro,' said the king, while laying an encouraging hand on his shoulder, 'and the best way to overcome the sorrow of bereavement is to keep busy.'

As an illustration, he related how even his most esteemed knights were helping the lowliest of foot soldiers gather and stockplie rocks as ammunition for the siege engines, the knights bringing the stones balanced before them on their saddles, the soldiers carrying them on frames slung round their necks. And, he pointed out, there was hardly a man among them who wasn't mourning the recent death of a brother in arms.

To Pedrito's surprise, the king then reached out and felt his biceps. 'And you could carry rocks with the best of them, eh? Ah, *sí,*' he winked, 'but I've an even more strenuous job for you and your old hack, my friend, weary as I'm sure you both are after your travels.'

Before Pedrito could emphasise just how physically and mentally exhausted he actually was, King Jaume informed him that he himself had had no sleep for three nights now, and he expected an equally selfless commitment from all of his men.

'But just think of the prize that awaits us all, Little Pedro,' he enthused, '– the reconquest of Mallorca for our Lord God Almighty, and a share in the riches and assets of this beautiful island for each and every one of us who labours and fights in His name.'

Pedrito could have reminded the king that he and his family had already enjoyed, in the form of their humble little *finca* at Andratx, the best share of Mallorca's riches and assets that they could ever have wished for, even if their overlords worshipped Allah instead of God. But to say this would have been tantamount to blasphemy in King Jaume's ears, and Pedrito had recovered sufficient of his will to live to render such a potentially suicidal statement highly unwise.

'So, *senyor,*' he said, with as much eagerness as he could affect, 'what is it you want me to do for you?'

'Well, as I mentioned back at the tent of En Oliver the night before last, I do have a very important task in mind – a delicate one that could be crucial to the outcome of this war. But first I need those muscles of yours.'

He explained that a Christian patrol had seen, from a distance, the Moorish king return to the city with about twenty of his horsemen, the assumption being that the rest of the Saracen troops who survived the most recent battle had headed for the mountains to join the thousands of their comrades already taking refuge there. That being the case, the Christian objective now would be to ensure that none of these routed forces either mounted a surprise attack on the camp or made their way back into the city to reinforce whatever remained of the original garrison. But, even more crucially, the bombardment of Medîna Mayûrqa by the Christian siege engines would have to deliver maximum damage as quickly as possible in order to sap the resistance of its inhabitants and, consequently, to force the Amir into submission.

'However,' the king cautioned, 'that could be easier said than done, because we've already seen that the Moors are preparing their own defences, and that includes at least one large *trebuchet* and some smaller *mangonels*.'

Pedrito raised his eyebrows. '*Trebuchet? Mangonels?*' He then raised his shoulders. 'Sorry, *senyor*, but I don't know what you're talking about.'

At that very moment, a large rock whistled over their heads and thumped into the ground several rows of tents behind where they were standing.

'That,' said the king, rising gingerly from the ducked position, 'came from a *mangonel*, a type of *trebuchet*, but smaller and without a sling attachment. The Moorish version is called an *algarrada*, I believe.'

Pedrito was none the wiser, and it showed.

The king was becoming impatient. 'Look, I haven't time right now to give you a lecture on the history and finer points of war engines. Suffice it to say that, at the moment, we have two each of the most up-to-date variants almost ready to use.' He nodded to an open space on the side of the stockade facing the city, where the machines he referred to were being prepared. 'You'll notice that both types have a vertically-swinging boom – in effect a catapult arm powered by counterweights. The larger machines are the *trebuchets* – the ones with slings attached – and they're used for hurling projectiles *over* walls as well as into them. As you can see, their frames are the height of three men, and their booms when released almost as high again. The smaller ones, the *mangonels*, launch their ammunition in a low trajectory aimed *at* the target. They're more powerful than *trebuchets*, but less accurate.'

'Thank God for that,' said Pedrito with a leery look. He hooked a thumb towards the landing place of the recently delivered rock. 'A bit more accurate than that and we'd be spitting teeth.'

The king gave him a wry smile. 'Yes, but at a great distance from our bodies, my friend. Those machines are for battering holes in castle walls, so it would take a pretty thick head to survive a direct hit, don't you think? Anyhow, this is neither the time nor place for whimsical chatter. The hard fact is that I've taken part in many sieges, and I can tell you that the *mangonel* the Moors are using here is the best I've ever come across. What's more, they've positioned it on their ramparts well out of range of our machines, so that's why I need all the muscle I can muster – and fast.'

Pedrito could see that the king was revelling in this situation, one ideally suited to his instant-action way of thinking. As he hurried Pedrito out of the compound, he divulged, and with obvious pride, that the masters of five ships donated by the French city of Marseilles had advised him that they could construct a type of *trebuchet* to equal, or even better, the range of the Moor's *mangonel*. Furthermore, they'd said that they would gladly build one out of the yards and spars of their own vessels, if the king could mobilise sufficient manpower to help dismantle the heavy timbers and lug them all the way up here from Porto Pi.

Thus Pedrito and old Tranquilla spent most of what was destined to become a very long day indeed. And, as it would transpire, an unimaginably fateful one for Pedrito as well.

### *LATER THAT DAY, IN 'EL REAL', THE CHRISTIAN CAMP OUTSIDE THE NORTHERN WALLS OF THE CITY OF MALLORCA ...*

During the afternoon, periodic shots had been exchanged between the besiegers and the besieged, but the projectiles were hurled more to enable fine adjustments to made to the war engines than as serious attempts at inflicting damage. Nevertheless, the presence of flying boulders did nothing to alleviate the tribulations of heaving and hauling bulky lengths of timber from ship to shore and from shore to camp. By early evening, Pedrito was in a state of near collapse. But his day wasn't over yet – not by a long chalk.

The king handed him a bundle of cloth. 'This is a Moorish robe and head scarf. I had them stripped from one of their battlefield dead, and I want you to put them on, Little Pedro.'

Pedrito glanced at the bundle, then at his own soiled clothes. He then peered at the king through narrowed eyes. 'I may smell like a dog, *senyor*, but I'd rather smell of my own smells than those of a dead man. Anyway, my shirt and *pantalons* are better than a robe for doing manual work, no matter how high they stink.'

'Don't worry,' the king laughed 'I had all the blood stains and scraps of flesh scrubbed from the robe, and the headdress has been checked for lice – plus, my man went to great lengths to find a tall Moorish corpse, so you needn't worry about showing too much leg. Now, go and wash all that sweat and muck off yourself, then come back and I'll tell you what I have in mind.'

The spring water trickling through the camp may have been on the bracing side of cool for Pedrito's liking, but it did at least refresh his aching muscles, and once his skin had shivered off its goose pimples, he had to admit that it felt wonderful to have a clean body again. It didn't feel quite so good, though, to be the butt of soldiers' ribbing once he had donned the Moorish garb. The white robe was full, flowing and, as the king had predicted, long enough to reach his ankles; the blue head scarf of sufficiently generous dimensions to wrap turban-style round his head, with ample cloth remaining to bunch over his mouth and shoulders. From what he could discern from the distorted image reflected in the metal shield the king held up for him back in the royal enclosure, he did indeed look the real thing, swarthy skin, dark, deep-set eyes and all. He slightly resented, however, the king's declaration, no matter how mischievous, that he had been transformed into 'every bit the shifty, heathen Arab' he wanted him to be.

To make matters worse, even Nedi growled and took several swift steps backwards to peer furtively at him from behind his master's legs.

The king did his best to suppress a smirk. 'He obviously doesn't recognise you in those clothes, eh?'

'He's probably just confused by the lack of smell,' Pedrito suggested, trying to give the impression of indifference. 'First smell, then hearing, next sight – that, in descending order, is the sharpness order of a dog's senses.'

Nedi barked a nervous bark, wagged his tail briefly, cocked his head and, without venturing out from behind the refuge of the king's legs, stared nonplussed at Pedrito.

'I think his hearing has recognised you,' the king said, deadpan. 'Only smell and sight to go before he latches onto you like a barnacle again, no?'

This was the first time the king had made reference to his dog's relationship with Pedrito, and there was no telling from his expression whether he resented it or not. Pedrito decided to play it safe.

'I can only apologise sincerely for his absence yesterday, *senyor*. I had no idea he'd followed me out of camp the night before. I mean, even when he did let me know he was there, he took off again and I honestly thought he would have headed right back to –'

'Given the chance,' the king interrupted, 'the dog chooses the master, not vice versa. And I can tell you, *amic*, that smell, sound and sight, no matter how sensitive, are nothing compared to the magical ability a dog has to communicate with the man *he* chooses to own.' King Jaume's hitherto inscrutable expression melted into a broad smile. 'And if Nedi does ever decide to adopt you instead of me, who am I to question his choice? After all, he's a dog, and I'm merely a man.'

Pedrito found himself unable to reply. It wasn't that he couldn't think of any words to say, but simply that they stuck in his throat, so touched was he by this young king's generosity and his sense of humility towards creatures of a supposedly lesser order than himself. Pedrito thought again about the story the king had told him of how, during a long siege, a pair of swallows had chosen his tent in which to to build their nest, and how, against all military advice, he had forbidden the tent to be moved before the little birds had hatched their young and had nurtured them through to the day when they were able to take to the skies by themselves. Yet this same man could kill a fellow human without a second thought, and for no other reason than that he held different religious beliefs from himself. It set Pedro wondering if the king assumed, perhaps, that all dogs and swallows were by nature Christians.

Meanwhile, the king had adopted a more serious mien. Leading Pedrito into the privacy of his tent, he proceeded to reveal why he had asked him to dress as a Moor...

'Although you're not a soldier, Little Pedro, I'm sure you can imagine that a siege of a well-defended city like Medîna Mayûrqa can be a long and uncomfortable experience, for those on either side of the walls. And while starving the besieged into defeat is the longer-term alternative to swiftly battering them into submission with our war engines, the continuous supply of sufficient food can be a problem for the besiegers too. That's obvious, no?'

Pedrito nodded.

'And, *amic*, when the city being besieged is on an island like this, the besiegers have two additional problems to concern themselves with. One is that enemy reinforcements may arrive by sea, as is the threat here. The other, as ever, is that there's a limit to the amount of provisions we can glean from the immediately surrounding area. But, unlike a siege situation on the mainland, there's no way of bringing food supplies from farther afield – except by ship, with all the risks that this would involve. Do you understand what I'm saying?'

Pedrito gestured that he did indeed. He was also beginning to suspect that he understood why the king had got him dressed up like an Arab. His suspicions left him feeling distinctly apprehensive.

Precisely how justified this feeling might be was promptly revealed by the king. 'I need you to get inside the city walls – and tonight!'

Pedrito's apprehension increased commensurate with the bluntness of this revelation, as did his heart rate.

'I hope you're not thinking of catapulting me over from one of your *trebuchets*,' his mouth said, indulging itself in that risky old habit of not first consulting his brain. 'Flying's one thing, but landing in one piece could be another matter entirely.'

Fortunately, King Jaume's response was more droll than reproachful. 'We never hurl the living into enemy cities, my friend – unless, of course, the living are carrying leprosy or the plague.

Even then, it's much easier to hurl the dead.'

Pedrito had heard enough rumours about siege procedures in his time to know that the king was unlikely to be joking.

In any case, the king got straight back down to business by informing Pedrito that his mission was to get himself into the city, by whatever means he could, and then to ascertain the true size and weaponry of the Moorish garrison, also whether or not a fleet of ships bearing reinforcements was really on its way from Africa. The king reminded him that all they had to go on at present was the word of Ali, the Saracen deserter, and while he had no reason to disbelieve him, confirmation or otherwise of Ali's assertions was now vital to the Christian effort. 'Oh,' he appended, 'and there's also the matter of where, how and from whom we may be able to obtain a reliable and plentiful supply of provisions, without the risk of sending foraging parties too far afield. After all, there are still many thousands of the enemy holed up in the mountains around here.'

'And there are still many *more* thousands of them holed up in the city there, but you don't mind risking this one-man foraging party, it seems.' Pedrito instantly wished he hadn't said that, but, surprisingly, the king seemed to take it in good part.

'Ah, but don't forget you're posing as an Arab, *amic*, and as I told you before, you would pass for one any day.'

'Hmm, that makes me feel a whole lot better,' Pedrito mumbled.

Once more, the king let Pedrito's apparent recalcitrance go without rebuke.

The two young men stood looking at each other, both wondering what the other was thinking. Then, without saying a word, Pedrito got down on his knees and scooped up some earth, which he proceeded to rub all over his clean robe, before doing the same to his face and arms. He responded to the king's quizzical frown by explaining that this was all part of his instinctive plan for gaining entry to the city.

The king arched an eyebrow. 'Yes, well, I think I'd prefer not to know the details. But whatever they are, you'll need this.' He handed Pedrito a small dagger. 'Tuck that away under your robe somewhere.'

Pedrito shook his head. 'One dagger against a garrison of soldiers? I don't think so. No, thanks all the same, *senyor*, but if I can't survive on my wits, I'm done for anyway.'

'Well, you'd better keep *all* your wits about you, because survive you must. The information I've asked you to root out could be the difference between the success and failure of this crusade.' The king then took a leather purse from the pocket of his surcoat. 'If you won't take a weapon, then at least take this. It's some Moorish money we found on the previous owner of your clothes. It may come in handy. You never know – you may have to buy something to eat.'

Pedrito gave an uneasy little chortle. 'Starving isn't what I'm worried about. No, it's those boulders flying about that bother me. So, can I take it you won't be launching any into the city while I'm in there?'

The king's response was unequivocal. 'This is war, and we certainly won't be sitting here taking the enemy's missiles without giving as good as we take – or better, especially after the new *trebuchet* is ready. No, no, make no mistake, as soon as there's enough light to see the city walls tomorrow morning, we'll be hitting them with everything we've got, so you'd better get yourself in there and out again as fast as you can.' Noting Pedrito's worried look, he cleared his throat and added, 'And, uh, may God go with you.'

Pedrito dipped his head reverentially, then muttered into his chest, 'This time, just make sure that Nedi doesn't.'

## 17

# THE GATE OF CHAINS

*LATER THAT DAY, ON THE WESTERN PERIFERY*
*OF MEDÎNA MAYÛRQA...*

While the new camp was under construction, it had been decided that those foot soldiers still awaiting tented accommodation should accompany the sailors back to their ships at Porto Pi each evening. This both afforded the soldiers a sheltered place to sleep and provided the ships with a degree of protection should the Moors' threatened seaborne reinforcements arrive under cover of darkness. So it was that Pedrito tagged onto a large body of men as they headed coastward at dusk.

It was taken for granted that this activity would be closely monitored by the Moors on the city-wall ramparts, so the trek south was made by a route well out of crossbow and missile range. With his own interests to the fore, Pedrito made sure that he was on the far side of the column and well hidden from the Moorish lookouts. It went without saying that their suspicions would have been raised by the sight of a man in Arab garb marching with Christian forces.

The strategy he had decided upon was to try and gain entry to the city by one of the gates farthest from the northern perimeter, against which the Christian bombardment would commence at dawn. What the king had asked him to do promised to be a risky enough business as it was, without leaving himself open to annihilation by a 'friendly' flying boulder. Accordingly, he stayed with the Christian column until it reached the coast at a point where the road south to Porto Pi was crossed by one leading eastward to the city. There, he hid in a pine grove and waited for darkness to fall.

\*

Yet again, the island was illuminated by the moon rising in a cloudless sky, thereby lighting Pedrito's way along the beach until he could see the twin towers of the gate the Moors called *Bab-al-balad* rearing above the city walls ahead of him. It was obvious, even in the dim light, that the towers and adjacent ramparts were heavily manned by archers. It had to be assumed, therefore, that if Pedrito could see them, they in turn would be able to see him, conspicuously dressed as he was in a white robe. For that reason, he decided to forestall any likelihood of becoming the target for a hail of arrows by making his presence blatantly obvious.

'Allah is great!' he shouted in Arabic, while waving both hands above his head.

'*Matha tureed?*' a guard called back. 'Who are you, and what do you want?'

Pedrito pointed over his shoulder. 'I'm a farmer from west of here. My home was destroyed by the infidel invaders, and I seek sanctuary within the city walls, *inshallah*.'

'Not by this gate,' came the firm reply. 'It's barricaded against any attack by the Christian dogs, as are all entrances to the city, except the Gate of Chains, along the waterfront there by the mole. They open the postern occasionally to let men who've been fishing from the quay back in with their catch. Try there.'

Pedrito bowed deeply and flamboyantly. '*Shukran, akh*. Thank you, brother, and may peace be upon you and your house. Allah is great.'

So far, so good. Out in the bay, he could see a curve of Christian ships blockading the harbour, their outlines silhouetted against the moonlit water. Perhaps their presence should have been of some comfort to him, yet it only served to emphasise in his own mind just how alone he was. It also brought home to him that he was probably only being used as a cat's paw in one small element of this mighty conflict. Although both King Jaume and Robert St Clair de Roslin had put forward the suggestion that he would now be keen to avenge the wrongs done to his family by contributing in any way possible to the downfall of the Moors, Pedrito still felt no animosity towards them as a people. He knew that Muslims and Christians could live side by side in Mallorca, each respecting, to a reasonable extent, the other's beliefs, customs and culture. This had been his own experience while growing up on the island, and he'd never had any reason to wish that situation to change. Yet change it would. Intertwining religious, political and commercial forces far greater than he had ever imagined had been unleashed by King Jaume and his high-ranking Christian supporters, including the Pope himself. Nothing Pedrito could do would alter that.

So, why was he continuing on this dangerous assignment, when he could just as easily have disappeared into the mountains at nightfall, never to cross paths with the Christian king again, no matter what the outcome of current hostilities? Trust, that was the reason. The king had put his trust in him, and Pedrito's conscience would never allow him to betray that. Besides, he'd grown to like the charismatic young monarch. Despite the disparity of their backgrounds, there was something common to their natures, based on frankness and a freedom of spirit, perhaps, that had helped create a bond of friendship between them. No, Pedrito wouldn't let the king down, although he found it hard to share his alleged belief that what he'd asked him to do this night would have all that much bearing on the outcome of the crusade. But then, as the king had pointed out, Pedrito wasn't a soldier, so doubtless there were subtleties of war which he didn't understand. What he did understand, though, was that getting as far away as possible from those rock-hurling siege engines made absolute sense, and this, if precious little else, gave him a sense of relief at being where he was at present.

It also helped that he was now in a place with which he was fairly familiar. Here was the palm-fringed seafront of the city that King Jaume had admired from the heights of Na Burguesa after his victorious encounter with the Moorish king's army a few days earlier. Pedrito had frequented these wharfs and quays countless times in his youth, when landing fish from his father's boat to sell in the bustling waterside markets. But that had usually been in daylight, and there had been no thought of venturing inside the stout city walls, which now towered above him in an intimidating way that he'd never felt before.

The other thing that struck him was just how devoid of life the area was – apart from the occasional squealing, scurrying rat, that is. Not another solitary human shadow apart from his own fell on flagstones that would normally be resounding with the voices of hundreds of mariners, trinket-sellers, beggars, pickpockets, pimps and prostitutes, all bent on spending or making money in the age-old ways typical of seaports everywhere. And although there were still several vessels berthed alongside the mole, whether pirate galley, fishing boat or merchantman, none showed a lamp or any sign of occupation whatsoever. It was clear, then, that all those who had chanced to be on the waterfront of Medîna Mayûrqa when the first ships of the great Christian armada entered the bay from Santa Ponça had taken themselves safely within these same city's walls that now stood between Pedrito and the accomplishment of his mission.

He could see guards patrolling the battlements high above him and could hear their muttered snatches of conversation as they passed each other. He assumed that they had also seen him, so he shouted, '*Marhaba*! Allah is great!' just in case any trigger-happy crossbowman decided to take a potshot. But his salutation was ignored completely, Pedrito's supposition being that, if he had been granted freedom of passage by the lookouts back at the *Bab-al-balad* gate, he posed no threat to the security of the city anywhere along the seafront wall. Then again, the guards here probably thought he was only one of the usual waterside fishermen, on a nocturnal quest for any nice, plump octopus that might be lurking in a nearby rock pool.

He ventured over the wharf towards the Gate of Chains, which led from the harbour to the area of the city where both the principal mosque and the royal palace were situated. As he'd expected, the massive wooden doors of the main entrance were closed and barricaded, but there was a glimmer of light seeping through the surrounds of the little side gate. He gave the postern door a sharp knock, and almost immediately a small hatch was drawn aside, framing the scowling face of an elderly man, whose wrinkled features appeared uncannily prune-like in the underlit glow of his lantern.

'Who are you and what do you want?' was his greeting.

Pedrito offered the same reply he'd given in response to the identical question put to him by the sentry at the *Bab-al-balad* gate. He indicated his soiled clothes and muddy skin as proof of his struggles. 'Please, *please* show me the mercy of Allah and allow me sanctuary within these walls.'

The gatekeeper's reply was a grunted, 'If I had a single *dirham* for every destitute peasant who has come knocking at this door during the past few nights, I'd be a rich man.'

'There is no god except Allah,' Pedrito bluffed, 'and you, oh venerable one, have the bounty of his mercy in your hands.'

'When I see the colour of your money in my hands, then you'll see the bounty of his mercy. Until then, sleep with the rats on the quayside.' With that, the prune slammed the hatch shut in Pedrito's face.

So much for bothering to rub muck all over himself, Pedrito thought. From his robe, he took the leather pouch the king had given him and jangled its contents close to the hatch.

'Allah be praised,' the gatekeeper declared as his wizzened face appeared again in the opening. 'His bounty is boundless.' He thrust an upturned palm through the hatch. 'And I, a poor man, extend his gift of mercy to the downtrodden victims of the infidel invader.'

Pedrito placed a coin in his hand.

'You expect to receive the gift of mercy for *this*?' the gatekeeper scoffed. 'Don't be a complete idiot. Even the bounty of Allah has a going rate!'

Pedrito placed another coin in his hand.

'Now you're only half an idiot. Double this and your salvation from insanity will be complete.'

Pedrito placed two more coins in his hand.

The hatch slammed shut again, and the sound of bolts and chains being rattled resounded across the deserted quayside. The postern door creaked open, but only far enough to enable the gatekeeper to peep gingerly through the gap. 'Are you armed?' he asked, his eyes narrowing into slits of suspicion.

Pedrio assured him that he was carrying no weapons.

'Then raise your hands above your head, turn around and come through the door backwards. A detachment of archers is lined up inside here, so one wrong move by you and you'll be a human hedgehog!'

Pedrito did as instructed, and as soon as he had crossed the threshold he was told to keep shuffling backwards, hands high, for a further ten paces. While he stood there in the semi-darkness, the gatekeeper meticulously re-bolted and chained his door, all the while keeping one eye on Pedrito. He then wheeled round wielding a sword which he had produced from the shadows.

'Right,' he growled, 'come near me and you're a dead man! There's an inn some way up that street behind you. It's a rat-infested flea pit, but it's been good enough for the other peasant halfwits who've bribed their way past me, so it'll be good enough for you.' He brandished the sword threateningly. 'Now, be on your way!'

The first thing Pedrito did was to glance about him in order to ascertain the exact whereabouts of the detachment of archers who, allegedly, had been all set to use him for target practice. He wasn't all that surprised to see that the little yard in which he stood was entirely empty. There was, however, a huddle of guards lounging over the battlements above the gatehouse, and Pedrito was in no doubt that any one of those would have been ready and more than willing to alleviate boredom by welcoming him to the city with the sharp end of a javelin or crossbow bolt, should his demeanour warrant it. Consequently, he did as the gatekeeper had instructed and went quietly on his way.

He'd gone but a short distance when it became clear that he

wasn't in the city proper at all, but in a dingy and rather smelly warren of narrow, winding alleys tucked in behind the sea wall. This quarter, he concluded, would be the current domain, whether temporary or permanent, of those selfsame seafarers, ponces, whores, junk-vendors, down-and-outs and cutpurses who would normally be frequenting the harbourside at this time of night. And the street lighting for which Medîna Mayûrqa was renowned certainly hadn't been extended into this murky kasbah, where every shadowy opening and passage exuded even more menace than had the gatekeeper's version of hospitality. Pedrito was regretting more with each step that he'd turned down King Jaume's offer of a dagger.

Shortly, on rounding a corner, he noticed a glimmer of light coming from a small, barred opening in a castellated wall up ahead. As he approached, the stench of rotting fish and animal dung which permeated the kasbah was gradually supplanted by the sweet, tangy smell of citrus and the fragrant aroma of flowers, just as the throaty guffaws and squeals of simulated delight coming from behind shuttered windows were replaced by the soothing tinkle of running water.

Through the bars, he was at last granted a glimpse of the glory for which the capital city of Mallorca was famed. The opening was in what appeared to be a lesser city wall within the city's outer fortifications, and there, on the other side of a wide, palm shaded avenue rose the magnificent royal palace known as the Almudaina, its honey-stone facade, grand arches and delicately turned pillars illuminated by the warm glow of tow torches set into gardens surrounding a marble-paved courtyard. A series of elaborate fountains played at equidistant intervals between quartets of orange and lemon trees occupying the centre of this stunningly beautiful space, which was being patrolled even now by sentries dressed in gold-trimmed robes of the same pristine white that their king had been seen to wear in battle. By their very bearing, Pedrito could tell that these weren't expendable arrow fodder of the caste butchered in their thousands by the Christian invasion forces of late, but elite royal guards, selected for their ability to provide the most effective protection possible for their lord and master, Sheikh Abú Yahya Háquem.

Pedrito couldn't even begin to imagine what life was like behind those bejewelled walls for the mysterious Moorish King of Mallorca. While frequenting the quayside markets with his father over the years, Pedrito had heard many accounts of the Amir's fabulous wealth and awe-inspring presence, yet he had never actually seen him. He was said to be a brave and ruthless warrior who led by example, yet also a man who, as befitted his lofty station in the social order of the Moors, lived in unashamed luxury, his every whim catered for by suitably extensive assortments of personal attendants, bodyguards, advisors, musicians, cooks, confectioners, physicians, poets, slaves, wives and concubines.

Pedrito smiled a wry smile as he thought of how young King Jaume had admitted he secretly envied the Moorish elite their access to members of the latter two designations; wives and concubines, in constantly-available profusion for the exclusive pleasure of their master. He thought of how Sheikh Abú might currently be enjoying such perfumed delights within his sumptuous Almudaina Palace, while his Christian counterpart was obliged to make do with the company of sweaty, work-weary soldiers in a spartan encampment away to the north of the city. He then pondered how, in the event of King Jaume emerging victorious from the present war, his avowed intention of wiping every vestige of Islam from the face of Mallorca might result in the destruction of all that was so admirable about the city of which he was now enjoying a close-up view, albeit through little more than a pigeonhole.

His gaze drifted above and beyond the battlements of the royal palace to where the massive, gilded dome and intricately carved minarets of Medîna Mayûrqa's principal mosque glittered mesmerizingly in the moonlight. King Jaume had promised that, if granted victory by God, he would build a mighty cathedral to His glory on that very site. What chance, then, the survival of any other wonders the Moors had bestowed upon a city that had become such a fitting tribute to the pre-eminence of their culture?

Pedrito was stirred from his musings by the sound of a frail voice coming from a recess on the other side of the alley…

'Have pity on a poor cripple, young master. Alms, please – alms for a wretched soul who has had nothing to eat for two days.'

Pedrito was put instantly on his guard. He knew well enough that seedy dockside areas like this were the haunts of rogues and vagabonds who would cut your throat for a pinch of salt and were capable of more devious tricks than a sackful of Barbary apes.

'Step out into the open where I can see you!' he growled, thrusting a hand into a fold in his robe. 'And be warned – I have a sword here, and I won't hesitate to use it, no matter how many of you there are!'

He waited, his heart pounding, until a dejected, hooded figure hobbled out from the shadows. In what little light was filtering through the hole in the wall, he could see that it was a woman. She was walking with the aid of a crutch. She was small and stooped, and he could tell from the way her clothes hung on her that she was as skinny as a stick. As she came closer, it became apparent that the long mantle she was wearing had been stitched together from odd scraps of cloth.

She stopped in front of him and held out a shaky hand. 'Please, young master, give a hungry old woman something to buy a piece of bread. Please, in the name of Allah and all his mercy.'

As pitiable a figure as she cut, and as much as Pedrito was moved to offer her money, he couldn't help suspecting that she might be acting as some sort of decoy for accomplices who would leap out of the darkness and attack him the moment he produced his purse.

The woman raised her eyes to meet his, and as she did, the hood fell back from her head, revealing a face that, although etched with the telltale signs of a life of hardship and deprivation, still radiated a look that was unexpectedly devoid of bitterness. There was even a suggestion of dogged self-esteem in those pleading eyes now staring into Pedrito's.

'As you can see, young master, I am not a leper, neither do I care to wear a veil in the way of other women, because' – the woman paused to lift the hem of her cloak slightly – 'because a one-footed liability is unlikely to win any kind of husband, far less one who would require her to be kept in purdah.'

Pedrito felt a chill shiver run through him as the woman then pulled back the sleeve of her cloak with one hand to expose a crude metal hook strapped to her other wrist.

'With such bodily imperfections as these, what husband would care if another man looked upon my face?' The woman smiled knowingly as she watched Pedrito's reaction. 'I see you have the eyes of a compassionate young man, but spare me your sympathy. I need *no* one's pity. All I need is enough to buy a morsel of food.' She held out her hand again.

Pedrito had seen many pathetic victims of life's cruelties and inequalities during his years as a galley slave, but, although this old woman had been reduced to begging, there was an underlying air of dignity about her that stirred his admiration – even commanded his respect. Without saying a word, he dipped into his purse and placed a few coins in her palm.

'*Shukran*,' she said, then pulled the hood back over her head. 'Thank you, young master, and may Allah reward you generously in paradise.'

With that, she limped away, the tapping of her crutch echoing along the alleyway into the night.

## 18

# CLOSE ENCOUNTERS OF THE
# UNEXPECTED KIND

*THE SAME EVENING – IN THE CITY OF MEDÎNA MAYÛRQA...*

If the gatekeeper's brief description of the inn had seemed a mite less than complimentary, first impressions on entering it suggested that he had probably been understating the level of ambient squalor. Although Pedrito couldn't actually see any rats scurrying or fleas hopping, the general appearance of the place left him in little doubt that they were there in numbers all the same. As if to confirm his suspicions, a cockroach, itself about the size of a young rat, scampered over his foot and disappeared down a crack in the mud floor.

The inn, if indeed it warranted the title, appeared to be one large barn of a place, furnished with rows of rough wooden tables and benches. Along the length of two walls were curtained alcoves, which Pedrito took to be the sleeping accommodation, while along the other two walls were stalls in which were housed a selection of mules, donkeys, sheep and goats. In the middle of the floor, an open fire with a large cauldron suspended above oozed wood smoke that drifted into every corner of the room before eventually finding its way out through a hole in the roof. A small flock of hens pecked optimistically under the tables, while a puffed up cockerel strutted about eyeing his harem with an air of supercilious pride.

As far as Pedrito could make out in the meagre lantern light, the clientele with which the room was crowded included few, if any, refugee peasants. Perhaps the money such humble country folk had paid the gatekeeper had been their last, or perhaps they'd simply preferred to take their chances sleeping in alleyways rather than risk life and limb in the company of such a concentration of human detritus as was assembled within these miserable walls.

Slouched round the tables were the expected mix of harbourside undesirables, together with groups of conspicuously armed men, whom Pedrito took to be members of the Amir's army, a few huddles of shifty-looking deck hands in dirty, brine-bleached shirts, some sheepskin-caped muleteers and a cluster of Moorish pirates. This latter category was instantly recognisable to Pedrito, having been subjected for so long to the enforced company of their objectionable ilk. As if to add a final touch of melancholy to this uninviting scene, a bald-headed black man sat cross-legged and naked to the waist in the straw of one of the animal pens, his sightless eyes rolling in his head as he plucked the strings of a lute and moaned a wordless dirge to a pair of disinterested donkeys.

Pedrito now decided that, on balance, the truest description the gatekeeper could have given of this establishment would have been a stable polluted with human vermin, rather than an inn infested by rats and fleas. But, either way, it was a hell-hole from which he resolved to make himself scarce just as soon as he'd done what he came here to do.

A fat, greasy-looking fellow, dressed in a robe that might once have been white, was sitting by the fire, sweating profusely as he stirred whatever foul-smelling concoction was bubbling in the cauldron. '*Ahlan wa sahlan*! Welcome!' he shouted when he noticed Pedrito standing inside the door. 'You want a bed? A girl? We have the best. Or maybe you want food. We also have the best.' He tapped the pot with his ladle. 'Rabbit stew with onions.'

It instantly occurred to Pedrito that the alleys in the kasbah had been surprisingly devoid of cats as he passed through. 'Uh, no thank you,' he said to the innkeeper. 'Just, uhm – just some bread, olives and a cup of water, *min fadlak*.'

The innkeeper shrugged, burped freely and, with a twitch of his ladle, directed Pedrito to a solitary wooden stool placed against the wall by the door. He then bellowed Pedrito's order across the room to a grubby waif of a boy cowering by a screened-off opening, which Pedrito assumed led to some sort of kitchen or pantry. Two more well-fed cockroaches raced out as the boy slunk in.

No sooner had Pedrito made himself as comfortable as possible on his stool than he noticed he was being eyed with obvious suspicion by one of three soldiers eating from a communal bowl at a nearby table. He was a sinister-looking character – full-bearded, dark-skinned, with beady eyes exuding menace and a livid scar running down one cheek. His clothes, like those of his companions, looked as if they hadn't seen the inside of a washtub in recent memory, and comprised a short, sleeveless gambeson worn over a full-length shirt of coarse linen. This suggested to Pedrito that these weren't members of the elite royal guard which patrolled the Almudaina Palace grounds, but were more likely only lowly foot soldier of the sort who would be considered expendable by their battlefield superiors. And the dour expression worn by Scarface indicated that his allotted rung on the military ladder suited him just fine. He was a potential arrow-stopper, and proud of it.

'Haven't seen you in here before,' he barked at Pedrito, wiping a sliver of soggy onion from his beard with a loose fold of his head scarf. 'What's your story, eh?'

Pedrito gave him the same reply he'd given twice already tonight.

Scarface smirked. 'A farmer, huh? A fat lot of good you'll be if it comes to helping us defend the city against them Christian pigs.'

'Well,' said Pedrito, with what he hoped would pass for a gormless smile, 'I'm used to hauling ploughed-up rocks off the fields with my mule, so maybe I could help fetch boulders for your war engines, no? I saw the Christians towing what looked like two big rock-throwing contraptions up from Porto Pi on my way here.' He feigned a nervous look. 'I mean, I – I hope we've got machines in the city good enough to give them their own back, or – or I might have been safer staying hidden out in the country, no?'

The soldiers glanced at each other and chortled.

'Give them their own back?' Scarface pooh-poohed. '*Two* big rock-throwing contraptions, says you? Pah! We got a couple of *trebuchet* mechanical slings bigger than anything they got, plus fourteen really powerful *algarrada* catapults that'll smash their tents and everyone in them to smithereens once we gets them going right.'

'That's right,' one of his companions eagerly confirmed, 'and we should know, because we've spent all day setting them up on the ramparts either side of the *Bab-al-kofol* gate over on the north quarter of the city there. Our boys will pound that camp into the ground before them Christians have had time to shove their silly bits of siege artillery even half way within range of ours.'

Scarface couldn't have agreed more. 'Absolutely!' he enthused, then prodded his comrade on the shoulder. 'And don't forget, mate – if we needs to, we got plenty materials inside the city to build as many war engines as we wants, while the enemy only has what little heavy timber our lookouts seen them strip from their own ships today.'

'But – but surely the enemy would need to be really desperate to do that,' Pedrito gasped, wide-eyed with fake incredulity. 'I mean, they say out in the countryside that a big fleet has been sent by our brothers in Africa to attack the Christians, so surely they'd be stupid to damage their own ships.'

The soldiers shared another derisory chuckle.

'It don't never fail to amaze me just how gullible you country bumpkins on this island can be,' Scarface snorted. 'A big fleet from our brothers in Africa, says you? Listen, boy, us in the know here in the city found out days ago that that was never going to happen.'

Pedrito allowed his jaw to drop. 'Honestly? You mean – you mean it was just a false rumour put about to worry the enemy?'

Scarface dipped a hand into the communal bowl and pulled out an alleged rabbit leg. 'Rumour, says you?' he slavered between bites. 'Rumour? Depends what you means by rumour, don't it, boy?' He prised a shred of meat from between his front teeth with a dirt-ingrained finger nail, surveyed the morsel for a moment, rolled it between forefinger and thumb, then popped it back in his mouth. 'Rumour? Nah, us in the know always knowed it was more than that. Didn't we, lads?'

While Scarface continued to devour his dubious dinner, the third member of his group, patently keen to show off his superior urban awareness to an ignorant yokel like Pedrito, took up where his mate had left off. He readily divulged that there had indeed been a plan to summon reinforcements from Africa, but the Amir's message had never left the island, intercepted as it had been by a member of his own family, an uncle by the name of Abú Hafs Ibn Sheyri.

Pedrito donned his incredulous mask again. 'But why would the king's own flesh and blood want to do such a treacherous thing? I mean, we farmers always say that our family is even more important to us than our animals – well, almost.'

Sniggering, the three soldiers exchanged mocking glances, then Scarface resumed the role of group spokesman...

'That, boy, is what centuries of breeding with your own sisters and mothers has done for you peasants. You ain't capable of thinking except in straight lines.' After his two comrades had given that quip grunted nods of approval, he added, 'Yes, and even then, your tiny minds goes round in circles!'

Scraps of half-chewed meat and stewed onion flew in all directions from gaping mouths as the three arrow-stoppers laughed their fill at this brilliant punch line.

Pedrito had felt his hackles rising at the derogatory remark about mothers and sisters, and for a moment it had revived all the pain and sadness of his recent loss. But trying to alleviate his grief by rising to the bait of these buffoons would do him more harm than good. The odds would be stacked against him if he attacked them physically, and displaying a bit of intellect to put them in their place verbally – which he knew he was more than capable of doing – would be both a waste of breath and tantamount to admitting that he was an impostor, with all the disastrous consequences that this would invite. He decided, therefore, to maintain his country bumpkin persona.

'I'm sorry, sir,' he said, while scratching his head and smiling vacantly, 'but I still don't understand why the king's own uncle would want to stop help coming from Africa.'

'And you doesn't need to understand,' Scarface came back.

'Even us what's in the know here in the city doesn't need to understand. All we needs remember is that them sheikhs and amirs and caliphs and suchlike that rules the roost only holds onto power by staying one move ahead of them that's nipping at their heels – and that's usually one of their own. So, King Abú's Uncle Abú tries to knock him off his perch by stopping the reinforcements. How would that help Uncle Abú grab power, says you?' Scarface hunched his shoulders. 'Who knows? But whatever the ins and outs of his plan, the king got wind of it, he's still in charge, and his uncle, as likely as not, is rotting in a dungeon by now – *if* he's still alive.' Scarface tapped the side of his nose. 'That's what it means to be a member of one of them top families, boy, and that's why the likes of us common soldiers does as they tells us.' He pointed a rabbit-size leg bone at Pedrito. 'Yes, and *you*'d better learn double-quick to do the same, as long as you're inside them here big-city walls.' He pointed to his ear through his headdress. 'And don't forget, boy – big-city walls has eyes as well as them here things!'

Pedrito smiled inwardly. This mission was going a lot more easily than he'd dared hope. In the space of little more than a couple of minutes, he'd already ascertained the approximate number and location of the Moor's war engines, and had also been informed that there was no longer any threat of a backup fleet arriving from North Africa. Admittedly, the source of these items of military intelligence probably wasn't of the most elevated variety, but it was certainly about as reliable as he was likely to gain access to in the short time available.

Feeling buoyed up by this, he professed his unease at being trapped in the city when its garrison had already been depleted to such a large extent. He told of how he had seen the bodies of so many of the Sheikh's soldiers lying on the slopes of Na Burgeusa Mountain as he passed by earlier in the day. There had been hundreds of them, he said, maybe even thousands. Yes, and someone on the road had told him there had been even more killed in battles near Santa Ponça a day or two before. And, he went on, someone else had told him that those who survived these encounters had taken refuge up in the mountains. How, then, could the city be defended against the huge Christian army now that African reinforcements weren't going to come after all? He put this last question with what he hoped would be taken as a note of panic in his voice.

Scarface glowered at him disdainfully, before muttering that there were still as many soldiers in the city as those deployed to the mountains – three thousand, maybe four, maybe even five. Who was counting anyway? And then there were the civilians – fifty thousand of them, and every man, woman and child ready to fight like lions to keep the Christian pigs out.

Pedrito gathered his brows into a puzzled frown. '*Deployed* to the mountains? Sorry, sir – I don't understand.'

'You peasants just doesn't get the subtleties of battle strategy, does you?' Scarface gave an impatient shake of his head. 'Pathetic! I mean, it can't be *that* difficult to grasp, can it?'

Pedrito flashed him an uncertain smile. 'Uhm, what can't?'

Scarface inhaled a slow sigh of exasperation, then proceeded to elucidate. 'It's all a crafty move dreamed up by the Sheikh to lure them Christians into their present position, that's what. Understand now?'

Slack-jawed, Pedrito indicated the negative.

Scarface tutted impatiently, then marked three crosses in the grease of the table top with his alleged rabbit bone. 'This here's the city, right? And that there's the mountains, right? And this here cross in the middle of them two crosses is the Christan camp, right?'

Pedrito nodded, vacuously.

Scarface muttered an oath. 'It's what we calls a pincer movement in military parlance, right!' The leg-bone pointer came into play again. 'This here's our war engines – or rock-throwing contraptions, as you calls them – and they're pounding that there Christian camp, right? Right, and when them Christians has been pounded senseless, our lads charges down from the mountains and attacks them, while we does the same from inside the city.' He stared into Pedrito's eyes in search of any glimmer of battle-strategy comprehension that might be flickering there. 'Pincer movement, right? Simple. Just like you, boy.' He turned away and plunged his hand into the communal bowl again. 'Peasants?' he harrumphed to his comrades. 'Cretins, the lot of them. Telling you – this here rabbit's got more brains!'

'You're not wrong,' one of his mates concurred, 'and it's probably only half as inbred and all!'

This shaft of soldierly wit elicted even more food-spraying guffaws from the trio of troopers.

Pedrito smiled a suitably cretinous smile throughout, while contemplating, perhaps a tad morbidly, that even cat passed off as rabbit might soon become a luxury for those besieged inside these walls. Not even the inn's rat population would be safe from the stew pot then. And what about the soldiers' smug assertion that the situation of the separated remains of their army was actually a cunning pincer-movement strategy devised by their king to trap the Christians? Pedrito knew that even the most unmilitary of minds would suspect that the Moorish forces hiding in the mountains were hardly likely to pose an immediately sustainable threat to anyone, routed as they had been and forced to abandon much of their weaponry on the battlefield. No, as with the claim that the absence of seaborne reinforcements from Africa would be of little consequence, what these potential arrow-stoppers had eagerly swallowed was nothing more than a generous helping of morale-boosting propaganda, fed to them by an understandably concerned hierarchy. That was Pedrito's reading of the situation, anyway, and it was the conclusion he would report to King Jaume at the earliest opportunity – given, of course, that he managed to get himself back out of the city again.

During his exchange with the three soldiers, who, it eventually transpired, were actually mercenaries from the south of mainland Spain, Pedrito had been keeping a discreet eye on a group of six pirates sitting at a table a little farther into the room. And a pretty unsavoury-looking bunch they were. All were clad in the typical attire of Moorish corsairs, which in most cases amounted to minor personal variations on a fairly universal theme; heads wrapped in turbans; flowing capes draped over shoulders; open-fronted tunics girt at the waist with broad sashes; long, billowing 'Sinbad' pants gathered in at the ankle; wrists and fingers dripping with gold. Each man had a scimitar sheathed in a spangled scabbard dangling at his side, and, apart from the trim of respective beards, the only other noticeable difference in their appearance was the individual choice of garish colours for each item of clothing. As much as Pedrito, for good reason, had grown to detest the very sight of their breed, he was still obliged to concede that they did present a striking image, albeit one bristling with wanton savagery.

Four of the pirates were entertaining ladies of the world's oldest profession, who looked, even in the dim light of the inn, like prime examples of mutton dressed as lamb. Not that dress was one of their most obvious features. Rather the lack of it. Muslim rules governing female modesty clearly meant nothing to this clutch of sirens, nor did their well-used appearance seem to matter a whit to their present clients, who, fair to say, were showing signs of having consumed copious quantities of vision-deluding drink.

The increase in noise coming from their table had been consistent with the pirates' intake of wine. As with the women's immodest dress, no regard was being paid to accepted Islamic principles in relation to the drinking of alcohol, which was generally thought, at least by many non-Muslims, to be forbidden. Pedrito recalled, however, that his pirate-galley friend and mentor *al-Usstaz*, 'The Professor', had told him that some Muslims, particularly those of higher rank, chose to interpret the Koran's pronouncement on the subject as meaning that imbibing would actually be condoned by Allah, with the one stipulation that the common man should never enter a mosque for prayers in a state of drunkenness. In other words, prudent moderation was mandatory – at least in the case of the common man.

There was no doubt that these pirates could rightly be classified as 'common', and in the most derogatory sense of the word at that. Although Moors, the only gods these fellows worshipped were those of greed and violence, so there was no chance of them ever entering a mosque at even one of the five daily prayer times. They could feel absolutely free, therefore, to get drunk whenever they wanted, and now was clearly one of those occasions. What's more, they were acting as if they owned the place, which, it could be said, they effectually did. And this applied not just to this sleazy inn, but to the entire island. For without the revenues gleaned from plunder that the ruler of Mallorca received from the fleets of Moorish pirate vessels to which he granted safe haven, his little kingdom would never have become so fabulously rich. Yet, ironically, it was the persistent attacks on their merchant ships by Mallorcan-based corsairs that had stimulated the Catalonian call for this all-out war against King Abû in the first place.

But if any of this had ever been a cause for concern to the six pirates present here, they were certainly doing a fine job of disguising the fact. Uttering a string of curses, the two 'unattached' men got to their feet and, swaying as if on deck in a heavy swell, informed everyone within earshot that they were abandoning ship. They were off, they said, to find a sweeter-smelling brothel than this stinking slops bucket – one where the whores looked more like mermaids than the beached whales disguised as women who flogged their pox-ridden wares in here. This declaration elicited an explosion of raucous laughter, not only from their drunken shipmates, but also from their respective beached whales, who presumably accepted that it was ultimately more profitable to take such insults in apparent good humour than to spit in their clients' faces.

One of the two departing pirates had been sitting with his back to Pedrito, and from this angle he'd looked pretty much the same as the others, apart from being considerably bulkier. But the moment he turned round, Pedrito's heart skipped a beat. The gold ring piercing the septum between his nostrils instantly identified him as *al-Tawr*, 'the Bull', one of the most bestial of all the slave masters Pedrito had had the misfortune to encounter during his years as an oarsman on that damned galley. However, the nose ring wasn't the only reason why this lumbering brute of a man was called the Bull. When sober, he could just about be relied upon to threaten female captives with nothing more harmful than a salacious look and a few ruttish grunts. But when under the influence of drink, the Bull lived up to his name – or would, if not physically restrained by his shipmates and, more often than not, left to sleep off his lustful urges courtesy of a persuasive blow to the back of his head with the haft of a scimitar. Female captives were, after all, potential sources of rich rewards at slave markets, and premium prices could always be expected for younger girls presented as being *virgo intacta*. Unfortunately, this category of female prisoner also topped the Bull's list of preferences when in a fever of drink-induced lechery, and he had the scars on the back of his head to prove it.

He was indeed a nasty piece of work, given to unprovoked and vicious acts of aggression, to the extent of being known to run people through for no better reason than having disliked the way they'd looked at him. And now he was staggering towards the door where Pedrito was sitting. Suddenly, panic surged through Perdrito's veins. If the Bull recognised him, the clandestine mission King Jaume had dispatched him on would surely be terminated in a pool of blood, Pedrito's blood, right here and now. And recognise him the Bull almost certainly would, because he had been the leader of the slave-taking party from which Pedrito had escaped near the Catalonian hamlet of Sitges earlier in the year. Pedrito tugged the front of his head wrap down over his eyes, then dipped his head as if appraising the bread and olives on the plate now resting on his knees.

He heard the padding shuffle of the Bull's footsteps stop in front of him, cringed at the rasp of his laboured breathing, gagged at the pungency of his closeness. The all-too-familiar smells of the galley, stale sweat and urine, were now augmented by the nauseous whiff of spirit liquor. Pedrito thought again of *al-Usstaz* and how he had claimed that it had been a devout Muslim alchemist who, while experimenting with the development of subtle perfumes, had discovered, reputedly by mistake, how to distil brandy from wine. How ironic, then, that a religion which advocated temperance should spawn the creation of such a powerful intoxicant, and one ultimately so highly prized by those not subject to the righteous constraints of Islam. The Bull reeked of the stuff.

Pedrito held his breath as he watched grimy fingers hover above his plate, then grab a handful of olives. Without daring to lift his eyes, he waited, fully expecting the scarf to be whipped from his head at any moment. But when the Bull's hand eventually reappeared, it was only to fling spat-out olive stones back onto the plate. He then broke wind, cursed the inn and everyone in it, before finally lurching out of the door arm-in-arm with his mermaid-seeking companion.

Hardly had Pedrito's pulse rate returned to normal when it was sent racing again by the sound of a blood-curdling scream coming from the alley outside the inn. Hearing it so soon after his close encounter with the Bull reminded him chillingly of the despairing cries of the girls taken captive on the pirate galley. It also made him think of his little sister Esperanza and how she had fallen victim to just such a horrific fate. Instinctively, he got to his feet.

'Relax, boy,' Scarface the soldier drawled. 'Chances are it's only some of the lads having a bit of fun. Happens all the time in garrison towns like this, and them here Mallorcan floozies loves it. Thrives on a bit of rough and tumble, they does.' He nonchalantly held up his latest miniature leg of meat and surveyed it approvingly. 'Mmm, and they goes like rabbits and all!'

But his words were lost on Pedrito. Although he had managed so far to suppress the most repugnant thoughts regarding details of what might actually have happened to his family, all he could see in his mind's eye now was an image of his sister being maltreated by some filthy pirates like the Bull and his coterie of scum. In a trice, he had flung his plate onto the soldiers' table and was out of the door and into the alley.

It took only a few seconds for his eyes to adjust to the gloom. There, just as he'd envisaged, was the unmistakable outline of the Bull, abetted by his crony, setting upon a girl in a doorway opposite. Although Pedrito couldn't see her, hidden as she was by the Bull's bulk, he could hear her frantic pleadings, and it was obvious from the timbre of her voice that she was indeed young. Moreover, no matter what Scarface had so disparagingly said about the 'romantic' predilections of the city's women, it was abundantly clear that this one was not in any way enjoying the treatment she was being subjected to by these two debauched bilge rats.

'Hold her arms!' the Bull's mate growled. 'Fights like a wildcat, this one!'

'All the better,' the Bull puffed. 'Nothing like a bit o' spirit in a young *bint*, eh, Samak?'

His temper rising, Pedrito repeated the name to himself. '*Samak* – the Fish – and a rotten one, just like the way he smells!'

'Wearing the *niqāb*, eh?' Samak grunted. 'We'll have that off you, darling. Have a look at your pretty little face, uh!'

'Never mind her face,' the Bull panted. 'All I'm interested in is her... Ouch! She – she bit my hand, the bitch!' He raised his fist. 'Right, you'll pay for that, you dirty little slut!'

'Want to try that with somebody your own size?' Pedrito cut in, grabbing the Bull's wrist and wheeling him round. There was so much adrenalin pumping through Pedrito's body now that he was incapable of thinking clearly. What he did next, therefore, was purely an automatic act of survival. As the pirate lunged at him, he hooked a finger through his nose ring and tugged downwards with all his strength.

The sound that filled the alley now was more animal than human, and more like the shriek of a wounded mule than the bellow of a charging bull. Pedrito knew there was nothing more dangerous than a wild beast when injured, so, however illogically, he swiftly went about putting this one out of its agony by inflicting even more. He felt the sinew between the Bull's nostril's tear as he yanked his head lower still, felt the saliva splattering his hand as the Bull screamed a string of oaths, felt the crunch of breaking teeth as he brought up a knee to meet the Bull's jaw.'

'That was from all the young girls you've abused,' Pedrito snarled, then kneed him again, this time in the groin. 'And that was from me! I've been longing to do that since the first time I set eyes on your ugly face!' All at once, the pent-up anger and resentment caused by years of suffering at the hands of the Bull and his like was coming to the surface, and Pedrito wasn't holding anything back. As the Bull doubled over in pain, Pedrito smashed a fist into his face. With blood streaming down his beard, the pirate sank into an unconcious heap at Pedrito's feet.

Then Pedrito saw the Fish hurl the girl across the alley, where she collapsed, stunned, at the base of the wall.

'You bastard son of a sow!' the Fish snarled as he lurched towards Pedrito, his hand reaching for the hilt of his scimitar. 'Prepare to draw your last breath, you worthless piece of pig shit!'

Pedrito backed into the doorway, desperately glancing about for an escape route. But the Fish was barring his way, scimitar drawn and raised for the kill. Pedrito was unarmed, so there was nothing he could do but close his eyes and wait for the fatal blow. He'd often heard it said that, when faced with certain death, your entire life flashes before you, but all he could sense now was a paralysing terror and a sickening feeling of absolute helplessness. His knees buckled as the sound of blade scything through air assailed his ears. For a split second, his memory returned to the time when, aboard the royal galley, King Jaume had teased him with a similar threat of death by the sword. But there was nothing jocular about this situation. The Fish was about to kill him, and the best Pedrito could hope for was that the end would be swift, clean and reasonably painless.

Time seemed to stand still while he listened to the swish of the scimitar descending, then felt the touch of its cold steel. As the razor-sharp blade cut into his skin, he heard a dull '*thwack*'. Then nothing. He felt a trickle of blood on his neck. But he was still breathing, his head was still attached to his shoulders. Gingerly, he opened his eyes, just in time to see the Fish stagger backwards and collapse in a heap on top of his comatose mate.

'You should be careful who you pick fights with, young master,' said a frail, familiar voice. 'Lucky I was here to look after you.'

Pedrito blinked tears of shock from his eyes as they focused on the diminutive form of the old beggar woman to whom he'd given a few coins earlier. She was standing in the shadows just a couple of paces away, swaying slightly as she hitched her crutch back under her arm.

'I've used the head of this peg for a few unusual things over the years, but this is the first time I've had to fell someone with it.' There was an impish smile on the old woman's face, but it was quickly replaced by a look that was deadly serious. She motioned towards the girl lying dazed and trembling against the wall. 'Quick, get her onto her feet. We'll have to make ourselves scarce before these two animals wake up.'

Pedrito was too dumbfounded to say anything, so he dutifully did what he was told. Whispering reassuring words, he took the girl's hand and, supporting her by the elbow, gently helped her up.

The girl began to sob, her whole body quivering as the shocking reality of her ordeal finally gripped her. She looked up at Pedrito with terror in her eyes.

He put an arm round her shoulders and stroked her hair. 'It's all right, it's all right,' he murmured. 'It's all right – nobody's going to hurt you now.'

'Hurry, young master!' the old woman hissed, then prodded the unconscious pirates with the tip of her crutch. 'Even if this pair stay in dreamland for a while yet, there's always plenty more like them prowling about this rat warren at night. So, come on. If you value your lives, follow me home. *Now!*'

## 19

# A HEART-RENDING REVELATION

*A LITTLE LATER THE SAME NIGHT –*
*IN THE 'KASBAH' QUARTER OF MEDÎNA MAYÛRQA...*

The 'home' the old woman led Pedrito and the girl to was one of several lean-to shacks built side-by-side against the city's sea wall and facing onto a small, rundown yard with a well in the centre. This, she explained, was where some of the city's merchants stored the baskets into which they decanted fish bought from boats at the quayside. From here, they would take the baskets by donkey or mule to whichever parts of the city were recognised as their individual trading areas, there to sell their wares door-to-door.

The storage shack she ushered them towards doubled as a tiny stable, which, it was revealed, she shared with a donkey called *Masoud*, or 'Lucky'; an apt name, she said, as the donkey ate better than she did herself these days. She admitteded that times had never been particularly bounteous for someone with her disabilities, but since the Christian invasion and the consequent disruption of trading with the fishermen, the merchant who paid her a few *dirhams* to guard his store and look after his donkey had stopped coming down here, with the result that she was now reduced to begging in order to stay alive. At least she had a roof over her head, though, and for this she thanked Allah in all his mercy.

It had taken only a few minutes to reach here from the scene of the altercation with the two pirates; an urgent flight through one dingy, winding passageway after another, with Pedrito supporting the faltering girl as best he could, while also trying to keep up with the old woman, who, in defiance of her handicap, hobbled along at a surprisingly brisk pace. He had murmured soothing words to the girl as they went along, but the only responses she gave were little whimpering sounds and a few indistinct pleas about taking her home to her mother. As she was considerably shorter than Pedrito, all he could see of her was the top of her head, but he could tell by the touch of his hand on her waist that the long *abaya* robe she was wearing was of the smoothest silk. Also, there rose from her the hint of a perfume that was far too subtle for Pedrito to define, but which positively oozed opulence. How, he wondered, could such a delicate little flower as this have strayed at night into the squalor of the kasbah, with all its inherent dangers? Although he knew nothing about her or even what she really looked like, apart from that brief glimpse of her terror-filled eyes, he'd found himself feeling relieved that the girl's beguiling scent had remained unsullied by the attentions of those stinking pirates, and he was stirred by an inexplicably deep hope that she had suffered no physical harm at their hands either. Perhaps, he pondered, he was merely reacting in some indirect way to the hitherto unthinkable plight of his little sister.

'Here!' the old woman said before Pedrito was even over the threshhold of her shack. 'Take this jug and fill it with water while I light a lantern in here.' She beckoned the girl. 'Come, my dear – come inside with me. And try not to cry any more. No harm will come to you now, I promise.'

Her words lingered in Pedrito's ears as he drew some water from the well. As sincere as the old woman's promise had doubtless been, he was compelled to wonder just how she could possibly hope to honour it. In a few hours, the Christian assault would commence and, although this would be concentrated initially on one specific section of Medîna Mayûrqa's northern defences, there was no telling how long it might be before its effects were felt throughout the city. If the walls were breached quickly, there was a very real likelihood – going by the results of the preceding days' confrontations – that the Christian incursion would be swift, incisive and typically merciless. And the inhabitants of the kasbah could expect no more quarter than those privileged to live in more affluent areas of the city.

'Shut the door behind you and bolt it,' the old woman told Pedrito when he returned from the well. 'And pour a little water into this bowl so that I can clean these grazes on our little lady's face here.' She had dispensed with her crutch now and was hopping about with surprising agility on her one foot. Clucking like a mother hen, she rested her behind on an upturned basket and began to tenderly dab at the girl's injuries with a wad of cloth, which, Pedrito noticed, was as scrupulously clean as everything else in this tiny shelter, including Lucky the donkey's stall, generously bedded as it was with fresh straw.

The girl was sitting with her back to the door on a wooden stool, which appeared to be the only item of furniture in the room, other than a dilapidated half barrel, on which was placed a lantern, the shack's sole source of light.

The old woman, ever watchful, had noticed Pedrito taking in his surroundings. 'And in case you're wondering where I sleep,' she said with the same puckish smile she had shown after flooring the pirate with the heavy end of her crutch, 'it's over there in the straw beside Lucky. We have an arrangement,' she winked. 'I respect the donkey's celibacy, and he respects my chastity.'

Once more, Pedrito was moved to admire the pluck of this unfortunate soul, who not only accepted her lot with stoicism, but managed to make the best of it with surprising flashes humour as well.

'Come round here,' she said to Pedrito. 'Fetch the lantern and hold it closer to me. I need to make sure these scratches are properly cleaned.' She tutted in disgust. 'Who knows what filth was under the fingernails of those smelly apologies for human beings.' She gave the girl a reassuring smile. 'But don't worry, *habib* – they're really only little blemishes. Nobody will notice them after a day or two.'

The girl was trembling all over, clearly still in a state of shock. She flinched as the cold water of the old woman's cloth touched a scuff of broken skin.

The woman turned to Pedrito and gestured with a nod towards the sleeve of her cloak which covered the hook she'd shown him earlier. 'I need you to give me a hand – literally. Hold her face steady while I wipe away the grit from this scratch.' She smiled comfortingly at the girl again. 'This may chafe a little, *habib*, but I'll be as careful as I can, I promise.'

Pedrito placed the tips of his fingers under the girl's chin and gently lifted her face up to the light. She winced as the old woman swabbed the scratch, but not even the resultant grimace could deter Pedrito from thinking that this girl had the most beautiful face he had ever seen. It was olive-skinned and perfectly oval, with a dainty little nose and enormous dark eyes, which, even when filled with tears as they were now, would be capable, Pedrito thought, of capturing anyone's heart. They had certainly captured his. Pedrito was smitten, and he knew from that instant that the feelings this girl had aroused in him earlier were not of the brotherly kind after all.

She may have been small of stature, but something told Pedrito that her figure, although concealed beneath the flowing silk of her *hijab*, would be, in all probability, perfectly formed. As he brushed a wisp of long raven hair from the girl's face to expose another graze, the velvety touch of her skin sent a shiver running through him. The girl, sensing this, lowered her eyes coyly. But as she did, Pedrito thought he noticed the faintest suggestion of a smile playing at the corner of her lips.

The old woman glanced up at him and smiled that knowing little smile of hers.

Pedrito felt his cheeks colour. 'I, uhm – I think,' he stammered, 'there's another little graze just, uh, just there to the left of her eye.'

The old woman nodded, smiled to herself, but made no comment.

To cover his embarrassment, Pedrito decided to point out yet another blemish, this one on the girl's forehead. 'I heard the pirates saying something about a veil, a *niqāb*, so maybe they made that mark when they pulled –'

'Why don't you ask the little lady yourself,' the old woman butted in. 'But perhaps you should tell us your name first, no?'

Pedrito had become aware that, since entering the old woman's domain, she had stopped addressing him as 'young master' and had adopted an altogether less subservient demeanour. While still the epitome of good manners, she left him in no doubt that she was queen of her own castle, no matter how humble. And it was now obvious that she had decided that breaking the social ice would be a good way to begin bringing the girl out of her defensive shell.

'I – I'm really sorry,' Pedrito flustered. 'I should have said. It's … it's Pedrito. My name is … Pedrito.'

'Pleased to meet you, Pedrito,' the old woman came back breezily. 'I'm called Farah, and I hope you'll excuse me if I don't shake hands. I've only one, as you know, and it's otherwise occupied at present.' She let out a little giggle, as if privately enjoying this little dig at her own infirmity. She then looked directly at Pedrito and said, 'Pedrito – Little Pedro in Spanish, isn't it? Surely that's a strange name for a big, burly lad like you, no?'

Pedrito shuffled his feet uneasily. He thought that recounting the story of his foundling origins would bring to mind too many fond memories of his parents and aggravate the still-raw pain of their loss. Then again, he realised that the old woman and the girl whose injuries she was caring for would undoubtedly have bitter stories of their own to tell, so why shouldn't he have the courage to tell them his?

'My parents,' he began, 'called me Pedrito when I was a tiny baby, and the name just sort of stuck, I suppose. And yes, since I grew up, being called *Little* Pedro has made me the butt of a few jokes, I admit.' He shrugged his shoulders. 'But –'

'But it's a nice name.'

Pedrito and the old woman exchanged glances that were a blend of surprise and relief. The girl's voice, soft as it was, had betrayed hardly a tremor.

'It's a nice name,' the girl repeated, as if finding confidence in her defence of Pedrito, 'and you shouldn't pay attention to anyone who makes fun of it – even though it *is* a Christian name.'

She was looking into Pedrito's eyes now, and he felt his knees go weak again, but for an entirely different reason from the one that had caused the same reaction from Fish the pirate's scimitar.

'Pedrito,' the girl said again, then paused to offer him a melting little smile. 'My name is Saleema, and I'm grateful to you for saving my life.'

Pedrito found himself stammering again. 'Well, uhm, no – it was nothing, because – well, it was actually Farah here who saved *both* of our lives.' He gave Farah a sheepish look. 'And, well, I should have thanked you before for that, so I'm – well, I'm sorry and...'

Farah giggled again. 'I'm thinking that maybe Cupid just happened to come into that alleyway in the form of an old cripple with a head-crunching crutch, yes?' She grinned delightedly as she watched the two young people go all fidgety and look everywhere except at each other. 'Who needs little arrows, eh?' She laughed aloud now, before saying, 'Anyway, Pedrito, I'll spare your blushes. You were about to ask the little lady about this scratch on her forehead, weren't you?'

But Saleema beat him to it. Farah's clever little ploy of breaking the social ice had triggered a cathartic reaction in the girl, who now seemed impatient to confide the details of what had led to her falling prey to those two drunken pirates. She poceeded to reveal that she was the daughter of a Moorish shepherd, who had a small farm in the hills some way inland from the bay of Santa Ponça. A year earlier, when she was just sixteen, the w*ali*, the overseer of that part of the island, had told her parents that she had been recommended by him to join the Mallorcan king's court. The w*ali* said that he had watched Saleema grow from childhood into a beautiful young woman, and it was his opinion that she would meet with the king's favour – as a concubine.

Pedrito caught his breath, while Saleema paused to glance at him. She then went on to explain that to have such a compliment bestowed on one of their daughters was generally considered to be a great honour by humble Muslim families like hers, although any disinclination on her parents' part to accept the invitation would have been ignored anyway. She had been summoned to become a member of the king's harem in the Almudaina Palace, so a member of the king's harem she duly became.

It had broken her heart to leave her mother, and she had cried herself to sleep every night for weeks after becoming installed with over a hundred other girls – most of them older, though some even younger – in the sumptuous surroundings of the king's private quarters within the palace grounds.

Pedrito noticed that Farah had frowned and nodded her head almost imperceptibly at this admission of Saleema's. But she remained silent. Also, for the first time, Pedrito was able to take a close look at Farah's face in the direct light of the lantern, and he was suddenly made aware that she was not, perhaps, as old as he had previously thought. Although there was no denying that her features revealed the evidence of a life of hardship, there was an underlying vibrancy about her look as well. Pedrito was intrigued, but any revelations about Farah's past would have to wait until Saleema had completed her own. She was in full flow now, and clearly deriving great relief from being able to get it all off her chest.

She related how the first few months in the palace were spent being tutored in the etiquettes of the royal household by former concubines. These women had passed their prime, in their king's eyes at any rate, but had been favoured by being retained as members of his large train of female servants, along with whatever children they may have had by him. During this time, the king would pay periodic visits to the harem to make, according to his whim, a 'selection' from within the ranks of his more experienced concubines, while also appraising the assets of the novices and discussing their progress with the head eunuch. In this context, 'progress' meant the girls' aptitude to learn and accept the king's somewhat individualistic partialities in the ways of the flesh.

Pedrito was relieved to hear Saleema add that even the thought of being touched by that strutting peacock of a man – old enough to be her father, if not her grandfather – did nothing to her own flesh but make it creep.

Fortunately, as the months passed, the feeling of worthlessness that came from being pampered on the one hand and regarded as a mere chattel on the other had been balanced by a sense of thankfulness for not yet being chosen to join the king in the isolation of his personal chambers. Saleema drew a wry smile from Farah when she declared flippantly that it was a wonder the old rake had the energy to satisfy all his wives, never mind attempt to sample frequent 'side dishes' picked from his extensive menu of concubines.

Pedrito liked this girl's spirit. Although a Muslim and, for all he knew, a devout one, she didn't appear to subscribe to the received Islamic tenet that women should automatically accept that they were subordinate to men.

Then, as if to substantiate this impression, she said, 'My father gives my mother more respect than he does the ewes in his flock of sheep – as well he should – so why should I allow myself to be regarded as nothing more than a young doe by a lecherous old buck rabbit?' It was for this reason, she continued, that she had resolved to escape from the royal palace before the king had finally decided to 'honour' her with a command to join him in his gossamer-draped burrow. And her chance had come earlier this very day.

The palace, she explained, had been in an unprecedented state of disorder as measures were taken to reinforce its defences against any possible attack by the Spanish invaders. Although the king had been going to great lengths to assure everyone in the city that the Christians would soon be driven back off the island, it had become obvious nonetheless that he was taking no chances with his own security. So, while the palace guards were preoccupied in supervising the bolstering of the Almudaina's fortifications, Saleema borrowed a hooded cape from one of the kitchen maids and slipped out of the palace by a door normally used only by the lowlier members of the royal staff. She had then made her way through the busy streets, neither knowing where she was nor where she was going, until finally finding herself at dusk in the kasbah quarter. There had still been plenty of people about, and after asking for directions to the nearest city gate, she found a little alcove in a quiet passageway and hid there until nightfall. Then, alone now in the deserted maze of alleys, she crept through the darkness towards, she hoped, the Gate of Chains and, *inshallah*, to her freedom.

'I was frightened, and I wasn't even sure if I was going in the right direction any more. Then I saw a glow of light coming from what appeared to be an inn, so I ... then those two men ... they tore the cloak from me and –' She stopped abruptly, wringing her hands, tears welling in her eyes again.

'History repeats itself,' Farah muttered, almost inaudibly, then added, 'though not completely, thanks be to Allah.'

Pedrito wondered what she'd meant by that. He hesitated for a moment, unsure whether or not he should pry into something that may have been nothing more than a casual remark. But, as ever, his innate sense of curiosity got the better of him.

'History repeats itself, you said. Sorry if I'm poking my nose in where I shouldn't, but –'

Farah wagged a finger. 'You don't want to hear about it, believe me.' She handed Pedrito the bowl. 'Here. I've finished tending our little lady's injuries, so put some fresh water in that and clean yourself up. Look at your face and hands – all smudged with dirt – and there's a cut on your neck – and look at your knuckles, all grazed and bloody too.'

Pedrito couldn't resist a chuckle. 'Yes, well that's what comes of punching a bull's nose with a ring in it.'

'A bull?'

'*Al-Tawr* – that's what they call the pirate I had the difference of opinion with back in the alley.'

Farah frowned again. 'And how, may I ask, do you happen to know his name?'

Pedrito shook his head. 'You don't want to hear about *that*, believe me.'

But Farah was insistent. 'Ah, but I do want to hear about it.'

'Just as I want to hear why you said history had repeated itself, maybe?'

Now Farah shook her head. 'Nobody's interested in my story. This kasbah is full of all sorts of freaks and cripples, and nobody cares about our past – least of all us freaks and cripples. No, we just get on with the life fate handed us and say nothing. It's the best way, I promise you.'

There were a few moments of silence, then it was Saleema who spoke: 'You saved our lives, Farah. Surely you can understand why we'd want to know a little about yours.'

She stared at Farah in a searching way, eliciting a look from her that suggested to Pedrito that, although these two women were complete strangers, some sort of affinity existed between them – a vital link that only they could sense. Saleema, who now seemed to have regained her composure, got to her feet and helped Farah up from the basket she had been sitting on, then onto the comparative comfort of her stool. This done, she indicated to Pedrito that he should take Farah's place on the basket, before taking the bowl of water from him and starting to clean his scuffed knuckles. She then glanced sidelong at Farah, her brows arched in anticiptaion. 'Well,' she said, 'we're waiting.'

Pedrito's admiration for this girl's spirit was increasing by the moment. Instead of wallowing in self-pity, she was picking up on Farah's positive lead and actually taking control of the situation. Even Farah herself was obliged to concede an admiring little smirk. She realised, apparently, that she had met her match in this determined little lady. So, with a sigh and a shrug, she started to tell her story...

Like Saleema, she had been taken from her parents' home in the countryside to become a concubine of the king – the same Sheikh Abú Háqem, in fact, who ruled Mallorca to this day, and whom Saleema had just described as a lecherous old rabbit. But this had been over twenty years ago and he had been a comparatively young man of not quite thirty. Farah had only been fifteeen years old herself, and still totally innocent. Yet despite this – or possibly because of it – within a few months she had been taken by the king as one of his many wives, and had soon become established as his favourite. The attentions and luxuries that were then showered upon her would have been enough to turn the head of any unsophisticated young girl, and Farah readily admitted that she became totally besotted by it all. She was a queen, to all intents and purposes, and she revelled in every extravagant aspect of her position.

Before long, she fell pregnant, and it seemed to her that her cup of good fortune was filled to overflowing. She prayed to Allah that her child would be a boy, as he would become the king's firstborn ligitimate son, and therefore heir to untold wealth and privilege.

Saleema had drawn up a basket beside Pedrito, and they both sat spellbound as Farah continued her tale...

During her pregnancy, her every fancy had been indulged by an army of handmaidens, and the king himself had devoted an inordinate amount of his time to be with her. Gifts of jewellery, exquisitely embroidered robes, exotic fruits and endless selections of elaborate sweetmeats specially concocted by the king's personal confectioners were lavished on her continually. And Farah loved it all.

But such favours bestowed upon one particular wife are bound to provoke jealousies in a palace awash with female competition, and in Farah's case the result was to prove fateful in a way she could never have imagined.

Yamínah, the wife whom she had replaced as the king's favourite, sought the services of a soothsayer to make a prediction on the suitablity as heir to the throne of Farah's unborn baby. The king was made aware of this, yet despite an avowed mistrust of mystics, he offered no objection. The child's worth, he assured Farah, would be judged by the wisdom of Allah, and not by a handful of lizard bones scattered on the floor by some wizzened old hag clad in sackcloth. He therefore decreed that, in the interests of domestic harmony and for no other reason, Yamínah could have her way.

The soothsayer's prophesy, delivered to the king in suitably baleful tones after she'd run her fingers over Farah's abdomen, was that the child would indeed be a boy. At this, the king smiled cynically and, with a forbearing gesture, bade her continue. The soothsayer's reaction was to glare at Farah, her face contorted into a grotesque scowl. Then, after much woeful moaning, she declared, 'But on his body, the infant will carry the mark of the devil!'

The king's response had been to dismiss the old crone with another gesture, but one notably less lenient than before, after which he'd laughed and joked with Farah about stupid supersititions and how thoroughly he repudiated them. Yamínah had been appeased, peace and goodwill had been restored to his household, and Farah should think no more of this silly exercise. The boy child, *their* boy child, would be a fine, healthy and worthy heir to the kingdom of Mallorca, and for this he put his trust in Allah.

At first, Farah had automatically accepted the king's reassurances, but after a while it dawned on her that, if he truly rejected the soothsayer's prophesies, why would he have referred to the 'boy' child, when there was no other way of telling that her unborn baby would indeed be male? Consequently, the suspicion was sown in her mind that, if the king trusted one aspect of the soothsayer's predictions, then it followed that he must at least be inclined to give a modicum of credence to the other.

She became more haunted by this possibility as her pregnancy progressed. Moreover, the king's increasingly infrequent visits to her chambers served to exacerbate her anxiety, and to such an extent that, by the time she finally went into labour, Farah had become convinced that the resentful Yamínah had succeeded in laying some sort of curse on her baby. Such intrigues, in the mind of a young and still relatively innocent country girl, were seen as routine features of life in the court of a king.

'Look,' the midwife had gasped moments after delivering Farah's child, 'he has the devil's mark, just as the soothsayer foretold!' She had then thrust the newborn infant into Farah's arms, almost as if passing her a burning log. 'See there – a birthmark – the stamp of the devil!'

The king, who had been waiting discreetly in an anteroom throughout the birth, then entered, his expression grim. One look at the tiny blemish on the skin of his son and heir was all it took.

'This creature is the work of the infidel's god,' he growled. He turned to the cowering midwife. 'See to it that its heathen life is ended without delay, and have the body burned!'

Farah's voice began to quaver as she related to Pedrito and Saleema that the king had then swept out of her quarters without saying a word to her, or even taking the briefest of glances at her face, which was still sweat-soaked and flushed from the agonies of bearing his child.

There had been only one thought in Farah's mind now, and that was saving her baby's life, even if it meant endangering her own. She knew very well that defying the king in such a situation would mean being subjected to some terrible form of punishment, *if* she was caught. But she would cross that bridge when she came to it. Her first priority was to escape, but to do that she needed help, and quickly.

The same fates that had condemned her newborn baby to death then sent her a guardian angel, in the most unexpected form of Layla, one of the ex-concubines who had been assigned to Farah's train of personal servants. Whether Layla's action was a result of her resentment at having been rejected by the king, or whether it was because she felt a need to get back at the scheming Yamínah for some previous slight, Farah neither knew nor cared. All that mattered was that Layla had been in a position to overhear the king's command to the midwife and had taken it upon herself to come to Farah's aid.

The first thing Layla had done was to lie to the midwife that she, Layla, had been instructed by the king to get rid of the baby, so the midwife was free to go, without risk of being exposed to further contamination from the 'devil's brat'. Farah revealed that what followed had been similar to Saleema's experience today, in so far as she had slipped out of the palace disguised as a servant girl, but with three important disparities – there was no impending attack on the city to distract the palace guards, she was still weak from giving birth *and* she was carrying a newborn baby in her arms.

'Anyway,' said Pedrito, 'I presume this explains why you said that history had repeated itself.'

Solemnly, Farah nodded her head. 'But I added "though not completely", remember? I also said that you wouldn't want to hear my story, and I think I've probably told you enough of it already.'

'But you can't just leave it there,' Saleema objected.

Farah gave her a chastening look. 'Ah, but I can, and I think it's best that I do. The rest of my story doesn't make for pleasant listening, believe me.'

Saleema was about to attempt another protest, but Farah was having none of it. In familiar style, she wagged a finger. 'No, no, little lady, all you need to know is that I survived.' She looked askance at her crutch, which was standing propped against the donkey's stall, then smiled wryly and added, 'Well, most of me did.'

No one spoke for a while, the only sounds to disturb the silence being the guttering of the lantern's candle and the slow, heavy sighs of the snoozing donkey.

For reasons that he couldn't explain, Pedrito was starting to feel a strange urge – a compulsion, almost – to learn more about this fascinating woman. And it wasn't just his natural curiosity at work either. But he realised that even more important was her right to keep to herself whatever details of her life she chose. His inquisitiveness, then, would be held in check, and the rest of Farah's story, no matter how intriguing, would have to remain a mystery.

What he hadn't bargained for, though, was that Farah, irrespective of her physical disabilities, was still susceptible to the same craving for attention as any able-bodied member of the fair sex. She had told him when they first met that she didn't want anyone's sympathy or pity, and Pedrito had absolutely no doubt that this was true. However, a need for sympathy and a desire for attention, no matter how superficially similar, are two entirely different emotions in the female psyche, and if Pedrito hadn't known this before, he was about to be enlightened now.

'Of course, I never did find out if it was Yamínah who alerted the guards,' Farah blurted out after the silence had become almost unbearable. 'I mean, I suspect she did, and I even wondered for a while afterwords if she had actually set the whole thing up with Layla. But if that had been the case, Layla would have had to know in advance that my baby was going to be born with a birthmark, and that would have been impossible. Unless, of course, the midwife was in on the conspiracy and actually made the mark herself with some sort of dye. I never had a chance to put that to the test. Anyway, if the midwife did do that, it would have meant that the soothsayer's prediction had also been part of Yamínah's plot for my downfall.'

Saleema was quick to urge Farah on. 'You say you never had a chance to check if the birthmark was real. How do you mean?'

That was all the encouragement Farah needed. As was evident in the rapt expressions of the two young people sitting opposite, she had now been afforded the attention she sought – and their sympathy, far less their pity, clearly didn't come into it. Not yet, anyway.

Farah went on to tell how she had scarcely taken three paces outside the door when a cry rang out from one of the palace balconies. It was the voice of a woman alerting the guards to her escape. Farah couldn't be sure if it was Yamína's voice, but she had always supposed that it was. Not that it would have made any difference anyway, because her fate was already sealed. She had rushed across the palm shaded avenue outside the palace and on into the narrow alleyways of the kasbah, where she thought she would have a better chance of melting into the crowds. Fortunately for her, the shouts of the two pursuing guards were ignored, the humble inhabitants of the kasbah clearly more sympathetic towards a young servant girl fleeing with a babe in arms than towards a pair of scimitar waving soldiers.

Although in a state of panic and totally unfamilar with her surroundings, she'd had enough presence of mind to keep heading in the direction of the sea. Her idea was that, if she could only make it to the harbour, she might be able to stow away on a ship and thereby make good her escape from the island. But she was already in a state of exhaustion and getting weaker with each step. She could hear from the guards' shouts that they were gaining on her. Wracked with pain and gasping for breath, she had stumbled on, and then, just as she thought she was about to collapse, she saw the twin towers of the Gate of Chains rising up ahead of her.

It was a pleasantly warm evening, so the area was teeming with people on their way to and from the quayside markets. Dredging up every last grain of strength, she barged her way through the crowds and on into the bustle of the harbour. She had made it! The wharfs were lined with boats and ships of all sizes and descriptions. Surely she would manage to slip aboard *one* of them without being seen.

Farah interrupted her narrative to draw breath, and to assess the reaction of her two young listeners.

Saleema, wide-eyed with apprehension, respond swiftly. 'I'm not surprised you hadn't time to see if the baby's birthmark was real or not,' she gasped. 'That would have been the last thing you were bothered about. But what happened next?'

Pedrito, meanwhile, sat silent and expressionless – an anomaly that didn't go unnoticed by Farah. Nevertheless, she adopted an air of insouciance and continued with her story...

'Although the two guards were now only seconds behind me, I thought I might be able to give them the slip as I made my way through the crush of people on the waterfront. Then I saw them – two more soldiers, patrolling the quayside and heading straight towards me. The palace guards yelled at them to catch me. I was trapped. Nowhere to go. I knew that I was done for now, so my only concern was to save my child. In desperation, I ducked into a recess in the sea wall that was piled high with baskets, and there I hid my little baby, wrapped in the servant girl's cloak I'd borrowed.'

Farah may not have been seeking anyone's sympathy, but her eyes had misted over as she made this harrowing revelation.

Saleema was struggling not to burst into tears now herself. She reached out and took Farah's hand. 'And the baby? Was it saved? Did you manage to...?'

Farah lowered her eyes. Despite herself, teardrops began to trickle down her cheeks. 'The guards caught me as I tried to run away. I was paraded through the streets of the city as a messenger of the devil and a disobeyer of the king's commands. They punished me by taking me to the steps of the principal mosque, where, on the king's orders, they cut off my right foot and left hand – in public.'

Saleema was horrified. 'But that's barbaric – inhuman. I mean, the agony you suffered must have been terrible, but it's a miracle you didn't bleed to death as well.'

Farah shook her head. 'Ah, but that's the whole point. They don't want you to die. They make great efforts to keep you alive, because they want you to serve as an example. As if your screams when they're hacking off bits of your body aren't enough to discourage others from breaking the rules, they want you to go about as a helpless cripple for the rest of your days as well.' Farah stifled a sob. 'But the worst of it was that I never saw my baby again.' She lowered her voice to the merest whisper. 'And many are the times since then that I've wished I'd died with him.'

A stony silence descended on the shack once more, this time broken only by Saleema's sniffling as she patted Farah's hand.

Pedrito still said nothing, but the blood had drained from his face.

This was also noticed by the constantly-alert Farah. 'You look pale, Pedrito,' she said after a while, her tone more searching than concerned. 'The thought of someone having their hands and feet cut off make you feel squeamish?'

Pedrito could have told her that he had seen that and worse during his years as a slave of Moorish pirates, but somehow all such atrocities now seemed to pale into insignificance. To his way of thinking, even divulging this aspect of his past would not have been appropriate at this moment. He'd felt a strange sensation gripping him ever more chillingly as Farah's story unfolded – a feeling that had started out as fascination, but had progressed through sorrow for her plight to outrage at the brutal way she had been treated by the father of her child. But there was more to this feeling than such predictable reactions might have been expected to produce, and, painful though it might prove to be, he knew there was only one way to find out if his intuition was right.

'A birthmark,' he said to Farah. 'You said your baby had a birthmark.'

Farah raised her shoulders. 'There was a small mark, yes. But as I told you, it could have been made by the midwife. I never found out.' She bristled slightly. 'Anyway, as the little lady here said, it was the last thing on my mind at the time.' She then looked at Pedrito in a way that suggested she was being stirred by a feeling which aroused her curiosity and, for fear of being hurt, also put her on guard. 'But why do you want to know?' she asked, cautiously.

Pedrito first apologised for prying, then answered her question with one of his own. 'Did you notice if the mark had a particular shape, or was it just a –?'

'It was a cross!' Farah cut in, a tremble of anger in her voice now. 'A cross – a tiny cross – the sign of the Christians, the sworn enemies of the Muslim people!' She shook her head vigorously. 'Why else do you think the king said my baby was the work of the infidel's god?' She lowered her eyes, unable to stem the tears any longer. 'My baby's life, and all for the sake of a tiny cross!'

While Saleema did her best to console Farah, Pedrito sat in silence, trying desperately to untangle the confusion of his thoughts. He realised that pressing the subject of the birthmark with Farah must have rubbed salt into old wounds, while also making him seem needlessly insensitive in Saleema's eyes. Nevertheless, just one vital detail remained to be broached, and the only way to go about it was to be blunt. Easier said than done, however, when on the verge of breaking down yourself.

'And where,' Pedrito began, his own voice quavering now, 'where on the – on the baby's body was the…?'

Slowly, Farah looked up at him, her tear-filled eyes revealing nothing now but a sort of pleading vulnerability – a look that Pedrito had seen many times in the eyes of pirate-galley captives when about to be sent to unknown fates in the slave markets of North Africa. In this case, it distrubed him to think that Farah's answer to his final question might result in her being condemned to even greater depths of pain than she had already been subjected to in life.

And what of his own feelings? Did he really want to face the heartbreak of hearing something that would shatter the hopes which, despite his efforts to resist them, were now invading the most guarded corners of his mind?

'Behind my baby's ear,' Farah whispered. 'A tiny cross behind his left ear.' She rested hear head against Saleema's shoulder. 'Christian god or Muslim god,' she sobbed, '– I prayed to any god who was listening that my baby's life would be spared. Then I kissed him on that little mark, the very mark that threatened to rob him of his life. And then – and then I said goodbye.' With a great shuddering sigh, Farah wiped her eyes on her sleeve, then looked directly at Pedrito again. 'But I never found out if that final prayer was answered ... or even listened to.'

Pedrito was in tears now himself. His tears weren't of sadness, however, but of a joy he thought he would never know again, following that black moment, just a few days earlier, when old Baltazar had broken the news of his family's tragic demise.

Smiling through the tears, he spread his arms. 'Well,' he said to Farah, 'do you like how your little baby turned out?'

She was still staring at him. 'You?' she gasped, the look in her eyes flitting back and forth between disbelief and a kind of bridled euphoria. 'No, it – it can't be!'

But it was, and Saleema didn't hesitate to prove it.

Pedrito felt like a present being unwrapped by a little girl on her birthday, as Saleema, giggling and weeping in a jumble of emotions, hurriedly pulled off his head scarf and fumbled with a shock of his shoulder-length hair.

'It is! It's true!' she piped in an eruption of excitement. 'Look!' she beamed, tears of delight glinting in her eyes while she yanked Pedrito's head round as if expecting it to rotate like an owl's. Blissfully unmindful of the discomfort it might be causing him, she then pulled his hair aside and jabbed a finger behind his left ear. 'See, Farah! See – a little cross, just like you said! It's him! It's *really* him – your little baby boy!'

Farah and Pedrito continued to sit motionless, their eyes locked, seeing everything, yet revealing nothing. Then, hesitantly, like a child afraid to disturb her reflection in a pool for fear of destroying it, Farah reached out and tenderly touched his cheek.

## 20

# THE FLIGHT FROM THE CITY'

*SOME HOURS LATER – IN FARAH'S SHACK ...*

The first cockcrow was already heralding a new day by the time Pedrito had recounted his own story to Farah and Saleema. So, here they were, three people with similarly humble origins, thrown together by diverse quirks of fate that had threatened to destroy their lives, but now offered glimmers of hope which none of them could have dreamt of just a few hours earlier. Glimmers of hope, but hazy ones. For, no matter how warm their feelings towards one other, all three were caught up in a war that could have dire consequences for everyone in the vicinity of Medîna Mayûrqa, on both sides of the conflict and on either side of the city walls. Saleema's problems, however, were even more acute, in that her escape from the Moorish king's harem would surely be rewarded with punishment commensurate with such a contemptuous act – if she were caught.

Pedrito had already confessed to the two women that he'd given his word to the Christian King Jaume that he would return to his camp with news of the city's garrison and defences. He'd explained that, although he owed no allegiance to this crusade against the Moors, and would have preferred, in fact, that the war had never been started, his return home to Mallorca had come about because of it, albeit indirectly. In the process, he had been befriended by a young king who trusted him to keep his word, and nothing would prevent him from trying to honour that trust, even if the military information he was able to pass on would matter little either way to the eventual outcome of the conflict.

Neither woman had indicated that they bore him any grudge for this. Indeed, they had admitted that, like him, they wished that people of the two religions could have continued to live in relative harmony on the island, just as they'd done for centuries. But if that wasn't to be, what, they wonderd, would happen to Muslims like them if the Christians should win this war? And what, Pedrito asked in return, would happen to Christians like him if they didn't? But, for the moment, the answers to such questions were secondary. First, Pedrito pointed out, they had to survive, and under present circumstances, that might prove to be fairly problematical.

'It'll soon be dawn,' he said, 'then all manner of rocks and things will be raining down on the north of the city, and it may not take long for the bloodshed that follows to spread down here.' He then addressed Saleema directly. 'In any case, we have to get you out of the city before the palace guards come looking for you, so we'd better get going before daybreak.'

Farah's hand had been resting on Pedrito's all the while. Her fingers now gripped his tightly.

'Take care of the little lady, and look after yourself too. I can only pray that whatever god brought you back to me will protect you both.' She smiled through her tears and whispered, 'And promise me you'll come back to see me again one day. Who knows – maybe the soldiers will leave a haggard old crone like me alone, hmm?'

'You won't be here to find out!' Pedrito countered.

Farah frowned. 'I don't understand. There's nowhere else I can go.'

'Yes there is. You're going where we're going – wherever that may turn out to be.'

Farah uttered a forlorn little chuckle, then nodded towards her crutch, which was still propped against the donkey's stall. 'I'd only slow you down, and I wouldn't be able to go far anyway.' She gave Pedrito a stern look. 'No, you and Saleema must go alone – and now! And don't worry about me, because –'

'Because you're coming with us,' Pedrito affirmed.

Farah was about to object again, but Pedrito put a finger to her lips. 'You're coming with us.' He then gestured towards the donkey. 'And on his back, you won't slow anyone down.'

'Yes! That's a great idea!' Saleema chirped.

To emphasise her disagreement, Farah both shook her head *and* wagged a finger. 'Absolutely not! The donkey belongs to my landlord!'

'So what?' Pedrito shrugged.

Farah was appalled. 'I may be reduced to begging, but I'll never steal from anyone!'

Pedrito was already in the donkey's stall and untying his tether. 'Depending on how long the siege lasts, Lucky here could either starve to death or be eaten by the starving – probably both.' A cock crowed again. 'Now, no more arguments. Let's get out of the city before the sun comes up.'

\*

As chance would have it, the Gate of Chains turned out to be only a short distance from Farah's shack, and the prune-faced gatekeeper proved to be in an even less pleasant mood than when Pedrito had crossed his threshhold the previous evening. He was fast asleep, slouched on a chair in the open doorway of his little gatehouse.

Farah poked him on the shoulder with the tip of her crutch. 'Wake up, Shafeeq!' she hissed. 'Wake up, you lazy old goat, and open up! I need to be on my way!'

'Farah?' he blinked. 'Farah! What in the name of Allah's beard are you doing sitting on a donkey?' He rubbed his eyes. 'And what's the idea of disturbing me in the middle of the night?'

'You're supposed to be minding the gate, not sleeping, so open up or I'll report you to the captain of the guard!'

It was obvious that this pair of kasbah characters knew each other well, although Farah had warned Pedrito and Saleema that the gatekeeper would still be an awkward old rascal to deal with.

'I've seen you somewhere before,' he grunted at Pedrito. 'Begged your way in through this gate not that long ago, didn't you?'

Pedrito was tempted to vehemently dispute the 'begged' element of that question, but he thought it best to hold his tongue.

The gatekeeper then squinted at Saleema, who was standing, head bowed, in an old hooded cloak Farah had given her. 'Who's this tramp? And where do the three of you think you're going anyway?'

Farah jerked her head in Pedrito's direction. 'The little one's the big lad's young brother. They've decided to take their chances back at their farm after all.'

'Half-witted peasants!' the gatekeeper muttered, then glowered at Farah. 'And what about you?' he sneered. 'Not going to stay and help fight off the Christian army, eh?'

Farah gave him another poke with her crutch, though a bit more energetically than before. 'This stick might be useless against a Christian sword, Shafeeq, but it's good enough to take your eye out, so open up and let us out!'

'Why are you going with these two bumpkins anyway? You'd be safer staying right here in the city.'

'Not that it's any of your business, but I just happen to be related to them. Their mother's my sister, and I want to see if she survived when the Christian armies overran their farm.'

The gatekeeper gave a gutteral laugh. 'None of you are going anywhere unless I say so, and I only say so for a price – as your big, pea-brained nephew here already found out to his cost.'

Farah rounded on him. 'You know very well I haven't any money, and even if I had, you'd be the last person I'd give it to! And to think your parents called you Shafeeq – the kind, compassionate one. What a joke!'

But Shafeeq wasn't about to allow a little insult like that deter him. 'If I wasn't kind and compassionate, I'd be shouting to the guards on the ramparts up there – telling them to come down and arrest you three for trying to leave the city without permission.'

Farah hunched her shoulders. 'Go ahead. I'll report you to their captain for taking bribes.'

But this only evoked another mocking laugh from the gatekeeper. 'And who do you think I'm sharing the money with, you silly old bat?' He turned to Pedrito. 'So, come on, big boy – get that money bag of yours out and buy a little more of my kindness and compassion, huh!'

Pedrito knew there would be no point in objecting to this old bandit's demands. It was almost dawn, they had to leave the city fast, the Gate of Chains postern was the only way out for them, and old prune face here had the key. Without further ado, then, Pedrito produced his purse, pulled out the same number of coins it had cost him to get in and handed them over.

A snort of derision escaped the gatekeeper's nostrils. 'That's the price for one. Seems to me there are three of you now, no?' He made a come-hither gesture with the fingers of his right hand. 'Cough up!'

Pedrito duly counted out the required amount.

Smirking, the gatekeeper shook his head. 'No, no, no, boy! I can hear more money jangling in your pouch.' He then repeated the same hand gesture as before. 'I'll have the lot!'

It was Farah who took it upon herself to baulk at this. 'You can't just send us out there with nothing in our pockets. In Allah's name, have a heart, man!'

'You've *never* had anything in your pocket anyway, Farah, so don't give me that.' The gatekeeper fixed his beady eyes on Saleema. 'But who's to say this one hasn't got a bit of money tucked away somewhere?' He stepped towards her. 'Maybe I should do a body search, eh? Take off that hood so I can see your face, and then raise your hands above your head, boy!'

Pedrito's heart was in his mouth. How were they going to get out of this one? While his brain retreated into panic mode, Farah stepped coolly into the breech.

'We all know about your disgusting little perversions, Shafeeq. Nothing you like better than groping young boys, right? Hmm, but you won't get your grubby hands on this one.' She prodded the gatekeeper in the belly with her crutch. 'Now back off, or you'll feel the point of this where it *really* hurts!' She turned to Pedrito. 'All right, give him all the money you've got. It'll be worth it just to see the last of his depraved, wizzened face.'

The gatekeeper chuckled delightedly to himself while Pedrito shook what remained of the contents of the purse into his cupped hands.

Then, with the postern door finally open to the sound of waves lapping gently against the quayside, Farah said, 'One last thing, Shafeeq – you've taken all our money, so I want you to shout to the guards and tell them to let us go on our way. We don't want to step out there just to be herded up and brought back inside again.'

Shafeeq grinned as he trickled the coins from one hand to the other. 'You're not the first to leave the city tonight, and I doubt if you'll be the last.' He flicked a coin in the air. 'As long as they can afford the price of kindness and compassion, of course!'

'Well, we've paid through the nose for that,' Farah retorted, 'so kindly see to it that we're allowed to go in peace.'

'Go in peace?' he guffawed. 'And who's going to stop you, huh? The more useless idiots like you who leave the city the better. All the less mouths to feed if the siege happens to last a while.' He slapped the rump of Farah's donkey. 'Now, get out of my sight and let me go back to sleep!'

*

It had been Pedrito's initial intention to take Farah and Saleema to the safety of his adoptive parents' *finca* near Port d'Andratx, but he soon realised that the journey might well prove too long and arduous for Farah. Despite her gritty attitude, the lack of food had obviously had an adverse effect on her already frail physical condition. Furthermore, the road to Andratx would take them past the scenes of those first bloody encounters between the Christians and Moors, the same stretch of countryside inland from Santa Ponça where Saleema had said her own parents' *finca* was located. Naturally, her first wish would be to be reunited with them, but from what Pedrito had seen of the devastation that had been wreaked upon some of the farmsteads thereabouts, he decided it would be kinder not to expose the girl to such potential grief so soon after her traumatic experiences of the previous day. Where, then, could he find a secure refuge for his mother and Saleema, at least until he had fulfilled his obligation of reporting to King Jaume? It was Farah herself, who, as if sensing Pedrito's dilemma, came up with a possible solution.

After clearing the south-western perimeter of the city at daybreak, they had reached the road leading up from the coast at Porto Pi and were taking cover in a thicket of *monte bajo* while column after column of Christian forces trudged by on their daily trek northward to the vast new camp being constructed at El Real. While Pedrito knew that he could safely have presented himself to the leaders of the troops, who were fully aware of his mission, he thought it might have created problems to be seen in the company of two scruffily-dressed Muslim women, so keeping out of sight until the forces had passed appeared to be a more sensible course of action.

'Your Christian king will be expecting you,' Farah said to him at length. 'And I can see you're anxious to keep your word.'

Pedrito still wasn't anywhere near coming to terms with the fact that King Jaume's adversary in this war was actually his own father, so all he could manage to do was offer his mother an awkward little smile. 'Well, a promise is a promise. But, to be honest, my main concern at this moment in time is to find somewhere safe for you both to stay until we see which way the war's likely to go.' He stroked his chin. 'It isn't easy. I mean, I'll be expected to be on hand at the Christian camp, and at the same time I'll want to be able to make sure whenever I can that you're both all right too.'

Saleema looked at him in the way that a damsel in distress might regard a knight on a white charger galloping towards her turret.

This wasn't lost on the ever-observant Farah, who smiled discreetly, then said to Pedrito, 'I was born and brought up in a little settlement called Génova.' She hooked her thumb over her shoulder. 'It's up on the slopes of Na Burguesa Mountain there – not far from where you said the most recent battle took place.'

'I know where you mean. It was on a rise near there that King Jaume took his first look at Medîna Mayûrqa. Fantastic views of the city.'

'Yes, and you can see all the way round to where your new

Christian camp is being set up as well.'

Intrigued, Pedrito raised an eyebrow. 'So?'

'So, where better to be able to watch which way the war's going?'

Pedrito was beginning to understand what his mother was getting at, but only just. 'And it's not too far from the camp at El Real for me to come over and check on your safety occasionally, right?'

'And for us to check on your safety as well,' Farah came back. 'King Abû has war engines too, you know.'

But Pedrito was far from convinced. He shook his head. 'No, there would have been terrible damage done to the Génova area when the Christian soldiers raked through at the end of that battle. There may not even be a house still standing.'

'Maybe so, but who's talking about houses?'

Confused, Pedrito frowned. 'But you can't just sleep behind a wall. It's getting cold at night now, and there could still be more autumn storms. Gales. Thunder and lightning. Rain coming down in sheets. You'll need a roof over your heads!'

'There's plenty of room at my parents' *finca*,' Saleema piped up. 'We could be there in a couple of hours or so, and my mother and father would be delighted to have Farah as their guest.'

Pedrito didn't hesitate to pooh-pooh this suggestion. Although he couldn't let on to Saleema, there was every chance that her parents might not even be alive now. 'Trouble is,' he said, 'I haven't time to go that far with you at the moment, and I'm not letting the pair of you go on your own. It's a bandits' free-for-all along that road now, you know. Besides, even if you did make it, you'd be too far away for me to come and check on you regularly.' He shook his head again. 'No, you'd be much better tucked away for a while up in the hills there by Génova.' Pedrito responded to Saleema's downcast expression by promising that he would, however, take her home to her parents at the earliest possible opportunity. He then cast Farah a searching look. 'But you'll still need a roof over your heads. And you say this won't be a problem, even if there isn't a house left standing up there?'

Farah dug her heel into the donkey's ribs. 'Just follow Lucky and me,' she said with a self-assured nod of her head. 'I know the very place.'

*

There was certainly ample evidence of the aftermath of battle to be seen as they made the ascent towards Génova hamlet. Large sections of the drystone walls retaining the tilled *bancales* had been knocked down, allowing the ochre soil to spill over the terraces and bury any crops that hadn't already been trampled flat by the retreating troops and their pursuers. Farmhouses had also been damaged, some showing signs of having been torched, others comparatively unscathed, but most with their livestock enclosures torn open. Clearly, either the fleeing Moors had been hell-bent on denying the victorious Christians access to captive supplies of meat, or the Christians had seen fit to make ongoing life as difficult as possible for the local Moorish people, innocent and unthreatening as they might be.

Though many of these farms appeared to have been abandoned, a few, surprisingly, were still occupied, as witness the stoical attempts being made by folk to make good the damage done to their homes and fields. Hens were still pecking away in some back yards, and a scattering of sheep and goats could be seen grazing freely here and there on the pine-studded hillsides. There were even a few families, armed with long canes, determinedly knocking the autumn crop of almonds from their trees in the time-honoured way. Life, despite everything, was going on.

Yet there existed a harsh reminder that death was also present. Although out of sight, the scene of the most recent battle was only a short way over the lower folds of the Serra de Na Burguesa. From there, the fetor of decomposing flesh now drifted upwards on a gentle sea breeze which, only a few days earlier, would have breathed an invigorating whiff of brine into the island's mountain air.

With Pedrito and Saleema following gamely behind, Farah urged Lucky onwards and upwards through a patchwork of little farms until they came to a narrow shoulder of flat land, where the ground rose steeply through woods on one side and fell away steadily towards the coast and the island's central plain on the other. As Farah had said, there was an uninterrupted view all the way from Porto Pi northward round the city to the Christian encampment at El Real.

Viewed from up here, the tents of the camp appeared no bigger than neatly arranged rows of wheat grains, and while it was impossible to actually see the Christians' siege engines, bursts of dust erupting from the city walls revealed that the bombardment of Medîna Mayûrqa was already under way. Also, what looked like tiny balls of fire could be seen rising in high arcs from the camp to plunge down inside the city's outer defences. Pockets of flame flickered among the buildings where these projectiles landed, producing plumes of smoke that spiralled upwards into the cloudless morning sky. While there was no such visual indication of reprisals by the Moors, Pedrito assumed, from what he had been told by the three mercenaries at the inn, that their fearsome *algarradas* would be returning the Christian artillery assault with equal ferocity.

However, he was standing some three miles away from the action, so not the faintest echo could be heard of the terrible din that must have been accompanying these first serious salvoes of the siege. Silence, in fact, was a conspicuous feature of the landscape that Pedrito now found himself in. It was as if the things of nature, though far from this latest outburst of human violence, had reacted in the same way as they had to the earlier encounters between the two armies. Not a bird sang, not a leaf stirred. Even the soothing jangle of sheep bells which had resonated round the hillsides down by the hamlet of Génova could no longer be heard. This little sliver of uninhabited land was steeped in an eerie hush that, to Pedrito, seemed totally at odds with the breathtaking beauty of the place. Saleema, who had been clinging to his hand all the way up the mountainside, shivered as she too became aware of this.

In contrast, Farah appeared hardly troubled at all, the only negative aspect of her demeanour being a trace of disappointment in her voice when she began to relate how this secluded spot had been a favourite place for her and a few friends to come and play when they were children. Even then, the little wedge of land had only been used to graze sheep and goats on weeds that grew between the gap-tooth rows of ancient olive and almond trees after the spring and autumn rains. The presence of those selfsame trees suggested that this tiny *finca* had once been carefully tended, but had ultimately been abandoned, perhaps because of its remoteness from the 'hub' of the scattered Génova community, or perhaps because the fertility of the soil had been exhausted by over-grazing, as was often the case on the poorer mountain farms.

Be that as it may, according to Farah there had at least been some life about the place back then, even if only when used as a playground for the handful of children who could be bothered coming up here. But, she sighed, by the looks of things now, it seemed that even the local kids had long since forsaken what she and her friends had regarded as a special hideaway of their very own – a secret eyrie from where they could look out over what they thought was the entire world.

Pedrito could see what she meant, but what her reminiscing hadn't explained was why, apart from its secluded and elevated location, she had chosen this place as a refuge for herself and Saleema. He looked around for a sign of somewhere that would provide a roof over their heads, but there wasn't even a ruined wall for them to shelter behind – only those few ancient trees, standing forlornly on an otherwise empty sliver of land.

Farah read his puzzled expression. 'Look over there,' she said, nodding in the direction of a rocky overhang at the landward side of the field. 'What do you see?'

Pedrito raised his shoulders. 'A rocky overhang?'

Farah widened her eyes, inviting further speculation.

Pedrito repeated his gesture. 'The base of a little cliff with some old vines clambering along it?'

Farah allowed herself a mischievous smirk. 'Precisely, and that's what will provide a roof over our heads.'

Mystified, Pedrito and Saleema looked at each other, then at

Farah. 'Those old *vines*?' they asked in unison.

Chuckling to herself, Farah gave Lucky the donkey a kick in the ribs. 'Follow me, children! Follow me!'

\*

What the vines had been concealing was a heap of boulders, which in turn hid the entrance to a cave.

'People must have lived in here at one time,' said Farah, holding her lantern up to what looked like primitive animal drawings on the walls, 'but not even the local shepherds knew about it when I was a child. That rockfall covering the entrance could have happened hundreds, maybe thousands, of years ago. So, who knows,' she shrugged, 'maybe us nosey kids from the village were the first to set foot in here in all that time?' She laid the lantern on a little ledge just above her head, then gave Saleema a reassuring smile. 'Anyway, it's home sweet home for us now, *habib* – for a while anyway.'

Saleema smiled back, though without much conviction. When she had made her dash for freedom from the Almudaina Palace, she had only been wearing flimsy slippers on her feet, which were now cut and bruised from the climb up the rough mountain tracks. As if that wasn't bad enough, she had had to rely on Pedrito to haul her up some of the steeper inclines, so her arms and back were now starting to ache in sympathy with the soles of her feet. Taking a deep, quivering breath, she glanced round the spartan conditions inside the cave, her facial expression suggesting that this sudden change from the luxurious surroundings of the harem could take a bit of getting used to. Her bottom lip began to tremble.

Farah patted her on the head, then, maintaining a cheery façade, she addressed Pedrito with mock haughtiness. 'Now then, my boy, if you'll help unload the rest of my wordly possessions from my pack animal's back, I'll start to make things comfortable for our little lady here.'

Once again, Pedrito found himself admiring the pluck of this woman. Although he wasn't yet able to easily regard her as his mother, so long had someone else occupied that special place in his heart, he couldn't help but recognise a steely determination in her that was also a trait of his own. That said, she had endured far worse tribulations in her life than he had, and even now, when she must have been on the verge of collapsing from hunger and the fatigue of the journey, she was still able to find the generosity of spirit to think more of someone else's immediate wellbeing than her own. It was a rare attribute, and one worthy of trying to emulate.

Saleema seemed to pick up on this. Wiping a tear of self-pity from the corner of her eye, she took Farah's arm and helped her sit down on a rock. Then, dusting off her hands, she chirpily said, 'Well then, Pedrito my boy, you heard what your mother said, so let's unload the donkey and start to make this cave a home!'

In reality, there wasn't that much to unload. Farah's wordly possessions amounted to a couple of blankets, a few basic kitchen utensils, a cup, a bowl, an earthenware pot, a bottle of oil, a little pouch of salt, some candles, and a small piece of flint with its striking iron – all in addition, of course, to the lantern, which she had already drawn into service.

While Pedrito and Saleema went about their task, Farah explained that, a little farther into the cave, there was a hole in the roof, and if you lit a fire immediately below it, the smoke would be drawn up to emerge through a small opening in the ground a few hundred paces higher up the mountain. As children, she and her friends had recognised the twin values of this natural chimney – one, that it kept the cave entirely free of smoke, and two, that the place where the smoke eventually emerged gave no clue as to the actual location of the cave. She then disclosed that, round a corner just a little way beyond the 'fireplace', there was another chamber, much larger than the one they were in now, where, over the ages, a small lake had been formed by water seeping down through the limestone to drip from stalactites dangling from the roof like giant, misshapen carrots. That water, Farah assured them, was the sweetest and purest you could ever hope to taste.

So much for warmth and water, thought Pedrito, but what about food? Without that, the natural 'comforts' of the cave would soon count for nothing. He put this to Farah.

She chuckled again. 'Well, the field outside may not be producing much these days, but what little food it does provide will keep us going for a bit.'

Pedrito and Saleema looked at her, their heads canted inquisitively.

Farah reached out and took the bowl that Saleema was holding. 'It's autumn, the season for harvesting almonds and olives and grapes, and there's plenty of those out there.' She tapped the bowl. 'So, if we fill this whenever we're hungry, we won't starve.'

Pedrito frowned. 'You'd need to soak the olives for a few weeks to get rid of the bitterness before you could eat them, though.'

Farah shrugged. 'Well, we've plenty of water, and I daresay we'll have plenty of time too ... *inshallah*'

She noticed the look on Pedrito's face becoming even more concerned. 'And, don't worry – I'll make sure we get some meat as well.'

'Meat?' he frowned.

'Well, maybe not *exactly* meat, but as near it as a barren little field like that can provide.' Farah paused for a few moments, enjoying the looks of utter puzzlement on Pedrito and Saleema's faces. 'Again, it's autumn,' she went on, 'and we're bound to get some more rain.' She indicated the lantern on the ledge above her head. 'And at night, after the rain, we'll take the light and go hunting.'

'*Hunting?*' Pedrito and Saleema chorused.

Farah giggled as she glanced down at her sole surviving foot. 'All right, I admit I wouldn't be much good at chasing wild goats these days. No, something a bit slower, a bit easier to catch would be my limit now. But luckily, there's always been plenty of wild fennel growing along the bottom of the cliff here, and being country kids yourselves, I'm sure you know that there's nothing snails like better than to climb up the stalks on a nice, damp night.'

'*Snails?*' Saleema squeaked. 'Eat ... *snails?*

Farah nodded, then drew attention to Saleema's tattered slippers and lacerated toes. 'Unless you fancy going on a wild goat chase up the mountain yourself, of course.'

Pedrito interrupted the ensuing silence by gallantly – though not too plausibly – claiming that he quite liked snails himself. 'Yes,' he said through a wooden smile, 'I haven't eaten them for years, of course – not too much wild fennel growing on a pirate galley – but when I was young, my mother –' He stopped abruptly, the clumsiness of what he had just said hitting him like a slap in the face. He felt his cheeks flush.

Equally embarrassed, Farah lowered her eyes.

Saleema cleared her throat and followed suit.

'Uhm-ah, what I was going to say,' Pedrito eventually stammered, 'was that snails – well, you really need some bread – you know, to uh…'

'And we'll have bread as well,' said Farah, quickly retaking the initiative. She gave Pedrito a heartening smile. 'Never fear, just as soon as I've rested a bit, I'll go down to one of the farms by the village and scrounge some.' She winked playfully. 'Can't fail. Won't be every day they get a queen begging from them, eh?' The tension broken, she laughed along with Pedrito and Saleema, then tossed her head in a pretend fit of pique. 'Well, all right then, an *ex*-queen!'

With the sound of laughter ringing round the walls of the cave, Saleema sat down beside Farah and gave a her a hug. 'You're still a queen in my eyes,' she said, then planted a kiss on her cheek. 'And together we'll make this a palace fit for a queen!' Looking around, she moved her arm in a flamboyant sweep. 'Who needs silken cushions, marble floors and tinkling fountains when we've got all this?'

As concerned as he still was about their welfare, Pedrito drew a welcome grain of relief from seeing this bond develop between the two women. Farah had already shown her indomitable character in every situation she'd encountered since Pedrito's fortuitous meeting with her in that grim alleyway. Now Saleema, although still a relatively callow girl of seventeen, was starting to display a similar fortitude and wry sense of humour. And, Pedrito told himself as he weighed up her current situation, she was going to need plenty of both, and then some! He was perturbed, and it clearly showed.

'Come on now, don't worry about us,' Farah told him with a commendable air of self-confidence. 'We'll be just fine, once we've gathered some food and made beds to sleep on. So, off you go and report to your Christian king. As you said, a promise is a promise.'

Pedrito hesitated before replying. His heart told him that he should be staying here to support these two brave but vulnerable women. Why should he put King Jaume's interests before theirs? Even if he never went back to the Christian camp, he, Farah and Saleema could probably live indefinitely in these hills, no matter which side eventually won the war. But then his head told him that, while such a course of action might prove to be a way out of their predicament in the short term, it was likely to do precious little for their longer-term prospects. No, it was obvious that fulfilling his commitment to the young monarch would provide the best hope for the future that he had at present. But what if the Moors should be the eventual victors? How would they react if they found out he'd not only sided with the Christians but had gone out of his way to conceal two Muslim women in a cave? That, Pedrito told himself, was a bridge he would cross if he ever came to it. For now, he would have to make the best of matters as they stood.

'The Christian king can wait a while yet,' he said to Farah, then spoke to Saleema. 'If you can make things as comfortable as you can in here, there's something I have to go and do in the meantime. Give me an hour, two at the most, and I'll be back, I promise.'

Saleema nodded, her look one of resigned confusion.

Farah gave her a consoling pat on the hand. 'You can always trust a man to make himself scarce when there's housework to be done, *habib*.'

*SEVERAL HOURS LATER –*
*BACK IN THE CAVE ABOVE GÉNOVA...*

The sun was sinking low in the afternoon sky by the time Pedrito eventually returned.

'It took a bit longer than I thought,' he said, somewhat

sheepishly.

Farah and Saleema looked up from where they were sitting on either side of a good-going fire that had been built with chunks of dead olive wood. They were clearly pleased to see him, though perhaps even more pleased to see what he was carrying.

For his part, Pedrito was pleasantly surprised to see the 'home comforts' that had been created in the cave. As well as gathering wood for the fire, which both provided much-needed warmth to the dank air and cast a comforting glow around the rugged stone walls, Saleema had managed to collect sufficient material to make beds for herself and Farah. Well, perhaps calling them 'beds' would have been a bit of an exaggeration, Pedrito admitted to himself on closer inspection. But at least the makeshift mattresses that had been put together from springy layers of dwarf palm fronds, dry heather, brushwood and moss would provide a modicum of cushioning on top of the stony floor. Hardly the feather pillows that Saleema had been accustomed to until yesterday, but amounting to considerably more comfort than the cave had offered just a few hours earalier. Saleema had done well, and Pedrito told her so.

But Saleema, like Farah, seemed more interested in what Pedrito was carrying than in what he was saying.

'Two pigeons?' she gasped.

'And *three* rabbits?' Farah marvelled.

Pedrito raised an apologetic shoulder. 'Well, I've seen the day when downing a few more pigeons in flight wouldn't have been a problem, but I'm a bit out of practice. There wasn't much chance to keep my skills honed during those years I spent pulling an oar for my sins.'

'Skills at what?' Saleema queried.

Farah smiled one of her knowing smiles, but said nothing.

Pedrito pulled his sling from a fold in his robe. 'At using this,' he told Saleema. 'You get a bit rusty if you don't keep practising.' He smiled sheepishly again. 'And, well, that's why I've been so long.'

'The pigeons were too quick for you?' Saleema teased.

'Yes, and the rabbits weren't far behind them, believe me!'

'I used to be a bit of an expert with one of those myself when I was a kid,' Farah proudly announced.

Pedrito lowered his brows. 'With a *sling*? A *girl* an expert with a *sling*?' He gave Farah a doubting look. 'You're joking … aren't you?'

'No, I'm serious! I was a match for any of the boys – outside in the field there, knocking stones off the branches of the trees. Yes, and from quite a distance too.' Farah was getting on her high horse. 'And I don't mind telling you that I once hit a pigeon in flight myself. Yes, I remember it as if it was yesterday. Oh yes indeed, we spit-roasted it over a fire right here where I'm sitting now.'

Pedrito held up his hands. 'All right, all right, I believe you, I believe you. Honestly, I didn't mean to –'

'Insult me?' Farah laughed. 'Don't worry, it takes more than that, believe me.' She became pensive for a moment, then said haltingly. 'You, uhm – you wouldn't happen to have a spare one, would you? I mean, it could come in handy for hunting – you know, if we ever get tired of eating snails.'

Without thinking, Pedrito looked at Farah's one and only foot.

'I know what's going through your mind,' she immediately came back. 'And, yes, you're right – I'd fall flat on my face if I tried to swing a sling round my head now.' She glanced hopefully at Saleema. 'But with our little lady holding me upright…'

'I'd be delighted to,' Saleema chirped, 'especially if you could teach me how to use it as well.'

With mischief dancing in her eyes, Farah twitched her head in Pedrito's direction. 'I think you'd enjoy it more, *habib*, if you were given lessons by the young master here. It takes someone steady to stand behind you and guide you through the arm movements, you see.'

Saleema blushed and stared at nothing in particular on the floor.

Pedrito faked a cough. 'You're, uh – you're more than welcome to this one,' he blurted out, handing Farah his sling. 'I, uhm – I can make myself another one easily enough.'

'Excellent!' Farah beamed. 'Thank you very much indeed.' She adopted her mock-regal mien again. 'Now then, young sir, allow us to repay your generosity by inviting you to dine with us.' She snapped her fingers at Saleema. 'If you would be so good as to pluck a pigeon, my dear, I shall deal with one of the rabbits.' Smiling a queenly smile, she said to Pedrito, 'A banquet fit for such a grand palace as this, no?'

'No doubt about it, madam,' Pedrito replied. 'And if I may be permitted...' He paused to step back outside, returning a moment later holding a small sack. 'I've brought a little surprise to add to the sumptuous bill of fare.'

'Just tell me it isn't snails!' Saleema pleaded.

Pedrito shook his head. He dipped his hand into the sack, then held up a white-coated finger. 'Found it in an abandoned barn back down near Génova.' He licked his fingertip. 'Flour – fresh as the day the miller ground it.'

'See!' Farah said triumphantly. 'I told you we'd have bread as well, didn't I?' She rolled her eyes heavenward. '*Some*body up there likes us, and at this moment in time, I couldn't care less whether he's Muslim or Christian, black, white, green or blue!'

'My sentiments entirely,' Pedrito concurred. 'Now, if you'll permit me, madam, I'll skin that rabbit for you.'

\*

Nothing of much consequence had been said during the meal – just snippets of small talk between bites of much-needed food. For, despite the jocular banter that had taken place after Pedrito's return from his foraging expedition, a slightly awkward atmosphere still persisted between himself and Farah. He felt a genuine affection for her, and he was sure the feeling was mutual, but it was going to take time to forge the cherished mother-and-son relationship that had existed between himself and, until yesterday, the only mother he had known and whose loss he hadn't yet had time to properly mourn. To her credit, Saleema, young as she was, had been aware of this and had tried to ease the tension by injecting little lighthearted topics of conversation into proceedings whenever there was a lull. She had even managed to tell a story about her childhood which explained why eating snails was so abohorrent to her now.

Pedrito doubted that it was true, but it didn't matter. What counted was that Saleema was showing a genuine sensitivity towards the feelings of others. This mirrored the quality he so admired in his mother – the *real* mother who was sitting with them here – and he felt good about that.

Lucky the donkey was already snoring on his feet on the other side of the little cave when Pedrito finally stood up.

'It's getting dark,' he said. 'Much as I'd rather stay here, I'll have to make my way down the mountain and over to El Real.' He hunched his shoulders. 'The Christian king – a promise is a promise.'

Saleema nodded her understanding, though with downcast eyes.

Pedrito looked at Farah. She was nodding too, but more due to the irresistible onset of sleep than in response to what he had just said. She looked drained and exhausted, older than her years, a frail little creature kept going by nothing more than a dogged determination to survive. Her eyes fluttered shut and she sank sideways onto her crude mattress, cushioning her head childlike on her forearm. Pedrito wondered what, in contrast, the man who had done this to her would be reclining on now. And that man was his father, whose blood coursed through his own veins. The mere thought of it made him shudder.

'I'll be back,' he whispered to Saleema, who was trying, albeit none too successfully, to stop her lip from trembling again. He placed a finger under her chin and raised it gently, the pleading look in those huge, dark eyes making it all the more difficult for him to do what he knew he must. Without saying another word, he turned and strode towards the cave's entrance, his heart heavy, the uncertainty of what lay ahead, not just for himself, but more agonisingly for Saleema and Farah, filling him with an awful sense of misgiving. His intentions were beyond reproach, but their potential success, or failure, would now lie largely in hands other than his own.

## 21

# VICTORY OR DEATH

*THE FOLLOWING MORNING –*
*THE CHRISTIAN CAMP OF 'EL REAL'...*

The fenced-off royal compound was an oasis of relative calm in the midst of a huge military settlement alive with activity. The hubbub of shouted commands, whinnying horses, the clanking of hammers on anvils, the thumping and rasping of mallets and saws reminded Pedrito of the chaos that had prevailed during the initial mass landings at Santa Ponça, except that there, an atmosphere bubbling with the anticipation of adventure prevailed, whereas here, chaos had been replaced by order and the air was charged with the pulse-quickening inevitability of a final fight to glory – or oblivion.

Although most of the vast expanse of tented accommodation was now almost complete, relays of men and beasts were still busy hauling newly-felled timber from the surrounding countryside to finish off the palisade that would soon encircle the entire encampment. Immediately beyond that, other squads were working frantically to dig a ring-ditch as yet another line of defence. Throughout it all, however, the 'swoosh' and 'thwack' of missiles being hurled by the opposing armies served as a reminder that destruction was the ultimate object of the exercise, no matter how well constructed the defences.

Standing outside his tent, King Jaume listened while Pedrito recounted details of his fact-finding foray into the city. Pedrito had already seen for himself some of the damage that had been done to the Christian enclave by projectiles propelled into it by the Moors' mighty *algarrada* war engine. The proof of its power was manifested in the terrible carnage inflicted on those men and horses unfortunate enough to have been in the wrong place when the rocks battered into the camp. Yet the king seemed surprisingly disinterested in what Pedrito told him about where, according to information gleaned at the inn, the most effective of the *algarradas* were located.

'We've already found that out the hard way,' the king said with a rueful shrug. 'It was easy to see where the missiles were coming from, and doubtless the Saracens thought their engines were beyond the range of ours. They know better now, though.' He gestured towards the southern perimeter of the camp, where rising above the roofs of the tents were the twin stanchions of the mighty *trebuchet* the Marseilles sailors had built from the timbers of their own ships. 'The Moors have no match for the distance that beast can hurl whatever we load into its sling. So, the best of their *algarradas* have been obliterated, and anything they've aimed at us since has landed short of here.'

Pedrito then stressed that he'd been told there was ample material within the city to build replacements for the most powerful machines. Again, King Jaume appeared only mildly interested.

'That's the way of any siege, Little Pedro, and eventually the side with the best artillery equipment gains the upper hand. At the moment, that side is us, and it's up to us to keep it that way.' He then assumed a more urgent manner. 'But what of the Moors' reinforcements from Africa – those the turncoat Ali tells us about? Their arrival will be a much greater threat to us than the building of a few more war engines. Did you find out the size of the fleet and when it's likely to reach here?'

King Jaume greeted with a bellow of delight Pedrito's revelation that it appeared to be common knowledge, even among the rank and file of the Medîna Mayûrqa garrison, that, because of an act of treachery by the Moorish king's own uncle, no such seaborne reinforcements had ultimately been summoned.

'Well now, that puts an entirely different compexion on things,' the king beamed. 'We'll continue to post a few sentry ships out beyond the bay, just in case. But we can now remove most of the contingency troops from our vessels at Porto Pi and put them to work here. Yes,' he grinned, 'and your news is all the sweeter because of the "treachery" factor.' He slapped Pedrito's shoulder. 'It warms my heart to learn that elements of my own kith and kin have their counterparts within the Moorish aristocracy. Seems that back-stabbing parasites have a taste for blue blood, whether it's Muslim or Christian, no?'

'Except that, in your favour, *senyor*, family disloyalties are now a thing of the past,' Pedrito diplomatically proposed, noting the approach across the enclosure of a glum-looking En Nunyo Sans, the king's senior general, but also a cousin, who had once been guilty of plotting against him with their mutual kinsman, En Guillen de Muntcada. Both of these nobles had eventually come round to renouncing their breach of royal trust, though not before the king had paid them handsome 'sweeteners'. And to add to the irony, En Guillen and his own cousin, En Remon de Muntcada, had ultimately died the death of heroes while fighting for their king here on Mallorca only a few days earlier.

King Jaume chose not to respond to Pederito's potentially contentious observation about family disloyalties, electing instead to greet En Nunyo with the cheering news that the feared fleet of Moorish reinforcements didn't actually exist after all.

Despite this, the scowl En Nunyo had been wearing scarcely lifted. 'Good news indeed,' he said with the thinnest of smiles, 'but I have news, *Majestat*, that may turn out to be even more worrisome than yours is heartening.'

Frowning himself now, King Jaume asked him to explain.

One of the Christian patrols, En Nunyo disclosed, had just returned with word of a large force of Moors having come down from the mountains to a place called Canet, some four miles north of the Christian base here at El Real.

King Jaume's face fell. 'Canet's where the spring rises to feed the stream this camp straddles, isn't it?'

En Nunyo nodded. 'The spring that supplies our entire army with water. The scouts say as many as five thousand Saracens are up there They have about a hundred cavalry with them, and it's obvious they're there to protect teams of diggers who're trying to divert the stream. I've just had a look where it runs under the palisade here, and even now the little water that's still dribbling through is thick with mud.' He shook his head. 'We're facing a complete disaster – the possible end of the crusade.'

Thinking hard, the king stroked his beard. 'Five thousand men, you say? Hmm, and if we send an equal number to engage them, it'll leave the camp susceptible to attack by forces from inside the city.' He looked at Pedrito. 'A twist on the *unlikely* pincer-movement the Saracen soldiers told you about at the inn, eh? *Sí*, and an extremely cunning one at that, don't you think, Master Blànes?'

Judging it prudent not to get involved in the military musings of the king, Pedrito remained silent. Nevertheless, he thought it highly unlikely that the three 'arrow stoppers' he had spoken to would have had even the slightest inkling of the stratagem now being employed by comrades of theirs who had taken refuge in the mountains after being so soundly defeated in battle. This development was more probably the result of impromptu action taken by an opportunist commander within the ranks of those same fugitive forces. In any event, if potentially catastrophic consequences for the entire Christian expedition were to be avoided, this unforeseen problem would have to be resolved, and swiftly. No easy task.

En Nunyo Sans, however, appeared undaunted and duly declared himself well up to the callenge. He would take the cream of his own company of mounted men-at-arms, and, if the king would make their number up to a hundred with his own choice of knights, he would launch an attack on the Saracen cavalry at Canet with such speed and ferocity that they would be cut to pieces in no time. That had been the pattern of the previous confrontations between the two sides, and he saw no reason to believe it would be any different this time.

The king responded by pointing out that there was the not-insignificant matter of five thousand Moorish infantrymen to take into account. Wouldn't their presence tilt the balance overwhelmingly in the enemy's favour?

'Perhaps,' En Nunyo airily conceded, 'but who's to say that those alleged infantrymen will turn out to be anything more dangerous than a collection of walking wounded, their ranks bulked out with chicken-hearted Moorish peasants rounded up like sheep from their mountain farms?' En Nunyo was nothing if not confident. Give him a hundred good knights with their trusty followers, he declared, and the camp's water supply would soon be restored.

Pedrito was struck by this unexpectedly bullish attitude of En Nunyo's. There was nothing here of the hesitancy that had preceded his commitment to earlier engagements with the Moors. Perhaps the desperation of the present situation was bringing out the best of his soldierly qualities, or maybe the glorious death in action of his relatives, the intrepid cousins Muntcada, had finally sparked a desire to show off a more gung-ho side to his nature than had previously been apparent. Either way, he was making it known to the king that he was ready and willing to assert his position as senior general of the Christian forces. And in so doing he had displayed a commensurate amount of aristocratic arrogance, including, Pedrito had noticed, a disdainful glance in his own direction when uttering the words 'chicken-hearted Moorish peasants'.

Pedrito harboured no illusion that he was regarded as anything other than a common upstart in the eyes of many of the high-ranking nobles and churchmen on this mission. The admittance of such a vulgar person into the inner sanctum of the royal house clearly went against the grain in some quarters, and Pedrito could fully understand their attitude. But, as the king himself had fostered the relationship without any self-seeking effort being made by Pedrito, he felt reasonably comfortable with the situation, while remaining fully aware that he was *persona non grata* in the eyes of certain influential people, and as such would be wise to watch his back at all times. He had already learned from his mother's experiences what it could mean to fall foul of resentful elements within the covetous corridors of such a close-knit patrician community.

That said, how, he wondered, would he be regarded by this crusade's dignitaries, including King Jaume himself, if details of his own 'regal' lineage were made known to them? Pedrito had already decided, however, that this potentially explosive piece of information would be best kept to himself, for now at least.

Before the king went off to muster a group of knights to ride with En Nunyo, he announced that Pedrito was being put into the service of the expedition's chief engineer, En Jaspert de Barberá, whose primary duty now was to make urgent preparations for the undermining of the city walls. He also took a moment to tell En Nunyo that, as soon as he had resolved the situation at Canet, he would have to see to it that detatchments of troops were deployed to the vicinities of each of the city's gates, thereby ensuring that no Moors could either enter or leave. Now that there was only need to station a few soldiers on the ships at Porto Pi, there would be sufficient manpower available to form such barricades without any serious diminution of the essential forces garrisoned within the camp.

Pedrito was taken once again by how the king had assumed so much more authority since the demise of the Muntcadas. He was now very much the commander-in-chief of the entire operation, overseeing and controlling every aspect of the campaign, and not even En Nunyo Sans took it upon himself to question his decisions. King Jaume had accepted his senior general's claim that he could handle the Canet situation, so the word 'if' didn't come into his thoughts regarding the successful outcome of the mission.

Accordingly, Pedrito saved himself the trouble of suggesting to the king that, having had next to no sleep for the previous three nights, he might reasonably be allowed to rest a while before taking up his duties with En Jaspert. He already knew enough of the king's character to predict that he would only be reminded that he himself was sorely deprived of sleep, and therefore expected every man to follow his example without question or complaint.

It also came as no great surprise to Pedrito to find that the duties he was expected to fulfil for the king's chief engineer relied more on muscle power than any requirement to take up arms. In this the

276

king was being as good as his word by continuing to respect Pedrito's declared unwillingness to kill any Moor, despite the heinous treatment meted out to his adoptive family by pirates of the same ilk.

And if, because of Pedrito's closeness to the king, he had expected any special treatment to be afforded him by En Jaspert, he would have have been brought down to earth with a jolt. As when instigating a headlong charge into enemy lines at the battle of Na Burguesa (while his superior En Nunyo held back), this no-nonsense nobleman was wasting no time in preparing an assault on the stout walls of Medîna Mayûrqa – an assault more subtle, in some ways, than the battering being inflicted by the Christians' siege engines, but an assault that might ultimately prove to be at least as decisive. And to achieve this end, every man under his command would have to put his back into what was asked of him, even if this also meant turning that back into a potential target for the enemy.

Just inside the stockade fence, the construction had commenced of a huge vehicle that resembled a wooden house on wheels, and it was to this that Pedrito, after exchanging his 'borrowed' Arab robes for his familiar old sailor's shirt and *pantalons*, had been directed by the king. He was soon informed by one of the carpenters that this cumbersome-looking affair was called a *mantellina*, or, affectionately, a 'she cat'; an apt enough name for a contraption that was intended to creep stealthily towards its quarry, which, in a siege situation like this, took the form of the city walls. But the 'cat' herself would pose no direct threat to her prey, for that would be the responsibility of her kittens, or rather the 'litter' of burly men who would ultimately shelter under her belly.

The *mantellina* was being assembled from timber components shipped from the mainland, and when Pedrito arrived on site, the framework of the base was already mounted on eight sturdy wheels – four on each side – on top of which a pitched roof was being made of hurdles overlaid with planking. But as robust as this protective canopy was, it would still have been prone to damage by enemy projectiles. So, to bolster its resistance, a layer of brushwood topped with a thick quilt of earth would have to be applied. It was to this latter task that Pedrito found himself assigned.

He joined a team of other stalwarts, each lugging two large bucketfuls of soil at a time from the ditch workings outside the palisade. To minimise the distance they would have to carry their loads, they were directed to the diggings closest to where the *mantellina* was being built, which, of necessity, was the point of the camp nearest the city walls. And you didn't have to be a ballistics expert to realise that this area of operations was also the one most exposed to incoming missiles. It came as some consolation to Pedrito to know that, according to the king at any rate, those missiles were likely to fall short of their targets. Nevertheless, some rocks were landing uncomfortably close to where the buckets were being filled, and it crossed Pedrito's mind on every trip outside the stockade that the Moors' long-range *algarrada*, which, to everyone's relief, had been destroyed, might be replaced by equally effective machines at any moment.

Meanwhile, he was able to see at close quarters the operation of the mighty Marseilles *trebuchet*, which was positioned close to where the *mantellina* was being made ready. A fifty-foot-long timber boom, originally a ship's mast, was pivoted between two even stouter uprights, and attached to one end of this swivelling pole was a sling of the same principle as Pedrito's hand-held version, though of massively greater proportions. On the opposite extremity of the boom, a counterweight, made up of boulders contained within a net of heavy-guage rope, dangled like a monstrous wasps' nest.

The sheer scale of this siege engine was truly awesome, as was the savagery of its action. After the counterweight had been cranked as high as possible from the ground and the cradle of the sling armed with suitably destructive ammunition, a trigger mechanism was released, allowing gravity to pull the counterweight down with such momentum that, as the opposite extremity of the boom shot upward, the sling was sent flying with a sound akin to the air being slashed by a giant whip. Then, at the very moment the cradle reached the apex of the sling's trajectory, the ammunition – most commonly a large rock – was discharged towards its target at alarming speed.

Even from this distance, Pedrito could see that the attentions of the Marseilles *trebuchet* were having the intended effect on the city walls. The puffs of dust he had seen rising when looking down from the mountainside above Génova were in reality great clouds of pulverised mortar peppered with chunks of shattered stone. But for all that, it was abundantly clear that the walls were of such a thickness that bringing them down by this means alone would be a long and arduous task, no matter how many siege engines might ultimately be employed. And this was precisely why En Jaspert de Barberá was making all haste to have his 'she cat' completed and sent creeping towards that selfsame objective.

Suddenly, a cheer rose up as En Nunyo Sans and his company of knights, followed by a column of their squires, rode out northward from the opposite boundary of the encampment. Although a considerable distance away, Pedrito could plainly see the black-and-white horizontal halves of a Knights Templar banner flying in the vanguard. He was duly reminded of young Robert St Clair de Roslin's disclosure that the only battle honour recognised by this order of warrior monks was 'Victory or Death'. To retreat was forbidden, unless outnumbered at least three-to-one; an article of faith which the king had evidently borne in mind when assembling a band of the most potent men-at-arms to support En Nunyo on his vital mission.

*

As the day wore on, the atmosphere of urgency enveloping the camp prevailed, despite the energy-sapping effect of the autumn sun on man and animal. The king himself, true to his custom on such occasions, rode conspicuously to and fro, standing high in the saddle while shouting words of encouragement to his people. And, just as when the establishment of the El Real base had been in its earliest stages, no distinction was drawn between nobleman, knight or vassal when it came to doing whatever was necessary to secure the impregnability of the camp and escalate the bombardment of the city.

Keeping the momentum going in such gruelling conditions, however, required the arousal in the Christian troops of an unflagging commitment to the cause. This was being achieved by the fiery eloquence of a robustly-built and ruddy-faced Dominican monk called Friar Miguel Fabra, who, according to one of Pedrito's fellow earth-movers, was well experienced in the art of whetting a soldier's appetite for the hardships of war. Pedrito marvelled at the passion this monk's words instilled in even the most exhausted of men as he moved among them. Indeed, Pedrito mused, the friar's rhetoric was as inflamed as his complexion and every bit as striking. King Jaume, or his ecclesiastical advisors, had obviously recognised the importance of such an inspirational figure when putting the 'non-combative' elements of this mighty invasion force together. Friar Miguel may not have wielded a sword, yet the power of his oratory alone was probably worth more in military terms than an entire platoon of men who did.

A battery of siege engines, comprising both *trebuchet* and *mangonel* varieties, was now established along the southern fringe of the camp. Although none had the destructive capability of the Marseilles machine, they were finding their range and hitting their prescribed targets with increasing accuracy. Accordingly, the northern walls of the city were taking a terrific pounding, and in the hope of inflicting horrific injuries on their defenders, flaming barrels filled with oil were being hurled over at intervals by the *trebuchets* as well. The screams of the victims rising above the clamour of the barrage served as chilling proof of the effectiveness of these lethal incendiary devices, which Pedrito instantly realised were actually the 'tiny balls of fire' he had seen when watching proceedings from the heights of Génova the day before.

But the Moors weren't taking this onslaught without reprisal. Just as predicted by the mercenaries Pedrito had spoken to at the inn, replacements for any war engines destroyed by the Christian artillery were being built and brought into play with impressive speed. What's more, the range of these new *algarradas* was increasing at a commensurate pace, so that every fresh salvo of rocks launched from the city ramparts landed ever closer to the El Real palisade. This, in turn, prompted the Christian counter-offensive to become concentrated afresh on the obliteration of these replacement machines. The siege of Medîna Mayûrqa had developed, then, into a mercilessly violent game of tit-for-tat. And Pedrito, for all that he wasn't an active participant, was right in the thick of it.

\*

Once the protective mattress of earth had been laid over the roof of the *mantellina*, a retaining blanket of hides was secured on top. Only then did her creator, En Jaspert de Barberá, announce that his 'she cat' was ready to prowl. Between the 'cat' and her quarry, there was a deep ditch, the essential first line of defence of any walled city, and it was to facilitate the digging of a tunnel under this that En Jaspert's cumbersome feline had been built. The ditch was of considerably less daunting dimensions than the dry river bed that protected the city's western perimeter, and which had been the deciding factor in the Christians establishing their encampment at its current location. Nevertheless, it still represented a formidable obstacle that would have to be negotiated before the undermining of the city walls could commence.

With a gang of diggers, or sappers, concealed inside her, the 'cat' had to be pushed manually across the rough expanse of no-man's-land to the very edge of this dry moat. To move the lumbering beast over such terrain would have been onerous enough at any time, but when those involved were also being assailed by rocks and arrows directed at them from the city's battlements, the task was fraught with a very real danger to life and limb.

Thankful that he and his fellow earth-movers had been replaced by fresh muscle power for this particular undertaking, Pedrito watched from the palisade as the 'cat' was heaved forward inch-by-inch. The men pushing her were being given some degree of cover by companies of archers moving along on either side behind large wheeled screens. The archers, though, also became exposed to enemy fire as soon as they ducked out to release their own arrows. Consequently, to give *them* some cover, the targeting of projectiles from the Christian war engines was temporarily redirected from the city walls to the soldiers manning their ramparts.

The ensuing casualty rate on both sides was horrific, with those Christians slain or wounded replaced immediately by men scurrying out from the camp. This, then, was siege warfare – relentless and brutal, with every man hell-bent on achieving the same goal; the annihilation of his opposite number, without a thought for who or what he might be. Not even the awful deeds he had seen committed during his years in the hands of Moorish pirates had prepared Pedrito for what he was witnessing now. It was as if attackers and defenders alike had been gripped by a murderous frenzy. The unfettered barbarity of it all made Pedrito cringe, yet those battle-hardened men around him, including the firebrand Friar Miguel himself, scarcely batted an eyelid, seeming more excited than dismayed, in fact, by the bloody spectacle unfolding before them.

And little did Pedrito know that the *real* battle for Mallorca was only just beginning.

*LATER THAT AFTERNOON – 'EL REAL' CHRISTIAN CAMP...*

As soon as the 'cat' had reached the edge of the moat and her litter of sappers were seen to have made a successful start to their tunnelling, the construction of two more of En Jaspert's *mantellinas* was ordered – one by the king himself, the other by the Count of Empúries, a veteran of many such sieges, who had now been put in charge of the entire mining operation. Time was of the essence, and every available man, irrespective of rank or title, was put to work.

Not so Pedrito, however. To his immense relief, a messenger arrived to summon him to the royal compound, where King Jaume was waiting, flanked by two guards, whose brief was clearly to keep a watchful eye on a young Moor cowering in front of them.

'This fellow was apprehended by our sentries outside the north gate,' the king told Pedrito. 'He was making signs that suggested he wanted to speak to someone, so they took him to a man in my train called Abel Babiel – a rabbi from Zaragoza, who's with us to ensure a fair return for that city's financial contribution to this crusade. But he's also known to have a knowledge of Arabic.' The king shrugged impatiently. 'Anyway, it seems he could make little sense of this man's babbling. Said he must be speaking some sort of Mallorcan dialect or other, and that's why I sent for you. *Sí*, and you may as well tell him right away that, if what he has to say turns out to be a waste of my time, he'll have babbled his last.'

The king was making no attempt to disguise the fact that he was tired, harrassed and preoccupied with ongoing military matters, so in no mood to be be trifled with.

Pedrito noticed that the young Moor, although in a slightly dishevelled state, was dressed in expensive robes and, despite his nervousness in the presence of the king, had a quietly dignified air about him. The Arabic he spoke was indeed heavily tinged with the vernacular of rural Mallorca, a patois with which Pedrito was totally familiar. Consequently, it took no time for him to ascertain the purpose of the lad's arrival at the entrance to the Christian stronghold. Unlike the defector Ali, who had swum to King Jaume's initial landfall on the islet of Es Pantaleu bearing what some regarded as a fairly fanciful prophecy of the successful reconquest of Mallorca, this young Moor said he brought the promise of real material benefits that would significantly boost the prospect of a Christian victory. All Pedrito could do, however, was relay his message to the king and let him decide whether to believe him or – as was very likely in his present mood – behead him.

'He says his name is Akeem, and he comes as an emissary from a wealthy Moor called Ben Abbéd, the *wali*, or governor, of the towns and surrounding districts of Inca and Pollença to the north-east of here. He says his master also owns large tracts of land in that most fertile area of the island, including the magnificent estate of Alfàbia.'

The king scowled. 'So?'

'So, he says his master believes that your siege of Medîna

Mayûrqa is likely to bring about the downfall of the Moorish king, although it will be essential to obtain a reliable source of food to sustain your army for however long the siege lasts – which could be months.'

'Does this Ben Abbéd character think I don't already know that?' King Jaume snapped. He glared at Pedrito. 'And I hadn't forgotten, Master Blànes, that finding out how to obtain such supplies was one of the tasks I set for you on your foray into the city.' With a sardonic raising of an eyebrow, he tilted his head. 'And do I recall being told what you found out?'

'No, because I found out nothing, *senyor*, and when I'm given the opportunity, I'll tell you why.' Pedrito knew he was asking for trouble by being so abrupt, but he was also aware that shilly-shallying would achieve nothing. He was just as tired as the king and had plenty worries of his own to cope with, less momentous though they might seem to His Majesty. Meanwhile, a young Moor had risked his life to venture into enemy territory, and Pedrito was determined to help him deliver his message, no matter how volatile the king's present state of mind. So, with deliberate calm, he asked Akeem to continue with what he had to say.

The smile that tugged at the corner of King Jaume's mouth when the translation of Ben Abbéd's overture had finally been conveyed to him was a blend of pleasant surprise and instinctive mistrust. He addressed Pedrito.

'He says that his master will do *what*?'

'That if you promise to view his master's position favourably after the war, he will guarantee you a regular supply of all the food you need to sustain your forces for the duration of the siege. On top of that, he will prove his goodwill by immediately placing into your control territories that amount to one third of the entire rural area of island – from Andratx to Pollença along the mountainous west, and from Inca eastwards to Manacor on the plain.'

The king raised his eyebrows. 'Fine words, and no mistake!' He frowned again. 'But talk is cheap.' He stared stony-faced at Akeem for a few moments, then shook his head. 'No, this reeks of a Saracen ploy. Tell him, Master Blànes, that this Ben Abbéd fellow will have to do more than make extravagant promises. Ask him how he intends to give me proof of his allegiance. *Sí*, and tell him also that if this turns out to be some sort of trick, I will personally make him and his master wish they'd never tried to get the better of a Christian king.'

Pedrito turned to Akeem. 'The Christian king thanks your master for his most generous offer, which he will be pleased to accept.'

Akeem's face opened into a broad smile. He bowed deeply and offered the king his obeisance – in Arabic.

The king looked askance at Pedrito. 'He seems surprisingly pleased to be threatened with his life, no?' He pursed his lips, nodded slowly, half closed his eyes, then added under his breath, 'And I advise you not to play the politician, Little Pedro. I can easily summon Babiel the Jew to check what you're saying. I'm sure he'll get the gist of the Arabic you two are speaking, bastardized as it may be.'

'I'm sure he would,' Pedrito agreed with an innocent smile. 'But I know a little of the Moorish nature, and I can tell you that threatening them with the scrutiny of a Jew isn't the best way to get their cooperation – especially when they're offering the hand of friendship.'

King Jaume looked as though he was about to have a seizure. 'Just get him to answer my question, will you! And get a move on!' He rolled his eyes. 'God knows I've enough on my plate without having to stand here waiting for the foibles of the Saracens to be explained before I decide whether or not to have this one executed!'

Pedrito gave Akeem a reassuring smile. 'The king says he would value an opportunity to meet with Ben Abbéd. Perhaps, uhm – perhaps you could invite him to come here?'

Akeem replied that he would be glad to, adding that he was sure his master would regard the invitation as a great honour. He bowed to the king again, before reiterating his words of obeisance – in Arabic.

King Jaume, nostrils flaring, fiddled with the pommel of his sword.

Pedrito touched Akeem's shoulder. 'And, uh – perhaps your

master would agree to come unarmed, with only a small group of retainers, and, let's say, with a sample of the type of provisions he would be prepared to supply?'

Indeed, this had been the crux of the message he had been sent to deliver, Akeem replied with an eager nodding of his head. All the Christian king had to do was say where and when, and Ben Abbéd would regard it as a great privilege to comply with his wishes.

'Tell him tomorrow morning after matins – on open ground – a league to the north of here,' was the king's curt response to Pedrito's diplomatically amended translation of this exchange. '*Sí*, and be sure to repeat, Master Blànes, that he and his master will find no hiding place from my sword if this turns out to be some kind of Saracen treachery!'

Not having understood a single word, Akeem looked at Pedrito, wide-eyed and hopeful.

'King Jaume bids you convey his compliments to your master,' Pedrito lied through a comforting smile. 'He looks forward to meeting him and to thanking him personally for his generous offer of allegiance.'

*

The sun was dipping towards the southernmost ridges of the Serra de Na Burguesa when En Nunyo Sans rode back into camp at the head of his troops. He brought with him news of a total rout of the Moorish opposition. He also brought with him a gruesome memento of the encounter.

'One of the Amir's foremost warriors,' he said, throwing a bloody sack at the king's feet. 'At least that's what he implied just before I cut his head off. Called himself *Fatih-billah*. Means something like "great conqueror by the grace of Allah", according to one the Templars who picked up a bit of Arabic during his exploits in the Holy Land.'

'It would appear that the grace of Allah was in short supply on this occasion,' King Jaume came back, then took the sack on the tip of his sword and emptied its contents onto the ground. 'Hmm, and his gift of good looks was clearly wanting in this fellow's case as well.'

Pedrito almost threw up.

The king didn't even flinch. 'I'll show the Amir what I think of his so-called great conqueror in due course,' he muttered. 'But first, En Nunyo, tell me of the mission. You say the Moors were totally thrashed again?'

En Nunyo went on to confirm that any resistance offered by the enemy had been swiftly and ruthlessly wiped out by his men – most prominently by the squadron of KnightsTemplar, who had spearheaded the attack in their customary do-or-die way. 'As you know, *Majestat*,' he enthused, 'even the horses of those Templars are fearsome fighters, trained to kick and bite the mounts of their enemies.' He allowed himself a self-satisfied chuckle. 'Those Saracens hadn't a hope. We left a good five hundred of them dead – the heads of many brought back here as trophies on the lances of my men. The rest were sent scurrying back to the mountains.' En Nunyo shook his head emphatically. 'You won't see any more resistance from that miserable mob of goat-herders, *senyor*.'

'And what of the spring at Canet? Has the vandalism been put right?'

'My men are busy re-directing the stream even as we speak.' En Nunyo raised an assured finger. 'Have no fear, *Majestat* – the water will be running pure, sweet and plentiful through this camp again by nightfall.'

The king's delight was obvious. 'You and your men have done right well. Now, let's show the Moorish king what we think of the great conqueror who tried to dehydrate us into defeat.' He motioned to one of his guards. 'Pick up that ugly Saracen head and follow me.' He mounted his horse and prepared to trot off in the direction of the palisade, but paused and called over his shoulder to Pedrito, 'And you come along as well, Master Blànes. I want you to experience an aspect of siege warfare that you may not have considered before.'

*

The men manning the Marseilles *trebuchet* were ordered by the king to interrupt the launching of their usual missiles while his 'personal messenger', as he put it, was loaded into the cradle of the great machine's sling.

Pedrito gagged as he watched the gory head of *Fatih-billah* emptied once more from the sack. He stared transfixed at the glaring, lifeless eyes, the crimson slime still oozing from slashed neck veins, the blood-matted beard framing a grimace that, even in death, seemed to spit defiance and hatred at its adversaries.

'You will recall,' King Jaume called out to the crowd of men now milling around, 'that the Saracen King insulted me, my army and moreover our Lord Jesus Christ by holding aloft the impaled head of one of our people during the Battle of Na Burguesa. Well, I said then that the infidel swine would pay for that.' He pointed towards the city. 'And, by Saint Mary, he will, just as soon as we've entered his sty yonder!' The king then dismounted, sauntered over to the loaded sling and gave the severed head a kick. 'Meanwhile, I will reply to his disrespect at Na Burguesa by returning this to him.' With a few muttered words, he instructed En Nunyo Sans to have his men bring forward all other such 'trophies' that had been won at today's Canet encounter, then shouted, 'And with interest!'

At that, he gave the order for the trigger mechanism to be sprung, and with a great cheer from the gathered assembly, his gruesome gift to King Abû Yaha Háquem was dispatched from the *trebuchet* to soar high over no-man's-land before plunging out of sight behind the city walls.

Pedrito noticed that the inspirational monk, Friar Miguel Fabra, had positioned himself at the side of the siege engine and had pronounced some sort of mumbled, though flamboyant, benediction as the Saracen head took to the heavens. And he repeated this performance for every one of the next dozen or so heads delivered likewise into the midst their former comrades. Meanwhile, the rock-hurling barrage by the other machines in the Christian battery continued uninterrupted.

King Jaume had remounted and remained in a prominent position throughout, his eyes glinting with satisfaction, his teeth gritted in a vengeful smile. His look reminded Pedrito of the day he first saw him on the deck of his galley when about to set sail from the mainland. Then, his boyish features had been radiating a glow that seemed to combine excitement for the coming adventure with a kind of childlike apprehension, if not full-blown trepidation. Now, though, that almost innocent look had become poisoned by the venom of battle and his smile polluted by the bitter taste of death. A shout ringing out from the city ramparts changed his expression yet again, however.

'What's that damned Moor trying to tell us, Master Blànes?' he scowled. 'Good God Almighty, waging war with the infidel would be a whole lot easier if only they had the grace to speak in a decent Christian tongue!'

The soldier doing the shouting was now joined by several others, who were shoving a huddle of naked, shackled men towards the edge of the battlements. The first soldier called out again.

Pedrito strained his ears, then told the king that the shackled men were Christians, taken prisoner at one of the earlier battles. The threat being made by the Moorish soldier was that, if the bombardment of the city didn't stop forthwith, the captives would be suspended on crosses along the face of the wall on which the barrage of rocks was currently focused.

A gutteral laugh rumbled in King Jaume's chest. 'So, they think they can hide behind a screen of defenceless Christians, do they? And they revile the memory of our Lord Jesus Christ by threatening to condemn our brothers to death on the cross!' He twisted round in his saddle and shouted to the commander of the nearest battery of siege engines. 'Tell your men to continue pelting the city walls with everything they've got. *Si*, and tell them not to let up, no matter what!'

As soon as it became plain to the Moors that their warning was being ignored, they duly bound their prisoners to crosses and lowered them over the battlements, where they were immediately exposed to the full force of the Christian onslaught. Amid the ensuing clamour, a lone, quavering voice was heard to call out from the row of victims spreadeagled against the wall. Of the few words he uttered, the only one audible to Pedrito was 'God'.

'There! Did you ever know a more devout follower of Christ?' King Jaume exclaimed to everyone within earshot, his sense of hearing considerably more acute, apparently, than Pedrito's. 'Even in the face of death he urges us to continue our assault on the Saracen cowards. And for the glory of God at that!' He then urged his siege engine commanders to redouble their efforts. 'See!' he shouted, pointing over no-man's-land. 'See how your boulders batter the walls close enough to our men to shave the beards from their faces, yet none is even scratched.' He brandished his sword above his head and yelled at the top of his voice, 'Those brave Christian soldiers have faith in our Lord God in whose name and for whose glory we fight this war! So batter away, lads, and fear not for the lives of your bold comrades yonder! God and His Son our Saviour are already rewarding their faith, and *your* faith, for all to see!'

While he had everyone's attention, he then called for a *ballista*, a wheeled catapult resembling a massive crossbow, to be rolled forward. This vicious machine, so powerfully constructed that its bowstring had to be drawn by a windlass, was capable of launching several projectiles at once, and with breathtaking velocity at that. On this occasion, however, King Jaume commanded that it be loaded with only one large javelin.

He motioned towards the setting sun, told the bowman precisely what to aim at, then declared, 'Let us bid our Saracen foes good night with something appropriate to dream about!'

Pedrito watched the projectile streak from the *ballista* with that now-familiar sound of the air being slashed by a giant whip. The javelin struck the shield of one of the Moorish soldiers with such force that it penetrated the metal as if it were paper, then continued on through the soldier's body, eventually coming to a halt having fatally skewered a second man standing behind him.

The king winked at Pedrito. 'What your ancient Balearic Slingers might have called killing two birds with one stone, eh?' Without waiting for a reply, he then ordered the soldier in charge of the Marseilles *trebuchet* to load its sling with a few more severed heads from the Canet encounter. '*Sí*,' King Jaume said with a resolute jerk of his head, 'and that'll teach them to treat prisoners of war with respect in future!'

## 22

# AN ANGEL FROM THE NORTH

*EARLY THE FOLLOWING MORNING –*
*'EL REAL' CHRISTIAN CAMP...*

The last thing King Jaume had said to his entourage at nightfall was that his ignoring of the Moors' threat would ultimately prove to be to the advantage of the Christian soldiers who had been so cravenly used as human shields. Everyone should mark his words – God would reward those men's unwavering devotion to Him by shaming their Moorish captors into returning them unscathed during the night to their dungeon, from which they would be released as heroes just as soon as their brothers in arms had entered the city.

Sure enough, it became evident at daybreak that the crucified men were indeed gone, but (perhaps significantly) so had the section of wall they had been hanging on. To a doctrinal waverer like Pedrito, this suggested that there was more chance of the men having been annihilated by the Christians' nocturnal bombardment than of their captors having been shamed into clemency. However, the king stood by his reasoning of the night before. This was reiterated by the redoubtable Friar Miguel Fabra during Mass, and appeared to be accepted without dispute by his congregation of combat-conditioned soldiers. This was war, God was on their side, and such illustrations of His support would be questioned at the doubter's peril.

Despite his exhaustion, Pedrito had slept fitfully, and it wasn't only because of the snoring and flatulent eruptions of the group of royal guards with whom he was sharing a tent. No, it was the images of Farah and Saleema invading his dreams every time he did drift off that were the main culprits. His crippled mother and the vulnerable girl in whose care he had left her had been constantly in his thoughts during waking hours, and the associated concerns for their safety became amplified in his sleep-hungry mind as the night wore on.

His overriding wish now was to be with them, not just to check on their wellbeing, but to take them somewhere that would provide the comfort they deserved, and which would also afford them protection from the desperate characters who would surely now be afoot in the war-torn countryside. But the more he thought about it, the more it became obvious that Farah's choice of their current sanctuary was still as good, or probably better, than anything he could come up with himslef. Even so, he still had a burning compulsion to go to them. But that would require the king's sanction, and he hadn't even told him of their existence yet. This was going to be a tricky revelation to make, given the religious and genetic complications involved, so the moment would have to be chosen with care.

'I trust you slept well,' the king beamed as he ushered Pedrito into his tent to join him for breakfast.

Pedrito nodded and offered a drowsy smile.

The king stretched. 'Ah, yes, Little Pedro,' he yawned, 'that's the first decent sleep I've had in several nights myself, and I have to admit that it makes me feel hungry.' He tore a chunk of bread off a loaf that a servant had brought to the table, accompanied by a large wedge of cheese and a jug of goat's milk. 'And it's good to have a real base again. Gives the cooks a chance to do what they're here for.' He patted his stomach. 'Simple fare in the field can seem better to a soldier than a lavish banquet produced in the kitchens of his own castle.'

'Yes, the smell of new-baked bread always reminds me of home as well,' Pedrito said without thinking. He realised too late that this may have given the impression that he'd been indulging in a bit of self-pity. And, in truth, he probably had.

King Jaume cast him a searching look. 'Hmm, still hurting from the loss of your family, eh?' He gave him a pat on the back. 'But as I told you before, keeping busy is the best way to get over bereavement, and that's precisely why I've made sure you haven't had an idle moment.'

'I'm grateful to you for that, *senyor*,' Pedrito replied with as much enthusiasm as he could muster.

The king poured him a cup of milk. 'Come on, *amic* – eat up and drink up! We have a busy morning ahead of us!' He gave a slightly self-conscious laugh. 'And, uh, if I seemed a mite blunt with you yesterday on the matter of your not having found out anything about the potential supply of provisions during your visit to the city, I apologise. I had a lot on my mind, and what with the lack of sleep and so on…'

Pedrito nodded. 'I know exactly what you mean, *senyor*. I've, well – I've had a lot to think about myself of late. Nothing as weighty as the things you have to concern yourself with, of course, but…' He rolled his shoulders uneasily. 'Well, more sort of personal matters, really, but things I'd like to talk to you about anyway … sometime, you know, when you can spare a few moments.'

'No problem at all,' the king breezed. 'Always glad to listen to the private problems of my people.' He then made what Pedrito took to be an unwittingly dismissive gesture with a lump of cheese. 'But first, you said yesterday that you would tell me about the local availability of food supplies for our forces – or rather why you hadn't been able to glean any information on the subject.'

'Exactly, and it ties in with the personal things I want to explain. You see, I chanced to meet two people while in the city – two women, actually – and because of their particular predicaments, which I sort of became involved with, I had to get out of there as fast as I could, and so I had no time to –'

The king cut him off with a wave of his hand. 'I knew it!' he guffawed, almost choking on his cheese. 'Women, eh? Underneath that goody-goody front, you're just like me. I mean, given half a chance, you're after them like a randy young bull let loose in a pen of heifers, right?' He stifled Pedrito's attempted remonstrations with a hearty slap on the shoulder. 'And I must say I'm glad to hear it, *amic*! Honestly, I was beginning to wonder if all that time spent with Arabs had bent you in the same perverted direction as them.' He gave Pedrito a lewd wink. 'Know what I mean?'

'No, no, no, it's not that,' Pedrito flustered.

'It isn't?' the king queried, devilment twinkling in his eyes. 'Don't tell me you're going to disappoint me after all.'

Pedrito was getting himself into a flap. 'No, I won't – what I mean to say is – well, what I want to tell you is – it wasn't a bull-and-heifer situation that –'

Laughing delightedly, the king interrupted him again, this time by throwing a crust of bread at him. 'Hey-y-y-y, I'm only teasing you, Little Pedro! And it's all right – I don't want to hear about your *indiscretions* with those two women. And anyway, we won't need to worry about where our provisions are going to come from, if it's true what the quisling Moor Akeem said yesterday, that is.' He took on a serious look. 'And that's why I invited you here this morning. I need you to translate when I meet this Benahabet character.'

'It's Ben Abbéd, *senyor*.'

'Call him what you want. He's still a sly, scheming Saracen to me – and will be, until he proves otherwise.'

Pedrito felt something bump against his ankle, and looked down to see a tousled black head in the process of putting itself on the outside of the piece of bread the king had thrown. 'Hello, Nedi,' he grinned. 'Where did you appear from all of a sudden?'

'Probably the other side of the camp,' the king suggested. 'Has a fantastic nose for food, that dog.'

'Don't they all?' Pedrito chuckled as he popped another crust into Nedi's upturned face. He gave the dog's head a ruffle. 'You're a lucky boy. I met someone in the city who had to beg on the streets for a scrap of bread like that.' He looked over at the king. 'And, ehm, that's what I wanted to talk to you about, *senyor*. You see –'

King Jaume held up a hand. 'It's all right, Little Pedro, I know all about the hardships a siege can inflict on the innocent. I've seen the evidence all too often, believe me, but as cruel as it may seem, a military commander just has to harden himself to it.'

'No, that's not what I –'

'Yes, yes, and I know you think my giving the order for the heads of the enemy to be catapulted into the city seemed heartless.' He smiled knowingly. 'I saw how disgusted you were when the first one was loaded into the *trebuchet* yesterday evening.'

'Yes, but –'

'Yes, and that's exactly why I insisted you went along to see it happening. War's a dirty business, *amic*, and you have to give as good as you take – better, even.' King Jaume thumped the table. 'Those Saracen cowards tried to cut off our sole supply of water. Hardly an act of bravery, huh?'

Pedrito hunched shoulders.

'Precisely, Little Pedro. There's nothing more heartless than to sneakily deprive an army of its water.' He wagged a finger admonishingly. 'So don't you go thinking I'm a heartless man. I stand by the most honourable Christain values, including praying for the souls of the besieged who are starved to death.' He gave a slow, pious nod of his head. 'Ah yes, because I've always brought about their demise for the further glory of God, and He will endorse the righteousness of my actions here by granting me victory once again. You'll see.'

Pedrito could sense a one-sided conversation developing here, so he sat in silence while the king continued his address on the legitimacy of war's cruelties. It was patently obvious that informing him of the existence and parlous circumstances of Saleema and his mother would have to wait until a more appropriate moment.

*A LITTLE LATER THAT MORNING –*
*A LEAGUE TO THE NORTH OF 'EL REAL' CAMP...*

King Jaume seemed to have made a shrewd choice of location for his rendezvous with Ben Abbéd – the centre of a wide area of flat land, with good lines of vision in all directions, and therefore no risk of being ambushed. All the same, an advance detatchment of twenty knights and their followers had been sent out from the camp to observe the *wali*'s arrival, and only when they were satisfied that there was no sign of intended treachery did they signal that it was safe for the king to come forward. Even then, the advance detail took the added precaution of riding round to the far side of the Moorish party to ensure that no others joined them, and also to cut off their escape route, should their forthcoming conduct justify the need for one.

The king, mounted on his charger and wearing a chainmail hauberk, approached the meeting place flanked by archers and members of his personal guard, all fully armed and battle-ready. He had an intuitional mistrust of this Ben Abbéd fellow, so no chances were being taken.

Pedrito, as had become his wont, followed at a respectful distance, riding the steady old hack he'd waggishly nicknamed Tranquilla after her nervy behaviour on the road to his family home at Andratx a few days earlier. When the king was about a hundred paces away from a little almond grove in which the Moors had stationed themselves, he halted his company and beckoned Pedrito to his side.

'It's impossible to make out how many of them there are or what their pack animals are carrying, if anything,' the king muttered. 'Trust a devious Saracen to set up his stall in the only clump of trees for miles around!' He nudged Pedrito with his elbow. 'Trot off in there and see what's what. Have a word with this Benahabet, or whatever his name is, then come back and let me know what you think.' Noticing Pedrito's concerned look, he then added, 'And don't worry – if you haven't returned in five minutes, we'll charge in and slaughter the lot of them.'

Suitably reassured, Pedrito did as instructed.

In the event, the king's suspicions proved to be unwarranted. What Ben Abbéd had brought to the rendezvous was a generous and tantalising array of the season's produce from his estates. A team of twenty mules had been laden with sacks of barley and flour, with chickens, kids and lambs, with amphoras of wine, and with a mouthwatering variety of fruit, including baskets brimful of plump grapes so tenderly handled that a guarantee was given that not a solitary one would be found to have been bruised. What's more, Ben Abbéd, a tall and swarthy Moor, whose robes and bearing identified him as a man of substance, had taken the trouble to have this cornucopia of nature's gifts displayed in the most decorative of ways, given the restrictions imposed by an improvised presentation in the middle of an isolated almond grove.

King Jaume was impressed and didn't hold back from letting it be known to his benefactor...

'Tell him, Master Blànes, that we are delighted with what he has on offer. Splendid – absolutely splendid!' He squinted up at the sun, then glanced at his surroundings. 'And, uhm, tell him it was most considerate of him to chose this shady copse for our meeting.'

In response, Ben Abbéd, bowing reverentially and gesticulating extravagantly, ushered the king towards an open-sided tent that had been pitched in the middle of the grove. Here, with the ground covered by a rug of intricate arabesque design, a cushioned couch had been positioned beside a table displaying samples of all the produce brought for the king's appraisal. He was invited to be seated while a quartet of veiled, though conspicuously curvacious, hand maidens served him morsels of his choice on delicate little silver dishes.

'*Sí*,' the king enthused, 'most impressive! Hmm, most impressive indeed!'

Pedrito noted that, while the king was uttering this final superlative, it was the serving girls rather than what they were serving that he was devoting his attention to. If the young monarch's reputation hadn't preceded him (and it was most unlikely that it would have), then Ben Abbéd had made a very fortuitous choice of personnel when preparing this exhibition. Any doubts he may have had about the king's cooperation – or, indeed, vice versa – were soon to be proven groundless.

Within half an hour, the conversation conducted via Pedrito had resulted in an understanding between the two men which confirmed everything young Akeem had offered on his master's behalf the previous day. In return for the king's assurance that his position would be 'respected' after the war, Ben Abbéd would pledge to provide – each and every week that the siege lasted – supplies equivalent to those he had brought today, and in sufficient quantities to satisfy the entire army's needs. All he would require from King Jaume in the meantime would be one of his flags, so that his men conveying the provisions could pass unharmed through ground already held by the Christians. This, the king readily agreed to.

A deal had been struck, and to endorse his commitment to his side of the bargain, Ben Abbéd solemnly affirmed that his offer to place approximately one third of rural Mallorca into the king's control would be implemented at the earliest opportunity. As soon as the king found it convenient to appoint two of his nobles to act as governors of the relevant areas, the peaceful transfer of their administration and associated revenues would be put into motion without delay.

This, the king readily agreed to as well. And in so doing, he made no attempt to conceal his liking for the 'fellow' he had so recently dubbed a sly, scheming Saracen. Formal pleasantries were exchanged in the most amicable of atmospheres before the two partners in this unlikely alliance finally prepared to go their separate ways – Ben Abbéd back to the spleandour of his Alfabia estate, and King Jaume (with Ben Abbéd's twenty laden mules in his train) back to the relative austerity of his encampment.

Of all the paradoxes this meeting had produced, the one that struck Pedrito as the most bizarre was that it was still possible to hear the horrific noises of siege warfare drifting over the plain into this tiny oasis of bonhomie and opulence. This spawned the thought that it might require weeks of death and destruction on an unthinkable scale to enable King Jaume to take the capital city, yet a few minutes spent bartering food in exchange for the promised continuation of a rich *wali*'s privileges had already won him a third of the island's entire hinterland.

Pedrito mentioned this to the king after he had bid *adéu* to his new friend.

'Ah, but that's war for you, Little Pedro. It throws up the most unexpected changes of fortune – good or bad, depending on which side you're on, but invariably tied to the survival of someone of influence.'

Pedrito sighed. 'Every turncoat has his price, I suppose.'

'*Sí*,' the king smiled while waving to the departing Ben Abbéd, 'and that one came surprisingly cheaply!'

### THAT EVENING, 'EL REAL' CHRISTIAN CAMP...

Though a little disconcerted by the spirited resistence the forces within Medîna Mayûrqa were showing in the face of the unrelenting bombardment of their city, King Jaume was heartened by the good progress being made by the Count of Empúries and his three teams of sappers. However, while their tunnelling work beneath the moat continued, the Moors' missiles were now inflicting considerable damage to the southern extremities of the Christain stockade, and to those defending it. Fortunately, though, such activity was sporadic, the pattern and timing of the attacks dictated by how quickly the Moors could replace or repair any war engines knocked out by the Christians. King Jaume's men were still having the better of these artillery exchanges, but the speed of the Moors' repairing of the resultant damage to the city walls, together with an increasingly evident spirit of resistance, indicated a long and painful siege for both sides.

But that, as the king had told Pedrito on more than one occasion, was war. And the good news for his people was that, thanks to the 'forward-looking' Ben Abbéd, they would now have the ability to starve the enemy into submission, should they persist with their determination not to surrender the city. The king considered this worthy of celebration, and what better way to celebrate than by enjoying the unexpected bonus of all those edibles brought into camp on Ben Abbéd's mule train. So, even in the midst of the ongoing combat, the campaign's leading nobles and churchmen joined the king in his tent that evening for a right royal feast.

*

Pedrito had been afforded the privilege of joining members of the king's retinue of younger knights for their apportionment of the fare, to be served in the open air at tables set round a fire in the centre of the royal enclosure. After the pleasant warmth of the day, the evening air was noticably chilly, as is normal in Mallorca at this time of changing seasons. It soon became abundantly clear, however, that the falling temperature was of no concern to the gathered company of young warriors. Even without the benefit of the fire, their spirits had been lifted sufficiently by the occasion to set the blood surging hotly through their veins. And the potency of Ben Abbéd's sweet Mallorcan wine doubtless played its part in boosting this sensation of euphoria.

Pedrito had witnessed the same effect that just such a welcome release from the rigours of warfare had had on another group of young Christian soldiers when huddled round a fire to share a simple supper after the Battle of Na Burguesa. And although the meal here was considerably more sumptuous, an outpouring of identical banter developed in its wake. Harmless insults were bandied about amid raucous eruptions of laughter, while each man sang the praises of his own place of birth more effusively than the next. The understandable outcome of a temporary escape from the fear of death in the first instance, and the unwitting exposure of a carefully concealed longing for home in the second. That, at least, was Pedrito's reading of the situation.

Albeit that he had been welcomed wholeheartedly into the body of this rather select company of young men-at-arms, Pedrito had slipped away quietly when their post-prandial skylarking started. And famished though he had been, the sight of so much food when it appeared had actually ruined his appetite. The prospect of his mother and young Saleema sitting in that dank cave eating snails had filled him with a feeling of guilt. How could he possibly enjoy all that had been laid before him here when they were having to survive on so little? Why, even Nedi the dog was eating better on scraps dropped from the table.

And so he spent the latter part of the evening sitting alone with his thoughts near the perimeter of the compound, the sound of the young knights' jollity on one side, the clamour of war engines being cocked, loaded and discharged on the other. It struck Pedrito as a curious blend of the merry and the malicious, a notion put into words by King Jaume when he sidled up behind him after the banquet in his tent was over.

'That's war for you, Little Pedro – a bitter broth of blood, sweat and tears, with the occasional dash of nervous laughter added to sweeten the mixture – *if* you're lucky.'

Startled, Pedrito stood up. 'It seems you've been reading my thoughts, *senyor.*'

The king shook his head. 'They're everyone's thoughts, and they never change, no matter how often men find themselves in situations like this.' He shivered, pulling his cloak around him. 'But why are you sitting so far from the fire? Wasn't the company of my young heroes good enough for you?'

'No, no, it wasn't that,' Pedrito protested apologetically. 'It's just that I –'

The king started to chuckle. 'It's all right, *amic*, I was only teasing again. But anyway, the lads have all gone off to their quarters now, so why don't you come and sit with me for a while back there – you know, have a chat while there's still a glow in the ashes?' He rubbed his midriff. 'I've eaten so much I'll have nightmares if I go to sleep before I've had a chance to digest some of this.'

Although the king was by no means tipsy, Pedrito could tell by his demeanour that he had been enjoying his share of Ben Abbéd's wine. And he told one of his servants to bring another two cups of it just as soon as he and Pedrito had settled down by the fire. Perhaps, Pedrito thought, the right moment to tell the king about his mother and Saleema had come at last. But not just yet. First, he would allow the king time to talk about whatever *he* wanted to. It seemed that he was in the mood to indulge in a bit of small talk, to unwind after taking part in what may well have been some highly-charged military conversations with his dinner guests, so best to give him his head.

'An angel, Little Pedro, an absolute angel,' he said after his first slurp of wine.

'Who, me?'

The king chuckled again. 'No, no – I mean no offence, but not you, although I'm sure you will be – some day, but not for a while yet, we hope. No, no, I'm talking about the Moor, Benahabet.'

'You mean Ben Abbéd.'

'Call him what you will,' the king said with a dismissive flourish of his hand, 'to me he's still an angel.'

Pedrito stifled a snigger, while also suppressing the urge to remind the king that he had referred to the same man as a sly, scheming Saracen that very morning. 'Ben Abbéd, an *angel*?' he queried.

The king took another gulp of wine. 'Absolutely. I've been thinking about it, and it's the only way to describe him.'

Pedrito shot him an incredulous look. 'A *Muslim* angel? But I thought we Christians were taught to believe that only followers of Christ went to heaven.'

'Very true, very true. But this Muslim was obviously sent to us by our God – the *only* God, the Father of our Saviour, Jesus Christ.'

Pedrito scratched his head. 'So God, *our* God, communicates with Muslims, is that what you're saying?'

The king pulled a facial shrug. 'Quite clearly, yes. How else would this Benahabet –'

'Ben Abbéd.'

'Whatever. How else would he have had the wisdom to provide us, God's army, with the wherewithal to defeat the disbelievers?'

'But he's a Muslim. He believes in Allah, not God.'

The king leaned over and prodded Pedrito in the chest. 'God moves in mysterious ways, Little Pedro, and it isn't for us to question them. Never forget that.'

Pedrito decided to remain silent for a while, fighting the impulse to say something that he feared he might regret. But, as usual, his tongue eventually won the contest with his better judgement.

'You told me on the first day at sea that your mission was to convert the Mallorcan Muslims to Christianity, and destroy those who refused.'

'So?'

'So, will the same go for Ben Abbéd?'

King Jaume gave a derisory little laugh. 'You clearly aren't familiar with the politics of religion, *amic*.' He paused to take another sip of wine. 'But for your enlightenment – and I say this in the strictest confidence – I discussed that very matter over dinner tonight with Berenguer de Palou, the Bishop of Barcelona himself, and it was agreed that the matter of Benahabet's religious persuasion would be held in abeyance – until after the war, at least.'

'In other words, he can buy the right to be a Muslim by providing the Christian army with food. Is that how it works?'

The king tapped the side of his nose. 'Politics, religion, war – you have to know how to come out on top in all of them, and it's for God to decide whether the action I take in His name is correct or not. If He grants me victory – and I believe He will – it will prove that I've made the right decisions. It's as simple as that.'

'Simple?' Pedrito snorted. 'Well, I'm afraid I'm too simple to understand, *senyor*.'

The king swallowed a yawn. 'Little Pedro, as I told you before – and no offence intended – that's why God made me a king and made you a peasant.'

'No doubt, *senyor*. No doubt.'

The king drained his cup, then nodded towards Pedrito's. 'You aren't drinking your wine. Don't you like it?'

'I haven't tasted it, but I'm sure it's excellent.'

'It is indeed, so no point in letting it go to waste.' The king tilted his head. 'Uhm-ah, may I?'

Pedrito indicated that he could.

'I don't know why you persist in only drinking water, *amic*. As that drunken old monk of a tutor always drummed into me, fish shit in it.' He raised Pedrito's cup. '*Salut*! Your very good health!'

Pedrito nodded his reciprocation, deliberating during the few moments of silence that followed whether this might be an opportune moment to broach the subject – and complicated side issues – of having chanced to discover his natural mother in the city.

But it was the king, slouched back against the table and gazing sleepily into the embers of the fire, who spoke first. 'You know how I've been using you to act as a translator for me?'

'Yes, and I'm only too pleased to help. Glad of the opportunity, in fact.'

'And you'll recall that I mentioned a man called Abel Babiel?'

'The man from Zaragoza, who speaks a bit of Arabic?'

'The same. Anyway, if it should happen that there's a parley between myself and the Moorish king – and such things do happen in the course of any siege – Senyor Babiel may well insist on acting as my interpreter.'

'Fair enough,' Pedrito acknowledged, in some inexplicable way relieved that he might not have to confront his true father. 'I know my place. No problem.'

The king sat up and looked directly at him. 'Ah, but there *is* a problem.'

Pedrito shook his head. 'Not as far as I'm concerned. Honestly.'

The king leaned in close again. 'Politics. Politics and religion, that's the problem.' He thought for a moment. 'And, eh, money … naturally.'

'All too complicated for me,' Pedrito chortled. 'And too steeped in intrigue as well. Yes indeed, being a simple peasant does have its advantages.'

'Except you're not just a simple peasant – you're my trusted interpreter – "trusted" being the operative word. *Sí*, and I'm afraid that merely adds to the problem.'

Pedrito watched the king stroke his beard meditatively for a bit, then said, 'So, you don't trust Senyor Babiel, is that it?'

King Jaume replied in a manner that suggested he was thinking aloud as much answering Pedrito's question. He muttered that it wasn't that he didn't trust this man Babiel. After all, he had raised enough money in Zaragoza to contribute considerably to the undertaking of this crusade, so that was surely worthy of trust. But at what price? That was the problem – or part of it. Abel Babiel was a Jew, and the agreed bargain was that his people would be granted a commensurate allocation of Mallorca's asset's on the successful completion of the Christian reconquest of the island.

'Seems reasonable enough,' Pedrito suggested. 'It's the same deal all your other supporters have been promised, isn't it?'

'Hmm,' the king droned, still in contemplative mood. 'But if I do have a final face-to-face with the Moorish King, how will I be able to judge if what Babiel tells me is a true translation? He may twist the Amir's words to suit his own ends.'

'So, you *don't* trust him,' Pedrito laughed. 'It's as simple as that.'

This seemed to shake the king out of his reverie. 'There you go with your naïve thinking again.' He gathered his brows into a frown. 'Nothing's ever as simple as that – not when it comes to dealing with a Jew at any rate.'

'Oh, I don't know,' said Pedrito, with more than a hint of dissent in his voice. 'I mean, my father used to sell fish on the quayside to merchants who were Jews, and although they always drove a hard bargain, they were never less than straight. You knew where you stood with them. And the Moors thought so as well. Treated them the same as us Christian – let them worship as they pleased, as long as they did it discreetly.' He hunched his shoulders. 'All right, just like us Christians, they were charged higher taxes than Muslims, but that wasn't a huge price to pay for peaceful co-existence. In any case, I never heard a Jew complaining about life under Moorish rule, and I never heard a Moorish merchant saying the Jews were untrustworthy.'

A wry smile crossed the king's lips. 'Ah, but that's where your peasant background lets you down. You haven't had the benefit of a proper education, you see.'

Pedrito gave him a quasi-vacant look. 'Well, never too old to learn, *senyor*. I'm all ears, so tell me what I need to know.'

King Jaume proceeded to explain to Pedrito that one of the first things he had been told by the Knights Templar who brought him up was that there were Jewish soldiers in the first Moorish armies to overrun Spain. 'Arabs, Jews, Saracens,' he went on. 'Whatever they call themselves, they're all Semites, the sons of Noah, all members of the same tribe.'

'But your man Babiel has committed himself to a Christian cause.

He's here taking part in a crusade, so does it matter what his forebears were?'

The king uttered a mocking little laugh. 'Senyor Babiel has come here in the company of Christian soldiers, there's no denying that. But he comes with an abacus in his hand, not a sword, and that's the difference.'

Pedrito had seen the king in this frame of mind before – absently revealing his innermost thoughts, not with any intention of stimulating a discussion, but rather in an attempt to lighten the load of his responsibilities while temporarily distanced from the critical presence of his senior barons and clergymen. Pedrito happily took it upon himself to feed him questions that might help the cathartic process along. Would it therefore be the king's objective, he asked, to make all Mallorcan Jews convert to Christianity, or suffer the same fate as dissenting Muslims?

The king was quick to reply that he had no such intention. 'Indeed, I have nothing against them practicing their own religion, as long as it's done in private – you know, in a way that doesn't offend the Christian establishment.'

'But if they're of the same tribe as the Arabs, why treat them differently?'

'Because our Lord Jesus Christ was a Jew, and Mohammed wasn't. Simple.'

Pedrito nodded pensively. 'But Jesus is the son of God, so does that mean that God is Jewish?'

King Jaume chose to ignore that question. Silence reigned for a while, then, gazing thoughtfully into the dying embers of the fire, he murmured, 'He's a clever man, your Jew. Good with money. Some of them even manage the financial affairs of Moorish rulers in parts of Spain. *Sí*, and make no mistake, they'll eventually do the same for some of the new Christian rulers as well.'

'What's wrong with that?' Pedrito came back. 'Surely it's a wise ruler who makes use of a subject's skills, be he a soldier or a bean-counter.'

The king glanced sidelong at him. 'Without a doubt. But it's when the abacus becomes mightier than the sword that the troubles will start.' He looked back into the fire. 'As I've said many times, it's the Church – they can make or break kings. And the day will come when they'll break the Jews, if they get hold of too many purse strings.' It was as if he was speaking to himself now. 'Even the Knights Templar won't be immune from the power of the Church. Just look at them – a century ago they amounted to nothing but a few impoverished French monks dedicated to ensuring the safety of Christian pilgrims on their way to Jerusalem's Temple Mount. Now, because of their crusading exploits, their prodigious order has amassed so much wealth through the granting of lands and privileges by the rich and righteous that they've become the bankers and financiers to much of Christian Europe.' He nodded his head dolefully. 'Money means power, and one day, if the Templars' power is seen as a threat to the Church, they'll be broken too.'

Pedrito remained tactfully silent while King Jaume stared into his wine. '*Sí*, God moves in mysterious ways,' he mumbled, 'and all a mortal can do is try to follow them...' He hesitated before adding, 'According, naturally, to the guidance of His representatives here on earth.'

'You mean the leaders of the Christian Church?' Pedrito asked rhetorically, but cautiously.

Again, the king appeared not to have heard. He shivered, pulling his cloak about himself once more. Then, as though shaken from a daydream, he looked Pedrito in the eye and said, 'I am not a heartless man, Little Pedro. I do what I do for the glory of God, but I'm not a heartless man ... even if you do disapprove of my ordering the severed heads of the enemy to be hurled back where they belong.'

Clearly, the king's mood had now graduated from mellow to conciliatory, so Pedrito decided to seize the moment.

He faked a cough. 'The, ehm, the two women I told you about – the ones I met in the city...'

The king arched an eyebrow, an impish smile lighting his face. 'Aha, the confession of your sins. Do you want me to summon a priest so that you can receive forgiveness like everyone else who joined this crusade? Better late than never.'

Lowering his eyes, Pedrito laughed nervously. 'No, *senyor*, no. I, well, what I have to confess is far from being a sin. Quite the opposite, in fact.' He allowed his eyes meet the king's for a second. 'Although...' He coughed again.

'Go on, *amic*!' the king urged. 'Although what?'

Pedrito shuffled his feet uneasily, then blurted out 'Although, *senyor*, I fear there may be aspects of what I have to say that won't meet with your approval.'

Intrigued, the king pursed his lips. 'Not a sin, yet I'll disapprove of it, eh?' He tutted loudly. 'But there you go again – talking in riddles. Come on, man, you know I've no time for any of that. Say what you have to say!'

Pedrito took a deep breath. 'Well, one of the women turned out to be my mother.'

King Jaume scowled at him for several tense moments. 'If this is some sort of jest,' he eventually growled, 'I'll take it ill out. You told me with tears in your eyes the other day that your parents had been killed by Moorish pirates, and I offered you my condolences.' His frown deepened as his voice rose. 'Now you tell me you met your mother in the city. Do you take me for an idiot – or have you taken leave of your senses?'

Pedrito could understand why the king's patience, and temper, was short, attempting as he had been to escape for a little while the worries of warfare by having a relaxed and unburdening chat. What's more, he was tired and perhaps beginning to feel the effects of his intake of Ben Abbéd's wine. All the same, Pedrito wasn't finding it easy to come out with what he had to say, and he felt stung by the king's sudden aggressiveness. After all, his allegiance to the king had been a major factor in his deciding to come back here when he could just as easily have stayed in the cave above Génova to help protect and support his mother and Saleema.

'I mean no disrespect, *senyor*,' he snapped, 'but I certainly haven't taken leave of my senses!'

The king took a sharp breath and held it, as if in the process of deciding whether he had just been on the receiving end of a veiled insult.

'Nor,' Pedrito quickly appended, as the king, his hackles rising, attempted to speak, 'do I take you for an idiot.'

King Jaume exhaled loudly. Then, with a wry smile and a rolling movement of his hand, he bade Pedrito continue.

Calmly and without emotion, Pedrito first reminded the king that it had been his adoptive parents, the people who had taken him into their home as a foundling, who had been the victims of marauding pirates. The woman he had met in the city, however, was his natural mother – someone whose whereabouts or even existence he hadn't known anything about until a chance encounter with her in the lowly kasbah quarter.

King Jaume's immediate, and absolutely valid, reaction was to ask how Pedrito could be certain that someone he'd never even heard about before was truly his mother.

It was a long story, Pedrito replied, the details of which could wait for now. The king could rest assured, however, that there was absolutely no doubt that this woman, Farah, had given birth to him and had been obliged, through circumstances beyond her control, to abandon him on the quayside shortly afterwords.

The king nodded reflectively. 'As En Guillen de Muntcada once said, such is the fate of the newborn infants of young women like that.'

Pedrito glared at him. 'Young women like *what*?'

Now it was the king's turn to react uneasily. 'En Guillen was talking generally, of course, so I'm sure he wasn't casting aspersions at you, but –'

'I remember exactly what he said,' Pedrito interrupted. 'As you'll recall, I was there, and what he said was that foundlings are the bastard offspring of whores.'

The king, as befitted someone of his status, defended himself by going immediately on the offensive. 'Ah yes, but as *you*'ll recall, I censured En Guillen severely about that, and I made a point of doing it in front of you. Believe me, I wouldn't normally give a nobleman – and a relation of mine to boot – a dressing down in the presence of a – a –'

'A peasant like me?'

Awkwardly, King Jaume inclined his head to one side, then the other. 'Well, all right, if you like – yes.'

This attempted show of indifference was far from convincing; a reaction that Pedrito found quite disarming. Here was the figurehead of arguably the biggest and most daring seaborne invasion ever carried out by Christian Spain, yet he still had an almost child-like vulnerability about him. He was a walking enigma, capable of kicking the severed head of an enemy aristocrat into the sling of a siege engine, while also feeling uncomfortable about offending someone he thought of as a peasant, even if a friendly one.

Pedrito siezed the opportunity to play to this side of the king's nature. 'I simply had to get her out of the city before the Christian soldiers reached that part of it.' He looked appealingly into the king's eyes. 'She's my mother. She could have been killed.'

The king returned his look with one of mild suspicion. 'And that's why you left without taking time to find out about possible sources of provisions for our army, as I'd charged you to do? Couldn't you have delayed for a while? After all, it could be weeks, even months, before we're able to occupy that area of the city.'

'But surely none of that's important any more. After all, unkown to any of us, Ben Abbéd was already preparing to supply you with enough food for the army's requirements.'

'Meaning?'

'Meaning that everyone needs a guardian angel. Ben Abbéd has turned out to be yours, while fate saw to it that I was in the right place at the right time to be my mother's.'

King Jaume smiled another wry smile. 'You have an alert mind, Little Pedro, and I admire that.' He raised a finger and rocked it back and forth. 'But I must take you up on two points. First, if you were in the right place at the right time, it was because of God, not fate.'

'No doubt,' Pedrito conceded without demur.

'Second, my instinct tells me that there was more to your swift exit from the city than you've admitted.' He cocked his head inquisitively. 'No?'

'I have nothing to hide or be ashamed of in that respect,' Pedrito countered. 'The fact is that my mother is a cripple. So, waiting in the city any longer than was necessary wasn't an option. *My* instinct told me that I had to get her out of there right away, and I did just that.'

The king pursed his lips again. 'A cripple, you say. I'm sorry to hear that. But, and I hope you'll excuse my curiosity, how so exactly?'

Pedrito could see the way the king's mind was working. And, although the truth was bound to come out eventually, perhaps it might be easier to let him think he was working it out for himself here and now.

'As a young woman, she had a foot and a hand cut off,' Pedrito said flatly.

The king arched his eyebrows. 'Hmm, a Muslim punishment, I believe?'

Pedrito confirmed that this was indeed the case. 'Left hand, right foot. A punishment demanded by her husband.'

The king winced. 'How inhuman! But what on earth had she done to deserve such barbaric treatment?'

'She'd given birth to a child. That was her only crime.'

'Ah, now I get it!' the king nodded. 'Adultery, eh? She'd given birth to a child not sired by her husband. *Sí, sí, sí,* now I can see why she incurred the full wrath of –'

'The child *was* her husband's,' Pedrito cut in. 'The problem was that it had the mark of the devil on it.'

'Of the ... *devil?*'

Pedrito pulled his hair aside to expose the small birthmark behind his ear.

'A cross!' the king gasped. 'But – but that's the emblem of Christianity, not the sign of the devil.'

'In a Christian's eyes, yes.'

The king raised a hand. 'Hold on! Hold on! Let me get to grips with this. You're saying that *you* are that child – the child abandoned by your mother and the cause of her having a hand and foot cut off. Is that what you're saying?'

Pedrito pointed to his birthmark. 'Yes, because I was deemed to be a Christian child.'

King Jaume was already stroking his beard in that pensive way of his. 'But I take it that your father and mother were, are, both Muslims, *sí*?'

Pedrito indicated that this was so.

The king looked at him through half closed eyes. 'So, it follows that you, too, are a Muslim.'

Chuckling to himself, Pedrito shook his head. 'No baby is born anything – Muslim, Christian, Jew or whatever. Infants can't decide what religion they're going to follow, if any. That's fed to them by their parents, or whoever brings them up.'

'Ah, but that's where your lack of education lets you down again, Little Pedro. The bible tells us that we're born in God's image – that's *God*'s image, not Allah's or any other false deity's, so it follows that...' The king's words trailed off as he began to consider the matter more carefully.

Pedrito picked up the thread. 'You were born in the image of your parents, who were presumably fair-skinned. I was born in the image of my parents, who weren't quite so fair-skinned. But unless we know what God looks like, how can we say what those who worship him are supposed to look like?'

The king stared at him blankly, then took a slurp of wine and muttered, 'Careful what you're saying, *amic*.'

'All I'm saying is that, if you had been brought up as a Muslim, you'd be a Muslim, no matter what you look like. And the same goes for Christians.'

King Jaume's eyes were now beginning to show the effects of his intake of wine. He focused them on Pedrito's face, smiled woozily and said, 'So, what is it you're trying to say, Little Pedro?'

'Simply, *senyor*, that I have Moorish blood in my veins – the blood of my parents – and if they had brought me up, I would have been brought up as a Muslim, even with the mark of a Christian on me. But the people who raised me were Christians and they taught me to be a Christian like them. So,' he smiled, 'that's what I am – even if I do look like a Moor.'

The king's chin dropped onto his chest as he began to laugh quietly to himself. 'All too complicated for a simple king like me, my peasant friend. All to complicated for me.' Then, after a few moments of contemplating his empty wine cup, he gave himself a shake, focused blearily on Pedrito's face again and grinned. 'But enough of theology!' He reached out and punched Pedrito playfully on the shoulder. 'Tell me about the other woman. You said there were two. And,' he winked, 'I'll eat my best saddle if she wasn't a frisky little filly, eh! So, own up, you dog. What dissolute deed was the *real* reason for your hasty exit from the city?

## 23

# A WOMAN IN MISCHIEF
# IS WISER THAN A MAN

*THE FOLLOWING MORNING –*
*THE MOUNTAINSIDE ABOVE GÉNOVA SETTLEMENT...*

Pedrito's conversation with the king the previous evening had ended without any further mention being made of Pedrito's mother or, more significantly for Pedrito, his father. King Jaume, in his 'relaxed' mood, had been more interested in hearing anything Saleema might have mentioned about the delights of the harem from which she had escaped. Although there had been precious little to tell, even touching briefly on the subject had evidently conjured up favourable images in the young monarch's mind of a palace awash with delectable (and constantly available) young concubines, judging by the smile on his face when he eventually fell asleep at the table, that is.

However, no matter how much under the influence of Ben Abbéd's wine he may have been last night, the king had been up with the larks and looking as bright as a button in the morning. He had summoned Pedrito to his tent immediately after discussing orders for the day with his military commanders, and he soon made it obvious that he had remembered at least the more important elements of what he had been told about the plight of Farah and Saleema.

The sensitive subject of the two women being Moors would be ignored for the present, he informed Pedrito. This was a matter that would be for no-one's ears but their own, of course – the hard fact being that 'unpleasant complications' would arise for Pedrito if even a whisper of his fraternising with the enemy leaked out. Then, repeating his assertion that he was not a heartless man, King Jaume told Pedrito to fill panniers with a selection of foodstuffs from the stores and make his way on his old hack to where the women were sheltering. What their fate might be in the long term was a bridge that would be crossed in the fullness of time, he said, but for the present, it was Pedrito's paramount duty to see to the welfare of his mother – and, he added with a twinkle in his eye, to the 'comfort' of the young concubine Saleema as well.

All the king had asked of Pedrito in return was his word that he would be back at camp by nightfall. His skill as a translator – not to speak of the strength of his muscles – could be called upon at any time. For it shouldn't be forgotten, he was at pains to emphasise, that Pedrito was, when all was said and done, a Christian!

Now, as Pedrito, mounted on Tranquilla, ascended the track leading to the sliver of land where the cave was situated, his mind was filled with conflicting emotions.

Relief was what he felt with regard to King Jaume not having shown any interest in the identity of Farah's husband. In fact, if he had asked, Pedrito would have been obliged to lie. The last thing he needed to further complicate his current familial situation was for the Christian king to know that the Moorish king was his trusted translator's father. At the same time, Pedrito himself was in a quandry about the rights and wrongs of siding with the enemy of his own flesh and blood. But his natural father – a man whose very existence he hadn't known about until a couple of days ago – had been responsible for an act of horrendous cruelty upon his mother, and that aroused in him a feeling of justification, albeit a confused one, for helping to bring about his downfall.

But what were his feelings for his mother? His admiration for her courage and a sense of afinity with her spirit of determination were certainly strong, and there was no doubting that he was deeply concerned about her wellbeing. Beyond that, however, the bond that had existed between Pedrito and his adoptive mother was one that

316

hadn't yet been replicated. Although well aware that it might not be easy, he had resolved, nonetheless, to do all he could to help give this new and unforeseen relationship a chance to develop. His hope was that time and nature would do the rest. Meanwhile, Pedrito realised that the situation would be equally hard for his mother to deal with. Faced with the predicament that she must try to replace her own son's lifelong maternal ties to someone else, her feelings would be just as much in turmoil as his own.

She was sitting beside Saleema on a rock outside the cave when Pedrio came over the rise. It was Saleema who noticed him first. He could see that she hadn't recognised him initially, dressed as he was in his shirt and *pantalons* instead of the Arab robe and head scarf he had been wearing before. Alarmed, she nudged Farah and started to help her to her feet.

'It's all right,' Pedrito shouted, 'it's only me!'

'Pedrito?' Saleema called back, holding the tips of her fingers to her lips. 'Is – is that you?'

'Who else would climb all the way up here to visit a pair of scruffy cavewomen like you?' Pedrito grinned as he jumped down from Tranquilla's back and led the old horse through the sparse stand of trees. 'What's that you're busy with anyway?'

Saleema laid down the bowl she had been holding and ran towards him.

Farah had now struggled to her feet and was hobbling along in Saleema's wake. 'We were just shelling some almonds,' she beamed. 'We're preparing something exotic for lunch, and you're welcome to join us. It's almond soup. You know, almonds, milk, stale bread and wild garlic!'

'What, no snails?' Pedrito joked.

Saleema threw her arms round him, then, with tears tricking down her cheeks, she looked up at him and smiled. 'Oh, Pedrito, you've no idea how good it is to see you again!'

Farah now joined them in a three-way hugging session. 'Yes, we've missed you really badly. Mind you, you needn't have worried about us.' She gave Saleema a surreptitious dig in the ribs with her elbow. 'We've been doing fine, haven't we, *habib*?'

Saleema hesitated for a moment. 'Oh, yes, yes, fine – absolutely fine,' she said, though not all that persuasively. 'Yes, as your mother says – no need to worry about us.'

Pedrito smiled at this show of stoicism, which was well-practiced and genuine on Farah's part, but with a bit yet to go on Saleema's. Nevertheless, she was trying, and who better to model herself on than Farah. Pedrito was proud of them both, and although still filled with misgivings about their situation, he was glad to be here in their company once again.

What's more, as muddled as his feelings towards his mother may still have been, the way his pulse had started to race at the mere sight of Saleema confirmed that what he felt for her was indeed different from the brother-and-sister association he'd thought had been his motivation for attempting to rescue her from the clutches of the two drunken pirates outside the inn. Also, the way she had looked into his eyes a moment ago had spoken volumes about the way she felt for him. Under other circumstances, he would have been absolutely delighted, but as things stood, his head told him that a romantic involvement with a Muslim girl was one more complication in his life that he certainly didn't need. What his heart might eventually have to say about this was an entirely different matter, of course, and he was acutely aware of that as well.

'So, I take it you haven't got any snails?' he teased after disentangling himself from their arms.

Farah dropped the corners of her mouth. 'Sorry – no rain, no snails. It's almond soup or nothing. And, uh – no goat, no milk, so it'll be the almonds-and-water variety, I'm afraid.'

'Tempting, very tempting,' Pedrito fibbed, while unhitching one of Tranquilla's saddlebags, 'but I think we may have something even more tantalising here.'

\*

The food that Pedrito had brought up from the camp may have been simple siege-army fodder, but it was at least more varied and wholesome than the slim pickings his mother and Saleema had been obliged to exist on since the last time he was with them. As he had anticipated, Farah's hope of regaining the slingshot skills of her childhood had proved over optimistic, even with Saleema's physical support, so no more pigeons or rabbits had graced their makeshift pantry in the cave. His mother told him that she had, however, made good use of the flour he'd left them by baking a simple but surprisingly tasty flat bread, which had seemed like becoming the staple of their diet until Pedrito's timely return today.

He had also managed to appropriate a few horse blankets and a couple of quilted saddle rugs to help improve their rough-and-ready sleeping conditions. The nights were sure to get progressively colder as winter approached, so anything that would contribute to making their hermit-like existence a little more bearable would always be welcome.

The day was bright and calm, with a warm autumn sun shining against the cliff face along from the cave entrance, where Saleema had set an improvised dining table on a slab of fallen rock. Farah, meanwhile, had decided to prepare the meal inside the cave. The smoke from a fire in the open, she had pointed out, would only have given away their whereabouts to potential intruders.

While the two women were attending to these domestic chores, Pedrito had taken his leave of them on the pretext of doing a bit of foraging for what he had called 'an essential addition to their daily sustenance'. This time, though, no trusty sling had been in his hand, but instead, a length of rope, which, like the blankets and rugs, he'd purloined from the royal stabling compound back at El Real. Despite twinges of conscience, he'd persuaded himself that he hadn't really been stealing from the king, but rather 'borrowing' a few items that His Majesty would never miss – presuming he was even interested in such minor details of his tack store inventory anyway.

'Your almond soup problems are over!' Pedrito called out to Saleema when he came back into the little field. He was leading a goat on the end of his rope. 'This young lady will supply you with more than enough milk for all your needs, I reckon. Yes, and she'll find enough food for herself if you tether her in the woods here.'

Saleema's face was wreathed in smiles. 'First a donkey, now a goat. All we need is a plough and a few hens and we'll have the makings of a farm here!'

'Well, I'm not sure about the plough, but maybe I'll be able to find a few hens for you next time I come back.'

Farah emerged from behind the curtain of vines covering the cave entrance. 'Did I hear something about a goat?' She squinted through the sunlight at Pedrito. 'Where on *earth* did you get that? I hope you didn't steal it! You know what I think about stealing!'

Pedrito couldn't help chuckling to himself. He hadn't been scolded like this since he was a child, when his mother – his *other* mother – would do exactly the same thing; jumping to conclusions about his wrong-doing before bothering to establish the facts. It was a typical motherly thing, he'd concluded back then, and he automatically reacted in the same way now – by telling the truth.

'No, I came by her fair and square,' he said, hitching the goat to a tree.

'But she's just given birth,' Farah came back. 'I can see that from here, so where's her kid?'

Well, that had been the downside *and* the upside of the situation, Pedrito began. He had noticed some sheep and goats grazing freely on the hillsides by Génova hamlet on their way up here the other day. They were obviously animals that had escaped when the retreating and advancing armies wrecked their enclosures. So, his thinking today had been that it would be worth his while having a snoop around that area, in the hope of finding a stray nanny goat that could do with a good home.

'That would still have been stealing,' Farah objected.

'Not if I was doing the goat a good turn,' Pedrito replied.

Farah looked at him suspiciously. 'How can anyone do a goat a good turn? You'd have been doing her owner a good turn if you'd left her for *him* to find.'

Pedrito stole a glance at Saleema, who was standing behind Farah and doing her best not to giggle.

'But who's to say her owner is still alive?' he reasoned. 'I mean, many of the farmers around that part would have been killed by the Christian soldiers. Either that, or they'd have taken to the mountains until this war blows over. Anyway, it seemed plain to me that this particular goat needed to be taken care of, and that's what I did.'

'And her kid?' Farah quizzed. 'You surely didn't leave it behind to fend for itself.'

The young goat, Pedrito explained, had just given birth when he came upon her on the edge of a clearing in the pine woods. Her kid, however, had been still-born. 'She was licking it and speaking to it and nudging it when I arrived on the scene. In a really desperate state, she was. You know how it is with animals.'

Pedrito noticed Saleema's chin quivering, the smile suddenly gone from her face.

'The poor creatures just don't understand what's happened,' Pedrito continued, 'especially when the young one's their first.'

Farah lowered her eyes and murmured, 'Young mums and their babies. Even Mother Nature can be cruel.'

'All the more reason for us to be good to this little lady,' said Pedrito, scratching the top of the goat's head. 'And she'll be good to you in return. I mean,' he laughed, trying to lighten up the atmosphere a bit, 'just think of all the excellent almond soup you'll be able to make now!'

'Ah, well,' Farah sighed, 'I think we may have more tasty things to make with it than that, if we're spared.' She shuffled forward, cupped her hand under the goat's chin and looked down at its upturned face. 'You may have sad eyes, *habib*, but they're kindly eyes, and we'll soon have them looking happy again as well, never you fear.'

Saleema came over and joined in the fuss-making. 'Yes, we'll be good to you, little one,' she told the goat, before ribbing Farah about why she had called it *habib*. 'You already call me your darling, so how will I know who you're speaking to if you give the goat the same name?'

'A good point,' Farah agreed. She thought for a moment, still looking into the goat's eyes, then said, 'We had a goat just like you when I was a child down there by Génova. She was called *Annam*, which means "Heaven's Blessing", and I think it could turn out to be a blessing for you and for us, little lady, that we've found each other today. So, your name will be *Annam* from now on. How does that suit you, eh?'

The goat replied with what sounded like an approving bleat.

'That's decided, then,' Farah laughed. She tickled the goat's chin, then turned to Saleema. 'And I think she deserves some of my bread as a welcoming present, don't you? So, off you go and fetch her a little piece from the cave.' She watched Saleema go, then said to Pedrito, 'She's very young and, at times, it shows. You know, a little bit giggly. On occasions, even a little bit weepy, especially when she thinks of her family. But she's a wonderful girl, with a good heart and a lovely, giving nature. And a prettier little princess would be hard to find anywhere.' She looked directly at Pedrito's face. 'Don't you think so?'

Caught off guard, Pedrito cleared his throat. 'Well, ehm, yes, I suppose – now you come to mention it...'

Farah smiled her customary knowing smile. 'Hmm, and she'll make a fine wife for some lucky fellow one day ... when all these troubles are over.'

Pedrito was stuck for words.

Farah, however, had plenty more to say. 'And you know, Pedrito, she talks about you all the time.'

Pedrito cleared his throat again.

Farah patted his shoulder. 'It's all right, it's all right, you don't have to say anything. I see how you look at each other, and I think it's safe to say you think about her as much as she talks about you, eh?'

Pedrito tried, unsuccessfully, to stem the rush of blood to his cheeks.

Farah laughed. 'I'm a wicked woman for teasing you like that. But I just want you to know that what I see in you both makes me very, very happy. Yes, I think finding the little goat today wasn't the only blessing that heaven has sent me of late.'

Pedrito felt a lump rise in his throat.

'Now, come on,' said Farah, linking an arm with his, '– help me over to the cave. I have a meal to prepare for us. Oh, and incidentally, I can promise you it won't be almond soup!'

\*

The culinary dividend paid by the years Farah had spent making the most of next-to-nothing in her humble kasbah shack was evident the moment Saleema laid the steaming dish on her improvised stone table. Pedrito hadn't paid too much attention to the random mix of grains, vegetables, bones and meat off-cuts that one of the cooks had bundled into Tranquilla's saddle bags back at El Real, but he knew that, whatever they were, they would amount to nothing more sumptuous than the ingredients that went into the dull daily rations dished up to the rank-and-file Christian soldiers. And he didn't bother to ask Farah what the swiftly garnered supplies had comprised either. The toothsome aroma drifting up from that dish said more than he could put into words, so to ask for details of the constituents from its creator would have been inappropriate – as well as a waste of precious time. Pedrito couldn't wait to taste this mouthwatering concoction.

'Herbs,' was what Faraha said on noticing Pedrito lick his lips. 'Herbs and wild *setta* mushrooms. They're free to collect in the woods, and they're the secret of a good stew.' She tapped the side of her nose. 'Some country things learned in your childhood you never forget.'

'That's right,' Saleema chirped. 'I used to gather herbs with my mother too.' For a fleeting moment her face fell, then she assumed her cheery manner again. 'That's why I knew which herbs to pick when Farah and I went looking.' She gave a nod of appreciation in Farah's direction. 'I've had to rely on your mother to tell me which mushrooms aren't poisonous, though. My memory isn't as good as hers, it seems.'

'Not bad for an old woman who's been living in the city for most of her life,' said Farah with a little self-cogratulatory smirk.

'Absolutely,' Pedrito agreed, while eagerly eyeing the helping of stew that Saleema was spooning into his bowl. 'Not many herbs growing inside Medîna Mayûrqa, I suppose.'

'Ah, but that's where you're wrong,' said Farah. 'And herbs are the least of it. There are gardens and orchards aplenty within the walls of the city, where water abounds and they grow things more exotic than most country folk have ever seen.' She shook her head pensively. 'Yes, and to think I had all of those things on a silver plate whenever I wanted them. For a while anyway.' She shrugged her shoulders and smiled resignedly. 'But once I arrived in the kasbah, I had to learn to make what I could of the left-overs I found on the quayside after the markets had closed for the day. And that usually included a bunch of herbs and a few *setta* mushrooms – wilted, admittedly, but good enough to put a bit of taste into a simple stew.' She gestured towards Pedrito's bowl. 'And the proof is in the eating, as they say.'

'I used to say that the smell of newly-baked bread reminded me of home,' Pedrito revealed after downing his first mouthful, 'but I have to confess that the smell of this stew coming out of the cave had me thinking twice. Mmm, and now that I've sampled the taste … well, I think I'll have to change my way of thinking.'

'And you haven't even tasted my bread yet!' Farah quipped, motioning towards the loaf Saleema had brought to the table earlier.

'No,' said Pedrito, 'but if the look on the goat's face when she did is anything to go by, I'm in for a treat.'

Saleema tore a wedge off the loaf and passed it to him.

'Dip that into your gravy,' Farah urged, 'and you'll think you've arrived in heaven.'

Pedrito smacked his lips, then, looking at Farah and Saleema in turn, said, 'Well, I think I've certainly arrived home, and if heaven turns out to be any better than this, then we're all in for a treat.'

'I'll take that as a compliment, although it's the first time I've been compared to a bowl of stew!' Saleema laughed.

Farah, conversely, had covered her lips with her hand, tears welling in her eyes at Pedrito's mention of having come home. He let her know with a little nod and a smile that he understood how this had touched her.

And so the meal continued amid increasingly convivial conversation, the three participants becoming more relaxed in each other's company as time went by; bonds, although markedly different in substance, being fostered gradually between Pedrito and the two women.

The makeshift table round which they were sitting was bathed in the warm glow of sunshine reflected by the adjacent cliff face, the foliage of the broken rows of olive and almond trees casting porous shadows over the ochre soil beyond. Indeed, Pedrito thought, there could be many more unpleasant places than this to have referred to as home. For, despite its remoteness and dearth of recognisable comforts, it was an eyrie of peace perched only a few miles away from a city being ravaged by the violence of war.

Another paradox that had struck Pedrito on arriving here today was how clean and tidy Farah and Saleema had managed to keep themselves while living as rough as they'd been obliged to of late. Cleanliness was, of course, a trait of Muslim people in general, and its evidence had been a feature of Farah's humble dwelling back inside the city. Although even Saleema's fine silk robe was now showing some signs of the harsh treatment it had been subjected to since her escape from the Almudaina Palace, it was just as spotless, though no more so than Farah's mantle of rags. Pedrito felt like a tramp in comparison – a fact that he knew wouldn't have gone unnoticed by his two pristine companions.

The ever-candid Farah confirmed this after they had finished their meal. 'Does your Christian king approve of the members of his household being so grubby?' she said, tugging at the front of Pedrito's shirt. 'You look as if you've been rolling around in a ditch.'

Pedrito realised instantly that he would have been taken aback, if not highly affronted, by such frankness coming from anyone other than his... He paused to reassess his thoughts. But yes, his initial reaction had been right; the only person who would have said this to him without fear of his taking umbrage was his mother. As she'd done on a few earlier occasions, Farah was indeed treating him in the way any mother would. And her gibe about rolling around in a ditch was just for starters!

'What's more, my lad, the old horse that brought you here smells better than you do!'

Pedrito let out a silly laugh, then cast Saleema an apologetic look. What could he say? After all, Farah was only telling the truth.

'Ehm, well, I – I *was* actually in a ditch,' he stammered. 'But not rolling around. I was – well, I was actually helping to build a she cat.' Another involuntary little laugh escaped his mouth as he became aware of just how feeble (and nonsensical) that excuse must have sounded.

'Spare us the details,' Farah retorted. She pulled at his shirt front again. 'Now, get those filthy clothes off right away!'

'*Off?*' Pedrito glanced at Saleema again, this time his expression a curious blend of embarrassment and pleading. 'But I can't. I mean, I haven't got anything else to –'

'You can wrap one of the horse blankets around you,' Farah cut in. 'You should feel at home in that. Now, go and strip off inside the cave. Then give me your clothes to wash. They'll soon dry in the sun if we lay them out against the cliff here.'

By this time, Saleema was in a fit of giggles, which, for some inexplicable reason, prompted Pedrito to start sniggering himself.

'You're worse than a pair of infants,' Farah chided, though not without allowing herself a discreet smile. 'And once you've taken your clothes off,' she said to Pedrito, 'you can fill Lucky the donkey's bucket with some clean water and give yourself a good scrub too.'

Ten minutes later, Pedrito emerged from the cave wearing a blanket toga-style. His teeth were chattering. 'I don't know about that water in there being the sweetest ever, but it's certainly the coldest.' He pointed to his arms. 'Look at my skin. I'm like a plucked goose!'

'Better a plucked one than a dirty one,' said Farah, who was still seated at the stone table. 'And you'll soon warm up if you sit for a while in the sunshine here.'

Pedrito was carrying his grubby clothes in a bundle under his arm. 'And it's all right,' he said to Farah, 'I'll, uh – I'll wash these myself once I've thawed out.'

'No you won't!' Saleema declared. She stepped forward and snatched his shirt and *pantalons* from him. 'My mother always said men are no good at washing clothes. It takes a woman's touch.'

Looking distinctly ill at ease, Pedrito tried to grab the clothes back. 'No, no, it's all right, honestly. I'm used to seeing to my own clothes. Five years as a galley slave and all that.'

'Yes, and they look as if it's been five years since they were last washed,' Farah countered. 'Leave it to Saleema. She'll heat up some water on the fire and do the job properly.'

'No, really, I'd rather do it myself,' Pedrito protested, gamely, but in vain.

Saleema had already skipped past him, laughing delightedly as she headed for the entrance to the cave. 'And don't worry,' she called over her shoulder, 'I used to help my mother wash my father's clothes, so I'm not easily put off.'

Farah, with a roguish smile, gave Pedrito a 'what have you got to say about that?' kind of look.

Pedrito knew when he was beaten. 'There are certain things a fellow likes to keep private,' he sighed, 'and the maintenance of his *pantalons* is one of them.'

Chuckling to herself, Farah patted the rock she was sitting on. 'Come and sit beside me and let the sun get rid of those goose pimples of yours.' But no sooner had Pedrito done as invited than Farah let out a squeal. 'Look!' she gasped, her eyes on sticks. 'There, bounding this way through the trees! Some sort of weird black sheep! Except – except I've never seen a sheep with a dead hen in its mouth before!'

Pedrito burst out laughing. 'It's only Nedi – no need to worry.'

Farah grabbed his wrist. 'Nedi? What's a … Nedi?'

'It's short for *Nedador*, the Catalan word for "swimmer". He's a water dog, you see.'

'A *dog*! And a black one as well!' Farah shuddered. 'As children, we were always told such a creature is the devil incarnate.'

Pedrito laughed again. He pointed behind his ear. 'Yes, and this little mark of the cross was supposed to make me the devil's child, don't forget.' He then pointed to the top of his head. 'And can you see any horns sprouting here?' Pedrito tousled Nedi's mop of hair as he came to a panting halt by his side. 'And you won't find any horns hidden in here either.'

At that, Nedi dropped the dead hen in front of Farah. He gazed up at her, grinning breathlessly, his tongue dangling from one side of his mouth in that endearingly gormless-looking way of his.

'He's brought you a gift,' said Pedrito. 'Surely that deserves at least a pat on the head.'

Farah did as suggested, though a mite gingerly at first. 'But whose dog is it, and where did he come from all of a sudden?'

Pedrito explained that Nedi belonged to the Christian king, but was actually something of a free spirit who tended to do whatever appealed to him at any given time. 'And this is the second time he's followed me in this way. Keeps himself out of sight until it suits him, though.' He tickled Nedi's ears. 'Probably got a whiff of that excellent stew while you were busy chasing some poor farmer's hens, boy, right?'

Nedi dipped his head, nudged the hen onto Farah's foot with his nose, then looked up at her again – appealingly this time.

Farah's initial apprehension melted. 'Who could resist a look like that?' she smiled, giving Nedi's head a ruffle. 'A black dog who brings me a gift of food. Hmm, I think you're probably more of an angel in disguise than a devil, Nedi.' She looked at Pedrito, a frown of genuine concern creasing her brow. 'But he'll be killed if he's seen on his jaunts by any Muslims who hold strictly to the teachings – especially if they find out he's a Christian.'

Pedrito laughed out loud, then hooked his arm round Nedi's neck and hugged him. 'Nedi's not a Christian, are you, boy? Or anything, for that matter. No, you're a true child of heaven – everybody's friend, like all dogs, given a chance. Yes, and it's just a pity us humans are too stupid to learn from you.'

Nedi gave Pedrito's face a big slobbering lick.

Farah's eyes misted over again as she watched this unbridled show of affection. 'Not even the finest poets in the land could compose a verse to better that,' she murmured, then stroked Nedi's head. 'Who needs words, little one? Yes, who needs words, eh?'

'He'll probably need a drink, though,' said Pedrito. 'I'll go and fetch him some water from the cave.'

Farah touched his arm as he stood up. 'Oh, and while you're at it, if there's a spoonful or two of stew still in the dish by the fire, ask Saleema to bring that for him too – and a chunk of bread, if there's any left. One gift deserves another, after all.' She stooped forward and picked up the dead hen. 'Yes, and you'd better ask Saleema to put this one somewhere safe until we get round to cleaning and cooking it.' She gave Nedi a wink. 'And maybe we'll save a bit for you in case you decide to pay us a visit again soon, no?'

Not surprisingly, Saleema's initial reaction to Nedi when she saw him was the same as Farah's had been, but with the additional caution to Pedrito that a man should only have a dog for hunting, working with livestock or to guard his property. That, she said, was how most Muslims regarded dogs, adding that some were even of the opinion that any dog not being used for those practical purposes should be killed. And to be touched by a dog's tongue – well, the affected area would be regarded as so filthy that an immediate and thorough washing would be essential.

Pedrito couldn't hide his dismay. He already knew about such alleged Muslim attitudes, but the thought of Saleema sympathising with them came as a very unpleasant surprise indeed. 'Well,' he replied indignantly, 'Nedi's a friend, and that's all I expect of him. That said,' he continued, going proactively on the defensive, 'he *has* already shown he can hunt.'

'Hunt?' Saleema frowned.

'Of course! Unless you think that hen he brought here just happened to drop down dead in front of him!'

Farah, who had been watching this little bout of friction with a wry smile on her lips, started to chuckle. Then Saleema began to giggle.

'Something amusing that I've missed?' Pedrito huffed.

Nedi, still sitting by Farah, was watching proceedings with obvious interest – the main object of this interest being the bowl that Saleema was holding in her hand. She laid it down at her feet, then called to him, 'Come on then, Nedi! Come and get your little treat of stew and bread!'

Nedi didn't need to be told twice, but interrupted his advance on the bowl to give Saleema's face an introductory licking. Pedrito was astounded. Instead of flinching as he'd expected her to, Saleema returned Nedi's greeting by giving his ribs a good rub and planting a kiss on his nose. She and Farah were laughing heartily now.

'B-but,' Pedrito stuttered, his face a picture of confusion, 'I thought, Saleema – you know, the way you were talking – I thought you didn't like dogs.'

'And didn't you take the bait, hook, line and sinker? No, I love dogs – always have done.'

Pedrito glanced over at Farah. 'And you knew that too?'

'No, it's news to me.'

'But you were the one who started all the hilarity a minute ago.'

'Call it women's intuition. Something told me Saleema was only having fun with you, and I wasn't wrong, was I?'

Pedrito was laughing himself now. 'No, and I can't tell you how relieved I am either.'

Saleema went on to explain that her father had had dogs to help with his sheep for as long as she could remember. She had always treated them as pets and her parents had never objected. On the contrary, she stressed, her mother had told her father that men who treated dogs like dirt were no better than those who regarded their wives as chattels and women in general as lesser beings than men.

'Good for her,' said Farah. 'A woman after my own heart.'

But wasn't that going against basic Muslim principles, Pedrito hesitantly enquired?

'Good principles are one thing,' Saleema replied, warming to her theme, 'but no man has the right to treat another human as his own property, to do with as he sees fit. And that's why I decided to escape from the clutches of that lecherous old rabbit in the Almudaina Palace at the first opportunity.'

Farah cleared her throat. 'Ah-ehm, that's my husband you're talking about, young lady.'

'And *my* father,' said Pedrito, swiftly picking up Farah's jocular thread.

Saleema clapped a hand to her forehead in mock self-reproach. 'Oops! Forgot about that for a moment.' She slapped herself on the wrist. 'Silly me!'

Even Nedi joined in the ensuing outburst of high spirits, wagging his tail and grinning eagerly as his three companions held their sides laughing about what he neither knew nor cared. These were fun people, this was a fun place to be, and he was enjoying himself.

*

It was mid-afternoon before Pedrito finally changed back into his newly-washed clothes, having spent the intervening time sitting in the sun chatting idly with his mother and Saleema, while Nedi lay sprawled and sleeping contentedly at their feet. At another time, this would have constituted a typical family scene in rural Mallorca – or would have appeared so. But a fierce war was being fought not too far beyond the edge of this little haven of peace and amity, and the three people presently delighting in each other's company came from opposite sides of the associated 'sacred' divide. And although the personal bonds being nurtured between Pedrito and the two women were already strong enough to overcome this, the overriding fact remained that such relationships would be regarded as mortal sins by the more fervent elements that held sway in the two powers currently fighting for control of the island.

Even so, Pedrito knew where his priorities lay, and they certainly did not fall in with the inflexible sectarian stances of either side. His mother was his mother, and no amount of religious bigotry would change that. The situation with regard to Saleema was, however, very different. Any liaison between the opposite sexes of either religion was strictly forbidden by both, and could even be punishable by death. No matter how much it pleased his mother to see the buds of an amorous attachment emerging between himself and Saleema, Pedrito was painfully aware that he would have to tread very carefully in that area, if tears, or worse, were not to be the outcome.

He glanced at the sun. 'Well,' he sighed, 'I've to be back at the Christian camp by nightfall, so I'd better make good use of what daylight's left by gathering some wood to keep your fire going for a few days more.'

'I'll come and help!' Saleema volunteered with unbridled enthusiasm.

Much as Pedrito would have enjoyed her company, he knew that every minute spent alone with her would merely add to the difficulty of keeping their relationship on a strictly platonic basis. He gestured towards her tattered slippers. 'That's really kind of you, Saleema, but it's liable to be a bit rough underfoot, and –'

'Not a problem!' Saleema butted in. 'I've become an expert at picking my way carefully through the woods since we came up here. I've had to! How do you think we managed to collect all those herbs and mushrooms?'

'Yes, I – well, I can apppreciate that,' Pedrito flustered, 'but, ehm, I – I was going to take old Tranquilla with me anyway. You know – fill her saddle bags with sticks – so I'll manage fine, thanks.'

'Good idea!' Saleema beamed. 'I can always jump up on her back if my feet do get sore. Plus,' she added before Pedrito could get a word in, 'I know where there's a big fallen pine tree, and I can lead you straight there. Think of the time you'll save.'

Pedrito could see that to offer any further resistance would be futile. This girl had a mind of her own all right, and Farah was about to add strength to it.

'You'll be doing me a favour if you take her along,' she told Pedrito with a reassuring nod of her head. 'I like to have a little nap in the afternoon, and this little lady's constant chattering never makes it easy.'

While Pedrito had no reason to doubt this, the sly wink he noticed Farah giving Saleema did make him slightly sceptical. 'Cupid with a crutch' was how Farah had referred to herself when fate had thrown the three of them together back in that dingy kasbah alleyway, and Pedrito suspected that she had become set more than ever on acting out that very role.

'Lead on, then,' he said to Saleema, trying to appear as blasé as possible. 'I'll fetch old Tranquilla and catch up, never fear.'

Sure enough, Saleema did indeed lead him directly through the pinewoods to a little clearing where there was a fallen tree; a victim of a lightning strike, Pedrito thought, judging by the scorch marks on its trunk.

'A good find,' he said. 'The wood's nicely dried out and there are plenty of broken outer branches that'll be easy enough to snap into handy-sized pieces for your fire.'

Saleema flashed him a mischievous smile. 'What about the bigger ones, though? It would take a *really* strong man to break those over his knee.'

This time, Pedrito didn't take the bait. 'Yes,' he agreed, getting immediately on with the job in hand, 'I'll have to try and scrounge an axe to bring along next time.'

Saleema giggled and kneeled down beside him to gather up a bunch of twigs. 'These will come in handy for kindling, don't you think?'

'Certainly will,' Pedrito replied, without lifting his eyes from what he was doing. 'Certainly will.'

'Certainly will,' Saleema mimicked. 'Certainly will.'

Pedrito ignored her, which wasn't easy, knowing as he did that she was being deliberately flirty. There was nothing he would have liked better than to play along, but one glance at the lightning marks on the tree trunk served as a reminder (as if he needed one!) that playing with fire was the last thing he should be contemplating. Without even glancing in Saleema's direction, he began packing pieces of wood into Tranquilla's saddle bags.

'Why are you being so offhand with me?' Saleema asked after a while. She was standing close by Pedrito now – close enough for him to smell again the same faint but tantalising fragrance that had beguiled him when helping her through the maze of kasbah alleyways on that first night.

'I'm not being offhand. It's just that...' Steeling himself, Pedrito stole a glance at Saleema's face, but looked away again immediately. 'You know why, Saleema, and there's no point in –'

'I don't know why, and that's why I'm asking you.' She reached up and drew his chin round so that he was forced to look directly into her eyes. 'Don't you like what you see?'

'Too much,' Pedrito croaked, his throat going suddenly dry. 'That's the trouble, and you know it.'

Saleema batted her eyelashes in a way that had Pedrito going all weak at the knees again. 'Trouble?' she whispered. 'What trouble?'

Pedrito had to draw on previously untapped reserves of self-restraint to turn away and load the last few chunks of wood into Tranquilla's saddle bags. 'The trouble, Saleema, is that Allah wouldn't approve of one of his female followers having a fling with –'

'What's Allah got to do with it?' Saleema bristled. 'If Allah or God, or whatever he or they are called, isn't happy with the way I feel – and the way *you* feel too, so don't deny it! – then he, or they, don't stand for what we're told they stand for!' She jabbed Pedrito in the chest with her finger. 'Yes, and I'm not just having a fling either! I'm not one of your galley-slave tarts, you know!' With that, she turned on her heel and stomped off through the woods, as determinedly as her flimsy footwear would allow.

Pedrito wasn't surprised to find her waiting for him in the next clearing.

'My feet are sore,' she snivelled, all the vixen-like fury of a few moments ago replaced by a much exaggerated little-girl-lost look. 'Poor Saleema,' she crooned, eyelashes fluttering like bunting in the wind. 'Poor little Saleema needs to be lifted onto the nice old horse's back.'

Pedrito couldn't help laughing. He realised that he was being set up for one of the oldest female tricks of all, but came to the conclusion that there would be no harm in playing along just this once. He knew he was strong enough to resist. Well, he was, wasn't he?

'All right, Saleema, you win,' he smiled as he hitched Tranquilla to a convenient branch. 'I'll help you onto her back, if that's what you want.'

He duly placed his hands on either side of her waist and began to lift her up. But as soon as their faces were level, Saleema flung her arms round his neck and kissed him full on the lips.

When she finally pulled her head back, Pedrito nodded towards the setting sun. 'It'll soon be nightfall,' he remarked, hoarsely.

'I think so,' Saleema whispered.

'So, I'll have to be on my way.'

Saleema shook her head and drew his face down towards hers again. 'I don't think so,' she murmured. 'I really don't think so, Little Pedro.'

## 24

# SAVAGE SUBTLETIES OF THE SIEGE

*SOME WEEKS LATER –*
*THE CHRISTIAN CAMP OF 'EL REAL'...*

'The mountain air obviously agrees with you,' was what the king had said to Pedrito when he eventually arrived back in camp that night. 'It's put a glow in your cheeks. *Sí,*' he grinned, 'and a smile on your lips as well. I take it, then, that you saw to the, uh, *comfort* of your little concubine, as I guessed you would, eh?'

Pedrito chose not to encourage the king by responding directly to his chaffing. 'I'm afraid the mountain air seems to have agreed with Nedi even more,' he said instead. 'He followed me up there, but refused to come back with me when I left. Just sat by my mother's side and wouldn't budge, no matter how often I called him.'

King Jaume was nonchalance personified. 'Not to worry. He'll make his way back when it suits him – *if* it suits him. A law unto himself, that one.'

And no more was said about Pedrito's cross-religious entanglements, except for the king to give his confidential permission for Pedrito to make further compassionate visits to his mother whenever circumstances allowed. Those in charge of the kitchen stores would be told he was taking supplies to a remote lookout post, and the matter would be left at that until the war reached a successful conclusion, when Pedrito would have to comply with whatever rules of conduct were required to purge Islamic influences from the island's population.

This was a prospect that filled Pedrito with dread, but all he could do for the present was stick to his decision to serve King Jaume as best he could and trust to the young monarch's sense of tolerance – and influence over the more dogmatic elements within the clergy – when the time came.

Meanwhile, the siege of Medîna Mayûrqa continued with increased ferocity and determination. As the weeks passed, the mining of tunnels under the dry moat was augmented by trenches being dug by squads of men protected from Moorish crossbow fire by *mantellina*-like 'roofs on wheels'. These laborious but unrelenting advances on the foundations of the city's walls were accompanied by the ongoing exchange of airborne missiles, resulting in an apalling number of casualties being suffered on both sides.

Eventually, three defence towers were successfully undermined and brought crashing down as the wooden props placed in the excavations beneath them were set alight by the Christian sappers. Yet the Moors succeeded in repairing the damage inflicted on their northern bastions with such speed that no real Christian advantage was gained. Impasse appeared to be a frustratingly reiterated outcome of every aggressive tactic employed by King Jaume's men.

Then two brothers by the name of Ritxo from the Catalonian town of Lérida offered to lend their bridge-building experience to spanning the dry moat with a stout framework of timber topped with layers of earth. Theirs, they claimed, would be a bridge capable of bearing the weight of all the heavy war horses needed to carry their armoured mounts on a final assault through a breach in the walls, the latter to be achieved by a bout of concentrated artillery bombardment at the crucial hour.

Pedrito became acutely familiar with the dangers inherent in the execution of this bold military undertaking, employed as he was in the transportation of timber and earth during the two weeks it took for the bridge to near completion. He saw many of his companions fall victim to arrows and rocks launched from the city ramparts, and ultimately to the horrific effects of boiling oil poured down on them the closer to the walls the construction progressed. Survival was a matter of luck, despite the best efforts being made to shield the men involved with moveable wooden screens, while full use was also made of every *trebuchet* and *mangonel* to batter their Moorish assailants with everything that could be thrown at them. And all the time King Jaume made a point of riding conspicuously through the forward positions within the encampment, offering cries of encouragement to his increasingly weary troops.

Then, under cover of darkness one night, a small party of Moors slipped over the walls and succeeded in lighting fires under the bridge structure's complex arrangements of timber supports. This surely would have resulted in terminal harm being done to the product of two weeks of backbreaking work, so dearly paid for in human life, had the king himself not devised an ingenious solution. While groups of men did their best to contain the flames with brushwood flails, he detailed Pedrito and a hundred other sturdy young men to set out, fully armed – not with swords, but with spades – to dig a channel directing the water from a well at a nearby abandoned farm into the dry moat. It was touch and go for a while, but eventually the king's ploy had the desired effect and the fires were extinguished before too much of the already completed work was damaged beyond repair.

Nevertheless, a morale-sapping setback had been suffered by the Christian army, and the Moors succeeded in inflicting another shortly afterwords. From inside the city walls, they had been secretly digging counter-mines towards those of the Christians, and when they finally hacked their way into the first of these, they attacked their opposite numbers with such fury that they succeeded in driving out all not put to the sword. Then, to add insult to injury, a group of cock-a-hoop Moors emerged from the tunnel and hurled verbal abuse at their Christian foes across no-man's-land.

It took yet another swift decision by King Jaume to nip in the bud what might have proved to be a telling psychological victory for the enemy in the grim struggle for Medîna Mayûrqa.

'Quickly!' he shouted to the commander of the nearest battery of war engines. 'Roll out two of our windlass crossbows – the most powerful ones. And load them with three long bolts each – one machine to be discharged immediately after the other.'

Two migfhty *ballista* catapults were duly trundled forward to just inside the stockade gates, their draw cables winched back and cocked, their javelins slotted into position. Then, on the king's order, the gates were flung open and the deadly darts released. The first salvo went straight through the bodies of their unsuspecting victims like daggers through pieces of cloth, the second thudding into the remaining Moors as they made a desperate attempt to get back into the mine.

A smile of satisfaction crossed the king's face. 'That,' he snarled through clenched teeth, 'will teach those vulgar Saracen moles that calling Christians names is extremely impolite.' He then climbed onto the framework of an adjacent *trebuchet* and shouted to everyone within earshot, 'Be of good cheer, brave lads! Once again, God has shown that He is with us in times of adversity. So, let us carry on with our good work in His name, and you have my word as the one whom God has chosen as your king that your reward will be great here on earth, and even greater should you join in heaven those valiant brothers who have died today in the furtherance of our holy mission against the disbelievers.'

Yet again, any spirits that may have been flagging within the Christian ranks were uplifted by King Jaume's infectious enthusiasm for the cause, ably bolstered, it has to be said, by lava flows of fire-and-brimstone rhetoric from the redoubtable Friar Miguel Fabra. And so work on undermining the foundations of the city walls continued with renewed vigour, while efforts were redoubled to complete the bridging of the moat.

*

As the days passed, the Moors' will to hold out revealed no outward sign of waning, so energetic was their countering of the Christian bombardment and so swift their shoring up of associated damage to their fortifications. Yet a hint of doubt creeping into their belief in maintaining this level of resistance was ultimately manifested by their king requesting a parley with someone of authority on the Spanish side. Accordingly, as was the accepted practice on such occasions, King Jaume instructed his senior general, En Nunyo Sans, to ride out with a small party of retainers to a prearranged rendezvous outside the Porto Pi Gate at the south-western corner of the city. It was presumed that this location had been suggested by the Moorish king because of its safe distance from the current theatre of hostilities and its relative proximity to the sanctuary of his Almudaina Palace.

Pedrito had been called upon as usual by King Jaume to translate when, under a white flag, the Moorish envoy had made the original approach to deliver his Amir's message. Nevertheless, the king was later obliged to inform Pedrito that, as expected, Abel Babiel, the Jewish financier from Zaragoza, had insisted on assuming the role of interpreter for the momentous meeting with the Saracen supremo. Just as Pedrito had anticipated, however, he felt more relieved than slighted by this disclosure, his natural curiosity to see the man who had fathered him tempered by misgivings about how he might react when confronted by the pitiless brute who had ruined his mother's life.

In the event, the parley turned out to be a total waste of time, the report delivered by En Nunyo Sans to King Jaume revealing only that, when asked what he wished to say, the Moorish King had replied, 'Nothing. What is it you wish to say to me?' After a further short but confused exchange of words, the meeting had broken up without anything being achieved.

King Jaume called together the Privy Council of his foremost nobles and churchmen to discuss this apparent snub, only for them to come to the somewhat presumptuous conclusion that the time would come soon enough when this insolent Moorish upstart would be glad to speak with due deference to his Christian adversaries – and, what's more, to come to terms. In the meantime, the siege of the city should continue as before.

All of this was related to Pedrito by the king immediately after he had drawn the assembly of his counsellors to a close. 'It appears to me,' he said, 'that something of what the Moorish king attempted to convey to En Nunyo may have been lost in translation, no?'

'Who's to say?' was Pedrito's diplomatic reply. 'Perhaps he just wanted to see what a Christian nobleman looked like close-up.'

The king shot him a cynical look. 'No, Little Pedro, you can sidestep the issue as much as you like – and I admire your tact – but I have to say that the translating ability of Senyor Babiel is being called into question here.' He stroked his beard in his customary pensive way. 'I shall have to be more guileful should a similar situation arise again.'

Pedrito was quick to reaffirm that he had no wish to intrude on any commitment the king had made with the Zaragozan gentleman who had donated so much money to this crusade.

'*Donated*?' The king gave a derisory chuckle. '*Lent* is the operative word! No, no, have no fear, Abel Babiel will want full repayment of what he has advanced, and with a hefty brokerage on top. And that's all in addition to the share of potential Mallorcan spoils he negotiated for his people.'

'So, what you're saying, *senyor*, is that you want to strip him of his duties as your interpreter, but without giving him the impression that you think he isn't up to the job. You don't want to risk offending him, correct?'

'To put it bluntly, Little Pedro – yes!' King Jaume fiddled with his beard again. 'Hmm, but easier said than done. As I suggested before, a Jew with an abacus can be a more potent force than a whole army of scimitar-rattling Saracens. And don't forget that soldiers of that wily persuasion helped the Muslim thieves take Spain from its rightful Christian owners in the first place.' He took a deep breath, smiled resignedly and patted Pedrito on the shoulder. 'But at least I know, *amic*, that I can depend on you to help me out if such a tricky situation concerning Senyor Babiel should arise again, *si*?'

Pedrito dipped his head in a stiff little bow of assent, though with his fingers crossed behind his back. While having no desire to default on his commitment to King Jaume, he was rapidly coming to the conclusion that, whatever the future held for him, it would be all the better for his not having to bear the memory of coming face-to-face with the man whose blood coursed through his veins, but whom he would never think of as his father.

It seemed that he had been relieved of his dilemma, when, shortly afterwords, En Pere Corneyl, one of the barons who had attended the earlier meeting of royal counsellors, came back to the king's tent with what he described as a potentially vital breakthough. A member of En Pere's retinue had just returned to camp from leading a patrol through the surrounding countryside, during which he had been approached by a man who introduced himself as Don Gil de Alagón, a former Spanish knight, who, after settling on the island, had converted to Islam and had adopted the surname of Mohammad. This man had offered to act as a go-between in negotiating a settlement that would end the siege to the satisfaction of both parties. Because he was on intimate terms with all the most influential Moors on the island, as well as being a fluent speaker of Arabic, this man felt certain that, if he were allowed to enter the city, he could convince King Abû Yahya Háquem to capitulate, thus ending the war without any further loss of life.

Pedrito felt a weight being lifted from his shoulders.

However, suspicion was writ large on King Jaume's face as he responded to En Pere's announcement. 'No military commander worth a straw submit's so meekly without demanding something in return, so what are the terms, *allegedly* acceptable to both parties, that this renegade Spanish knight believes he can elicit from the Moorish king?'

'Simply, *Majestat*, that the Moorish king would repay to you whatever the expedition has cost, together with a guarantee that all of the Christian forces would be allowed to return home to the mainland safe and sound.'

It seemed to Pedrito that the king's guffaw of contempt could well have been heard as far away as the Almudaina Palace itself.

'You are a good man, En Pere,' he said at length, 'and I have no doubt that you speak with the best of intentions. However, you have my permission to relate to the traitor, Gil *Mohammad*, or whatever infidel name he calls himself, that my mission, undertaken in the name of the one true God, is to return Mallorca to the followers of our Lord Jesus Christ. Therefore, even if I'm offered enough gold to pave all the ground between this camp and the mountains yonder, I won't return to the mainland until my mission is complete. So, En Pere, unless you, or any other of my train, wish to feel the sting of my wrath, never be tempted to convey such a blasphemous message to me again – ever!'

Thus ended Pedrito's short-lived respite from interpreter-related anxieties.

That aside, the king's decision proved to be a shrewd one – as did the earlier prediction of his Privy Council. Before another day had passed, a fresh plea for a parley had been delivered by an envoy of the Moorish king. Once again, Pedrito was summoned to the royal compound.

'I take it that you and Babiel the rabbi have never met?' King Jaume checked, after shepherding Pedrito into the privacy of his tent.

Pedrito confirmed that this was the case.

Smiling smugly, the king rubbed his hands together. 'Excellent! Now, here's what I propose to do in order to avoid another linguistic fiasco like the last time.'

He then proceeded to explain that the second meeting between En Nunyo Sans and King Abû would be held, as before, outside the Gate of Porto Pi. On this occasion, a small tent would be pitched on site, with only the two main protagonists and their personal attendants being allowed inside. Both En Nunyo and the Moorish king would be escorted once again by small companies of mounted guards, the respective units to wait on opposite sides of the tent until the meeting reached a conclusion.

'And now I come to the ingenious bit,' King Jaume winked. 'You, Little Pedro, will act as En Nunyo's orderly, and you will stand holding his horse for him immediately outside the tent while the negotiations are being conducted. In this way, you'll be able to listen to what's being said inside, and to judge if what the Saracen king says is being accurately translated for En Nunyo.'

'Sounds feasible enough,' Pedrito shrugged. 'But what if I think Senyor Babiel has made some mistakes? I mean, I can hardly shout corrections to En Nunyo through the canvas. That would surely defeat the purpose, wouldn't it? A bit of an insult to Senyor Babiel, no?'

King Jaume shook his head impatiently. 'There you go with your naïve thinking again.' He motioned Pedrito to come in close, then, looking furtively about, said out of the corner of his mouth, 'This is where the skill of politics comes in. You keep your mouth tightly shut outside that tent, while making sure your ears are wide open. You also make sure you remember everything that's said – and I mean *every*thing – and you don't speak a word to anyone of any mistakes made in translation by Babiel until you return to me here.'

'Then what?'

'Then, depending on the significance of what you have to say about such mistakes – if any – I will repeat your findings to my Privy Council of barons and bishops.'

Pedrito scratched his head. 'That's all very well, but surely that'll be a real slap in the face for Senyor Babiel, and I thought offending him was precisely what you wanted to avoid doing.'

The king shook his head again, but in exasperation this time. 'Politics – you just don't grasp the subtleties, do you?'

Pedrtio shrugged his shoulders again. 'Evidently not.'

The king lowered his voice to a whisper. 'The point is, *amic*, that Babiel will be instructed to return to his quarters after the parley and won't even know that all this has been going on behind his back. Understand now?'

'I'm beginning to,' Pedrito muttered. 'Politics – lies – deceipt. One and the same thing, if you ask me.'

'Nothing wrong with that, *if* your motives are worthy.' King Jaume cast Pedrito an incriminating look. 'As when borrowing – not *stealing* – horse blankets and saddle rugs from my tack store, eh?'

Pedrito felt the blood drain from his face. 'You – you mean you knew that I'd –'

'You don't survive being a king from the age of six to twenty-one without making a habit of knowing everything that goes on in your household, Master Blànes.' Scowling, he stared into Pedrito's eyes like a fox that's cornered a rabbit.

Pedrito gulped. 'You, ehm, you called me Master Blànes just then,' he said, unable to think of a more pertinent response.

The king continued to stare him out, saying nothing.

Pedrito persevered with his feeble attempt to divert the subject away from things 'borrowed' from the king's stable. 'What I mean to say is that you usually only call me Master Blànes when there are other people around. You know, when you're being formal ... sort of.'

A few more tense moments of silence followed, before the king said, 'That's politics for you. It's suits me not to let it be known that I call you by your fist name, far less your pet name. What's more important for you, though, is that I only employ such terms of familiarity towards friends – people I can trust – and there are precious few of those.'

The king had managed to make Pedrito feel really small. 'What can I say, *senyor*? All I can do is apologise, and I do – most sincerely. I didn't mean to steal from you. It's just, well, it's just that I didn't think you would –'

'Give you a few items of horse garb to help make life more comfortable for your mother up there in that cave?' The king tutted admonishingly. 'Honestly, Master Blànes, I thought better of you. I've told you often enough that I'm not a heartless man. Didn't you believe me? Wasn't it proof enough that I gave you permission to visit your mother *and* to take her food from my kitchens?'

Pedrito hung his head. 'I can't expect you to forgive me, or to even understand. But it was precisely because I was so grateful to you for providing food for my mother and Saleema that I didn't want to impose further on your generosity by asking for blankets and things – especially for Muslims.' He rolled his shoulders in his characteristically self-conscious way. 'And that's why, on the spur of the moment, I decided to –'

'*Borrow* them?'

Pedrito ventured a glance at the king's face, expecting to see that his earlier scowl had become even more menacing. However, to his surprise and relief, a twinkle had appeared in the king's eyes.

'I do enjoy teasing you, Little Pedro,' he said with a guarded smile. 'I suspected – hoped – that this was why you hadn't asked me for those things.' His smile widened. 'And so Saleema is the name of your little concubine, eh? *Very* becoming, I'm sure, and I trust she isn't too upset at having to snuggle up with you between horse blankets instead of the silk sheets of the harem?'

Pedrito thought it best to ignore this suggestively leading question.

The king frowned again. 'I put my trust in you, *amic*, because I believed you earned it. But please don't ever think that this automatically entitles you to anything. In future, if you want something from me, ask and I'll gladly give it – within reason, of course.'

Feeling suitably contrite, Pedrito lowered his head again, while thanking the king for his kindness *and* leniency.

'Kindness is part of my nature – just think of how I treated those little nesting swallows I told you about – but leniency is a quality I'm still working on – just think of how I treated the head of a certain Saracen who had the gall to describe himself to one of my nobles as "a great conqueror by the grace of Allah".' King Jaume then gave Pedrito a heartening slap on the back. 'But enough of all that. There's the little matter of a parley with the leader of the enemy to be getting on with, and you, Little Pedro, are to be your king's ears.' He tweaked Pedrito's cheek. 'How many ex-galley slaves will be able to boast to their grandchildren about that, eh?'

\*

As it transpired, Pedrito's dread of confronting his natural father proved to be unwarranted, for the simple reason that King Abû and his attendants were already in the tent when En Nunyo Sans and his company arrived at the rendezvous. Formalities were exchanged in grunts and sign language between the captains of the two opposing groups of guards, En Nunyo and Abel Babiel entered the tent, and the parley began without resort to undue ceremony.

It soon became obvious to Pedrito that Senyor Babiel's

knowledge of Arabic was indeed either somewhat sketchy or he was confused by the Mallorcan dialect being spoken. In any case, the negotiations were stilted to say the least, and Pedrito had to use all his powers of concentration to keep abreast of what was going on, and to decide if what was being said to En Nunyo by his interpreter was a true representation of what the Moorish king actually intended.

The first thing that struck Pedrito was the deep timbre of King Abû's voice. If his appearance matched the way he sounded, then he must have boasted a very commanding presence indeed. Yet his opening gambit had been more conciliatory than domineering...

'As I have never done any wrong to your king, it astounds me that he so violently seeks to gain control of this kingdom which was given to me by Allah. However, I am a man of the world, and a fair one. I realise that this expedition must have cost your king dearly, so I hereby guarantee to pay over to him whatever sum is involved and to ensure that all of you can return thereafter in peace and goodwill from whence you came. Tell your king to name his price, and he has my promise that it will be paid in full within five days.'

Since no reply was immediately forthcoming from En Nunyo Sans, King Abû expanded on what he had just said. 'And lest your king be under any delusion, please advise him that I have enough arms, provisions of all kinds and everything else that is needed to defend the city for longer than he can ever hope to besiege it. What's more, he is welcome to send witnesses to see for themselves that what I say is true.'

There was still no reponse from En Nunyo.

'And for his further reflection,' King Abû continued, 'I can assure your king that I care not a whit about the damage that your war engines and miners are inflicting upon our northern fortifications, for I have no fear of the city ever being entered on that side.'

En Nunyo finally replied by pointing out that, almost four years earlier, the Moorish king had in fact done King Jaume a great wrong by insulting an ambassador he had sent, in good faith, to ask for the return of two merchant ships from the city of Barcelona which had been captured by Moorish pirates and handed over, cargoes, crews and all, to King Abû himself. However, instead of being shown the courtesies appropriate to a royal emissary, King Abû had told him that he had never heard of this Christian King Jaume of Aragon whom he purported to represent.

The envoy had then taken it upon himself to suggest that King Abû must have been familiar with the existence and reputation of his lord and master, since he was the son of King Pedro of Aragon, who had defeated Abû Abdilla Mohammad, the mighty Sultan of Africa and Muslim Spain, at the Battle of Las Navas de Tolosa some seventeen years previously. Everyone in the world knew of that famous victory of King Pedro's, so it was grossly contemptuous of anyone, particularly a Moor, to claim that he had never heard of his son, whose own successful exploits on the battlefields of mainland Spain were already the stuff of legend.

En Nunyo then sought to remind the Moorish king that, instead of apologising to the Christian emissary, he had bluntly informed him that, if it had not been for his alleged ambassadorial status, he would have been severely punished for his insolence. When, eventually, this had been reported to King Jaume, he had sworn that he would delight one day in personally pulling the beard of the perpetrator of such a blatant discourtesy to one of his train.

'So, you can take it from me here and now,' En Nunyo stressed, 'that your offer to buy my king off will be greeted with all the contempt it deserves. In fact, I assumed you would already be aware that he recently conveyed as much to a turncoat quisling called Don Gil de Alagón, now masquerading under the name of Mohammad.' With the bit now firmly between his teeth, En Nunyo then made it very clear that King Jaume, despite his youth, had embarked on this campaign, one of the biggest ever undertaken by a Spanish monarch, because it was the will of *his* God that he should have the land and kingdom of Mallorca to hold in the name of Jesus Christ. He had made the most solemn vow that he would not leave the island until he had achieved that goal, no matter how long it took or how many of those who resisted him had to be destroyed in the process. 'Now, *senyor*,' En Nunyo concluded, 'you may speak to me of anything else you want, for what you have already proposed is not worth talking about.'

Instead of resuming his previous stance of defiance, King Abû elected to take a more pragmatic approach – and a surprisingly submissive one at that. He informed En Nunyo that, as his earlier terms had been rejected, he would now offer to pay five gold *besants* for the 'safety' of every one of the fifty thousand men, women and children in the city of Medîna Mayûrqa. He himself would leave the island with everyone who wished to follow him, on condition that he was provided with sufficient ships to cross over to the Barbary Coast of Africa. Those who chose to remain behind could do so.

Several things occurred to Pedrito as he listened to all of this from outside the tent. Firstly, he was impressed by the assertiveness displayed by En Nunyo Sans. He may occasionally have shown a tendency to err on the cautious side when going into battle, but when it came to a verbal contest, his confidence certainly could not be called into question. Secondly, giving credit where it was due to Senyor Babiel, laboured though his translations may have been, he'd got the gist of the most crucial aspects right. In the event, King Jaume need not have had any reservations in that respect.

Yet the thing that struck Pedrito most forcefully, albeit on a personal level, was how easily the Moorish king had capitulated. On this showing, it seemed that his mettle didn't match the manliness of his voice. Although already filled with loathing for the man, Pedrito still felt a strange twinge of disappointment that his own flesh and blood had acted in such an ineffectual way. As King Jaume had recently told him, changes of fortunes in a war are invariably tied to the survival of someone of influence. And here was a reputedly valiant king offering to sell his dominion over his land and subjects in order to save his own skin. Despite himself, Pedrito now felt an almost morbid compulsion to see the face of this perverse character.

But it was not to be. No sooner had Nunyo Sans made his somewhat smug declaration that he would present his leader with the terms of surrender now offered than King Abû swept out of the tent in a flurry of white robes. Then, keeping his back purposely turned to the onlooking Christian soldiers, he straddled his white Arab stallion. Without a backward glance, he galloped off towards the city at the head of his mounted escort, their lances raised, their pennants proudly fluttering as if departing a battlefield in triumph.

\*

The truce that had been called to accommodate what turned out to be such a potentially historic dialogue was to be surprisingly brief. King Jaume convened a meeting of his entire Privy Council immediately after hearing that the Moors had sued for peace, and he had no hesitation in telling this august gathering that he believed the tendered terms of surrender should be accepted. Not only would the crusade be ending in what it had been launched to achieve, namely the Christian reconquest of Mallorca, but a veritable king's ransom would also be paid by the Saracen King before he left for Africa. And this in additon to all the booty that would subsequently be there for the taking without another drop of Christian blood being shed. The young king concluded that God Almighty, His Son their Saviour and the Blessed Virgin had now delivered this land to them, just as he and every God fearing man who had followed him always believed that they would.

But not every God fearing man in the assembled company thought the matter to be as straightforward as that, and it was no less a voice of religious authority than En Berenguer de Palou, the Bishop Barcelona himself, who spoke for them first...

'Many good and brave men have been slain while serving God here, and their deaths should be revenged. That vengeance would be seen in God's eyes to be good and just. I tell you this as an intermediary of God, and you can therefore believe that what I say can be taken as God's will. However, you knights and barons seated here among us know more of military affairs than I do.' He gestured towards En Nunyo Sans. 'So, you must have your say as well.'

Accordingly, En Nunyo got to his feet and stated that it seemed to him that, if their lord King Jaume were to agree to a treaty as proposed by the Saracens, then he would achieve everything that he had come here for. 'Nevertheless,' he continued, 'I was but the bearer of the news, so I will say no more. Others are entitled to their own opinions.'

At that, En Remon Alaman, the nobleman of En Nunyo Sans' company who had advised the king to proceed with caution after the Battle of Na Burguesa at which En Guillen and En Remon de Muntcada had been killed, made a plea on behalf of the kinsmen and followers of those late lamented heroes. The Muntcadas, he said, had been an example of the best and most loyal vassals that any king could ever be served by, and they had lost their lives in unquestioning pursuit of that duty. However, there was now an opportunity, while the enemy was on its back foot, to properly avenge their deaths.

When the king made no immediate response, En Remon Alaman added that it should also be borne in mind that the Moorish king knew the island better than anyone here, and as he was a high ranking Saracen with appropriate connections and resources at his disposal, allowing him to retreat to North Africa would only invite a later invasion with such a huge army of well briefed Moors that King Jaume's tenure of Mallorca, gained at the price of so many Christian lives, would quickly be lost. Consequently, it was now incumbent upon the king to punish those who had slain his most dedicated servants, while also ensuring that the infidels would never pose a threat to his rightful possession of this land which the Lord God Almighty had granted him.

'As to our brave brothers who have died in battle,' the king replied, 'I can only say that what God ordains has to be fulfilled. And though I may gain land and riches by taking this island, those who are dead already have better reward, for they have the glory of God in heaven. But be that as it may, it must be remembered that I came here to serve our Lord and to conquer this land for Him, and since the proposal which has been made would realise that objective, it seems to me that I should accept. However, as you are my esteemed counsellors and leaders of all those who have sacrificed so much for me, I deem it right and proper that such a momentous decision as this should be left to you.'

It took but a brief exchange of mutterings and nods of the head for an agreement to be reached, then it was announced as with one voice that it would be far better to take Mallorca by force than to accept the offer extended by the enemy. Retribution for the deaths of the Muntcadas and their gallant like was merited, and should therefore be taken.

'And so it shall be,' said the king, though with little enthusiasm. 'But on your heads be it if rejecting my recommendation should prove to be costly.'

*

Scarcely an hour had passed before King Abû's reaction to the rebuffal of his offer was made abundantly clear. With the truce still in force, a Moor approached the Christian encampment under an appropriate flag and stopped midway across no-man's-land, where he began to shout defiantly in Arabic.

Pedrito was called to the stockade's southern gate by King Jaume, who had already been advised of the messenger's presence. 'He seems to be repeating himself, Master Blànes. Can you make out what he's on about?'

'He's simply saying that Allah is the one god, Allah is great, Allah is all-powerful, that's all.'

'Well, he's mistaken on all three counts,' the king muttered. 'Shout back and tell him that the Christian king forbids such sacrilege to be uttered in his presence, then ask him if he has anything worthwhile to say.'

The man didn't have to be asked twice. Reciting what was clearly a carefully worded dispatch, he declared at the top of his voice that his king had warned his men that the Christian invaders sought to make them slaves, and, worse than that, would do violence to their wives and daughters and would defile them to satisfy their own heathen pleasures. His king had vowed in the name of Allah that he would rather die than allow such crimes to be committed against his people and their sacred laws. He had therefore called on all the citizens of Medîna Mayûrqa, man woman and child, to fight with him so fiercely that one of them would be as good as two until the barbarian foe had been driven into the sea.

'So be it,' was the king's phlegmatic response to Pedrito's translation. 'Tell him to invite his king to do his worst, for that is precisely what I intend to do to him.' He then addressed the commander of his siege engines, who had been standing close by. 'Wait until the Moorish envoy has made it back into the city, then hit them with everything you've got. Oh, and by that,' he said as an afterthought, 'I mean dead bodies as well. There are plenty decomposing corpses strewn about the countryside, and it's high time we lobbed a few into the city to spread a bit of pestilence.' He dusted off his hands. 'We'll see how the all-powerful Allah copes with that!'

# 25

# A DILEMMA FOR PEDRITO

*EARLY DECEMBER – THE CHRISTIAN CAMP OF 'EL REAL'...*

It remained to be seen how Allah would cope with the gruesome form of plague warfare now being directed against the city, but what did become immediately evident was that his faithful followers had been spurred by this action into stiffening their resistance to the Christian offensive. Obviously, they were supporting to the hilt their king's appeal for each and every one of them to put up the fight of two.

This was carried out to such good effect that, only a few days after having gone against King Jaume's recommendation to accept the Moors' terms of capitulation, En Remon Alaman and the Bishop of Barcelona, two of his Privy Council's most vociferous opponents of the proposition, were suggesting to him that, on second thoughts, it could be advisable to enquire whether the Moorish king's offer might still be open.

For all that he recognised and respected the bishop's influence within the all-powerful establishment of the Church, and although he had always acknowledged the high regard in which En Remon was rightly held by his military peers, King Jaume left them both in no doubt as to what he thought of their proposal. To make such an approach to the Saracen king now, he told them, would put him in the position of a beggar kneeling with his bowl at the feet of someone who had only recently come to *him* as a beggar. The upshot of this, King Jaume fumed, would be to have himself portrayed as an indecisive mouse, and he would rather catch the pox!

Then, prudently turning away from the bishop and directing his displeasure specifically at En Remon, he barked, 'You would do well to take a leaf from the book of the Count of Empúries. When you were busy preaching vengeance to me and your fellow members of the Privy Council the other day, he remained steadfastly working in the mines with his men, having declared that he would remain there until their labours had resulted in the taking of the city.'

While his two counsellors stood in abject silence, King Jaume bluntly informed them that the die had been cast; the battle for Mallorca would continue as planned – but with redoubled conviction – and neither would respite be afforded any Christian soldier nor quarter given to the enemy until the war had been won.

*

As the days and weeks passed, the ferocity of the Moorish fightback became such that all the Christian mines and trenches either had to be abandoned or had been destroyed, with the exception of one tunnel, into which every effort then had to be concentrated. Under the tireless direction of the Count of Empúries, sufficient excavations were eventually completed to result in the collapse of a section of the city wall some forty paces in length. Yet the breach was so stoutly defended that the besiegers were forced to retire, while the besieged set about rebuilding their fortifications with daunting speed and ingenuity.

It was now early December, fully three months since King Jaume had set sail with his great invasion force of one-hundred-and-fifty ships and some seventeen thousand men from the mainland of Spain. Perhaps predictably, the onset of winter weather, combined with a feeling of weary dejection brought on by the seemingly unbreakable will of the enemy, was beginning to tell on the morale of the Christian troops. Then news of the capital city's dogged resistance somehow reached the outlying districts only recently transferred to King Jaume's rule by his unlikely ally and benefactor,

Ben Abbéd, the powerful Moorish *wali* of Alfabia. As a result, the threat of an uprising against the Christian occupation of the territories around the towns of Inca and Pollença became so real that both of the nobles whom King Jaume had installed as local governors were forced to return to the camp at El Real with their entire companies of men. Of a sudden, the outlook for the Christian reconquest of Mallorca had become disturbingly uncertain.

Nevertheless, inspired by their young monarch's zeal, driven on by prospects of booty, and reassured by ever more persuasive promises of a lavish life after death by their priests, the Christian troops persevered with the job in hand. Their spirits were eventually given another much-needed boost when the Count of Empúries' sappers succeeded in bringing down a second section of undermined wall – this stretch including a defence tower, which collapsed into the excavations as if struck by an earthquake. Surely this would herald the change in fortunes that every Christian soldier had been craving for so long. But yet again the Moorish resistance was so unwavering, the furious struggles to gain or hold ground so prolonged, that by the approach of Christmas there was still no indication that a final assault on the city was any closer to being launched.

*

Pedrito had been assigned throughout to one of several teams of men engaged in the essential tasks of felling and transporting timber for use as props and shoring-beams in the mines, as well as lugging away spoil from the associated diggings. It was exhausting, backbreaking work, made all the more unpleasant after seasonable rainstorms resulted in the ground being churned into furrows and ridges of heavy, clinging mud. It was also work fraught with the very real risk of injury, or even death, when obliged to venture within range of enemy positions on the city ramparts. Once again, the casualty rate among his colleagues brought it home to Pedrito that survival in such situations was very much a matter of luck, irrespective of efforts made to shield 'labourers' like himself from the attentions of Moorish archers and those manning their siege engines. No-man's-land still ran with the blood of Christians and reeked of their rotting flesh.

On the occasional rest days granted him, Pedrito had unfailingly foresaken catching up on much-needed sleep in order to make his way to the bolt-hole high above Génova hamlet where his mother and Saleema were living in increasingly punishing conditions. With the shortening of the days, such visits had become correspondingly more brief. Although Christian patrols had been constantly scouring the countryside between El Real and the mountains for Moorish militants, and summarily killing anyone suspected of fitting the bill, there were still desperate men at large, their readiness to attack and rob those who crossed their paths prompted as much by the need to keep body and soul together, perhaps, than by wanton banditry. In any case, Pedrito had to keep his wits about him when travelling.

That aside, every time he now set out, he took from the stores – not merely with King Jaume's permission, but by his insistence – whatever he considered necessary to ease his mother and Saleema's discomfort, right down to some hide and twine for them to make rudimentary shoes to protect their feet from the rigours of winter. Saleema was having to learn the hard way about life at the opposite end of the spectrum from the pampered existence she had been accustomed to in King Abû's palace. After all, Farah's ability to fashion and sew leather was severely limited by the physical effects of the punishment meted out to her at the behest of that selfsame potentate.

Indeed, whenever Pedrito saw how his mother struggled so bravely against the consequences of such cruelty, his heart was filled with loathing for the man responsible, albeit that he was his own natural father. Yet how ironic it was, Pedrito thought, that if it hadn't been for the tiny, cross-like birthmark behind his ear, he would now be fighting at King Abû's side against the Christian king who had so improbably become his friend. And, in all probability, Farah, instead of living rough in a remote cave, would still be luxuriating in the cushioned comfort of the Almudaina Palace.

Now, the closest things to luxury she could indulge herself in were the few fruits that Pedrito managed to glean from abandoned orange groves on his way from El Real. But he never once heard her complain about the miserable conditions in which she was now obliged to live. They were no worse, she would say, and better in some ways, than those she had endured for over twenty years in the grim kasbah alleyways of Medîna Mayûrqa. Nevertheless, Pedrito had noticed a gradual deterioration in his mother's wellbeing as the weeks passed. Although she put a brave face on things, the flame that once flickered so vitally in her eyes had now dimmed, to be replaced by a jaded look that was becoming progressively more difficult for her to disguise. She was exhausted, her fighting spirit finally yielding to the hardships that had been the bane of her life for so long.

Events usually followed a similar pattern on these fleeting mercy missions of Pedrito's. Nedi had stubbornly stayed on at the cave since the day he first turned up there in Pedrito's wake. He had decided, apparently, that this was where his presence was needed most, and that was that. And, in truth, it gave Pedrito a welcome measure of comfort to know that Nedi was acting as a guard dog for the two women in that isolated place. Meanwhile, King Jaume was understandably too preoccupied with waging a war to be unduly concerned about where his dog was.

So, all was well as regards Nedi, and it was always his bounding, barking, tail-wagging presence that was first to greet Pedrito when he appeared over the rise. Although Nedi's ultimate interest was directed towards what tasty morsels might be concealed in old Tranquilla's saddle bags, he did acquit himself favourably by delaying this investigation until he had subjected Pedrito to the customary attack of face licking.

Then, after less boisterous but no less ardent welcomes had been bestowed on him by his mother and Saleema, Pedrito would present them with whatever he had managed to garner from the El Real kitchens and stores. Mundane though they inevitably were, each item, when revealed, was always the source of great excitement. Even Annam the goat would barge her way into the animated huddle, leaving only Lucky, Farah's donkey, to remain sleepily aloof from such unbecoming antics over stuff that wasn't even weeds, never mind grass.

The donkey's attitude apart, however, these little outbursts of concerted exhiliration never failed to warm Pedrito's heart, while also reminding him how dismal and dreary life must have been for the two women during the long, lonely periods between his visits. But of more concern was his mother's state of health, and his anxieties were exacerbated by things Saleema told him on the few occasions they managed to be alone together...

'She coughs a lot during the night now. The atmosphere in the cave – even with the fire kept going all the time – the dampness seeps into everything, especially now that it's so cold at night. And I hear her groaning when she moves in her sleep, as if she's in pain – maybe her joints – the cold and dampness again, I think.'

Saleema was sitting beside Pedrito on a little bank at the edge of the tree-studded field outside the cave. They were gazing down over a panorama that extended from the seemingly endless expanse of the sea on their right, along the curve of bay to the capital city and beyond to the wide central plain of Mallorca, stretching all the way eastwards to the hazy summits of the Serra de Llevant.

'She always smiles and acts chirpily in the morning,' Saleema went on, 'but I know she's just making an effort for my sake. Doesn't want me to worry about her, you see.' She fell silent for a few moments, resting her head on Pedrito's shoulder. 'But I do – I worry about her more every day.'

There was nothing Pedrito could say to that. He was painfully aware of how urgent it was to find his mother and Saleema a more tolerable place of refuge, but he was no more able to think of where that might be than he'd been when he first helped install them here over two months earlier. And to make matters worse, he couldn't let on to Saleema what his mother had recently whispered to him about *her*...

'She cries herself to sleep when she thinks I've already drifted off at night. Talks to herself a lot during the night too – whimpers like a baby. She's missing her mother and father more and more.'

None of this did anything to make the quandry facing Pedrito any easier. In a perfect world, yielding to Saleema's desire to be taken home to her parents would both satisfy her personal longing and would provide a source of care and comfort that Farah desperately needed. But this was far from a perfect world. The risks of travelling through the battle-ravaged countryside between here and Saleema's home were perhaps even greater now than before. As Christian patrols cast their nets ever wider in hopes of finding pockets of Muslim resistance, those partisans who remained at large would have become more desperate than ever. On top of that, it was obvious that Farah was even less fit to undertake the journey now than she had been originally.

Then there was the matter to be considered of the time involved for Pedrito to complete the round trip from El Real to the hills inland from Santa Ponça where Saleema's father's farm was located. This would take the best part of two days, even if all went smoothly, and Pedrito feared he might be pushing King Jaume's benevolence too far by asking his permission to leave camp for so long at such a crucial stage of the siege.

Pedrito knew deep down, however, that the one factor which held him back more than any other from making the vital journey was the dread of what might be found when they eventually arrived at Saleema's home. He had seen for himself farmsteads that had been sacked in this area during the battles that followed the first Christian landings at Santa Ponça Bay, and it was highly likely that very few of the local inhabitants who hadn't already fled would have survived the associated bloodletting. Consequently, he couldn't bear the thought of Saleema's heart being broken by what she might discover when she did eventually fulfil her dream of returning home.

Yet, despite all these potential difficulties, it was clear to Pedrito that the status quo couldn't be allowed to continue for much longer. Somehow, he would have to find a means of getting his mother and Saleema away from the drudgery and discomfort of the cave. Saleema's emotional wellbeing depended on it – as, with increasing probability, did his mother's life.

To complicate matters even further, there was his personal relationship with Saleema to take into account. Sitting beside her overlooking such an entrancing view as he was now, it would have been easy to forget that the island was in the grip of a terrible and intransigent war, a bloody and murderous confrontation in which fate had placed them on opposite sides. Only the distant sight of flames, smoke and dust rising from the front line of combat to the north of the city served as a reminder that the feelings for each other that had grown so irresistibly were likely never to be allowed to develop further. The religious dogma of the eventual victors of the war would see to that. Besides, Pedrito was acutely aware that he might not even come out of the current hostilities with his life.

He was caught on the horns of a dilemma that seemed to become more inescapable with every passing moment – particularly at moments when Saleema did tantalising little things like tracing shapes on his knee with her forefinger, as she was at present. Although Pedrito tried to convince himself that this was nothing more than an idle extension of faraway thoughts that were occupying her mind, his own mind, courtesy of his knee, was far from being convinced.

She raised her head from his shoulder and looked up at him with those deep, dark pools of eyes in which he would willingly have drowned. 'When will you be able to take me home to see my mother and father?' she purred. 'You promised.' She then moved her hand from his knee and lightly drew a finger along the outline of his lips. 'And don't look so worried, Little Pedro. Your mother will be well looked after at our house, and I'll wait for you there until this war is over – *I* promise.'

Once more, Pedrito found himself at a loss for something appropriate to say. Consumed by a feeling of inadequacy and tormented by questions of where his priorities should lie, he looked away and gestured towards the sun dipping low in the western sky.

It was time for him to go back to El Real.

## 26

# HOPE IS GRIEF'S BEST MUSIC

*DECEMBER 24<sup>th</sup> – THE CHRISTAIN CAMP...*

It was beginning to occur to some of the Christian troops that the longer the siege lasted, the more likely it might be that they would become the victims of the war of attrition that they themselves had initiated. There was a suspicion in the ranks that, as the winter wore on, the pendulum of time would finally start to swing in the Moors' favour.

Although the Mallorcan weather at this time of the year is defined, as a rule, by pleasantly-warm, sunny days, the temperature does drop dramatically at night. Similarly, while rain isn't usually all that frequent, when it does rain, it habitually comes down in torrents, resulting in the ground being churned into a gooey quagmire, and in such a congested environment as a siege army's encampment in which humans live side-by-side with horses, a fetid, dung-polluted quagmire at that. These things, combined with creeping exhaustion, all added to the mens' aversion to being huddled together night after night in cold, squalid tents, and also contributed to a growing disenchantment with the entire campaign. There were even murmurings of coteries of foot soldiers planning to desert and make their way back to the mainland.

King Jaume was quick to recognise that not even the motivational urgings of Friar Miguel Fabra might be fiery enough to rekindle the essential flames of religious fervour if allowed to die in this way. He and his senior nobles concluded, therefore, that the time had finally come for an all-out physical attack on the city. To their more pragmatic military eyes, there were signs that three months of incessant pounding by the Christian artillery had finally begun to tell on the resolve of the Moorish defenders. Over the past few days, there had been a significant decline in the volume of missiles being launched from the few engines of war now remaining operational on the stumps of the city's battered ramparts. Also, disease emanating from semi-decomposed human carcases catapulted over the walls during the siege would steadily have been taking its toll on soldiers and civilians alike.

Just as crucially, however, there had to be borne in mind the threatened uprising in the northern territories of Inca and Pollença, the main sources of foodstuffs being so vitally provided for the Christian army by the area's turncoat Moorish overlord. If this steady supply of provisions were interrupted, it would be just a matter of time until, not only cliques of mutinous infantrymen, but what was left of the entire expeditionary force found itself heading back to the mainland. So, all things considered, it had to be now or never for making final preparations for the storming of the city, which, it was decided, would be undertaken on the last day of the year – exactly one week from now.

Tomorrow being Christmas Day, all military activity would be curtailed, except for whatever retaliation might be considered necessary to deal with any Moorish war engines still posing a threat. This interruption of hostilities was called primarily to honour the birth of Christ, but there also existed a more calculating motive; not only would the men be given a much-needed break from the punishing grind of siege warfare, they would also be afforded every means possible to celebrate Christmas Day in a festive way. Ahead of them lay an extremely testing few days, during which everything would have to be made ready for the death-or-glory attempt to take the city. Accordingly, anything that could be done to revive flagging morale would be done. King Jaume himself would make sure of it.

Today, though, would be just another day, with every man doing his allotted task to maintain the utmost pressure on the enemy – and with renewed vigour at that. For Pedrito and old Tranquilla, this meant continuing to help haul newly-felled timber, no longer for use in the mines, but for completing the construction of the battering rams, siege towers and scaling ladders which would be essential for the ultimate assault on the Mallorcan capital.

It was early morning when Pedrito, passing by the royal compound on his way to the woods, saw a familiar shaggy black shape hurtling towards him through the lines of tents. It was Nedi, making his first appearance in the camp for weeks, and showing signs of having run all the way from the mountainside above Génova. He started to bark loudly as soon as he saw Pedrito. But these weren't the 'woofs' of excitement he gave vent to when welcoming Pedrito to the field outside the cave. These were yelps of distress.

'What ails our long-absent friend?' asked the king, drawn from his tent by the commotion.

Before Pedrito could even acknowledge the king's presence, Nedi, instead of his usual licking attack on Pedrito's face, took the fingers of his right hand in his teeth and tried to pull him in the direction from which he had just arrived.

The king gave Pedrito a knowing look. 'He doesn't have to speak, this one, does he?'

'Something's wrong at the cave,' Pedrito muttered, his thoughts suddenly thrown into confusion. He tried to placate Nedi by patting his head and murmuring a few soothing words.

But Nedi was determined that Pedrito was going with him, and no amount of mollifying would change his mind. In frustration, he let go of Pedrito's fingers for a moment and barked frantically at the king.

'It's all right, boy,' the king assured him with a smile. 'I'll make sure he does what you say.' He then raised an eyebrow at Pedrito. 'Well,' he shrugged, 'what are you waiting for?'

Pedrito was in a quandary. 'But – but you said all of us would have to do the work of three or four men today. Getting ready for the attack on the city. Making the –'

King Jaume rested a calming hand on his shoulder. 'Go and see to your mother and the girl, *amic*. Tomorrow is Christmas, a day of respite for most of us anyway, so you and your old horse won't even be missed.'

Nedi, apparently of the opinon that too much time had already been wasted in idle chatter, grabbed Pedrito's fingers again and tugged him forcibly away.

'And, Master Blànes,' the king called after him, 'never let it be said that I'm a heartless man!' He let a few seconds pass, then added at the top of his voice, 'But all the same, make sure you're back here by dawn the day after tomorrow!'

*

Instead of following along unhurried and unseen as on the previous two occasions when he and Pedrito had made simultaneous excursions from camp, Nedi was now very much the pacemaker. And, tired though he must have been, the pace he set was too much at times for old Tranquilla, who also took advantage of the sporadic breathers allowed her to look nervously over her shoulder. It reminded Pedrito of how she had behaved on the night they made the fateful journey from Bendinat to his family home near Andratx. But Nedi couldn't be blamed for Tranquilla's actions this time. And in any event, Pedrito had more on his mind at present than whether or not the old hack's jitters about being followed were justified or not. What lay ahead of them was his only concern.

Every time Nedi paused to allow them to catch up, he stood barking at Pedrito, his ears drawn back in anguish, his every muscle straining to be on the move again. Whatever had happened at the cave was clearly a source of great anxiety to him, and even without words, he was succeeding in transmitting that anxiety in an emphatically lucid way.

Pedrito's heart had been in his mouth since the moment Nedi first tugged at his fingers back at El Real, and it had been beating faster and faster the nearer they got to where he was leading. To add to Pedrito's growing panic, Tranquilla made it patently obvious as soon as they reached the lower slopes of the mountain that she could no longer carry him on her back. As a result, he found himself obliged to clamber on foot up the rocky gradient in pursuit of a bounding Nedi, while also having to haul a reluctant Tranquilla behind him by the reins.

By the time he had made it all the way up to the sliver of level land by the cave, he felt as though his heart was about to burst from his chest, and the fact that there was neither sight nor sound of his mother and Saleema did nothing to assuage his condition. He could see the tethered donkey and goat grazing contentedly on weeds between trees at the far end of the field, so at least it could be assumed that a visit by robbers hadn't been the reason for Nedi's distress. Then again, perhaps there had been intruders interested only in the human occupants of the place. Pedrito had worried for some time about the smoke from their fire eventually leading someone to the cave, albeit that the smoke emerged through a hole much farther up the mountain. And as his mother and Saleema possessed nothing of material value, there could only be one reason for their being of interest to the type of lawless men currently roaming the countryside. His blood ran cold as terrible visions came racing back into his mind of what his adoptive parents and little sister must have endured when fallen upon by marauding pirates those five long years ago.

Nedi was now standing at the cave's entrance, his impatient yelps urging Pedrito on. Heart pounding, sweat stinging his eyes, his every breath a rasping gulp, Pedrito finally staggered headlong into the cave, half dreading what he might see there, half fearful that the cave would be deserted. Yet, even before his eyes had become accustomed to the gloom, he caught the sound of sobbing – hardly the most alleviating of sounds, but allaying the worst of his fears, nonetheless.

'Oh, Pedrito, thank heavens you've come. I just didn't know what to do.' It was Saleema's voice. She was clearly upset, but alive, and that was the most important thing.

Peering into the darkness, Pedrito could see that she was kneeling by the fire, which amounted to nothing now but a heap of dying embers. She was crouched over one of the crude mattresses that she'd helped cobble together when first faced with making the cave some sort of home.

'It's Farah,' she wept. 'I've been keeping her as warm as I could, but I ran out of firewood and – and I couldn't – I mean, I didn't want to leave her in case...' She paused to pull herself together, then went on to tell Pedrito that his mother had started coughing up blood during the night, and her condition had deteriorated so much by dawn that Saleema was convinced she was dying.

'I didn't know what to do,' she whimpered. 'All I could think of was to tell Nedi to go and fetch you. But as much as I wanted to believe that he'd understood, I honestly didn't hold out much hope.' She then reached out and gave Nedi a hug, showering him with praise, as well as tears.

Pedrito, meanwhile, knelt down beside his mother and gazed at her ashen face. He could see she was breathing, though only just.

Saleema told him that she had been lying motionless like that for hours, and nothing would make her stir. 'I honestly thought she was going to die. But – but I didn't know what to do. I tried to give her water to sip, but...'

Pedrito patted her hand. 'It's all right. Just being here beside her was the best thing you could have done.' He ruffled Nedi's head. 'And you did well too, boy. A real guardian angel after all, eh?'

As if responding to the sound of Pedrito's voice, Farah half opened her eyes, looked lovingly up at him and smiled. '*Lahm min lahmi,*' she said, her voice barely audible. 'Flesh of my flesh – come, give me your hand.' She raised her head slightly, took Pedrito's hand in hers and pressed it to her lips. Then, with the faint glow from the fire glistening in her eyes,' she reached up and stroked his cheek. '*Ibni wahid* ... my only son ... be happy.' She rested her head again, beckoned Saleema to come closer, then whispered to Pedrito, 'And look after my little *habib* ... you have both shown me more love than I have ever known.' Farah then closed her eyes, the smile she had smiled when greeting Pedrito a few moments earlier still lingering on her lips. 'I prayed you would come back to me one day, my little baby ... and my prayers were answered. Yes,' she sighed, 'I am a fortunate woman ... and a happy one.'

Pedrito buried her in the shade of an old olive tree on the fringe of the little field, where, as a child, she and her friends had marvelled at the wide vista of land and sea spread out before them, in the innocent belief that they were gazing down on the entire world. Saleema, with Nedi at her side, looked on in tearful silence as Pedrito built a little cairn of stones at the head of the grave, then stepped back and whispered a short but heart-rendingly poignant valediction...

'*Ma'asalama, ma'asalama ... Ummi*. Farewell, and be at peace ... my Mother.'

He turned round and stood comforting Saleema in his arms for a while, neither of them able to utter a word, or even feeling the need to. What they felt in their hearts said more than words ever could.

Then, as though wanting to let them know that he understood, Nedi gave a little whimper and nuzzled his head against Pedrito's leg. But only for a second or two. He then reared up and propped his paws in the crook of Pedrito's arm, panting his deceptively gormless-looking smile, first at him then at Saleema. Nedi had done something similar for Pedrito when he was grieving at the grave of his adoptive parents back at Andratx, and his intervention then had given Pedrito the encouragement he needed to pick up the pieces of his life and tackle the future with a sense of hope. It had the same effect now.

He gave Nedi's head another well-deserved ruffle, then said to Saleema, 'Come on then, little lady. It's time to take you home ... at last!'

## 27

# THE LONGEST MILE
# IS THE LAST MILE HOME

*LATER THE SAME DAY – ON THE ROAD TO SANTA PONÇA ...*

Saleema had greeted Pedrito's yearned-for words with a show of gratitude so physical that it almost knocked him on his back. Her excitement also let Nedi know in no uncertain manner that his unique form of canine counselling had done the trick again. He was patently and justifiably pleased with himself.

However, the truth of the matter was that Pedrito had been faced with no choice. Leaving Saleema to live in the cave alone would have been unthinkable, and taking her back with him to the Christian camp an absolute impossibility. So, the only option left was to set out with her for her family home, hoping against hope that what they found when they got there would be other than the scene of desolation that Pedrito had always feared.

But, for the moment, the fullness of Saleema's happiness was tempered only by the deep sympathy she felt for Pedrito's grief following the death of his mother, a sadness which also tugged agonisingly at her own heartstrings. Above all else, though, was the thought that, after a long and enforced separation culminating in a series of living nightmares from which she'd often feared there might be no escape, she was about to be reuinited with her mother and father. She was going home, and surely fate would soon lend her time to help soothe Pedrito's pain, and allow her to share with him the joy she had finally been blessed with.

For his part, Pedrito was experiencing what had become an all-too-familiar state of mixed emotions, although on this occasion the mixture was weighted decidedly against anything positive. He was with Saleema, and for this he was profoundly grateful. But countering that there were negative thoughts of what they might find at her home, of subsequently having to return to El Real to make ready for a do-or-die assault on the city, and, more immediately, of the fear that they might encounter trouble somewhere along the road they were now travelling. All of this on top of the sorrow inflicted by the loss of the person who had brought him into this world, and who had sacrificed her own life to save his. The woman he had only once called 'Mother' – but not, to his present shame and eternal regret, until he was standing over her grave.

The little procession that had come down Na Burguesa mountainside from Génova comprised Pedrito, mounted on Tranquilla, followed by Saleema, sitting side-saddle on 'Lucky' Masoud the donkey, with Annam the goat bringing up the rear on the end of a rope. Nedi had relinquished his usual shadowing role in favour of trotting jauntily along at Pedrito's side – a place now more appropriate, no doubt, for a dog of proven inspirational qualities such as his own.

After giving a deliberately wide berth to the macabre site of the Battle of Na Burguesa, Pedrito was now leading the way westward below the hillside where he and King Jaume had dallied for a while prior to the decisive phase of that bloody confrontation. This was the pretty stretch of coastline which the king had offered to name after Pedrito once the war was won. Costa d'En Blànes, he'd said he would call it – though with his tongue firmly in his cheek, to Pedrito's way of thinking at the time. Such light-hearted exchanges seemed a long way off now. The savagery of that very battle and the brutal drudgery of the three-month siege it led to had ensured that. King Jaume had still carried the air of an impetuous, devil-may-care young knight back then, but now he was a campaign-hardened commander-in-chief on the cusp of leading his army into a historic victory for Christendom – or to glorious death in defeat.

Such were the somewhat morose thoughts vying with Pedrito's admiration of the surrounding secenery as he went along at the head of his little caravan of refugees. They had been wending their way through the rows of almond trees that occupied the lower slopes of the hill and had now entered a clearing within a copse of pines fringing the shore.

Suddenly, Nedi stopped in his tracks and started to bark at something unseen up ahead. This prompted Tranquilla to dig her heels in as well, and nothing Pedrito did would make her budge. To make matters even worse, she then lapsed into her habit of staring wide-eyed over her shoulder.

Saleema let out a little cry of anguish.

'Don't worry,' said Pedrito, with as much reassurance as he could fake, 'they're only being spooked by the movement of the shadows. Sunshine, sea breezes and trees – always a problem for skittish animals.'

The expression on Saleema's face suggested that she was disinclined to believe this somewhat tenuous appraisal of the situation, and her intuition was about to be proved sound. With Nedi barking more frantically and Tranquilla incited into a spasm of nervous whinnying, six armed horsemen broke from the cover of a dense clump of trees up ahead, while six others did likewise from the rear. In a trice, Pedrito and his little party were surrounded. They had been ambushed. Saleema's screams of terror were immediately added to the din already being made by Nedi and Tranquilla. Only the donkey and the goat appeared unperturbed, making good use of the delay in forward motion to nibble enthusiastically at whatever edible greenery was within reach.

Pedrito's initial reaction had been that of utter dismay. One of his worst fears had materialised, and there would be little or nothing he could do to singlehandedly protect Saleema. Even with Nedi's assistance, any resistance he offered against such odds would be easily overcome. Then, as the men emerged from the shadows, he noticed that the one who appeared to be their leader was clad in a chainmail hauberk under a white mantle emblazoned with a large red cross.

'Ho, Master Blànes,' the fellow called out, his smiling face aglow beneath a fringe of red hair. 'What brings you to this neck of the woods?' It was Robert St Clair de Roslin, the novice Knight Templar from northern Britain who had established a friendly bond with Pedrito since their first meeting in a Salou tavern when he had been responsible, even though indirectly, for Pedrito being hired as helsman on King Jaume's galley. 'Hmm,' Robert added with a wink, 'and with a pretty wee lass for company too, eh! Aha, and a Moorish one into the bargain, if my eyes don't deceive me!' He spurred his horse towards Saleema, then dismounted to have a closer look. 'Aye, and a real bonnie one she is at that, so why the glum expression, my friend?'

It was a long story, Pedrito told him, but he would gladly give him the gist of it, if he had the time to listen. He then glanced around at Robert's companions and said hesitantly, 'But it can be for your ears only, I'm afraid.'

Robert readily assured him that this wouldn't be a problem. He explained that he and his troop had been patrolling the area between El Real and Santa Ponça on orders to deal with any bands of Moorish militants they came across. They were on their way back to camp, but had noticed Pedrito and his entourage making their way down through the almond groves and had decided to lie in wait for them here. 'Just to make sure you weren't murderous desperados,' he said with mock malice. At that, he dismissed his men and told them to wait for him at the edge of the wood a short way farther on.

After Pedrito had given him an abbreviated account of what had caused him to be here with Saleema – being careful, in the process, not to mention the identity of his natural father – Robert asked him if all of this was known to King Jaume.

'Leaving the camp regularly to help two Muslim women surely wouldn't have met with his approval, would it?' he probed.

Pedrito didn't reply, and pointedly so.

The ever-perceptive Robert, however, detected answer enough in his eyes. 'Well, no-one can ever accuse King Jaume of being a heartless man, and that's a rare attribute for a king.' He shot Pedrito an urgent glance. 'But don't you go telling him I said that last bit, mind!' He then looked admiringly at Saleema, who, being an Arabic speaker and therefore unable to understand the ongoing conversation in Catalan, was sitting quietly, though impatiently, in the shade at the edge of the clearing. 'Man, oh man,' Robert murmured, 'but she's a real wee beauty, right enough. And just see how she looks at you with those big dark eyes. Hmm, it makes me wonder if I've done the right thing.'

When asked by Pedrito to explain what he meant by that, Robert tugged at the front of his surcoat. 'See this white mantle of mine? Well, it's only us unmarried Templars who are allowed to wear it. We're bound by life-long vows of, ehm, *purity*, you see. The rest wear the black or the brown.'

Pedrito couldn't help smiling. 'So, you wish you hadn't taken the vows of chastity, is that it?'

Robert couldn't take his eyes off Saleema. 'Hmm,' he drooled, 'we're forbidden to even kiss a woman – and that's *any* woman, right down to our own mothers, aunties or sisters.' He turned to look Pedrito in the eye. 'You're a lucky man. All right, you've had your bad luck as well, and there's no denying that, but you've got a heaven-sent gift in yon lass there. And besides, I can see that there's more to her than just the looks of an angel. So, come what may, cherish her with every breath you take.'

'Oh, I will, I will,' Pedrito insisted. 'But all the same, I have to admit that the "come what may" scenario troubles me a lot.'

Robert tilted his head inquisitively. 'What in the name of Saint Mary are you talking about, man?'

'It's just that Saleema's a Muslim and I'm a Christian, and if King Jaume wins this war – well, we all know what the attitude of the Christian Church is towards –'

Robert cut him short by swatting the air with his hand. 'Ach, don't you go bothering about all that stuff! You've got a heaven-sent gift here – a God-given soulmate – and no mortal has the right to question the sanctity of that.'

Confused, Pedrito frowned. 'But I thought the very basis of the Templars' creed was anti-Muslim. Going on Crusades to rid

Jerusalem and the Holy Land of the Saracens. Helping re-take Spain from the Moors and destroy any of them who refuse to convert to Christianity. I mean, that's what King Jaume told me was the exact purpose of his mission here.'

Robert adopted a learned demeanour that belied his youth. 'Ah, but some things transcend religious divides,' he said in confidential tones. He gestured towards Saleema, then patted Pedrito's shoulder. 'What you have here is surely one of those things, so never let anyone or anything try to destroy it. Where there's a will there's a way, laddie, no matter how many bishops and archbishops say otherwise.' He looked surreptitiously over his shoulder, then hissed, 'But, hey – don't you go telling anybody I said that last bit, mind!'

Pedrito gave a little chuckle. 'You're a living puzzle, Robert, you really are.'

'Me? Never! Nah, they don't come any more transparent than me. You get what you see with the St Clairs of Roslin, and that's a fact.'

'I can't argue with that,' said Pedrito, 'but how can you devote your life – and *purity* –  to an order of Christian monks, yet cast doubt on the words of bishops and archbishops? That's what puzzles me.'

Dolefully, Robert lowered his eyes and contemplated his white mantle. 'I had no choice but to take the vows. My family, you see – the St Clairs, the barons of the lands of Roslin and Pentland in the Lowlands of Scotland. Devout Templars all of them, and guardians of the Holy Grail, no less.'

Pedrito frowned. 'The Holy Grail, you say?'

'Yes indeed! The drinking cup used by Christ at the Last Supper – brought back from the Crusades by a forebear of mine – and one day we'll build a fine chapel at Roslin to keep it in, you'll see!'

What Pedrito *could* see was that Robert was starting to wallow in a pool of nostalgia, so rather than probe further into his Holy Grail claim, which he was tempted to do, he listened in silence while Robert indulged himself in thoughts of home…

'Scotland,' he smiled, a faraway look in his eyes. 'Oh yes, it's a grand wee country, man. Majestic mountains and mighty rivers, where we hunt the stag and fish the salmon. Where men drink whisky instead of your sissy wine – or, ehm, as well as, in some cases. Where we eat real haggis, and none of your copycat *chireta* rubbish.' A rebellious scowl gathered on Robert's brow. 'Aye,' he growled, 'and where we don't have any of your damned wailing bagpipes to frighten our deer!'

'Sounds like a fine country,' Pedito tactfully conceded. 'A paradise on earth – even better than Mallorca, eh?'

Robert returned to the here-and-now with a conciliatory jerk of his head. 'Well, maybe the climate is just a *wee* bit better here. I'll give you that.' He prepared to remount. 'But you should come and see it for yourself some day. You'd like it.'

'Nothing I'd like better,' Pedrito sighed, 'but I've a few more Mallorcan hills to climb, if you see what I mean, before I can even start to think about your Scottish mountains.'

'No doubt, no doubt,' Robert replied, settling into his saddle. 'We've tough times ahead of us here in the coming days and maybe even weeks.' He pointed westward. 'But I don't think you'll encounter anything to bother you and your wee train between here and where you're headed now. Our patrols have done a fine job of mopping up any stray Moors who might have caused trouble, and any who managed to escape will have made their way north into the high Tramuntanas to join those wretched souls who survived the battles.' Robert stole one final approving glance at Saleema, then said to Pedrito, 'Fare ye well, my friend, and do whatever must be done to keep your little angel. For, mark my words as a man of God, He'll never send you down another as perfect as her.'

With that, he saluted theatrically, reared his horse dramatically, then swashbuckled off at the gallop to join his men.

*

Saleema had told Pedrito often enough where her family's farm was situated – three miles, more or less, north of the coast at Santa Ponça. And Pedrito didn't have to be reminded that this was the area, more or less, where the second massacre of Moors had taken place on the very first day of the campaign. How could he forget? This was where he had saved King Jaume's life by using his skill with the sling against a lance-wielding Moorish cavalryman. This was also where King Jaume had shown great delight when estimating the large number of Moors slain during his men's short, sharp rout of what had proved to be hopelessly inept opposition. On the day, some waggish young *cavallers* in the king's company had even dubbed the scene of this conspicuously one-sided encounter *Es Puig del Rei*, the King's Mountain. It was an epithet that had stuck and would probably be recorded in the annals of Mallorcan history – *if* the Christians emerged victorious from present hostilities.

When within sight of this place, but far enough away to be unable to see what evidence of the bloodbath still remained on the ground, Saleema pointed skyward.

'See, Pedrito – two vultures, circling above that hillside up ahead. A sheep must have died, or maybe a goat.' She shuddered. 'Growing up in these parts, I've seen this often enough, but it still makes my flesh creep.'

Pedrito couldn't bring himself to tell her that the flesh the vultures were eyeing was more likely to be what little remained rotting on the bones of men slaughtered in the *Puig del Rei* massacre than that of a recently-expired sheep or goat.

'Anyway,' said Saleema, 'at least they're unlikely to be my father's animals. Our farm is on the hill away to the north of that, so we have to take the track leading right at the next fork.'

Pedrito breathed a sigh of relief. Even if Saleema's estimation of its distance from the coast had been a bit out, at least the chances now were that her parents farm wouldn't have been at the heart of the Christians' rampage.

Presently, they entered a little sheltered valley, where orchards of orange, lemon and apricot still bore the scars of either having been raided by the inavders or deliberately harried by those retreating from them. However, just as Pedrito had seen around the Génova area when passing through with Saleema and his mother on their way to the cave three months earlier, there were signs that the local folk here had stoically set about restoring their farms to their former orderliness and productivity as soon as it had been safe to do so. Indeed, as at Génova, some families could be seen working on their properties, and one or two even stopped to wipe their brows and wave as Pedrito and Saleema rode slowly past in the late afternoon sunshine.

The smile of eager anticipation that had been lighting Saleema's face had faded as she caught her first glimpse of the damage that had been done to the cherished landscape of her childhood.

'Why?' she murmured incredulously. 'Why would anyone want to do such horrible things to such a beautiful place?'

Pedrito made no attempt to answer her, and he doubted that she had expected him to anyway. He was only grateful that what she was seeing here was notably less horrific than the scenes of desolation he had been obliged to venture into when looking for Christian survivors after the first merciless clash of arms that had taken place only a mile or so south of here. There, in the place King Jaume had later named *Es Coll de Sa Batalla*, the Vale of the Battle, the fertile landscape had been trampled into a wasteland strewn with human death on a sickening scale, the neat farmsteads ravaged in a frenzy of wanton destruction.

Now, with Saleema leading the way, they branched right again and began to climb a gentle slope where the fruit orchards of the valley floor gave way to terraced *bancales* on which the spidery branches of almond trees cast their shadows over the honey-coloured soil. Looking upwards, Pedrito could see that these cultivated slivers of land grew narrower as the gradient became steeper, ultimately yielding to the evergreen oak woods that typified the natural cover of Mallorcan mountainsides.

'My home is just over that little ridge up ahead,' Saleema said as she glanced over her shoulder at Pedrito, her eyes glinting with a blend of joy and apprehension. 'You wouldn't guess it from here, but there's another valley there – a hidden one – perfect for grazing sheep.'

Looking back, Pedrito could now catch a glimpse of the sea beyond the tree-fringed tops of the hills that rolled down towards the Bay of Santa Ponça. He felt a sense of relief that the arrival of the Christian fleet could have been seen from here, giving people in the vicinty time to take refuge before the invading forces penetrated this far inland. His concerns for the wellbeing of Saleema's mother and father began to diminish accordingly. Perhaps, he thought, the second of his worries about setting out on this journey was about to be proved as unwarranted as the first.

Meanwhile, Saleema was urging Lucky the donkey on with little clicks of her tongue, her impatience to see her parents again becoming more difficult to contain the nearer she got to home. Sensing this, Nedi ran ahead, barking excitedly. When Pedrito and the panting, wheezing Tranquilla caught up with them, Saleema was standing just over the brow of the ridge, staring down into a ribbon of land enclosed by the curved flanks of the hill rising up steeply on the far side. It was indeed a fine, sheltered place for grazing sheep, and fertile too, judging by the lush green sward growing between random stands of almond, olive and carob. In the centre of the valley, a whitewashed house nestled cosily amid a huddle of small barns and livestock enclosures. As was the custom in rural Mallorca, two tall palms stood guard at the entrance to this simple framstead. It reminded Pedrito of his own home, and he could understand now why Saleema had waxed lyrical so often about this entrancing place.

Why, then, was she standing here looking so perplexed? Surely, Pedrito said, this was the moment she had been dreaming of for so long, so why wasn't she rushing down there to give her parents the most pleasant surprise of their lives?

'It's the smoke from the chimney,' Sabrina replied uneasily.

Pedro looked towards the house. 'But there isn't any smoke.'

'Exactly. No sheep either.'

'Well, it's been a warm day, so maybe they haven't bothered lighting the fire.' Pedrito was trying to put as positive a slant as he could on the situation. 'And as for the sheep – well, maybe your father's grazing them further up the hill somewhere.'

But Sabrina was far from persuaded. She shook her head. 'No, it gets really cold at night up here at this time of year. Mother would have lit the fire hours ago.'

'Fine, but it's always possible she's with your father tending the sheep.'

Again Sabrina pooh-poohed Pedrito's attempt at reassurance, well-meant though she knew it was. 'No, in winter, Father would always have them down here in their pens by this time of day.' She motioned towards the setting sun. 'It's almost dusk, after all.'

'Yes, but it could just be that they've had to round up some stragglers,' Pedrito ventured, with what he hoped would pass for genuine nonchalance. He put an arm round her shoulder and contrived a little chuckle. 'I mean, you know what sheep are like.'

Saleema looked up at him and smiled back, though not very convincingly. She shook her head again, then gestured towards the field below them. 'The ground between the trees down there – it's too green. The sheep would normally have had it nibbled bare by now.'

Pedrito took her hand and gave it a squeeze. 'There's bound to be a perfectly good reason for that as well. So, come on, *habib* – let's go and see what's what. Everything will be just fine, you'll see.'

And when they reached the farm, everything *was* just fine – or appeared to be at first. The storage sheds and animal enclosures were intact, with no sign of having been interfered with. Pedrito drew up a bucketful of water from the well. It tasted sweet, so no-one had contaminated it, as was sometimes the case when a farm was abandoned on the approach of the enemy. Even the trees in the little orange grove at the side of the house were still heavy with fruit, so they hadn't been plundered either. This was taken as an encouraging sign by Pedrito, but it had the opposite effect on Saleema.

'It's well into the orange harvesting season,' she said, the look of concern on her face growing more intense by the second. 'Mother would have picked lots of them by now. And look, the ground is littered with fallen ones – all going to waste. She would never let that happen.'

She ran towards the house and through an opening in a wall at the back. 'This is the kitchen yard,' she told Pedrito, tears welling in her eyes. She nodded towards the corner. 'See there – weeds.

Mother would never let them grow like that. This little yard is her pride and joy.' She turned on her heel and ran her eyes over the outside of the house. 'And look – the windows are all shuttered.'

'Yes,' said Pedrito, 'but as I mentioned before, it's been a warm day, so keeping the shutters closed would be the normal thing to do, surely.'

Saleema shook her head. 'Mother always keeps these shutters open, even on the hottest summer days.' She drew Pedrito's attention to the wooded slopes rising up behind. 'This side of the house faces north, so there's nearly always some cool air coming down from the mountains.' Without waiting for Pedrito to comment, she scurried over to the kitchen door and grabbed the handle. 'Locked! This door's never locked – ever! I don't think I've even seen the key taken down from its nail behind the door – ever!'

Pedrito knew what she was getting at. Country folk on the island just didn't lock their doors, such was the degree of honesty and trust that existed in their communities. However, this was a time of war, so precautions beyond the usual could be regarded as sensible, if not absolutely essential. He started to tell Saleema this, but before he'd finished the first sentence, she'd set off running round to the front of the house. There, Pedrito found her trying to push open the heavy wooden door.

'Locked as well,' she panted, her voice trembling. 'Something's not right.' With a frantic look in her eyes, she ran off again, this time back towards the farmstead, where she stopped and stood staring into one of the little enclosures. 'This is where we keep the hens. And look – it's empty! And – and, there are even weeds growing in here too, which means there hasn't been anything pecking and scratching about in here for a *long* time!' Saleema turned and looked pleadingly at Pedrito. 'What could have happened?' she sobbed, tears running down her cheeks. 'What are we going to do?'

Pedrito folded his arms round her and stroked her hair while she snuggled her head against his chest. Saleema was a sensitive girl and it was obvious that she instinctively felt that harm had come to her parents. She was also an intelligent girl, so Pedrito knew there would be no point in trying to ease her anxiety with glib words of comfort. He could, however, emphasise the positive aspects of the situation, so that's what he decided to do...

There were no signs of violence, he told her. Nothing had been destroyed or even damaged. And as for the absence of livestock and the locked and shuttered house, well, that would surely suggest that her parents had made a planned and orderly departure, perhaps in anticipation of a possible Christian raid back on the very first day of the invasion. 'So,' he said, lifting her chin and wiping a tear from her cheek, 'there's every reason to believe your mother and father are safe and sound with all the other people who were sensible enough to take refuge in the mountains back then.'

'Oh, I really do want to believe that,' Saleema whimpered. 'But even if the Christian soldiers didn't come here, perhaps bandits came later, just looking for food. That would explain why there are no sheep or hens. And if my mother and father had resisted, as they would, the robbers might have –'

Pedrito placed a finger on her lips. 'Don't even *think* of it. Just believe that they're safe, and once this war's over, we'll find them, never fear.'

'And you'll help me?' Saleema sniffled, making a brave attempt at a smile.

'I promise,' Pedrito replied. He stroked her hair again. 'We'll do it together – just as soon as this war's over.'

As sincere as his words were, they were being challenged in his mind's eye by visions of the wholesale killing of Moorish fugitives that would take place in the mountains once the taking of the capital city had been achieved by King Jaume's troops. Going by past events, precious little opportunity would be afforded the vanquished to choose between conversion to Christianity or death. Then again, a Christian victory still couldn't be taken for granted, so the fate of Mallorca's displaced Moors might not ultimately be so bleak as it appeared at present.

The sun was now dipping behind the western mountains, casting chilly shadows of night over the valley, which seemed strangely at peace, despite being shrouded in a cloud of concern over the wellbeing of Saleema's parents, and in spite of the fact that a savage war was still being waged such a short distance away to the east.

'So, Little Pedro,' Saleema murmured, 'what will be do now?' She clung closer to Pedrito's chest as a cold shiver rippled through her body.

'You're tired,' Pedrito said softly. 'So am I – and so are Nedi, the old horse, the donkey and the goat. It's been a long, hard day for all of us.'

Saleema raised her eyes to his again. 'So,' she whispered, 'what are we going to do about that?'

'The only thing we can do,' Pedrito shrugged.

'Which is?'

'Which is find a cosy stable here and nestle down with the animals for the night.'

Sabrina stifled a yawn. 'And tomorrow?'

'Tomorrow, *habib*, we travel on. I'm taking you home – to Andratx.'

## 28

# THE END OF THE SIEGE

*CHRISTMAS DAY, 1229 –*
*THE CHRISTIAN CAMP OF 'EL REAL'...*

It had taken the best part of the morning to complete the trek to Pedrito's family home. He had been faced the previous evening with the same lack of choice that he'd had to accept after burying his mother earlier in the day, in that he couldn't leave Saleema alone at her parents' deserted farm, and her returning with him to El Real was totally out of the question. By the same token, it would have been unthinkable to abandon her to fend for herself at the uninhabited *finca* of his adoptive parents, but at least down there near the port of Andratx he had the option of leaving her in the care of his trusted neighbours on the other side of the *Torrent de Saluet.*

Old Baltazar Ensenyat and his wife couldn't have made Saleema more welcome, and the fact that she was Muslim and they Christian mattered not a whit to them. She was a destitute young girl in need of sanctuary, and their home would be hers for as long as she needed it to be. It appeared from his immediate settling down by the fire in the kitchen inglenook that Nedi took it for granted that the same applied to him. As for the donkey, well, Baltazar reckoned he could find enough field work to make it earn its keep for a while, and when it came to the goat, his attitude was that one more added to his little herd would be neither here nor there. Baltazar's wife had then reassured Pedrito that Saleema and her little menagerie would be treated as part of the family, so he could go off to his war taking comfort in the knowledge that they would be well cared for. 'Until you come back,' she appended. 'This time for good!'

\*

'This time for good... This time for good...' The phrase, so kindly spoken, yet not without a reproving edge, had repeated itself over and over again in Pedrito's head during the long ride back to the Christain encampment. And the image of Saleema, standing alone on the other side of the bridge after he'd he crossed the *Torrent*, was one that would haunt him for as long as he lived. Though fighting back the tears, there had been a smile on her lips as she gazed into his eyes after their final embrace. Neither had been able to speak. There had been no need to. The looks they exchanged had said it all.

'Until you come back – this time for good...' If only it were as straightforward as Senyora Ensenyat's gentle admonition. Pedrito knew only too well, as did Saleema, that there was a very real danger he might not live to come back at all. Even if the king didn't ask him to bear arms on the final push into the city, Pedrito took it for granted that he would be expected to be close enough to the king to at least provide him with a fresh mount, should his own chance to founder during the fray. That had been the way of things for the encounters at *Es Puig del Rei* and *Na Burguesa*, so there was no reason to expect it to be any different at the storming of the capital.

Pedrito had reported directly to the royal compound when arriving back at El Real shortly after sunset. Whatever Chrismas Day celebrations had been taking place were well and truly over by then, with the men obviously under strict orders to turn in early, in anticipation of a dawn start to five days of hard work making ready for the decisive assault on Medîna Mayûrqa.

'Robert St Clair de Roslin has told me about the sad loss of your mother,' King Jaume said on greeting Pedrito outside his tent. 'You're having more than your fair share of grief to bear, and all I can do for the moment is offer you my most sincere sympathies yet again.' He lowered his voice. 'Incidentally, I told young St Clair that, on pain of death, he must keep to himself the, as it were, religious complications of this matter.'

Solemnly, Pedrito shook his head. 'I'm sure he would never say anything to compromise you, *senyor*.'

'Nor, I hope, would he expose *you* to the punishment my more zealous churchmen would insist upon if they got wind of your, let's say, *alien* attachments.'

Pedrito nodded in deference. 'I'll be forever grateful to you for your understanding and confidentiality, *Majestat*.'

'So, uhm, talking of confidentiality,' the king said, a slightly salacious tone to his voice, 'what, in strictest confidence, eventually transpired between you and your little Saracen concubine, eh? Young St Clair tells me she's a real beauty. I mean, did her parents turn a blind when you – you know – when you...?'

'Her parents' farm was deserted when we got there,' Pedrito said flatly. 'Completely abandoned.'

The king looked a tad abashed. 'A pity, but our lads have to do what they have to do when they overrun those Moorish –'

Pedrito interrupted him. 'There was no sign of that, *senyor*. Maybe her parents had fled to the mountains. Who knows?' He raised his shoulders dejectedly. 'Who knows whether they're alive or dead?'

The king stroked his beard. '*Sí, sí*, the side effects of war, eh? Always very regrettable when the innocent have to suffer, but a burden that the commander of an army on a holy mission must be prepared to shoulder all the same.'

Pedrito hoped that the king wasn't being quite so indifferent as this last assertion had made him sound. King Jaume was wont to claim that he wasn't a heartless man, and he had indeed proved that to be so – in certain ways. Yet there was another, more callous side to his nature which allowed him to condone or even partake in acts of extreme brutality without, apparently, a second thought. It was all part and parcel, Pedrito suspected, of the ambiguous and essentially self-seeking characteristics inherent in someone who aspired to be *El Conquisador*, The Conqueror, and as such, one of the greatest Spanish warriors ever. In any event, Pedrito took this to be the cause of what may well have been an unintentionally dispassionate statement about the inevitability and acceptability of the 'side effects of war'. And even if he hadn't acknowledged it as such, there was nothing he could have said in retaliation without putting the king's qualities of tolerance sorely to the test.

Instead, Pedrito safeguarded his neck by ignoring the remark and telling the king how he had ultimately had no choice but to leave Saleema in the care of old neighbours of his down near the port of Andratx, where he hoped to return once the war was finally at an end.

But it seemed that the king's thoughts had now drifted off elsewhere – to the city walls, perhaps, and how they would finally be penetrated, and to what death-dealing triumphs and fabulous prizes might await within.

'Quite so, Little Pedro,' he mumbled while staring absently at the ground. 'To lose one mother is surely bad enough, but to lose two…' Then, with a sudden return to present practicalities, he raised his head and declared, 'However, you must be hungry and exhausted after your travels, so I suggest you ask one of the cooks to prepare you something to eat, then get your head down and grab some sleep.' He gave Pedrito an encouraging pat on the shoulder before turning to go back inside his tent. 'Tomorrow is another day, *amic*. *Sí*, and you can wager your mother's life that it will be a busy one!'

\*

During the days following Christmas, the construction of assault towers was completed and the mighty, wheeled contraptions made ready for drawing up against the city walls. At the same time, scaling ladders were laid out in no-man's-land opposite the appropriate points of attack, while finishing touches were put to the protective 'roof' of a gigantic battering ram on wheels that would be employed to finally smash down the *Bab-al-kofol* gate, which the Spaniards had already renamed the *Porta de Santa Margarita*.

The king's contention that keeping busy was the best way to ward off the agonies of bereavement was applied to Pedrito again now, although he had to admit that he was being worked no harder than any other man, be he humble foot soldier or exalted knight. A relentless, round-the-clock pounding of the city was now being maintained, so a steady supply of rocks had to be ferried in from the surrounding countryside to feed the voracious appetite of the *mangonel* and *trebuchet* war engines. Additionally, essential components brought from the mainland for use in the assembly of the various items of assault apparatus had to be hauled up from transports docked at Porto Pi. It was to those two mind-numbingly repetitive tasks that Pedrito and his trusty old hack Tranquilla had been assigned. But it could have been worse, for at the same time gangs of men had been given the unenviable job of making final reinforcements to the timber and earth bridge which had been so intrepidly built over the dry moat, their constant exposure to enemy arrows and missiles covered valiantly, though never one hundred per cent effectively, by archers crouched behind portable wooden mantelets. Even more exposed to danger than the bridge builders were the men sent in to level the moat by using rubble that had fallen in where sections of wall had succumbed to the Christians' bombardment and undermining. These men were working at the base of what was left of the ramparts at this, the focal point of the confrontation, and were therefore easy targets for whatever was hurled down at them, whether solid or liquid, blunt or sharp, hot, cold or on fire. The mortality rate was horrific, as were the injuries of those who survived. Yet the fever of the fight that spreads like a plague through attacking forces at such times kept the impetus going day after brutal day.

While all this frantic activity was happening in an around the camp, patrols continued to scour the hinterland for pockets of Moorish resistance. It was on his return from one of these expeditions that its leader brought news of rumours spreading through the countryside that thousands of the routed Moorish soldiers who had taken refuge in the mountains were planning to regroup and force their way into the city to help its beleaguered defenders. This, in turn, compelled the king to deploy extra troops to augment those already blockading the capital's seven other gates. It was already known that there was sufficient food within the city to allow its inhabitants, including the miltary, to survive for many more months, so it was essential to do whatever was required to avoid the possibility of the siege dragging on until the Christians did eventually become victims of their own war of attrition.

If there had been doubt in anyone's mind that the final offensive had to take place on the last day of the year as planned, this latest turn of events would have dispelled it. It was now December 30$^{th}$, so the pressure to get everyone and everything in place for the next day's big push was more intense than ever. But patience was also an essential ingredient of these final preparations, and the king's was about to be severely tested.

As on previous occasions when he'd felt in need of some diverting conversion to ease his apprehensions, King Jaume had summoned Pedrito to his tent shortly after nightfall. But before the king had taken his first customary sip of wine, a servant announced the presence of a knight from the Count of Empúries' train called Lop Xemeniç de Luziá, who sought an audience on a matter of great urgency. On being given the king's permission, the young knight entered the tent looking more like a mud-covered labourer than a well-turned-out man-at-arms. Excitedly, he revealed that he had just come from the mines, from which two of his squires had been so bold as to tunnel up inside the city walls.

'They report that there are many dead in the streets, my lord, and there are no guards on watch above the gate.' Lop Xemeniç could hardly contain himself. 'I implore you to order the camp to arms immediately, *Majestat*, for it's my opinion that the city's as good as taken. Honestly, there's no-one to defend it. Also, they haven't even started to repair the breach in the wall our artillery made today, and I'm certain a thousand or more of our men could enter before a single Saracen knows what's going on!'

Pedrito fully expected the king to sieze upon this as good enough reason to revert to his old impetuous ways. After all, wasn't this precisely the type of God-given opportunity he'd been awaiting for fully three months? But King Jaume was about to show that, as evidenced by other recent actions, he was not only three months older, but three months wiser now as well.

He flashed the young knight a superior smile. 'Patience is a quality you would do well to cultivate, my friend. Impetuosity, you see, is the trip-rope of the naïve, patience the ladder to success of the mature.'

Pedrito smothered a chuckle with a cough, while the king proceeded to berate the cresfallen Lop Xemeniç about the folly of attacking a town at night, particularly a dark one such as this. The actions of men were unpredictable enough during the turmoil that prevails at the start of any attempt on a city, he stressed – even in daylight. But to attempt such a feat at night, when no man could even distinguish between friend and foe, would be to invite chaos and undignified defeat. He then gave the young fellow one of his incongruously owlish looks and stated, 'For, if our men enter the town tonight and are driven out, we shall never be able to take it again. Mark my words.'

Lop Xemeniç said that he would, then left the royal tent, suitably enlightened, though patently disappointed.

King Jaume followed his departure with eyes that were now shining more with a glow of determination than glinting with flickers of apprehension. He laid his cup down on the table, its contents still unsipped. 'Well, Little Pedro,' he yawned, 'I suggest you go to your tent and get some sleep. Tomorrow is another day. *Sí*, and you can wager your mother's...' He pulled himself up, cleared his throat and continued, 'That is, you can rest assured it will be a busy one!'

*THE FOLLOWING MORNING, 31<sup>st</sup> DECEMBER, 1229...*

An altar had been raised, where, before daybreak, the Christian troops heard Mass and took the Sacrament from the Bishop of Barcelona, before exiting the camp and assembling in no-man's-land opposite the battered walls flanking the *Bab-al-kofol* gate. The sheer magnitude of this formation of fighting men made an impressive sight, with thousand upon thousand of foot soldiers ranged in front of rank after rank of cavalry. As had happened in advance of earlier battles, everything was enveloped in an eerie hush, broken only by the occasional snorts and whinnies of reined-in horses, either impatient for what they sensed lay ahead, or fearful of it.

With a rosy ribbon of light spreading along the eastern horizon, a gentle breeze drifted inland from the sea, dispelling the mists that had been lying like a gossamer shroud over this scene of impending death and destruction. Pennants and banners fluttered silently on lance heads above the horsemen, while the drawn swords of the infantry caught early shafts of sunshine and scattered them through the vast gathering like flickering stars.

It reminded Pedrito of a similar effect created by the sun glinting on the Moorish army's shields across the Bay of Sa Palomera when he was with the king on the islet of Es Pantaleu at the very start of this campaign. But the atmosphere had been so very different then. The beauty of the island had yet to be sullied by the violence brought to its shores aboard the ships of the great Christian armada, and birdsong still heralded the dawn.

It was through the unnatural quiet accompanying this morning's first light that King Jaume, fully clad for battle in winged helmet, coat of mail and mantle of red and gold, rode majestically from the camp and positioned himself in front of his mighty army.

'Ho, my men!' he shouted, standing high in his stirrups, as was his style on such occasions. 'Now is the day, the hour, the moment you have fought so valiantly to gain, and for which so many of our brave brothers have given their lives!' Echoing the Bishop of Barcelona's earlier sermon at the altar, he stressed what the conquest of the island would mean to Christianity, before reminding the men that they, like him, had sworn to God that suffering a mortal wound would be their only reason for giving up the fight. He quickly added that they should have no fear, however, of dying in the face of Christ, then repeated his promise of the fabulous spoils that would be shared among all those who survived the day victorious.

It was a stirring oration, delivered in a manner of which even the fire-breathing Friar Miguel Fabra would have approved. At its climax, King Jaume drew his sword, pointed it across no-man's-land and yelled, 'So come, lads! Attack in the name of our Saviour, Jesus Christ, and enter the city which the Lord has already deemed to be ours!'

But no-one moved.

King Jaume raised his eyes to heaven. 'Holy Mary!' he bellowed. 'We have come here to serve Thee and Thy Son to the greater glory of Thy name. I beg Thee, therefore, to intercede with Thy Son that He may relieve me of this affront, and that He may fill my whole army with courage!'

Then, his eyes burning into those of his troops who dared look at him, he shouted, 'Up, my men! In the name of God, why do you hold back?'

No-one moved, so he repeated the appeal, though still to no avail. On the third attempt, he addressed the nobles directly. 'Well, gentlemen,' he roared, pointing again to the city walls, 'are you afraid of these cattle? If not, for Christ's sake have your men attack!'

After several tense moments of silence, during which it seemed as if the long months of struggle might be about to end in ignominious failure, first one noble barked an order to his troops, then another and another, until, albeit hesitantly, the whole army began to move forward.

Pedrito had been observing this drama from the sidelines, and he was relieved to see that, despite the king's inclination to lead his forces into the assault, En Nunyo Sans and two other barons succeeded in restraining him and accompanying him to an elevated point midway towards the city, where he could best offer the troops the visual and audible stimulus of his presence. Pedrito joined him there – a discreet distance behind, as ever, but still in a position to have a good enough view of the developing action.

Suddenly, someone in the midst of the faltering mass called out, 'St Mary! St Mary!', and as the cry spread through the ranks, the pace of the advance increased accordingly. The foremost infantrymen reached the city walls running, spurred on by the chanting troops behind them. Although several in the vanguard were taken out by crossbowmen positioned on the crumbling battlements, they in turn fell victim to the arrows of Christian archers pressing forward in front of the cavalry.

Fully five hundred foot soldiers had penetrated the breach in the wall before it had been cleared sufficiently for any horsemen to enter, and the resistance they met was fierce. The Moorish king himself was seen to be commanding his forces, mounted, as before, on his distinctive white stallion, his cries of '*Rodo*! *Rodo*! Stand firm! Stand firm!' ringing out over the clamour of the developing battle.

A solid formation of scimitar-brandishing Moorish foot soldiers with bucklers on their forearms met the first of their opposite numbers head on, and would surely have driven them back had a group of Christian cavalrymen not charged into the fray. But they themselves were stopped in their tracks by a line of lance-wielding Moors emerging through the forward ranks of their comrades.

The surge of men and horses trying to make their way in through the breach was now checked by the impasse ahead of them, with the result that those actually engaging the enemy were so restricted for space that they could hardly put a hand out for fear of it being hacked off by one of their own. Chaos reigned.

Cries of, 'Help us, Saint Mary, mother of our Lord!' were heard coming from the midst of the leading mounted knights.

'*Vergonya, cavallers*! – Shame on you!' King Jaume yelled at them from his vantage point, his face contorted by the sheer frustration of not being in the thick of it himself.

En Nunyo Sans and his two companions had to physically restrain the impassioned young monarch from spurring his horse on, while desperately urging him to bide his time until the gate to the city had been smashed open. His troops, they counselled, would benefit more from his personal support at that decisive stage of the attack.

'What's more,' said En Nunyo, 'as you've been reminded before, *Majestat*, the success of this campaign depends largely on you staying alive, so your rushing headlong into that melee would be to risk everything – again!'

Duly admonished, though evidently not placated, King Jaume immediately turned his attention to goading on those men struggling to heave the cumbersome battering ram across the rough terrain of no-man's-land, his attitude clearly being that, if he was obliged to hang back until the gate was demolished, then the sooner the deed was done the better.

He twisted round in his saddle and shouted to Pedrito, 'Take that backup charger of mine you're riding and help tow the ram into position on the bridge over the moat yonder!' Noticing Pedrito's look of surprise, he added, 'I know, I know, it may be beneath his dignity to be used as a work horse, but this is war, and we must all pull our weight – in his case, literally. Now, get a move on! We haven't a moment to waste!'

And so Pedrito found himself involved once more with a lumbering house on wheels similar to the 'she cats' he had helped build to protect the Count of Empúries' miners, except that the 'kittens' inside this one would be using their muscle power to force a way through the city's defences instead of burrowing under them.

While this was going on, scaling ladders and mobile assault towers were being set against the walls. Those soldiers clambering up the ladders were wide open to being assailed by all sorts of projectiles and lethal liquids aimed at them from above. And even if they survived such 'sophisticated' countermeasures, there was still the ever-present danger of their ladders simply being tipped backwards by those manning the ramparts. Meanwhile, the Christian assault troops fortunate enough to be climbing inside the towers were at least afforded the protection of timber-clad walls, and therefore had a reasonable chance of reaching their goal unscathed. Nevertheless, when the draw bridge at the top of their shelter was lowered onto the battlements, they also found themselves exposed to whatever the waiting enemy could hurl at them.

The hush that had blanketed the scene before the start of the offensive had now been replaced by the roaring of soldiers engaged in hand-to-hand combat, by the clanging of sword against sword, by the screams of the wounded and the screeching of terrified horses. And yet more infantry and cavalry continued to crowd through the breach in the wall.

Outside, a desperately impatient King Jaume had taken personal command of the demolition of the *Bab-al-kofol* gate. His ears closed now to the cautionary entreaties of En Nunyo Sans, he sat atop his horse bellowing at the men engaged in driving the great battering ram forward. Pedrito likened his rhythmic barking of 'On! On! On!' to the drum beats he and his fellow oarsmen had been forced to keep time to while powering that damned pirate galley through the seas.

Time after time, the king urged his men on, the loud 'Boom!' of the ram's collision with the gate becoming more mingled with the sound of splintering wood with each charge, until eventually the heavy doors gave way and the city was open at last for the Christians' taking – though not without sacrificing an obscene amount of life to the glory of the two opposing dieties in the process.

\*

The fierce resistance that had been shown by the Moors defending the breach quickly waned in the face of the huge surge of troops now pouring in through the nearby gate. The Moorish king was among the last to retreat, but once the rout had started, it rapidly became unstoppable. The advancing Christians hacked down everyone in their way, so that the main thoroughfare leading south through the city was soon strewn with the dead and dying. In desperation, women and children on the flat roofs of their homes threw anything that came to hand at the Spaniards slaughtering their menfolk. But it was like trying to stem the tide with a sieve.

So swift and all-conquering was the advance that King Jaume, who had been in the van of his personal company of cavalry, had time to pause at the first mosque he came to and summon the Bishop of Barcelona from the rearguard to commence 'cleansing the building of all filthiness of the Mohammedan superstition.'

'I will name this church after *Sant Miquel*,' he declared from the entrance, 'and as soon as the Bishop has rendered it fit for Christian worship, I will have my galley's figurehead – a carving of the Holy Mother and Child – installed in a place of prominence as a symbol of our Christian ascendancy over the Saracen infidels who have profaned the sanctity of this island with their presence for so long.'

Then on he rode through a palm-shaded avenue lined with magnificent houses that rose from lush gardens filled with exotic flowers and shrubs, and irrigated by water spouting from fountains of intricately sculpted marble. Only at the northern perimeter of the city had significant damage been done by the Christians' war engines, but now that the victorious troops were on the rampage, nothing could escape their destructive frenzy as they fanned out through the network of inner-city streets.

Riding behind the king's troop, Pedrito could only marvel at the unashamed opulence of the Moorish architecture and the manicured courtyards that graced every step of the way. No wonder, he thought, that Medîna Mayûrqa, the capital of this island outpost, had been compared with the finest cities in the vast Arab empire that stretched from the mountains of India in the east to the shores of the Atlantic Ocean in the west. But it seemed that such a glorious endorsement meant nothing to the unruly bands of Christian foot soldiers who had already given themselves up to an orgy of pillage and plunder – with the associated activities of rape and murder – while the more disciplined of their comrades carried on with the business of finishing off any surviving members of the Moorish garrison who still had an inclination to fight.

By late afternoon, it was estimated that some thirty thousand people had fled the city, their departure ignored by a Christian army now more intent on taking booty from their homes than caring about any future threat they might pose to themselves. Meanwhile, it was assumed that many other Moors had taken refuge wherever it could be found within the walls, though still at least twenty thousand of their fellow citizens – men, women and children – were summarily slaughtered and lay in heaps round every corner. So much, Pedrito thought again, for being given a choice between conversion to Christianity or death.

However, none of this appeared to unduly bother King Jaume as he followed his army's trail of mayhem and carnage through the streets. It was a side-issue, Pedrito guessed, that came as a matter of course with the successful taking of any citadel. Presumably the king had seen it all before, even if not on such a grand scale. In any case, his only concern now was to track down the routed King Abû Yaha Háquem and bring him to heel. And where better to find the Saracen dog who had thwarted his territorial ambitions for so long than in his own lair, the sumptuous Almudaina?

'Holy Mother of God!' King Jaume gasped on entering the wide, palm-fringed forecourt of the royal palace. He reined in his horse. 'Have a man's eyes ever been regaled by the sight of a more glorious building?'

One of his accompanying knights then gestured towards the gilded minarets piercing the sky a short way behind the Almudaina's balustraded parapets. 'Perhaps that one, my lord?' he suggested.

'A-a-a-h,' the king sighed, 'the spires of the great mosque of Medîna Mayûrqa! How I marvelled at the jewelled beauty of its grand, golden dome as I gazed down on it from the heights of Na Burguesa. And how I swore that I would build to God's glory the finest church in Christendom on that very site, if the Almighty would only grant me victory here.' He nodded his head, a look of piety on his face. 'And now that He has, I vow that I will reduce that heathen temple to rubble and raise in its place a monument to Christ's domination of those who follow the infidel Mohammed's creed, to be seen and marvelled at for all time to come by everyone who sails to the city of Mallorca. *Sí*, and I will call this great cathedral *Sa Seu* – His House.'

What was to be seen when the king's party approached the Almudaina's walls was more to be abhorred than marvelled at, however. Piled against the gates were fully three hundred bodies of defenceless Moorish townsfolk, locked out by their own people, from whom they'd presumably begged sanctuary before being mercilessly butchered by marauding Christian soldiers.

'The side effects of war,' muttered the king, repeating the words he had spoken when told by Pedrito of the possible death of Saleema's parents, though perhaps with even less conviction this time. Coolly, he addressed one of his knights. 'Have these bodies cleared, then prepare to demolish the gates.'

Just then, young Robert St Clair de Roslin rode up. He dipped his head before the king then said, 'I have news for you, *Majestat* – news of the Sheikh, the Saracen king.' He nodded towards the palace gates. 'Aye, and I can tell you he isn't in there.'

'And are you saying you know where he *actually* is?' the king barked.

'No, not exactly, *senyor*, but –'

'But me no buts, man! You either know or you don't!'

'Well, I – I don't know myself,' Robert stammered, 'but – but I know who does.'

The king tutted in exasperation and motioned him to get on with it.

'Two of your soldiers from the town of Tortosa south of Tarragona, my lord – they say they can take you to the house where he's hiding. They say a Moor told them in exchange for his life.'

'A *Moor* told them?' The king frowned. 'But how could they understand what he was saying?'

Robert hunched his shoulders. 'They say they understand a bit of Arabic.'

'And they speak the truth?'

'I believe so, *senyor*, for they say their information is worth two thousand *libres* to you, and they're prepared to stake their lives on it.'

'Two *thousand*!' the king erupted. 'Do they take me for a fool? We know the Moorish king is in the city somewhere, so it's only a matter of time before we flush him out anyway.'

'No doubt, my lord, but – but –'

'I told you, but me no buts!'

'Aye, but I was about to say, *Majestat*, that those Tortosa laddies could save you valuable time, so maybe it could be worth paying the two thou–'

'I'll pay one thousand and not a bean more!' the king snapped. 'And if it turns out they're *wasting* my valuable time, I'll have their miserable heads. *Sí*, and you can stake *your* life on that!'

With this, King Jaume promptly detailed one of his train to go and fetch En Nunyo Sans, instructed two others to supervise the clearing of the corpses from the palace gates, then beckoned Pedrito.

'You will come along with young St Clair and me, Master Blànes. If those two men really can take me to the Sheikh, I'll need an interpreter.'

Pedrito had a heart-in-mouth moment. 'No, no, *senyor*,' he objected. 'I mean, it's kind of you to ask, but I really think you should get Senyor Babiel to translate on such an important –'

'I've no time to wait until we find Babiel,' the king snapped. 'What's more, you should think yourself lucky, for how often does a person of your humble origins get a chance to be involved in a parley between two kings?'

For all that he felt the moment had finally come for him to make a clean breast of it, Pedrito still couldn't bring himself to tell this king that the other king was his own father, and that he had been dreading meeting him face-to-face since the moment he'd found out how he had treated his mother. Pehaps, though, the best thing would be to keep King Jaume permanently in the dark about these personal details. All things considered, his knowing might do more harm than good.

'And anyway,' King Jaume growled while Pedrito was still in the throes of deliberation, 'I'm not asking you to act as my interpreter, I'm *telling* you!' He gestured towards the entrance to the square. 'Here's En Nuyo now, so let's go! *Ànims!*'

## 29

# THE SINS OF THE FATHER

*SEVERAL MINUTES LATER – INSIDE THE CITY...*

Darkness was falling as the two Tortosa soldiers led King Jaume and his company to a house only a short distance from the Almudaina Palace. Entry was through a small but graceful courtyard, dominated in the centre by a squat, spreading palm, and totally enclosed by arched walkways that supported the building's balconied upper storey. From somewhere unseen, water tinkled sleepily into a small pond in which marble cherubs bathed among the lilly pads in dimple-faced bliss. Here was a haven of peaceful shade to cool the most fevered brow on the hottest of summer days. Yet it was a modest refuge for one more accustomed to the expansive extravagance of a royal palace. This puzzled King Jaume to the point of mistrust, and he said so.

One of the two soldiers who had brought him here tried to put his mind at ease. 'The Saracen quisling who betrayed his master said that this is the house of one of his court officials – a scribe, somebody like that. There is little of value here, unlike the palace, where the Sheikh keeps vast hoards of priceless booty paid as tribute over the years by his pirate vassals. His reason for hiding here, *Majestat*, is the same as the little skylark who feigns injury to lure a predator away from her nest.'

Stroking his chin, King Jaume raised an avaricious eyebrow. 'Vast hoards, you say?'

'*Sí, senyor*,' the soldier nodded. 'That's what the man said.'

The king turned to one of his knights. 'Go back to the palace gates and tell them to stop clearing away the dead bodies. *Sí*, and make sure no-one, and I mean *no*-one, enters or leaves until I return. I don't want anyone getting his hands on those birds' eggs before I do. Now, go like the wind!'

Then up spoke En Nunyo Sans. 'Beware that this house is more than a mere decoy, *Majestat*. For all we know, it could be a trap, set as a cowardly means of taking your life at the very hour of your greatest victory.'

'Well reasoned, En Nunyo,' the king replied, 'and well counselled. It was for such qualities that I made you my chief general. Now,' he continued, jerking his head towards the doorway of the house, 'take two of my guards and go in there to make sure it's safe for me to enter.'

Although Pedrito's nerves were on edge in anticipation of the personal ordeal that might be awaiting him, he couldn't help but smile at the king's sardonic sense of humour, as well as at En Nunyo's obvious aversion to it.

'As you wish, my lord,' the king's cousin grunted, then selected two guards and directed them into the house – ahead of himself.

'Delegation in the face of mortal danger is the privilege of the privileged,' Pedrito silently concluded.

As it transpired, neither of the delegators had anything to fear. After a few minutes, En Nunyo appeared in the doorway to announce that the house had been searched and the only occupants were King Abû Yaha and three bodyguards.

'And you're sure it's the Sheikh himself?' King Jaume checked. 'I have no desire to waste time talking to an impostor while there's every chance that the real Saracen king is back at his palace preparing to make off with his ill-gotten loot.'

'As you will recall,' En Nunyo testily replied, 'I have already looked King Abû in the eye on those two occasions we parleyed at the start of the siege, and I can confirm, *senyor*, that the man inside the house here is indeed him. In fact,' he added with a shrug, 'I get the impression he has been expecting you.'

'*Expecting* me? But how could that be?'

En Nunyo looked directly at the two soldiers from Tortosa.

'Well, who's to say that the so-called quisling these men say betrayed their king might actually have been a messenger relaying his defeated master's invitation to his conqueror?'

King Jaume pursed his lips and nodded. 'Well reasoned, *amic*, and well counselled again. You may well have saved me a thousand *libres*.' He glared at the two cowering soldiers. 'More than that, if I find out that what he suggests is true, I'll personally take an axe to your miserable necks!'

The king and En Nunyo, escorted by Robert St Clair de Roslin and three other knights, then entered the house, with Pedrito, his stomach churning, following a few paces behind. An archway in a filigree screen opened into a sparsely furnished room illuminated by the soft glow of delicately carved wall lamps. King Abû Yaha Háquem stood in the centre, flanked by his bodyguards, the tips of their lances pointing innocuously towards the ceiling.

Pedrito was struck by the awesome presence of the man whose blood he shared. Tall and stately, he was clad in a flowing white burnous of finest silk, his dark, bearded face showing a serenity that belied the wretchedness of his situation. He acknowledged King Jaume with a slow bow and a flourish of his hand, before pulling his robe aside and drawing a jewel-encrusted dagger from his belt, then presenting it hilt-first to his subjugator. Next, and still without a word being spoken, he signalled his guards to surrender their lances to their opposite numbers.

En Nunyo Sans, unable to hide his delight, nudged King Jaume with his elbow. 'Now Mallorca is finally yours,' he grinned. 'Soon all the world will know of your great victory over the Saracen infidel. Now, *Majestad*, you can truly claim the title of *El Conquistador*, The Conqueror, the greatest warrior king in the history of Christian Spain.' He beckoned Pedrito forward. 'Tell the Sheikh what I just said, Master Blànes.'

His voice quavering, Pedrito did as instructed, though purposely avoiding eye contact with King Abû, whose reply was short and spoken without emotion:

'There is no conqueror but Allah.'

'Well, Master Blànes,' En Nunyo pressed, 'what did he say?'

'He, uh, he says that the Christian king is indeed a great warrior.'

'It's to his credit that he acknowledged the fact,' En Nunyo beamed, 'although he would have been courting trouble if he'd done otherwise.'

Pedrito glanced at King Jaume, who, unlike his more effusive cousin, maintained an inscrutable expression while keeping his eyes fixed on the face of his arch adversary.

After some moments of strained silence, King Abû spoke again – through Pedrito, but without looking at him.

'Tell the Christian king that the terms of my surrender of the land of Mallorca are simple: I must be given ships to sail, with guaranteed safety, to Africa with all the members of my household and whatever goods and chattels I choose to take from my palace.'

King Jaume remained silently impassive.

'Goods and chattels?' En Nunyo scoffed, nudging his royal cousin again. 'He means to empty that lark's nest of all its eggs and use them to fund a counter attack on us from Morocco. Beware the perfidy of this infidel, *Majestat*. He's like any wounded dog – still dangerous when shown mercy.'

Expressly ignoring those remarks, King Jaume spoke at last. 'Convey my compliments to the Sheikh, Master Blànes, and inform him that the terms of his surrender will be dictated by me, and by no-one else.'

King Abû stood stony-faced as Pedrito translated this pointedly unequivocal message.

'Tell him further,' King Jaume went on, 'that while I respect him as a fellow monarch, I have not forgotten that he insulted my emissary who, some time ago, came here to ask him to use his influence to stop his pirate cronies attacking the merchant ships of Spain. Instead of obliging, he slighted me by saying that he knew of no King Jaume of Aragon and Catalonia.'

While Pedrito translated, King Jaume directed a burning stare into the eyes of his vanquished enemy, who chose not to respond.

'Advise him,' King Jaume continued, 'that I vowed then that I would not rest until I had pulled the beard of the man who had treated me with such contempt.' He paused. 'The time has now come.'

The Moorish king continued to stare unflinchingly back, while remaining resolutely silent.

This was developing into a battle of wills, in which the odds were very much in King Jaume's favour, and he knew it.

'Tell him, Master Blànes, that I am a man sensitive to the feelings of others, so I will not make him suffer the ignominy of being humiliated in the presence of those in this room, including his own bodyguards.'

King Abû responded with an almost imperceptible dipping of his head.

'Inform him,' King Jaume went on, 'that a much more significant gesture will have to be made by him – one that will let the world see that he and his Muslim subjects are bowing to the supremacy of our Lord Jesus Christ, in whose name he has been so soundly defeated.'

A twitch of apprehension tugged at the corner of King Abû's mouth.

King Jaume smiled a wry smile, savouring the moment, then said, 'He will have to publicly renounce his Muslim faith and convert to Christianity.'

On hearing this translated into Arabic, King Abû reacted as if he had been kicked in the chest. He clasped his heart. 'I would rather die,' he growled through clenched teeth. 'The Christian king has my dagger. Let him turn it on me – now!'

Pedrito at once felt a modicum of admiration for the man he had been preparing to despise. For the first time, he stole a glance at his father's face, and was favourably struck by the determined look in his eyes and the defiant set of his jaw. But this positive reaction was to be disappointingly short-lived.

King Jaume took obvious delight in letting the Sheikh know that he had no intention of taking his life. That would be an easy way out for such a great fighting man who had suffered defeat at the hands of someone whose very existence he had previously declined to acknowledge. No, he stressed, if King Abû wanted to avoid the shame of being paraded in shackles through the streets of every city in Christian Europe, he would have to pay homage to Jesus Christ in a way that would be seen by the world and would be remembered for time without end. 'So then,' he said, 'will the Sheikh accept my invitation to be baptised, or will he choose public disgrace?'

Once more, a palpably awkward silence descended on the room, King Abû's steadfastly proud demeanour dissolving by the second into a look of total abjection.

'The Christian king claims that he is sensitive to the feelings of others,' he said at length, his eyes downcast, his shoulders sagging. 'If he will not grant me the means to go into honourable exile in Africa, can he, then, at least allow me to see out my days here in Mallorca, living in circumstances that befit my station, and in an appropriately secure location?'

King Jaume gave a little snort of derision. 'And what of the homage to Christ that I have already said will be a precondition of any act of clemency on my part?'

'Absolutely, *Majestat*,' En Nunyo Sans swiftly put in. 'What this Moor asks is tantamount to a reward for having been overthrown by the forces of our Lord and Saviour. He must show due respect to the one true Faith, or suffer the consequences.'

Again, King Jaume ignored the provocative suggestions of his cousin, instead instructing Pedrito to repeat his last question to King Abû.

'*Allahu akbar*,' was the Sheikh's grunted reply. 'Allah is the greatest, and I will never renounce Him.' He raised his eyes to meet King Jaume's. 'I repeat, I would rather die.'

This time, Pedrito translated the statement about Allah word for word. What was the point, he thought, of trying to make either man's religious principles sound any less immovable than they really were?

'So, he would still rather die,' King Jaume muttered. With a nod of acknowledgement to the Sheikh, he held out the dagger which had been surrendered to him earlier. 'I would not deny you the honour of proving the fortitude of your beliefs – even if you go to hell for committing the blasphemy of saying there is a greater power than the Father of our Lord Jesus Christ.'

All eyes were on the Sheik as he tentatively moved a hand towards the proffered weapon.

'Why do you hesitate?' King Jaume demanded. 'Don't you believe what your prophet Mohammed promised – everlasting life as a reward for a glorious death?' He took time to smirk at his attendant knights before adding, 'Especially when it's supposed to come with an endless supply of full-breasted virgins?'

With beads of sweat glistening on his brow, King Abû withdrew his hand as if it had been scalded. 'To take my own life would be an act of cowardice, and no coward shall pass through the gates of paradise.'

'So what?' King Jaume retorted. 'You'll already be heading in the other direction for insulting the one true God and his Son, Jesus Christ.'

A ripple of muted laughter ran through the Christian group.

Pedrito felt a twinge of disapproval at the way King Jaume was now baiting his deafeated foe, even if it was more for the entertainment of his company than his own satisfaction. In any case, any temptation Pedrito might have had to feel sorry for his father was about to be negated by the man himself.

With his chin on his chest, he pleaded in a barely audible voice to be allowed to live on in Mallorca. He now readily conceded that the location and nature of his residence would be the prerogative of the Christian king to decide.

His *residence*, King Jaume promptly informed him, would be a prison – a prison worthy of a king, but a prison nonethless. He would be treated with due respect, but without being afforded any of the trappings of his former life in the Almudaina.

When King Abû meekly bowed his acceptance, Pedrito started to feel a measure of shame creeping into his feelings. And there was worse to come.

King Jaume pointed out that a condition of the Sheikh being allowed to continue living on the island would still be his paying homage to Christ in a manner that would declare his subjugation to the world. And if he refused to convert to Christianity, King Jaume asked, how else could such a declaration be made?

Without lifting his gaze from the floor, King Abû then said that he was prepared to pass his favourite son, a fourteen-year-old, into the care of the Christian king, the boy's conversion to Christianity being an accepted condition of the bargain. Better a child of the new generation being paraded as a convert, he said, than someone of his own mature years.

While King Jaume grinned in undisguised delight, Pedrito cringed. He stood with his thoughts racing as King Jaume recounted, for the benefit of his entourage, that he himself had been given into the 'care' of an adversary of his own father's when only three years of age. A betrothal had been arranged at the time – to the potential benefit of both parental parties – and although the marriage had not materialised in his own case, he saw no reason to believe that a simlar arrangement should not be successfully employed here.

Why, he could visualise it already. He would have the Moorish prince baptised in his own name, Jaume, and he would have him married off to someone like the lovely Eva, the daughter of his friend, En Martin Roldan, the head of one of Aragon's most eminent lineages and an unstinting contributor to the cost of this crusade. 'Yes, I would then cede estates to the boy,' the king continued purposefully. 'Those around Illueca and Gotor near my own city of Zaragoza would be ideal, and I could give him a suitably prestigious rank. Hmm, Baron Jaume of Illueca and Gotor would sound good, I think.'

'Yes indeed,' En Nunyo Sans gushed, 'such a gesture would be the perfect manifestation of your new title of *El Conquistador*, the great Conqueror of the Muslim scourge of Spain – while also showing our people that you are a compassionate and generous monarch.'

While sycophantic mutterings were exchanged around him, King Jaume asked Pedrito to tell the Sheikh that his proposition was accepted. Arrangements should be made immediately for the handing over of his son to the Bishop of Barcelona, while the Sheikh himself should prepare himself for incarceration.

Pedrito did his bidding in a sort of trance, the words leaving his mouth almost of their own volition, preoccupied as he had become with the rapid descent into undignified self-preservation by the once-revered Moorish warrior standing slumped in front of him. Suddenly, his mind was filled with thoughts of the awful life his mother had been condemned to by this man's actions, and of how Saleema would eventually have been obliged to submit to his carnal whims.

He stared at his blood father, trying to work out if he could see anything of himself in him. But no, the undeniable reality was that the humble fisherman who had cared for him as a helpless foundling had more real merit in one calloused finger of his work-worn hands than this strutting peacock had in the whole of his silk-clad, perfumed body.

All at once, the pent-up frustrations and bridled anger that Perito had lived with for so long came surging to the surface like boiling lava. The presence of the two kings posturing in the name of their respective gods meant even less to him now than it had ever done. He would have his say, no matter what.

He stepped forward and glared angrily into the eyes of his father. The three Moorish guards, anticipating a threat to their master, made to intervene, only to be stopped by King Jaume drawing his sword and ordering his knights to do likewise.

'It appears, Master Blànes,' he said coolly, 'that you have a personal point to make with my Saracen adversary. Please feel free to proceed.'

All thoughts of acting as a translator had now gone from Pedrito's head. The gist of what he had to say in Arabic would either be understood by King Jaume in the light of what he already knew of his background or it wouldn't. Either way, Pedrito could not have cared less. His past life, his mother's life and death and any possibility of a future life with Saleema were bizarrely and inextricably tied up in what was now about to erupt.

'So, you sacrifice another son to suit your own ends!' he snarled into King Abû's face. 'You won't renounce Allah, but you're prepared to make your son commit what you regard as a sin in order to protect your own integrity in Allah's eyes.'

King Abû instantly drew himself up to his full height. 'Another son? I have many sons and I am a staunch protector of them all. How dare you speak to me like that, you Christian dog!'

'Ah, but I have every right to speak to you like that,' Pedrito replied, willing himself to be calm. 'And when it comes to that, I'm only a Christian because of you!'

'A Christian because of *me*? Pah, you speak in riddles, and I've no time for them!'

Pedrito allowed himself a wry smile. 'That's at least one thing you have in common with the Christian King. And talking of dogs, I have more regard for his – a black one – than I do for you!'

King Abû gathered his brows into a menacing frown, his deep-set eyes glinting like little black beads. 'You dare compare me to a black dog – the very embodiment of the devil himself?'

'Yes! And with good reason!'

King Abû reached instinctively for his dagger, but found only its empty scabbard. 'Damn your eyes! If I had a blade I would cut your worthless throat!'

Pedrito gave a scornful laugh. 'If you have to rely on a flunky doing your murderous work when it's a baby you take a dislike to, why should anyone believe you have the courage to tackle someone your own size – with or without a blade?'

The colour drained from King Abû's lips. 'Courage?' he hissed 'You doubt my courage?' He lunged at Pedrito. 'I need no knife – I'll kill you with my bare hands, you insolent peasant bastard!'

As Pedrito side-stepped, King Abû stumbled clumsily into the arms of Robert St Clair de Roslin, who took obvious delight in pushing him back into the middle of the floor, where Pedrito stopped him abruptly by extending an arm and putting a hand to his throat. King Abû immediately grabbed Pedrito's wrist in both hands and tried to pull himself away.

Pedrito duly increased his grip. 'A few years spent heaving an oar as a galley slave instead of a lifetime of cavorting between silk sheets with young girls might have given you the strength, old man,' he grinned, 'but as things stand, whether or not you draw another breath would appear to depend on me – a Christian dog and peasant bastard.' He glared directly into King Abû's eyes. 'How the tables have turned, eh?'

'Riddles,' King Abû wheezed, the veins at his temples bulging like bloated worms. 'You're still talking in riddles.'

Pedrito looked to one side and pulled his hair away to expose the cross-shaped birthmark behind his ear. 'Perhaps this will make things clearer for you!' he said, while simultaneously releasing his hold on the Sheikh's throat.

'The devil's mark!' he gasped, recoiling as if from a striking snake.

Pedrito stole a quick glance at King Jaume, whose nod of acknowledgement was all that was needed to confirm his comprehension of the relationship between his young helmsman and the defeated Saracen King.

'So, you remember me?' Pedrito said to his father.

King Abû's swarthy skin had now turned a sickly grey. 'The devil child,' he muttered. 'But – but, you were – you were –'

'Killed at birth by one of your flunkies?'

'No – I – no, I thought…'

'I had been left for dead somewhere down on the quay – or flung into the harbour to drown – or eaten by rats?' He stared unblinking at King Abû for several moments, both relishing his disquiet and pitying his state of utter dejection. 'Solving the riddles now, are you?' he eventually asked.

King Abû opened his mouth, but no words emerged.

'Then let me help you,' Pedrito went on. 'I did indeed become a Christian and a peasant, but only because those were the simple but benevolent ways of the people who saved my life after it had been rejected by you. And you called me a bastard.' Pedrito wagged a censuring finger in his father's face. 'That's a slight against my mother – your once-favourite wife, Farah – and I won't have her memory debased by anyone, least of all you!'

'I – I only knew she bore me a child with the mark of the devil and –'

'She bore you *me*!' Pedrito cut in. 'An innocent baby, your first-born son, who would have grown up to return all the love you cared to give me – and with interest – just as I did with the only parents I ever knew.' He looked his father up and down with patent disdain. 'And you call yourself a staunch protector of all your sons? Yes, just as you've protected yourself by giving one away to your enemies today! Life is clearly cheap for someone whose god encourages him to breed like a common rabbit while allowing him to assume the power of the god himself, no?'

'No! I would never act in such a way! *Allahu akbar*. Allah is the most great, and no man can assume his power.'

'Yet, in his name, you had my mother publicly crippled – a beautiful young woman, her life condemned to scratching a living in the squalid alleyways of the kasbah, just because her baby, a child you fathered, happened to be born with a small blemish behind his ear.'

The Sheikh stood in silence, his resentment simmering, as Pedrito turned to King Jaume and said, 'I apologise for speaking for so long in Arabic, *senyor*, but I hope you may have gathered from this' – he pointed to his birthmark – 'that certain things had to be said between myself and ... my father.'

'I think I may well have got the gist of it, Master Blànes,' the king replied, a tad contritely. 'And, ehm, I don't suppose I'll ever meet another galley slave who might have been – but for the vagaries of fate – a king like myself.'

Pedrito dipped his head and smiled benignly. 'As I've said to you more than once before, *Majestat*, perhaps I was actually more fortunate to be raised as a humble peasant.'

'*Sí*,' King Jaume agreed, with a wink that Pedrito hoped was loaded more with irony than arrogance, 'for at least it meant that you ended up on the winning side.'

## 30

# WHERE THERE'S LOVE THERE'S HOPE

*LATER THE SAME EVENING…*

'I suppose you'll be going off to meet your little harem plaything over by Andratx now,' King Jaume said to Pedrito in the courtyard of scribe's house. And there was no mistaking the meaning of his accompanying wink this time.

'No, no,' Pedrito protested with a forbearing smile, 'she's no plaything in my eyes. No, I was brought up to believe that I should show a woman as much respect as any man – more, in the case of his soulmate.'

'Oh, *soul*mate now, is it?' The king raised a mischievous eyebrow. 'Well, well, it seems we're going to have yet another convert to Christianity joining my court, eh? *Sí*, and you can count on me to lay on a lavish banquet in celebration of your marriage … *and* her baptism.'

'Ah, but you're jumping to too many conclusions,' Pedrito replied, his expression a little less tolerant than before. He thought for a moment, then gave a little laugh. 'Yes, and if you knew Saleema, you'd realise soon enough that she's her own person, and I respect her all the more for that.'

King Jaume cast him a cautioning look. 'I have to tell you, Little Pedro, that I am giving custody of the region of Mallorca which includes the territory of Andratx to Berenguer de Palou, the Bishop of Balcelona. It is to be part of his promised share of the spoils.'

Pedrito hunched shoulders. 'Fine. I can pay rent for our little

411

farm just as easily to him as my parents did to the Moorish *wali* of the area.'

'Aha, but now it's *you* who's jumping to conclusions, my friend. The Bishop of Barcelona will hold those territories for me in fief and will be entitled to his proportion of related revenues, even in his absence. So, naturally, the lands will require an overseer, a governor.'

'I follow all of that, *senyor*, but as long as I have tenancy of the *finca*, I won't mind who's collecting the rent.'

'But you won't be paying rent to anyone.'

Pedrito looked confused. 'Now it's *you* who's talking in riddles.'

The king smiled leniently. 'You may have been born a prince, Master Blànes, but you're still thinking like a peasant.'

'No harm in that,' Pedrito retorted, 'if my natural father's way of thinking tonight was anything to go by.'

'And I can understand why you say that,' the king conceded, then adopted a more admonishing manner. 'But perhaps you shouldn't think *quite* so badly of him.'

Pedrito now looked even more confused.

'Believe me,' the king went on, 'I have seen many more selfish, even cowardly, reactions from men who have been defeated in battle. And don't forget that I fought this war for Christendom, and the Sheikh's handing over of his son to Christ will do much to enhance the significance of my victory in the eyes of the world.'

'No doubt about that,' Pedrito acknowledged, realising too late that he should have injected more enthusiasm into his delivery.

Fortunately, King Jaume appeared not to have noticed. 'You will recall, I'm sure,' he said brightly, 'that I promised Ali, the young turncoat Moor, a just reward for being brave enough to swim out from Sa Palomera to the islet of Es Pantaleu to inform me of his soothsayer mother's prediction of my triumph here.'

'Yes, and before you'd even set foot on Mallorca,' Pedrito nodded.

'Well, if I grant some land at Sa Palomera to Ali – which I fully intend to do – surely it's only right and proper that I do even more for you – considering the greater contribution you've made to my efforts.'

Pedrito shook his head. 'While I appreciate your generosity, *senyor*, you mustn't feel that you owe me anything. As *you* will recall, on the very first day of our voyage here, you took one of the two tillers from me to help steer your galley through that terrible storm.'

King Jaume smiled reflectively. 'The day that would change my life, I'd said before setting sail. But it was keeping on through that first storm that turned out to be the deciding factor, no?'

'The first of a few deciding factors,' Pedrito ventured, mirroring the king's smile. 'But at the end of the watch that you helped me struggle through on that occasion, you told me you had done me a favour. I promised I would repay it, and I have done no more than that in any help I've given you since. So,' he concluded with another shake of his head, 'you owe me nothing. All I ask now is that I'm allowed to live in peace where my heart is – at home, on the little farm my father – my adoptive father, my *true* father – lived and worked on so contentedly all of his days.'

'And so you shall,' the king whispered keenly. He threw an arm round Pedrito's shoulder and gave him a hug. 'And so you shall.' Then he pushed Pedrito away and patted his cheeks with both hands. 'However, I have greater things in store for you as well,' he declared. '*Much* greater things!' He moved in close and lowered his voice again. 'For it's no secret that I was hardly one of the richest kings in Christendom when I agreed to lead this crusade, and now more wealth than I ever dreamt of is mine – even after every man with me has taken his share.' He swept his arm in a wide arc. 'And when all of the island has been purged of the infidel trespassers, I will populate it with good Christian stock from Catalonia and Aragon, and even from France. Good Christians like yourself, Little Pedro, who will help make Mallorca the heaven on earth our Lord God Almighty intended it to be.' He raised his eyes and offered up a silent prayer, before smiling at Pedrito and saying, 'But the details can wait for another day, *amic*. So, off you go now on that old hack of yours – home to your little farm, and' – he winked suggestively – 'to enjoy some time alone with your beautiful little Mooress, eh!'

\*

King Jaume had insisted on Robert St Clair de Roslin and two armed squires accompanying Pedrito to the city limits. Looting, wanton violence and murder were rife within the capital, with mobs of Christian soldiers running amok in a fever of greed and lust. Even oil lamps that had famously illuminated the streets had been torn from walls and thrown into houses newly stripped of their valuables. The flicker of flames and the sickly-sweet smell of fresh blood mingled with the roars of the rampaging victors and the screams of their victims as Pedrito and his escorts made their way towards the Gate of Chains.

This was the same gate by which Pedrito had both entered and left the city on the fateful night he had first been thrown together with his mother and Saleema. But now, instead of approaching it through the cramped dinginess of the kasbah, he was passing along a wide avenue which, only a few hours earlier, would still have stood as a shining example of many virtues of Moorish culture, from the magnificence of its architecture to the serenity of the scholars, poets, artists and philosophers strolling through lovingly manicured gardens.

What, he wondered, would be the thoughts of the Christian God, whose devotees had won this battle against those of His Muslim equivalent, if He could actually look down on the mindless destruction now being carried out to His eternal glory? What, he wondered, would be His verdict on those of His followers who had slaughtered thousands of vanquished Muslims, including defenceless women and children, without even a moment's thought of giving them a chance to convert to Christianity?

Yet King Jaume had made it known from the outset that full remission of sins would be granted to those who helped him achieve his goal. The papal legate who had bestowed the sign of the cross upon him before he embarked on this campaign had confirmed that such a concession had been authorised by God's personal emissary on earth himself. So, it followed that the appalling crimes now being committed during the sacking of the city would be regarded

414

by the perpetrators as sins from which they were instantly forgiven – given that they even saw their actions as sinful at all.

'I wish you good luck, laddie,' Robert St Clair said to Pedrito when they reached the gate. 'You'll need it. For, much as I envy you your beautiful wee Moorish lass, I wouldn't want your problems when the priests start doing what they came here to do.'

'I'll just have to hope King Jaume intervenes in our favour,' Pedrito shrugged.

'Aye, well, King Jaume thinks a lot of you, and there's no denying that. Even regards you as a friend. But never forget that he's controlled by the Church, and the rules are clear – Muslims either convert or ... well, at best they'll be expelled, *if* they can afford to pay for the privilege.'

Pedrito pondered the fact that none of the thousands now lying dead in the streets had been offered the option. Whatever money or valuables they possessed had been taken from them, along with their lives – no questions asked. 'It seems strange that it's regarded as a sin to marry a Muslim,' he reflected aloud, while looking back towards the sounds of brutality and terror echoing through the city, 'but not a sin to kill one – or many.'

'Ah,' Robert said sagely, 'but this is a holy war, don't forget.'

'It's certainly a religious one,' Pedrito muttered, recalling the contention made by *al-Usstaz*, his philosphising companion back on the pirate galley, 'but that isn't necessarily the same thing.'

'You'd better keep such provocative thoughts to yourself if your new landlord pays you a visit,' Robert advised. 'He's a stern man, that Berenguer de Palou, and he didn't become Bishop of Barcelona by condoning blasphemous utterings from anyone.'

'Yes, I know,' Pedrito replied. 'King Jaume told me exactly the same thing himself. But don't worry, I'm not about to commit verbal suicide. Anyway,' he continued, deciding a change of subject was called for, 'what of you, Robert? I suppose you'll be going back to your homeland, now that your work here is done?'

'No, no, no,' Robert chuckled. 'The stags will be safe from my arrows for a wee while yet. No, the real work of us Templars hasn't even started here. We'll be given our share of the lands and wealth of the island, as agreed – and without having to pay the king a one-fifth cut of the booty that he gets from everyone else, by the way. And in return we'll establish a proper seat for our order here – you know, to help Christian pilgrims on their way to the Holy Land. And then, if I'm lucky, I'll go on a crusade to Jerusalem myself one day. Oh aye,' he said expansively, 'the Scottish stags will be safe from my arrows for a wee while yet, right enough.'

'Then maybe I'll meet up with you again here on Mallorca,' Pedrito grinned. 'If you're ever down Andratx way, just ask anyone where my little *finca* is. You'll always be made welcome, humble though it is.'

Robert gave Pedrito's hand a hearty shake. 'Good luck again, my friend. I hope the angels who gave you the gift of your bonnie lass will bless you both with a long life together.' He feigned a cough. 'Ah-ehm, after endowing her with the wisdom to embrace the one true Faith, of course.'

### THE FOLLOWING DAY, 1ˢᵗ JANUARY 1230 – OVERLOOKING THE BAY OF ANDRATX, SOUTH-WEST MALLORCA...

When Pedrito approached the old Ensenyat's farm, dawn was only just breaking over the crest of the little hill they called Turtle Mountain on the road between the inland village of Andratx and its eponymous Port. Yet here was Nedi galloping towards him over the bridge spanning the *Torrent de Saluet*. And there, on the other side, was Saleema, standing just as Pedrito remembered her when they'd bid one another a poignant farewell a week that seemed like a lifetime ago.

'He's been scratching at the door for the past hour,' she said, taking Pedrito's hand as he got down from old Tranquilla's back. 'It's as if he knew you were coming.'

Nedi, meanwhile, had sat himself down between them, gazing up, first at one and then the other, the customary 'gormless' smile and dangling tongue indicating his delight at having his little family back together again.

Pedrito patted his head. 'Dogs know things us humans don't, eh,

Nedi?'

'I think so,' said Saleema, 'because, once he'd got me out of bed, he took me by the finger tips and pulled me along here as fast as I could run.'

Pedrito smiled wistfully. 'Just as he did to me at El Real when...' The words stuck in his throat. He tickled Nedi under his chin. 'Yes, dogs know more than we give them credit for, don't they, boy?'

'And the way he's sitting there,' Saleema said, 'I think he's acting as my chaperon.' She batted her eyelashes at Pedrito. 'Doesn't want you to get too close to me, hmm?'

Pedrito gave her a blank look. 'Maybe he isn't so smart after all then, huh?'

'Or smarter than you think.' Saleema sniffed the air. 'I've never smelt a battle-soiled soldier before, but if you're a typical example, I wouldn't want to get any nearer one until he's had a good scrub!' With that, she skipped off laughing towards the Ensenyat *finca*, with Nedi trotting by her side and Pedrito leading a weary old Tranquilla along behind.

*

'This time for good?' Senyora Ensenyat said to Pedrito when she and old Baltazar met him at the door. There was an enquiring smile on her face as she reached up to kiss his cheeks, but there was a distinctly more serious look on it when she pulled away. 'This time for good!' she growled, repeating the words that had haunted Pedrito on his way back to El Real and an unknown fate seven days previously. She poked him in the chest with her finger and gave him a motherly scowl. 'You've returned safely, as we prayed you would every moment you were gone, so make sure it *is* for good this time! Promise?'

Pedrito gave her a reassuring pat on the hand. 'I promise that if I ever have to leave here again, it won't be by choice – just as I had little say in the matter on the two previous occasions. First a bump on the head by pirates, then the call of a king, remember?'

'That's hardly the sort of promise this young lady needs from you,' Senyora Ensenyat scolded, hooking a thumb in Saleema's direction. 'You don't know how lucky you are, Little Pedro!'

Pedrito glanced at Saleema, who was standing behind the old lady, batting her eyelashes at him again, an impish smile dimpling her cheeks.

Her girlie wiles hadn't gone unnoticed by old Baltazar, however. With a wink to Pedrito, he laid a hand on his wife's shoulder. '*Preciosa*,' he said patiently, 'I think Little Pedro will know how lucky he is.' He then winked at Saleema. 'I know I would ... if I were fifty years younger!'

And so the sound of laughter rang out over the little valley, heralding what Pedrito hoped in his heart of hearts would be the start of a life of peace and simple contentment in a place he'd constantly dreamed of returning to during the dark years of his exile. Yet even as he was sharing this longed-for moment with Saleema and his elderly neighbours, the fever of plunder and bloodshed was still raging back in the city; a disease that would spread like a plague as King Jaume fulfilled his solemn vow to purge the entire island of everything and everyone Muslim.

This was an understandable source of anxiety for Saleema. She'd made no mention of it during the hearty homecoming meal that Senyora Ensenyat had insisted on preparing for a suitably scrubbed Pedrito. And, although she had avoided broaching the subject during the hours she'd spent strolling with him round the deserted sweep of Andratx cove that same afternoon, it was one that was bound to surface sooner rather than later. And it did.

As evening fell, they climbed the gentle rise from the shore and paused in the little vegetable garden of Pedrito's family home, there to watch the sun go down over the Punta Moragues headland at the western extremity of the bay. Pedrito led Saleema to a place where, perhaps centuries earlier, someone had removed the top few courses of rough-hewn stone from the *horta*'s enclosing wall and replaced them with a flat slab, broad enough for a few people to sit side-by-side. This was the very spot where he, his parents and little Esperança had spent countless evenings just like this, delighting in the views of the bay, the pine-cloaked arms of its enfolding hills, and beyond to the spangled waters of the Mediterranean Sea.

It was hard to imagine now that, five long years ago, those very waters had carried to this peaceful haven the Moorish pirate galley whose raiding party had so swiftly and brutally changed Pedrito's life forever. But it took only a glance towards a nearby corner of the *horta* for evidence of that barbarous incident to be brought starkly back into focus: the two simple crosses fashioned from almond sticks, the neatly raked soil between the rough chunks of limestonestone that marked the perimeter of the burial place, the two little earthenware cups containing posies of wild flowers at the base of each cross.

Pedrito swallowed hard and brushed a tear from the corner of his eye.

Saleema laid a hand on his. 'I came with old Baltazar and helped him tend the grave only yesterday. Senyora Ensenyat told me where to pick the flowers – down in the field where you were captured. She said she's been doing that every day since you were taken. Said she believed it would bring you and your parents a little closer.'

Lost for words, Pedrito drew Saleema's head to his shoulder. And there they sat, their thoughts intertwined like the fingers of their hands, while the glow of the setting sun painted the sea red and pulled a blanket of lengthening shadows over the surrounding landscape.

It was Pedrito who eventually broke the silence. 'I know you fear for the wellbeing of your own mother and father as well. But keep believing that they're safe, and I promise I'll do all I can to find them for you – just as soon as I possibly can.'

Saleema hesitated for a moment before saying, 'You mean, when you go with the Christian king to seek out the thousands of Moors who have taken refuge in the mountains?'

'Well,' Pedrito began uneasily, 'if he feels in need of an interpreter, as I'm sure he will…'

Saleema put a finger to his lips. 'Death by the sword is the same in any language, and I know that the chances of my mother and father surviving the Christian clearances are slim – even if they're still alive right now.' She took Pedrito's face in her hands and looked deeply into his eyes. 'All I have now is you. So, what is to become of us? I know that what we feel for each other is a sin in the eyes of your god, just as it is in the eyes of mine.'

Pedrito wagged a finger. 'Only in the eyes of those who claim to speak for those gods, but that's all.'

'Isn't that enough?' Samleema came back. 'Seems to me that the holy men have the final word on everything, including the right to take someone's life for breaking laws that were decreed by Allah – or God.'

'Laws that they *tell* us were decreed by Allah or God.'

Saleema frowned. 'But such thoughts are forbidden – punishable by death, surely!'

'How can anyone forbid you to think?' Pedrito countered.

Saleema's frown deepened. 'What you're saying frightens me, Pedrito.'

He gave her an understanding smile, then tapped his chest. 'Listen to your heart and you'll hear the angels sing. That's what my mother told me when I was little.'

'Hear the *angels* sing?' Saleema shook her head. 'I don't understand.'

'It means you'll be told what's right – what's good. God's word can come from your heart, sometimes more than it does from the mouths of those who tell us they're His chosen go-betweens. That's what I was brought up to believe anyway. And I never even met a priest in all my life until a few months ago, when I fell in with the Christian army that's butchering defenceless women and children in Medîna Mayûrqa even as we speak. Yes, and those same priests say they have the power to forgive the soldiers their sins because they're being committed in God's name. The same priests who blessed the dead, rotting bodies of enemy soldiers when they were being catapulted into the city to spread disease and death through the population. Tell me, are those the voices of *any* god?'

Saleema kneaded her forehead. 'I don't know … religion … I

don't know what to think.'

Pedrito mulled things over for a bit, then said, 'I remember discussing religion with King Jaume – one time when he'd had a cup or two of wine – and he said it gives people hope, so, whatever its faults, it would be a sin to take it away.'

'Well, I suppose there's something to be said for that,' Saleema reasoned.

'So, why don't you and I make *hope* our religion?'

While Saleema, eyes raised and a forefinger pressed to her cheek, was giving due consideration to that radical proposition, a shaggy black shape came hurtling towards them from the direction of the bay.

'Hello, Nedi,' Pedrito grinned. 'Been doing a bit of exploring, have you?'

By way of reply, Nedi proceeded to shake a coatful of sea all over them.

'Stop it!' Saleema squealed, pulling her knees up. 'You're soaking me, you inconsiderate creature!'

'Well,' Pedrito laughed, 'he *is* a water dog, after all. Yes, and not so inconsiderate either, are you, boy?' A reflective look came to his eyes as he patted Nedi's sodden head. 'We talk about hope, and that's exactly what you gave me, didn't you? Over there by my parents' grave, when I was in the depths of despair, with nothing to live for, by my way of thinking.' He glanced at Saleema. 'The look of encouragement Nedi gave me at that bleak moment may have amounted to a word from God as well, if you see what I mean.'

Saleema reached down and tickled Nedi's ear. 'So, what you're saying is that, if we look into Nedi's eyes, we'll hear the angels sing as well?'

'Well my mother – Farah, I mean – did say he was an angel, didn't she?'

Saleema gave a little laugh. 'That was after he'd brought a dead hen to the cave for her, wasn't it?'

Pedrito nodded his head, while returning the smile that Nedi was now panting up at him. Another few moments of silence followed, broken this time by Saleema starting to sniffle.

'What's wrong?' Pedrito asked. 'Not still feeling sorry for the hen, are you?'

Saleema's sniffle turned into a weepy giggle. 'No, no, I was just thinking of what your mother said after you'd told her that Nedi wasn't a Christian, or anything but a true child of heaven – everybody's friend.' A little whimper escaped her lips. 'And after you'd given Nedi a hug and he'd given your face a big, slobbery kiss, your mother said...' Saleema stopped to swallow a sob. 'She, uhm, she said that not even the finest poets in the land could compose a verse to better what Nedi had told you in just that one little show of unquestioning love.' She tickled Nedi's ear again. 'And Farah was right, wasn't she, boy? Who needs words, hmm?'

With an atmosphere of contentment descending with dusk on the *horta*, Saleema snuggled her head against Pedrito's shoulder, while Nedi sat at their feet following their gaze out towards the crimson waters of the bay. After a while, Pedrito, lulled into an ever more mellow mood, started to hum the strains of a simple melody.

'That's nice,' Saleema murmured. 'What is it?'

'That? Oh, just an old sailors' song. A Moorish one. It's about the winds – the eight winds that roam the seas of Mallorca. Each one has its own name, as well as its own character.'

Then, just as had happened on the day when Nedi's look had pulled Pedrito from the quicksands of despair, a gentle breeze began to drift in from the sea.

'So, what do they call that one?' Saleema asked.

'That's the *Migjorn* – the southerly note of the song. The wind my father said blew the shoals of sardines into the fishermen's nets. The *Migjorn* – the wind of hope, he called it.'

'Hope,' Saleema mused. 'Hope ... it's a word that's cropped up a lot since we sat down here, isn't it?'

Lost in thought, Pedrito didn't answer right away. 'It's also the name of my little sister,' he said at length. 'Esperança ... little Esperança with the laughing eyes.' He stroked Saleema's hair. 'Eyes as beautiful as yours.'

Saleema looked up at him in the way she knew made his heart skip a beat.

'Well, you know – *almost* as beautiful as yours – in their own way,' he flustered. 'Too beautiful, anyway, to be forced to look at the faces of the murderous brutes who came here and took her away.' Pedrito sighed deeply. 'I vowed on my parents' memory that I would find her – some day – somehow. Just as I'll find your mother and father for you – I promise.'

Sniffling again, Saleema squeezed his hand. 'They say that where there's life there's hope, yet all we can do for now is hope they're still alive.'

'And I'll tell you what,' said Pedrito, adopting a deliberately optimistic tone, 'to keep that hope alive, we'll call this little place the *Finca Esperança* – Hope Farm. How do you like that?'

'Sounds good to me,' Saleema chirped. 'Yes, and it'll go well with the names of our livestock too! I mean, there's Tranquilla your placid old horse, Masoud the lucky donkey and little Annam the heaven-blessed goat.'

'There you are then! Modest beginnings, maybe, but –'

'Hopeful ones?' Saleema cut in with a mischievous giggle.

'You took the words right out of my mouth,' Pedrito laughed. 'Modest beginnings, but hopeful ones.' He nodded in the direction of the last sliver of crimson disappearing behind the Punta Moragues headland, then leaned back and stretched his arms. 'Nightfall,' he yawned, 'and I honestly can't remember when I last had good night's sleep.'

Saleema stood up and pulled him to his feet. 'Well,' she said, gesturing towards the house, 'Senyora Ensenyat said she'd get your old room ready for you this afternoon, so...'

'So?'

'So, is a good night's sleep all you can think of?'

'What else?' Pedrito replied with a shrug of feigned indifference.

Saleema started to haul him homeward by the hand. 'I'm sure we'll think of something.'

Nedi, meanwhile, had picked up the mood of burgeoning

bonhomie, had taken the fingers of Saleema's free hand in his teeth and had started to pull her towards where he instinctively felt the fun would continue.

'I hear your angels singing,' Saleema told him, 'but tonight, you sleep with *them* – in the kitchen!'

## THE END

# APPENDIX

Remon and Guillen de Muntcada (otherwise Montcada or Moncada), the Catalan noblemen who fought and died at the Battle of Na Burguesa in 1229, have been popularly referred to as siblings – 'The Brothers Muntcada'.

However, while they can fairly be described as 'brothers-in-arms', their family tree shows that they were in fact cousins, and only second cousins at that.

It was Remon's father and Guillen's grandfather who were brothers – the sons of Guillen Remon de Muntcada, the Grand Seneschal of Catalonia, who died in 1173.

A memorial to the two brothers-in-arms stands by the roadside near Palma Nova in Mallorca.

\*

For full details of Peter Kerr and his books, visit

**www.peter-kerr.co.uk**